V&S Publishers has been in the forefront of bringing out innovative solutions to fulfil the needs of student community. While going through the school atlases available in the market, we observed that though they carry substantial cartographic details, some lacunae persist nevertheless. This we tried correcting, not just eliminating the inherent weaknesses, by providing clear, vivid and detailed geographical information that is ideal for class lessons, school projects, and homework. The effort has been published under the name Gen X Series – generating excellence in generation X - Atlas. Students will enjoy exploring the world with full-colour maps, photographs, and easy-to-use charts and graphs. The thematic maps of natural and other resources and inclusion of crucial school topics help explain more complex geographical concepts. This atlas is the perfect resource for knowing about the world.

Apart from brief introductory information about the geographic terms, Universe, and Earth, the atlas contains physical and political maps of continents in general; and about India and its States in particular. There are new informative pages and extensive coverage of fundamental thematic issues such as climate, natural vegetation, wildlife, agriculture, minerals, industry, demography, environmental concerns and natural hazards in a presentable layout. This edition includes recent geo-political and socio-economic developments and climatic and environmental concerns focusing on India and the world.

Broad Highlights of the Atlas:

- Learn about major rivers and deserts, highest and lowest elevations, ocean currents, and wind patterns.

- Locate towns and countries across the globe. Be confident to have the most recent updates to names, boundaries, capitals, and more.

- Statistics on agriculture, energy consumption, literacy, religions, and other important topics are summarized for students.

- Access data on population, languages, and monetary units plus a colour flag for each country.

Ideal for the classroom or library!

The external boundaries and coastlines of India on the maps shown in this atlas agree with the copy certified by the Survey of India, Dehradun vide their letter no. TB/811/62-A-3/A dated 10/03/2016

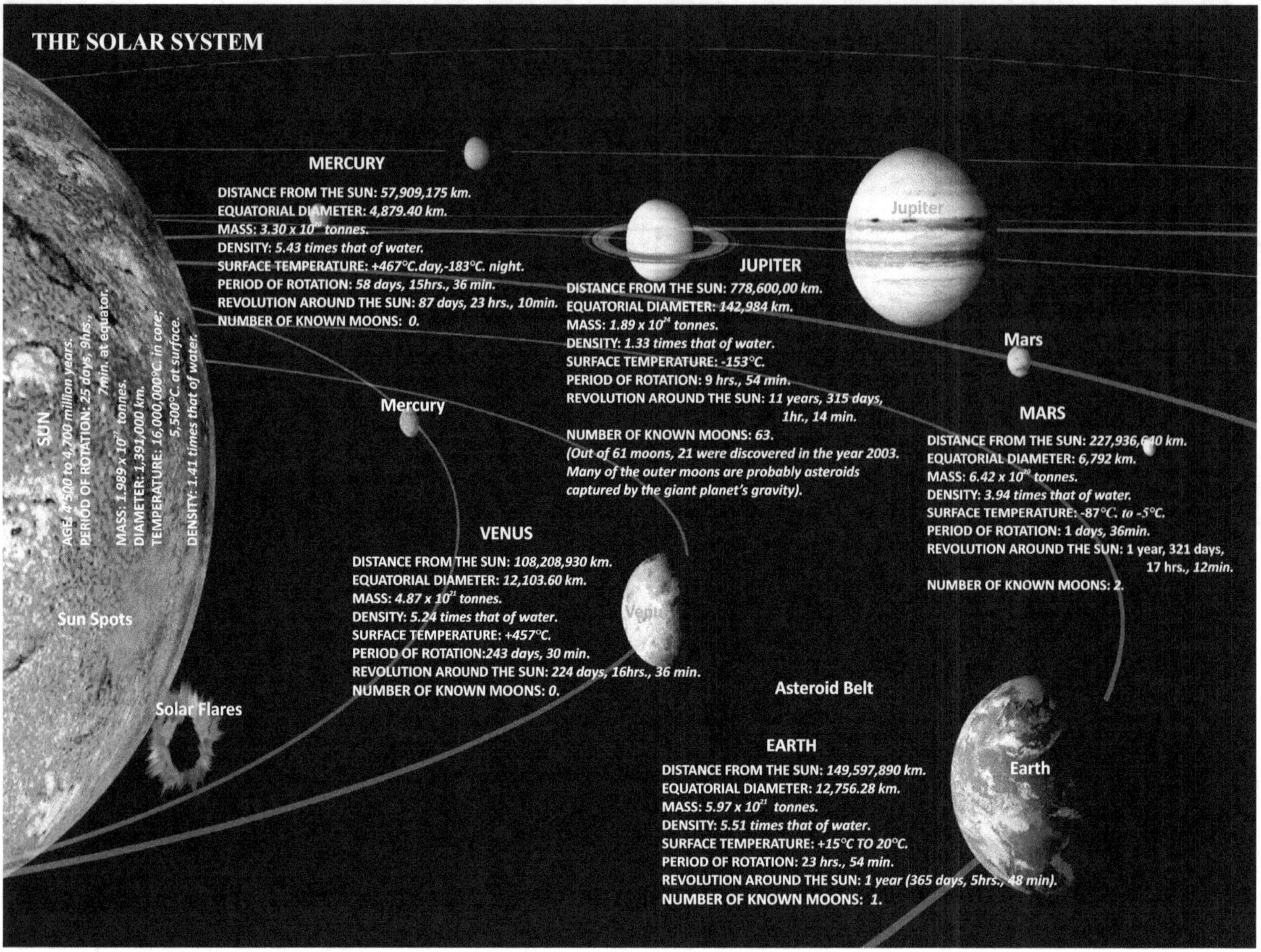

THE SOLAR SYSTEM

SUN
AGE: 4,500 to 4,700 million years.
PERIOD OF ROTATION: 25 days, 9hrs., 7min. at equator.
MASS: 1,989 x 10⁷ tonnes.
DIAMETER: 1,391,000 km.
TEMPERATURE: 16,000,000°C in core, 5,500°C, at surface.
DENSITY: 1.41 times that of water.

Sun Spots

Solar Flares

MERCURY
DISTANCE FROM THE SUN: 57,909,175 km.
EQUATORIAL DIAMETER: 4,879.40 km.
MASS: 3.30 x 10²⁰ tonnes.
DENSITY: 5.43 times that of water.
SURFACE TEMPERATURE: +467°C.day,-183°C. night.
PERIOD OF ROTATION: 58 days, 15hrs., 36 min.
REVOLUTION AROUND THE SUN: 87 days, 23 hrs., 10min.
NUMBER OF KNOWN MOONS: 0.

Mercury

VENUS
DISTANCE FROM THE SUN: 108,208,930 km.
EQUATORIAL DIAMETER: 12,103.60 km.
MASS: 4.87 x 10²¹ tonnes.
DENSITY: 5.24 times that of water.
SURFACE TEMPERATURE: +457°C.
PERIOD OF ROTATION: 243 days, 30 min.
REVOLUTION AROUND THE SUN: 224 days, 16hrs., 36 min.
NUMBER OF KNOWN MOONS: 0.

Venus

JUPITER
DISTANCE FROM THE SUN: 778,600,00 km.
EQUATORIAL DIAMETER: 142,984 km.
MASS: 1.89 x 10²⁴ tonnes.
DENSITY: 1.33 times that of water.
SURFACE TEMPERATURE: -153°C.
PERIOD OF ROTATION: 9 hrs., 54 min.
REVOLUTION AROUND THE SUN: 11 years, 315 days, 1hr., 14 min.
NUMBER OF KNOWN MOONS: 63.
(Out of 61 moons, 21 were discovered in the year 2003. Many of the outer moons are probably asteroids captured by the giant planet's gravity).

Jupiter

Mars

MARS
DISTANCE FROM THE SUN: 227,936,640 km.
EQUATORIAL DIAMETER: 6,792 km.
MASS: 6.42 x 10²⁰ tonnes.
DENSITY: 3.94 times that of water.
SURFACE TEMPERATURE: -87°C. to -5°C.
PERIOD OF ROTATION: 1 days, 36min.
REVOLUTION AROUND THE SUN: 1 year, 321 days, 17 hrs., 12min.
NUMBER OF KNOWN MOONS: 2.

Asteroid Belt

EARTH
DISTANCE FROM THE SUN: 149,597,890 km.
EQUATORIAL DIAMETER: 12,756.28 km.
MASS: 5.97 x 10²¹ tonnes.
DENSITY: 5.51 times that of water.
SURFACE TEMPERATURE: +15°C TO 20°C.
PERIOD OF ROTATION: 23 hrs., 54 min.
REVOLUTION AROUND THE SUN: 1 year (365 days, 5hrs., 48 min).
NUMBER OF KNOWN MOONS: 1.

Earth

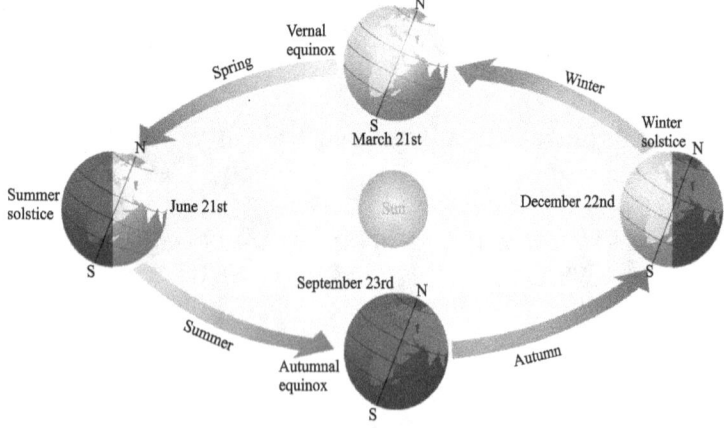

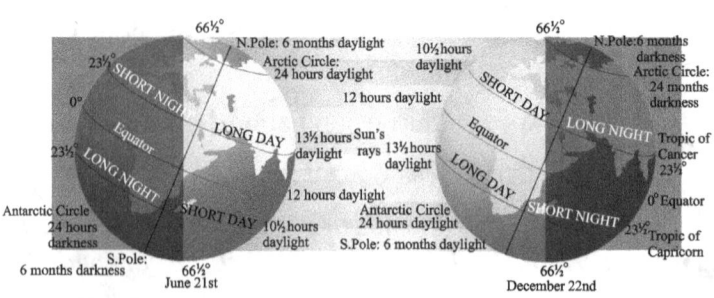

DAY AND NIGHT

The rotation of the earth's axis (which takes 24 hours) causes different regions of the earth's surface to be exposed to the sun at different times. The side of the earth which faces the sun experiences day and the opposite, unexposed side of the earth which is in darkness, experiences night.

THE SEASONS

Seasons occur in the course of the earth's revolution around the sun. The axis of the earth is titled and this causes each region of the earth to gradually move close to the sun and then further away from it. In the northern hemisphere, it is summer when the north pole is closer to the sun (in June) and winter (in December) when the north pole is further away from the sun, receiving far less heat and light. In the southern hemisphere, the opposite happens, in summer (in December) when the south pole is closer to the sun and winter (in June) when the south pole is further away from the sun.

CALENDAR

The Gregorian calendar now in use was devised in the 16th century. The sub-division of time into years, months, weeks and days is based on astronomical motions of the earth and the moon. One total rotation of the earth takes 24 hours (one day). It takes approximately 29 days (one lunar month) for the moon to revolve around the sun. It takes 365 days (one year) for the earth to revolve around the sun. It is very difficult to develop an accurate calendar which is dependent on so many varying factors, and therefore, our calendar has only 365 days. Once in four years, we compensate for this by adding an extra day to the year. This is called leap year.

SCHOOL ATLAS

Government Certified Indian Maps

High resolution Maps of India, Indian States, Continents and World Maps now in a user friendly up-to-date new avatar. Click on the Dropbox link to download files and explore maps by zooming in on different maps to satisfy your geographical inquisitiveness.

Upon clicking on the files the School Atlas will pop up on the screen. The navigation tool bar then is easy to use. It supports direct mouse dragging for navigating the image. It also supports common key buttons to move left, right, up and down (bottom) and zoom in and zoom out etc. On it are placed Buttons in a two-column format identifying, by name, India, different Continents, World and Polar Regions. Clicking any button will open that geographical location depicting its physical and political features. India and its States have been shown elaborately alongside thematic maps, climatic regions, vegetation, agriculture, minerals and industries, communications, transport – rail, road, air and sea routes etc to understand the relationship between geographic features and human-related activities.

The Government Approved Atlas is in accordance with latest NEPP guidelines and CBSE syllabus and meets the requirements of students in all classes across different boards and schools.

V&S PUBLISHERS

Published by:

V&S PUBLISHERS

F-2/16, Ansari Road, Daryaganj, New Delhi-110002
☎ 23240026, 23240027 • *Fax:* 011-23240028
Email: info@vspublishers.com • *Website:* www.vspublishers.com

 Online Brandstore: amazon.in/vspublishers

Regional Office : Hyderabad
5-1-707/1, Brij Bhawan (Beside Central Bank of India Lane)
Bank Street, Koti, Hyderabad - 500 095
☎ 040-24737290
E-mail: vspublishershyd@gmail.com

Follow us on:

BUY OUR BOOKS FROM: AMAZON FLIPKART

© Copyright: V&S Publishers
ISBN 978-93-579413-1-0
New Edition

Acknowledgments

The following notes are applicable for all the maps in this atlas where India - International boundaries and coastlines appear:

♦ © Government of India, Copyright, 2014

♦ The responsibility for the correctness of internal details rests with the publisher.

♦ The territorial waters of India extend into the sea to a distance of twelve nautical miles measured from the appropriate base line.

♦ The administrative headquarters of Chandigarh, Haryana and Punjab are at Chandigarh.

♦ The interstate boundaries amongst Arunachal Pradesh, Assam and Meghalaya shown on this map are as interpreted from the "North-Eastern Areas (Reorganisation) Act 1971,", but have yet to be verified.

♦ The external boundaries and coastlines of India agree with the Record/Master Copy certified by Survey of India.

♦ The state boundaries between Uttarakhand & Uttar Pradesh, Bihar & Jharkhand and Chattisgarh & Madhya Pradesh have not been verified by the concerned Governments.

♦ The spellings of names in this map have been taken from various sources.

♦ The external boundaries and coastlines of India on the maps agree with the copy certified by the Survey of India, Dehradun vide their letter No.TB/811/62-A-3/A dated 10/03/2016

CO

NTENTS

NTENTS

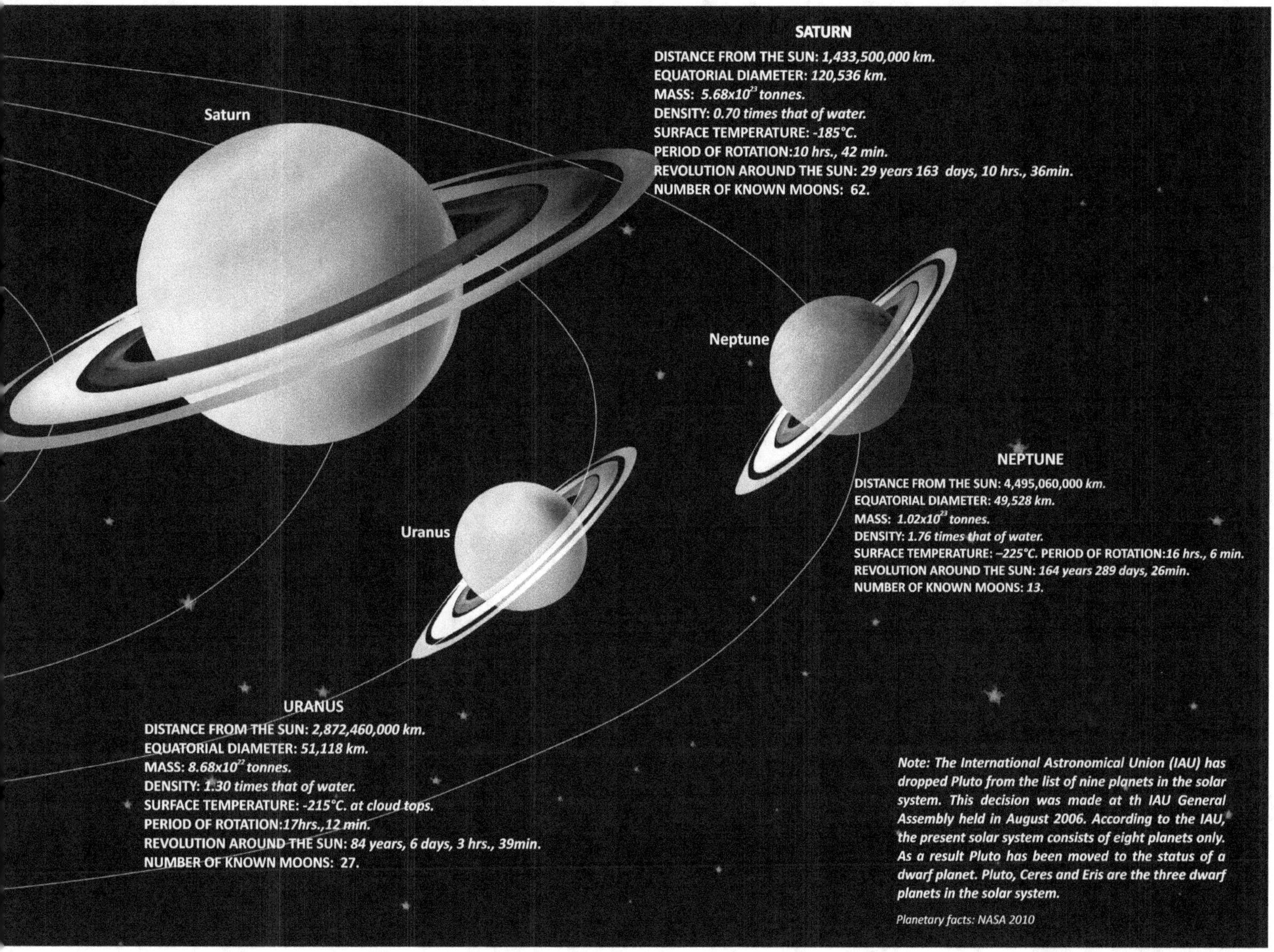

SATURN
DISTANCE FROM THE SUN: *1,433,500,000 km.*
EQUATORIAL DIAMETER: *120,536 km.*
MASS: *5.68x10²³ tonnes.*
DENSITY: *0.70 times that of water.*
SURFACE TEMPERATURE: *-185°C.*
PERIOD OF ROTATION:*10 hrs., 42 min.*
REVOLUTION AROUND THE SUN: *29 years 163 days, 10 hrs., 36min.*
NUMBER OF KNOWN MOONS: 62.
Saturn
Neptune
Uranus
NEPTUNE
DISTANCE FROM THE SUN: 4,495,060,000 *km.*
EQUATORIAL DIAMETER: *49,528 km.*
MASS: *1.02x10²³ tonnes.*
DENSITY: *1.76 times that of water.*
SURFACE TEMPERATURE: *–225°C.* PERIOD OF ROTATION:*16 hrs., 6 min.*
REVOLUTION AROUND THE SUN: *164 years 289 days, 26min.*
NUMBER OF KNOWN MOONS: *13.*
URANUS
DISTANCE FROM THE SUN: *2,872,460,000 km.*
EQUATORIAL DIAMETER: *51,118 km.*
MASS: *8.68x10²² tonnes.*
DENSITY: *1.30 times that of water.*
SURFACE TEMPERATURE: *-215°C. at cloud tops.*
PERIOD OF ROTATION:*17hrs.,12 min.*
REVOLUTION AROUND THE SUN: *84 years, 6 days, 3 hrs., 39min.*
NUMBER OF KNOWN MOONS: 27.
Note: The International Astronomical Union (IAU) has dropped Pluto from the list of nine planets in the solar system. This decision was made at th IAU General Assembly held in August 2006. According to the IAU, the present solar system consists of eight planets only. As a result Pluto has been moved to the status of a dwarf planet. Pluto, Ceres and Eris are the three dwarf planets in the solar system.
Planetary facts: NASA 2010

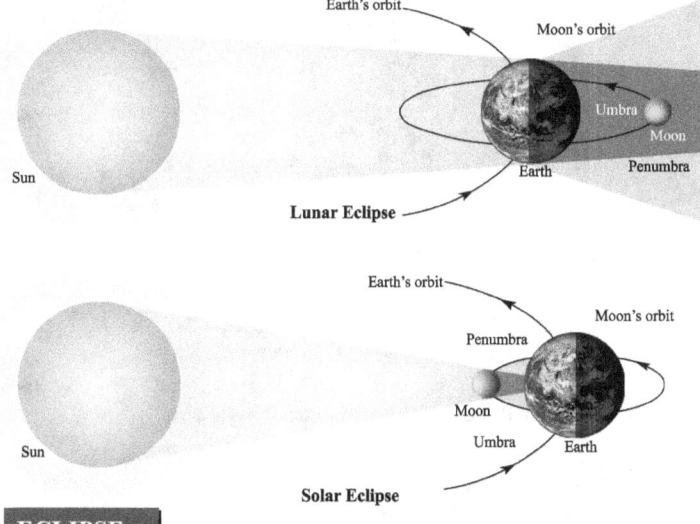

Earth's orbit
Moon's orbit
Umbra
Moon
Earth
Penumbra
Sun
Lunar Eclipse
Earth's orbit
Moon's orbit
Penumbra
Moon
Umbra
Earth
Sun
Solar Eclipse

Last quarter (half moon)
Warning crescent
Warning gibbous
Sun
New Moon
Moon
Earth
Moon's Orbit
Full Moon
Phases of the moon as seen from the earth
Waxing crescent
Waxing gibbous
First quarter (half moon)

ECLIPSE

The duration of the revolution of the moon around the earth and the duration of the revolution of these two celestial bodies around the sun is different. This causes peculiar positioning of the celestial bodies in such ways that the moon can block the sunlight from reaching the earth (solar eclipse), or the earth can cast its shadow on the moon (lunar eclipse). Since we can now calculate where these bodies will be at any particular time, eclipse can be predicted.

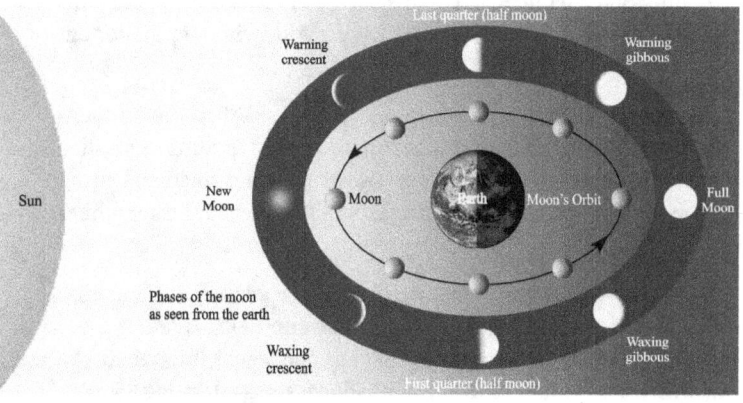

PHASES OF THE MOON

The moon, the only satellite of the earth, moves from west to east round the earth in 27 days, 7 hours and 43 minutes (sidereal month). The same face of the moon is always seen from the earth as the moon always has the same periods of rotation and revolution. The moon has no light of its own. The changing positions of the moon in relation to the earth and the sun are known as different phases of the moon. On full moon days the full face of the moon, illuminated by sunlight, is visible from the earth when the earth lies between the sun and the moon. On new moon days, the moon lies between the earth and the sun and therefore it seems dark from the earth. From the new moon to the full moon period, the moon waxes and from the full moon to the new moon period it wanes.

THE EARTH

The earth is spherical in shape, somewhat flattened at the poles and bulges at the equator. Its circumference around the equator is approximately 40,000 kilometres. The equatorial diameter is 12,756 kilometres but at the poles the diameter is 12,714 kilometres.

The Earth's axis : The axis of the earth is tilted at 66.5° to the plane of the earth's orbit; or at 23:5° to the perpendicular to the plane of the earth's orbit. If the earth's axis had been perpendicular to the plane of the orbit, the duration of day and night would have been equal throughout the world every day. Due to the tilting of the earth's axis, the length of day and night varies from one place to another.

Great circle : This refers to a hypothetical circle on the earth's surface, the plane of which passes through the centre of the earth. It divides the earth into two equal hemispheres. Of the latitudes, only the equator is a great circle but of the longitudes, every pair of longitudes is a great circle. For example, 120°E and 60°W together form a great circle. The shortest route between any two points on the earth's surface is the arc of the great circle which passes through them.

ROTATION OF THE EARTH

Rotation of the earth means the spinning of the earth on its axis. The direction of its rotation is from west to east. This gives us the phenomenon of day and night.

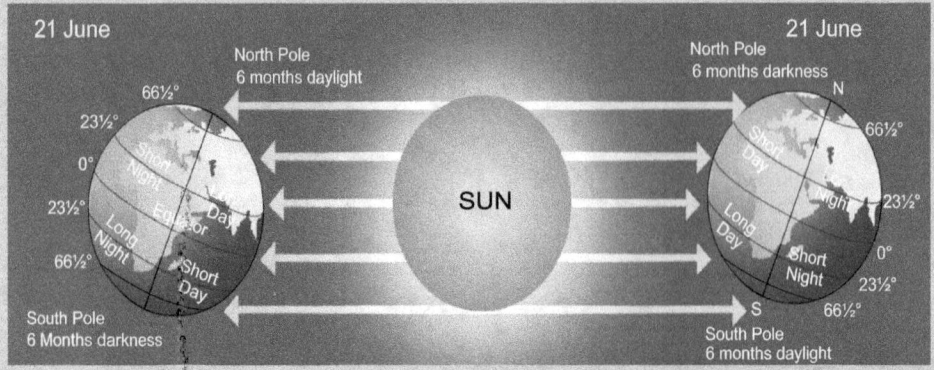

Parallelism of the Earth's axis : The earth's axis remains parallel to itself irrespective of the position it occupies during its revolution around the sun. This is called the parallelism of the earth's axis.

This is possible because the northern end or the North Pole of the earth's axis always points to the celestial North Pole or the position occupied by the Pole Star. While the position of the Pole Star is fixed, the actual star occupying this position changes.

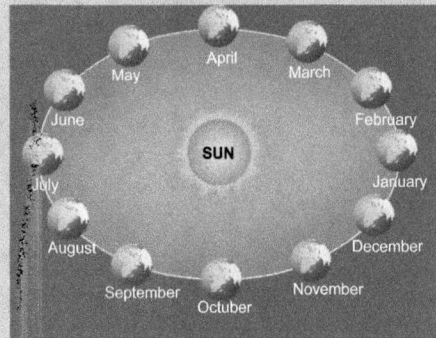
Parallelism of the earth's axis

Circle of Illumination : It is a great circle that bisects the earth's surface into the illuminated half and the half in darkness.

REVOLUTION OF THE EARTH

The earth revolves around the sun in its elliptical orbit even while rotating on its inclined axis. This results in the change of seasons. During its revolution, the earth occupies following four important positions :

Solstice : It occurs on the two solstice days. When the northern hemisphere is tilted towards the sun it is known as summer solstice or when away from the sun it is known as winter solstice. During summer solstice, the day is longest in the year and during winter solstice, the day is shortest and the night is longest.

Equinox : This is one of the two times in the year when there is no tilt towards or away from the sun. The sun being overhead, the duration of day and night is equal (12 hours each) throughout the world because the Circle of Illumination bisects all the latitudes.

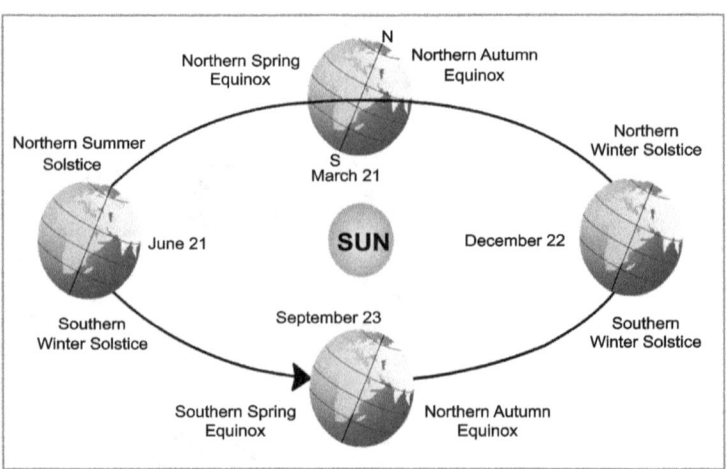
Revolution of the earth in its orbit around the sun

Revolution and Seasons : The position of the earth during its revolution around the sun determines the amount of incoming solar energy the two hemispheres receive. This results in seasons.

Precession of the Equinoxes : With respect to a fixed point in the celestial sky, this is the change in the orientation of the earth's axis. As a result, the axis traces a conical path in the sky. This conical motion is due to the gravitational forces of the sun and the moon acting on the earth's axis and its resistance to the forces. It takes nearly 26,000 years for the axis to complete tracing the conical path once. It is due to the precession of the Equinoxes that the same star does not occupy the position of the Pole Star. At present, the Pole Star is Polaris. The next Pole Star will be Vega.

EVOLUTION OF THE EARTH

The earth is 4.6 billion years old. To understand the evolution of diversity of life on the earth, we have to use Geologic Time or Geochronology. The total time period of 4.6 billion years is divided into four distinct eras and there are altogether eleven periods in these four eras.

Pre-Cambrian	Paleozoic	Mesozoic	Cenozoic
	Age of invertebrates 560 million years	Age of reptiles 245 million years	Age of mammals 66 million years

Mountain building activity was witnessed during the Tertiary period (period between 65,000,000 years and 1,700, 000 years ago). The Andes, the Rockies, the Alps and the Himalaya were formed either partly or wholly during this period. The Quaternary period is the last and the youngest period. During the Quaternary period, cyclic climatic changes took place on global scale. All the continents were formed during the Pre-Cambrian era. The chain of Himalayan Mountains is much younger.

Distribution of land and oceans on Earth and continental drift

Only after the Plate Tectonics Theory was developed the reason for the slow change of position of the continents could be understood.

The early supporters of continental drift believed that the jigsaw shapes of the present continents could be placed together to form an ancient land mass which, at some time in the past, split and drifted apart. But according to the theory of plate tectonics, the earth's crust was made up of seven major and many minor crustal plates.

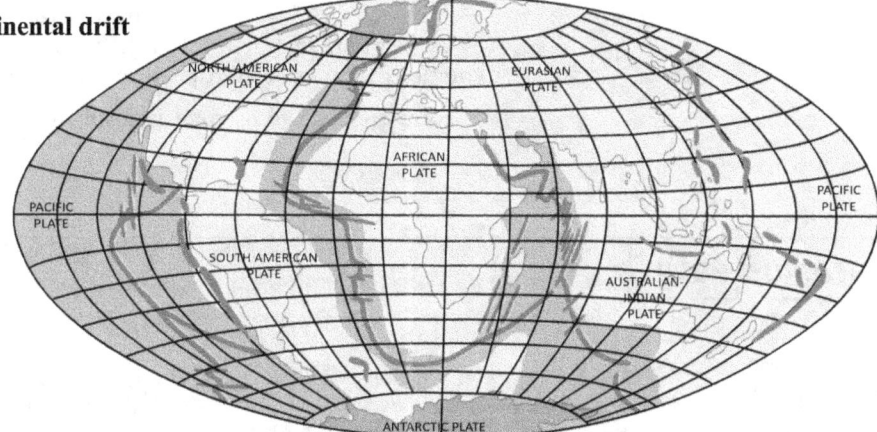

These plates fit tightly like pieces of a jigsaw puzzle to form the earth's crust. All these plates are in constant state of motion, resulting in slow drifting of the oceans as well as the continents.

STRUCTURE OF THE EARTH'S INTERIOR

The earth's internal structure can be divided into three parts — Crust, Mantle and Core.

The Crust : The continental crust in most places can be divided into an upper and a lower part. The base of these crustal rocks is marked by a sharp change in their rock density compared to that of the mantle rocks, which are much heavier. The zone that separates the crust and the mantle is called the Moho, named after the Yugoslavian scientist who detected it. The ocean crust consists of low density rocks and is 5-10 km deep.

The Mantle : The upper rigid part of the mantle can extend up to 100 kilometres below the Moho, and together with the earth's crust forms the lithosphere. The lower mantle extending up to 2,900 kilometres below the earth's surface is less rigid and is hotter. This is known as the Asthenosphere and is capable of being deformed over long periods of time. The phenomenon of plate tectonics or the movement of the earth's crust is caused by the movement of the lithosphere over the asthenosphere.

The Core : It forms about 33% of the earth's mass and has a radius of 3,500 kilometres. The outer core is liquid while the inner core is believed to be a solid nickel-iron alloy.

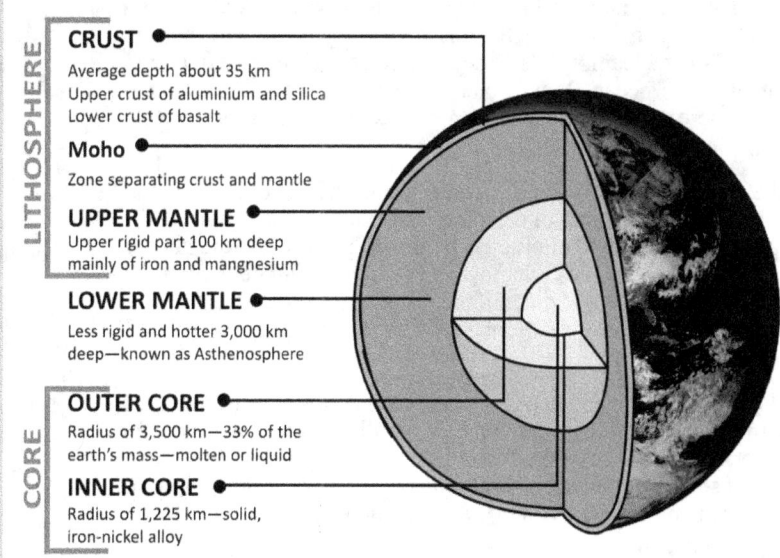

LITHOSPHERE

CRUST
Average depth about 35 km
Upper crust of aluminium and silica
Lower crust of basalt

Moho
Zone separating crust and mantle

UPPER MANTLE
Upper rigid part 100 km deep
mainly of iron and mangnesium

LOWER MANTLE
Less rigid and hotter 3,000 km
deep—known as Asthenosphere

CORE

OUTER CORE
Radius of 3,500 km—33% of the
earth's mass—molten or liquid

INNER CORE
Radius of 1,225 km—solid,
iron-nickel alloy

Structure of the earth's interior

BIOSPHERE

Biosphere is that area of earth in which all life forms exist. It includes a thin layer of air (atmosphere), water (hydrosphere) and earth (lithosphere). The biosphere contains all living organisms, including man, and all organic matter that has not yet decomposed. The biosphere is what truly distinguishes our planet from all others in the solar system.

The core of the biosphere is located right at the surface, where all earth spheres intersect. Life forms utilize gases from the atmosphere, water from the hydrosphere and nutrients from the lithosphere, as the biosphere is dependent on the other three realms. Thus, the four earth spheres are intrinsically connected. For example, soil contains mineral particles (lithosphere), water (hydrosphere), air (atmosphere) and organic matter, alive and dead (biosphere).

All physical processes on earth involve all realms in one way or another. For example, weather systems are generated in the atmosphere, bu't depend on factors such as evaporation of moisture from the hydrosphere and transpiration from plants in the biosphere. Moist air is then transported from one place to another by air currents that depend on the nature of the surface of the lithosphere. Similarly, volcanic eruptions occur in the lithosphere, but also affect the other realms substantially.

The atmosphere, hydrosphere, lithosphere and biosphere are together referred to as the Geosphere.

HYDROSPHERE

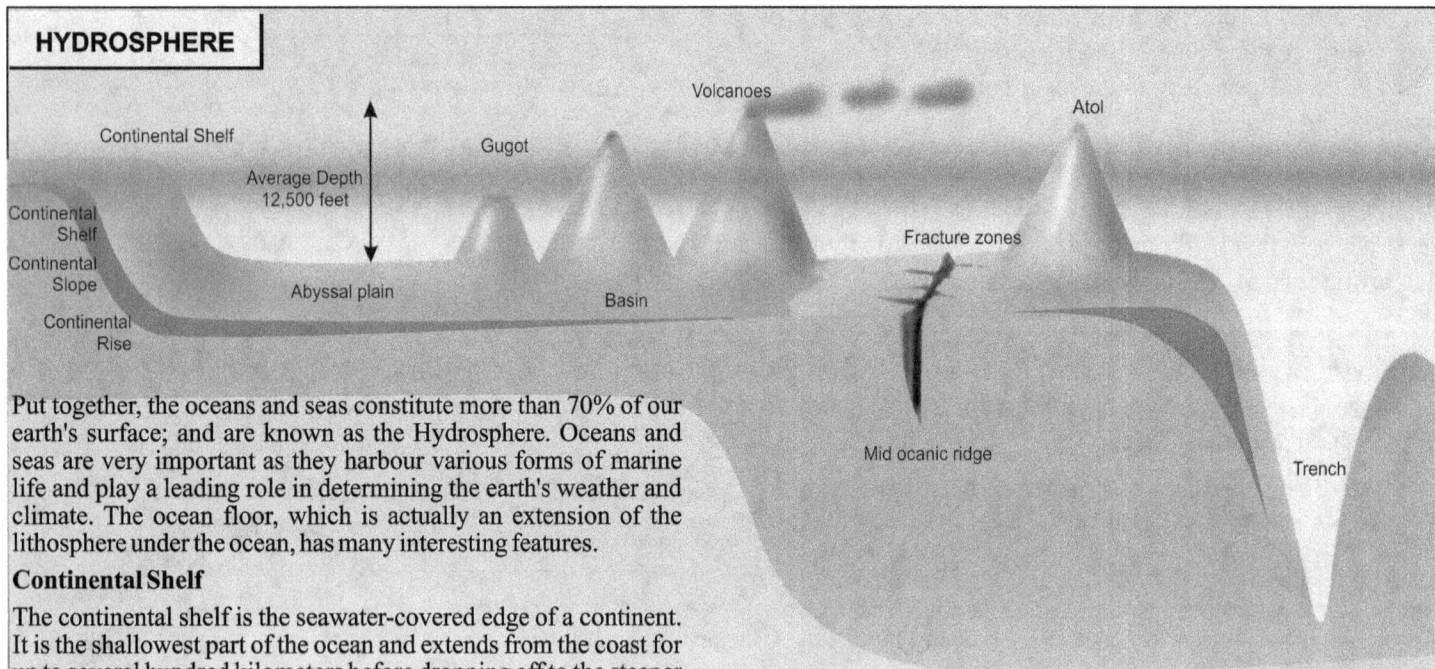

Put together, the oceans and seas constitute more than 70% of our earth's surface; and are known as the Hydrosphere. Oceans and seas are very important as they harbour various forms of marine life and play a leading role in determining the earth's weather and climate. The ocean floor, which is actually an extension of the lithosphere under the ocean, has many interesting features.

Continental Shelf

The continental shelf is the seawater-covered edge of a continent. It is the shallowest part of the ocean and extends from the coast for up to several hundred kilometers before dropping off to the steeper continental slope. These shallow and gently sloping plains contain most of the animal and plant life in the ocean. Most of the offshore drilling sites for oil and natural gas are located here.

Continental Slope

The steep continental slope connects the shallow continental shelf with the ocean floor. The slope is usually formed by powerful undersea avalanches called turbidity currents. The gently sloping pile of sediment that accumulates on the sea floor at the bottom of the continental slope is called the continental rise.

Abyssal Plains

Abyssal plains are the vast and flat expanses on the ocean floor; and are the deepest part of the ocean. Also known as deep-sea plains, the abyssal plains generally extend from the continental rise to the mid-ocean ridges.

Trenches

Trenches are long, narrow depressions on the ocean floor. Also known as ocean deeps, the depth of a trench can reach up to 11 kilometers. The Mariana Trench in the Pacific Ocean, which extends up to 10,800 m below sea level, is the deepest trench in the world.

Mid-ocean Ridges

Massive chains of underwater mountains that exist on the ocean floor are known as Mid-ocean ridges. Mid-ocean ridges are formed when two oceanic plates spread apart. As the plates diverge, molten rock material oozes up from the mantle and is grafted onto the edge of the receding plates to form new oceanic crust. The peaks of these ridges are higher than the peaks of most continental mountain systems. Many regions of great seismic activity cut across the earth's mid-ocean ridges. The mid-Atlantic ocean ridge is a chain of huge volcanoes slowly erupting under the sea.

The Earth's atmosphere that surrounds the Earth is a thin layer of mixture of gases. It is composed of 78% nitrogen, 21% oxygen, 0.9% argon, 0.03% carbon dioxide, and trace of other gases. This thin layer insulates the Earth from extreme temperatures. It keeps heat inside the atmosphere; and also prevents much of the Sun's incoming ultraviolet radiation from reaching the Earth.

The Earth's atmosphere is about 480 km thick. Most of the atmosphere (about 80%) is within 15-16 km of the surface of the Earth. There is no exact upper end place where the atmosphere ends; it just gets thinner and thinner, until it merges with outer space.

The Layers of the Atmosphere

Thermosphere

In the thermosphere, temperature increases with altitude. The thermosphere includes the exosphere and part of the ionosphere.

Exosphere

The exosphere is the outermost layer of the Earth's atmosphere. The exosphere exists from about 640 km to about 1,280 km high. Here, both the atmospheric pressure and temperature are very low.

Ionosphere

The range of ionosphere is from 70-80 km to about 640 km. It contains many ions and free electrons (plasma). Auroras occur in the ionosphere.

Mesosphere

The mesosphere is a zone where temperatures quickly decrease as height increases. The mesosphere extends from between 50 to 80 km above the earth's surface.

Stratosphere

The stratosphere is characterized by a slight temperature increase with height. The stratosphere extends from 18 to 50 km above the earth's surface. The earth's ozone layer is located in the stratosphere. Ozone, a form of oxygen, is crucial to our survival; this layer absorbs a lot of ultraviolet solar energy.

Troposphere

The troposphere is the lowest region in the Earth's atmosphere. On the Earth, it goes from ground level up to about 17 km high. The weather and clouds occur in the troposphere. In the troposphere, the temperature generally decreases as altitude increases.

Formation of the Atmosphere

The Earth's atmosphere was formed when gases like carbon dioxide, water vapour, sulphur dioxide and nitrogen escaped from the interior of the Earth due to volcanoes and other processes. Life forms on Earth have modified the composition of the atmosphere since their evolution.

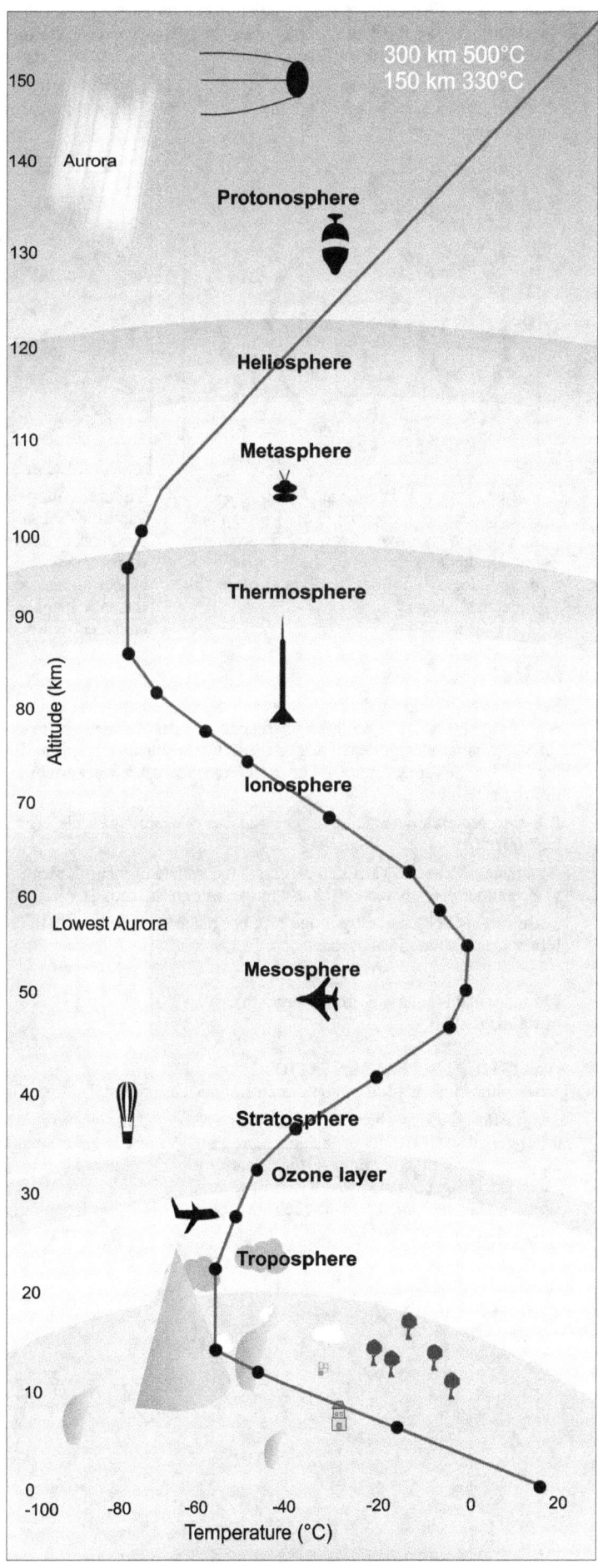

A Map is a representation of geographical space on plane surface. It helps us understand the interrelation of phenomena, e.g. soil, climate and vegetation of a region or heights or depths of physical features, in a spatial relationship. These phenomena are generalised, reduced and presented in a dimensionally systematic form on a plane surface.

Cartography is the art and science of mapping. There is no limit to the subject matter that can be mapped. Be it economic data, climatic information or other geographical facts, maps are the most effective means of communicating them. This diversity can be presented through General, Thematic and Topographical maps.

General maps : These maps portray spatial associations of a variety of geographical phenomena on a map. Accuracy of positional relationships of the items shown is of great importance. All political and **relief maps** fall under this category.

Thematic maps : These maps portray spatial variations of a single phenomenon or the relationship between phenomena. These maps represent a specific distribution theme or aspect under discussion. The large section of thematic maps in this Atlas presents important statistical data on various topics.

Topographic maps : These maps portray natural phenomena along with features, produced by human activity (i.e. cultural features), e.g. settlements, wells, bridges. These maps are usually drawn on a large scale to show the surface features in detail.

SCALE

Scale is an expression of the ratio between a distance on the map (which is always expressed as 1) and the corresponding distance on the earth's surface (this can change depending on the area available for printing and the focus of the subject matter). The unit of distance on both sides of the ratio must be the same.

R.E or Representative Fraction is the usual way of expressing scale, e.g. 1: 5,000,000

A statement 1 cm to 50 km also expresses the system of measurement, viz. centimetre, gram, second (CGS); metre, kilogram, second (MKS).

Scale can also be shown by a line or a bar placed on the map in the left/right upper margin of the page or in the Legend.

       0   50   100 km

The maps in this atlas vary from a large scale of 1:13,000 to a small scale of 1:198,000,000.

SYMBOLS

Apart from conventional symbols, colour patterns also help us understand maps. The colours in the General maps follow an isarithmic pattern. An isarithm is the same value or quantity, e.g. heights (drawn in contours), temperatures (in isotherms), barometric pressure (in isobars). Changing colours correspond to the changing values. Complete contour patterns depict the relief of the land. 3-dimensional topographical features appear on plane surface in colour gradations and contour lines. The width of space between the contours indicates the slope of the land. The less the width and the closer the lines, the steeper is the slope.

Relief shown in Contours

STATISTICAL REPRESENTATION

Geographical information can be presented through Bar Graphs, Line Graphs and Pie Graphs.

Bar graphs : Bars have been set vertically as well as horizontally. The length of each bar represents the proportion of the quantity of the category it stands for. Using both the axes (X and Y) several categories can be compared with each other over time, distance, quantity, etc.

Line graphs : The same information or any variation of quantity or quantities can also be indicated by Line Graphs.

Pie graphs : Pie Graphs or divided circle diagrams are those in which the circle representing the total of the values of a category is divided into sectors. Each sector is proportional to the quantity or value of the same category which it represents.

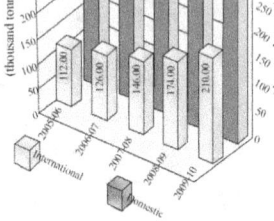

Bar Graph

Line Graph

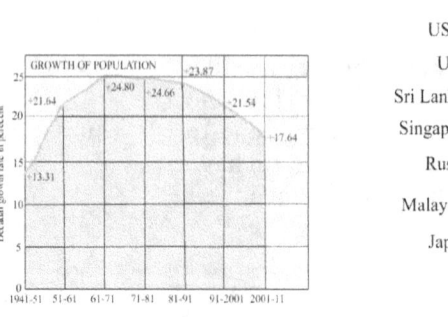

Pie Graph

LOCATION

A geometrical grid of latitudes and longitudes is used to locate the position of a place on the earth's surface. Mathematical formulae are used to project the information onto a plane surface.

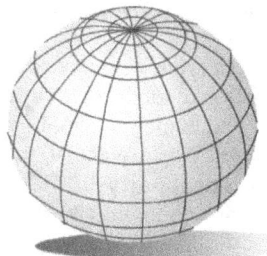

Grid system of earth

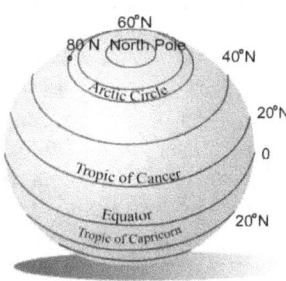

Latitude 40°N

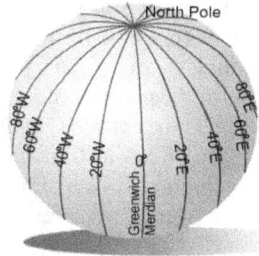

Longitude

A grid or graticule is a geometrical network formed by the intersection of parallels of latitude and meridians or lines of longitude which provides convenient reference points while projecting a spherical surface on a plane surface. These points are then used to positively locate any place on the plane map. Graticule Lines may be shown either as straight lines perpendicular to each other or curved lines, depending on the type of projection used for a specific purpose.

Latitudes (parallels) : Latitudes form the X axis of the grid. These lines run east-west along the earth's surface and are parallel, with their centres on the earth's axis and their planes at right angles to it. The Equator is the circle whose plane passes through the centre of the earth (0°) and is perpendicular to the earth's axis. Being equidistant from the poles, it divides the earth into Northern and Southern hemispheres. Its latitude is 0°. The greatest possible latitude is 90°, that of the poles.

Longitudes (meridians) : The longitudes form the Y axis of the grid. These lines run north-south along the earth's surface and meet at the two poles. Longitude is expressed as the angle made by a longitudinal plane at the earth's centre with that of the prime meridian, which is 0°. There are thus 180 longitudes east and west of the prime meridian.

Map Projections

A globe is the naturally accurate map of the earth.

Although the shape of the earth is that of an oblate spheroid, i.e. flat at the poles and bulging at the equator; for the sake of convenience, it is taken to be a perfect sphere. The globe thus is a reduced earth retaining all geometrical properties. Being a three-dimensional body, less than half of the surface is observed at any given time. The globe itself is cumbersome to handle and measurements are difficult. To overcome such practical difficulties, cartographers project the spherical surface on to a plane surface. The actual process of transformation of surface data is called a projection.

Distortions during transformation are inevitable because the two surfaces are not geometrically applicable.

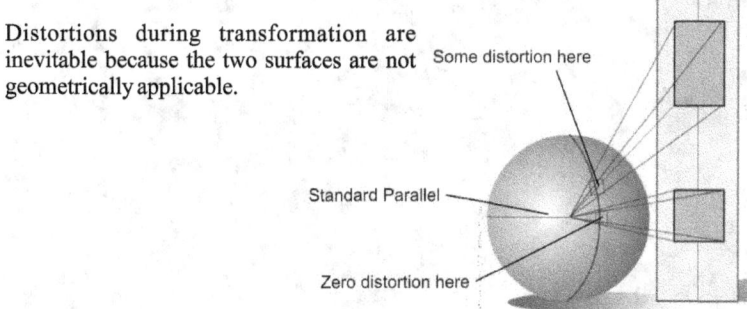

Same line of longitude

Many methods are employed to keep distortions to a minimum.

Retention of important geometric properties of the sphere like:

(i)   Angular relationships or retention of true shape
(ii)   Correct directional relations along a great circle
(iii)   Equal area
(iv)   Equal distance
(v)   Significant lines

Simple graphical projections with some adjustments of mathematical formulae are also used by cartographers. The details on the sphere are projected onto the plane surface. The points at which the plane surface touches the sphere are free from distortion, while elsewhere there is always some distortion in shape, area, scale, etc.

determine the type of projection to be made. Some of these properties may even be mutually exclusive.

Subject matter (e.g. political, physical), focus (e.g. particular latitudes, landforms) and scale of reduction may vary with the geometric properties.

SIMPLE PROJECTIONS

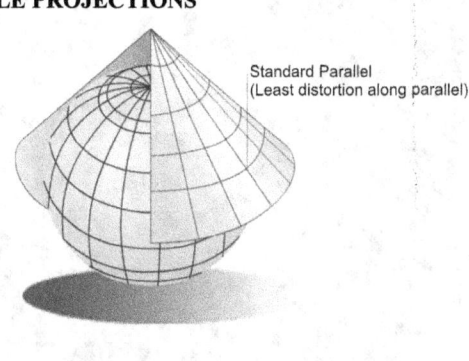

Conic

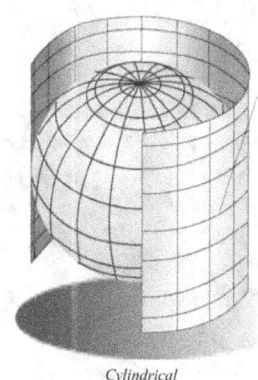

Cylindrical

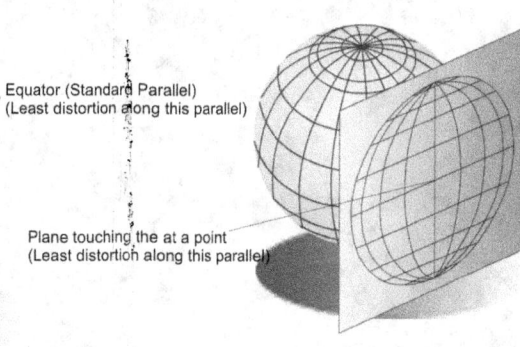

Azimuthal

Remote Sensing

Remote sensing is the science and art of obtaining information about phenomena without being in contact with it. Remote sensing deals with the detection and measurement of phenomena with devices such as sight (camera and scanners), heat (thermal scanners) and radio waves (radar) that is sensitive to electromagnetic energy. Remote sensing has a wide variety of uses; it provides a unique perspective from which large regions can be observed. Sensors can measure energy at wavelengths that are beyond the range of human vision. With remote sensing, global monitoring is possible from nearly any site on the earth.

The technology of modern remote sensing actually began in the early 1840s when pictures were taken from cameras secured to tethered balloons for the purpose of topographic mapping. By the First World War, cameras mounted on airplanes provided aerial views of fairly large surface areas that proved invaluable in military reconnaissance. In the 1930s, improvements in film and camera technology, including the introduction of colour film and infrared film allowed more detailed photographs to be taken. The Second World War (1939-1945) led to the rapid development of cameras and aerial platforms, as well as the training of a team of photo-interpreters on the ground. The immediate post-war years saw the widespread deployment of precisely engineered cameras by newly established air survey companies that led to the mapping of many new areas. Old maps were also updated and many inaccuracies were corrected.

Satellite Imagery

With the launch of the Soviet satellite Sputnik in 1957 began the remote sensing through satellite. This was followed by the NASA's Explorer in 1958. The first pictures from space were returned by radio link from a television camera on its US counterpart, Explorer 6 in 1959. A year later, the first of the TIROS (Television and Infra-Red Observation Satellite) meteorological satellites started to return systematic imagery of the earth's cloud cover. The TIROS weather satellites were launched throughout the 1960s and then were replaced in 1970 by the NOAA series, which continues to this day. Remote-sensing scientists now monitor changes to the earth's environment over timescales of hours using data from geostationary weather satellites. The USA's Landsat satellite system has been operating continuously since 1972, enabling changes to be monitored over decades.

Modern Cartography and Remote Sensing

Remote sensing has become very crucial to modem cartographers. It has opened the possibility of extensive geographical information with a vast image collection of the earth, other planets and other galaxies. Vegetation surveys can now be made from high altitudes to show the distribution of specific crops, weeds or native plants amidst a carpet of general vegetation. High-resolution satellite cameras can record details as small as a few metres in diameter on the surface of the earth. Satellites such as those in the Landsat series sweep the globe with continuous scans to provide detailed maps of the entire earth. Modern computers can store and transmit huge amounts of mapping data and then input such data into maps using sophisticated digitizers and plotting machines. Thus, the data obtained from remote sensing is assembled into highly refined electronic images that resemble photographs.

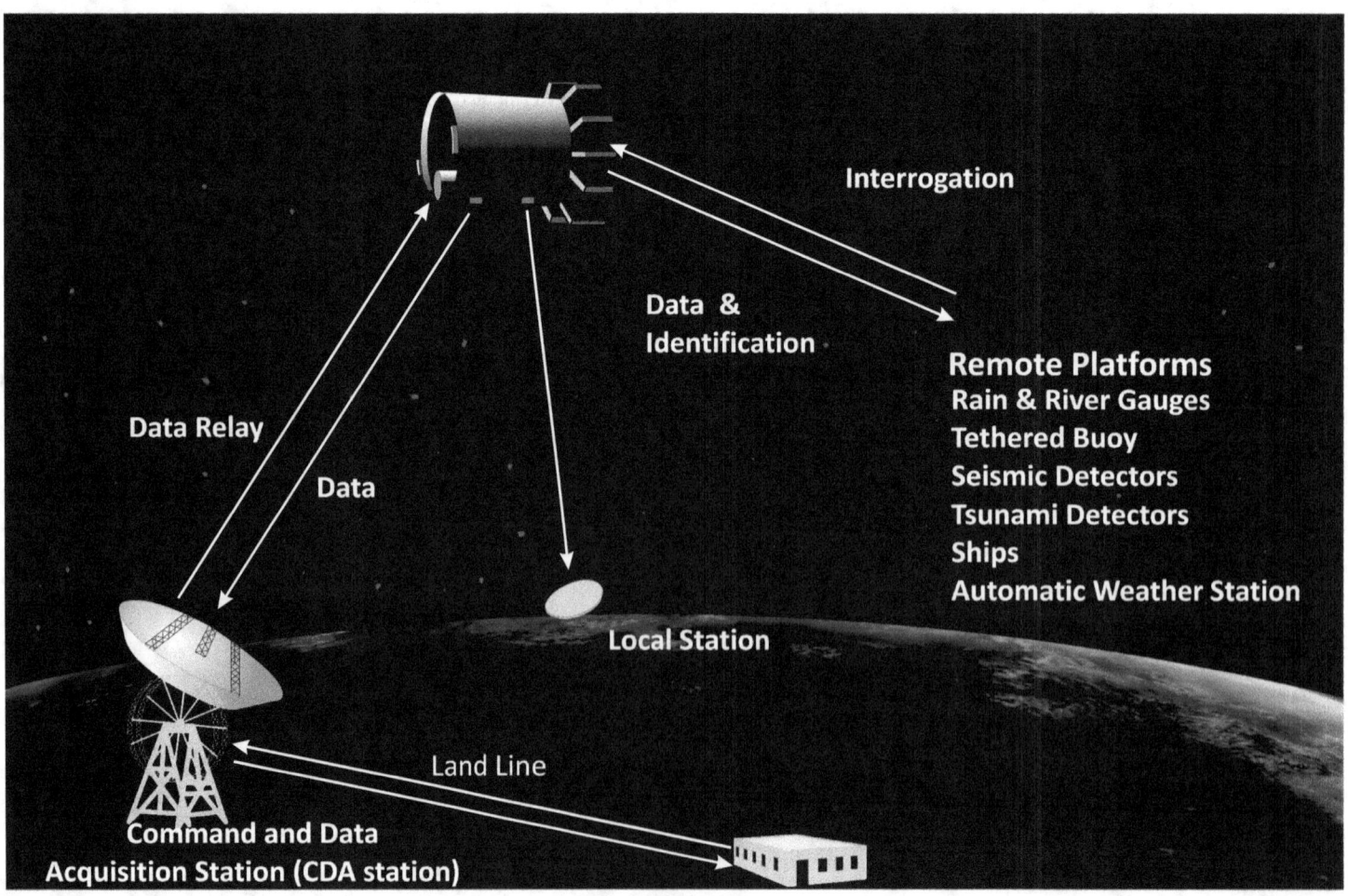

Global Positioning Systems (GPS)

Global Positioning Systems (GPS) are devices that give a person an earth coordinate position based on the reception of special satellite transmissions. Three or more satellites provide the energy beams on which a handheld GPS, through triangulation, bases its calculation of exactly where on the surface of the earth the GPS is located. Compact and handy, modern GPS units have a simple LCD screen similar to that on an electronic calculator and can be programmed to record and display the exact position of the unit, the user's ground speed and direction of travel, and projected arrival times along a specific route. In modern cartography, the GPS is used to verify the location of boundary lines. In future, GPS and related technology will play increasingly important roles in cartographic data collection.

Geographic Information Systems (GIS)

Geographic information systems (GIS) are a means of storing, integrating, analyzing and presenting geographic data. It consists of a combination of computers, databases and software, with skilled operators who can process and present different thematic data with reference to a single geographic framework. GIS technology can be used for scientific investigations, resource management and development planning. For example, a GIS may allow emergency planners to easily calculate emergency response times during a natural disaster or to find wetlands that need protection from pollution. The GIS works by relating information from different sources, capturing data, integrating it, forming a common projection, data structuring and data modelling. Complex analyses can be performed as the maps and data are stored or filed as layers of information in a GIS. GIS is now used in mapmaking, site selection, emergency response planning and for simulating environmental effects.

Global Positioning
Systems (GPS)

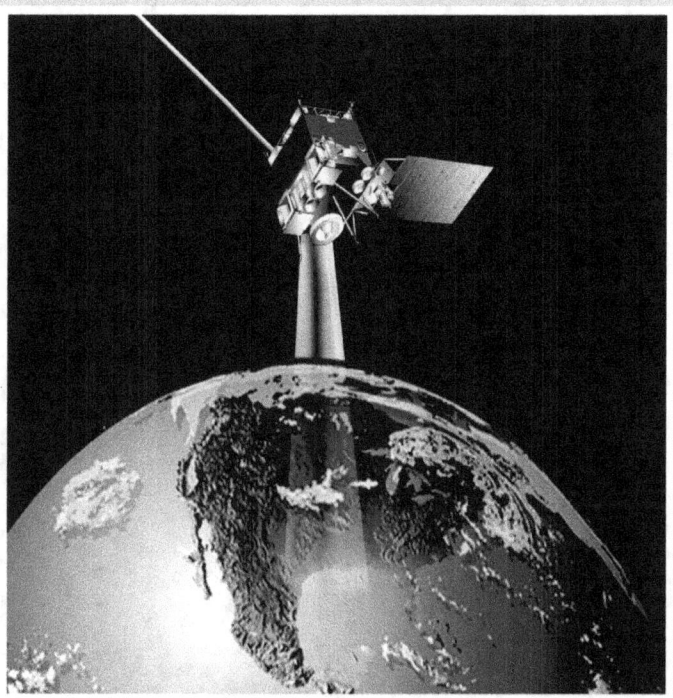

Geostationary Satellite

Remote Sensing Platforms
Aircraft
Light aircraft carrying aerial survey cameras are used even today for taking overlapping photographs that are useful in topographic map-making. High-altitude aircrafts such as NASA's ER-2 cover larger areas and carry experimental instruments that may later be developed for use on satellites.

Photographs from Space
Photographs taken from space shuttles are archived at NASA's Johnson Space Centre. They enable us to share the astronauts' view of the earth from low orbit.

Geostationary Satellites
Geostationary satellites move in a very high equatorial orbit. These satellites appear fixed above a particular location, as their movement exactly matches the rotation of the earth. This orbit provides a continuous view of half the earth, which is useful for communications and television broadcast satellites and earth observation platforms.

Polar-orbiting Satellites
Polar-orbiting satellites such as the NOAA weather satellite orbit at relatively low altitude above the surface of the earth, completing an orbit from pole to pole and back again in about 100 minutes. Their motion is usually synchronized to the sun. Onboard camera systems build up images line-by-line as the satellite moves along its orbit, transmitting the digital image data directly to a ground receiving station or recording it on-board for transmission at a later time.

NASA's Space Shuttle
NASA's space shuttle acts both as a launcher for satellite platforms and as an earth observation platform as well. Prototype instruments may be tested on limited-duration flights in the shuttle's cargo bay before permanent deployment on a satellite.

ABOUT THE EARTH

Total area	510,000,000 sq km
Land surface (29.2%)	149,000,000 sq km
Water surface (70.8%)	361,000,000 sq km
Equatorial circumference	40,077 km
Meridian circumference	40,009 km
Polar diameter	12,713.8 km
Equatorial diameter	12,756.8 km
Mass of the Earth	5.9×10^{21} tone

INDIA

Area	3,287,240 sq km
Population	1,026,610,328
Breadth	3000 km East to West
Length	3200 km North to South
Coast Line	6083 km
Latitude	8°0'N - 37°06'N
Longitude	68°07´E - 97°25'E
Area	Seventh largest
Population	Second highest

MOST POPULOUS COUNTRY

Country	2014 Population
China	1,368,853,362
India	1,236,344,631
United States	318,892,103
Indonesia	253,609,643
Brazil	202,656,788
Pakistan	196,174,380
Nigeria	177,155,754
Bangladesh	166,280,712
Russia	142,470,272
Japan	127,103,388

DEEPEST TRENCHES
(Depth in metres)

Mariana Trench, Pacific Ocean	11022
Tonga Trench, Pacific Ocean	10882
Japan Trench, Pacific Ocean	10554
Kurii Trench, Pacific Ocean	10542
Mindanao Trench, Pacific Ocean	10497
Kermadec Trench, Pacific Ocean	10047
Puerto Rico, Atlantic Ocean	9220
Peru-Chile Trench, Pacific Ocean	8050
Aleutian Trench, Pacific Ocean	7822
Cayman Trench, Atlantic Ocean	7680
Java Trench, Indian Ocean	7450

LONGEST RIVERS
(Length in km)

Nile, Africa	6670
Amazon, S. America	6450
Yangtze, Asia	6380
Mississippi - Missouri - N.America	6020
Yenisey, Angara - Russia	5550
Huang Ho, Asia	5464
Ob, Russia	5410
Cango, Africa	4670
Mekong, Asia	4500
Parana, S.America	4500
Lena, Russia	4400
Amur, Asia	4400
Irtysh, Russia	4250
Mackenzie, Canada	4240
Niger, Africa	4180
Mississippi, N. America	3780
Murray-Darling, Australia	3750
Volga, Russia	3700
Zambezi, Africa	3540
Purus, Brazil	3350
Maderia, Brazil	3200
Yukon, N. America	3185
Inuds, Asia	3100
Darling, Australia	3070

MAJOR INLAND WATER (Area in sq km)

Nettiling 5,066
Superior 83,350
Huron 59,600
Winnipeg 24,400
Caspian Sea 371,800
Aral Sea 28,687
Turkana (Rudolf) 8,500
Victoria 68,000
Malawi/ Nyasa 29,600
Chad 25,000
Balkhash 18,500
Tanganyika 33,000
Michigan 58,000
Ontario 19,500
Great Slave 28,500
Erie 25,700
Baykal 30,500
Mweru 5,120
Albert 5,300
Ladoga 17,700
De Nicaragua 8,200
Great Bear 31,800
Issyk kul 6,236
Qinghai Hu 2,278
Torrens 5,776
Athabasca 7,850
Reindeer 6,500
Poyang Hu 4,400
Vanern 5,500
Onega 9,700
Titicaca 8,300
Eyre 8,900

HIGHEST WATER FALLS
(Height in meters)

Angel, Venezuela	979
Tugela, South Africa	850
Utigord, Norway	800
Monge, Norway	774
Mutarazi, Zimbababwe	762
Yosemite, California	739
Espeiand, Norway	703
Mara Valley, Norway	655
Salto Kukenan, Venezuela	610
Dudhsagar, India	600
Sutherland, New Zealand	580
Kjell, Norway	561
Ribbon, California	491
Roraima, Guyana	457
Piedra Volada	453
Della, Canada	440

MAJOR OCEANS

Name	Ocean Area in sq. km.
Pacific Ocean	165,250,000 sq km
Atlantic Ocean	106,400,000 sq km
Indian Ocean	73,560,000 sq
Southern Ocean	20,330,000 sq km
Arctic Ocean	13,990,000 sq km

MAJOR SEAS

Name	Area in sq. km.
South China Sea	2,974,600
Caribbean Sea	2,765,000
Mediterranean Sea	2,516,000
Bering Sea	2,268,000
Gulf of Mexico	1,543,000
Sea of Okhotsk	1,528,000
East China Sea	1,249,000
Hudson Bay	1,232,000
Sea of Japan	1,008,000
Yellow Sea	752,443
North Se	575,000
Black Sea	462,000
Red Sea	438,000
Baltic Sea	422,000

MAJOR DAMS
(Height in metres)

Asia

Nurek, Vakhsh River, Russia	317
Bhakra, Satluj River, India	226
Kurobegawa, Kurobe River, Japan	186

Africa

Cabora Bassa, Zambezi River	168
Akosombo Main Dam, Volta River	141

Europe

Grand Dixence, Switzerland	284
Vajont, Vajont R.Italy	261

America

Oroville, Feather River	235
Hoover, Colorado River	221

Australia

Warragamba	137

PEAKS IN THE WORLD
(Height in meters)

Asia

Mount Everest	8848
K2 (Godwin Austin)	8611
Kanchenjunga	8586
Lhotse	8516
Makalu	8485
Cho Oyu	8188
Dhaulagiri	8167
Manaslu	8163
Nanga Parbat	8126
Annapurna	8091

Africa

Killimanjaro, Tanzania	5895
Kenya, Kenya	5199
Ruwenzori, Uganda	5109
Ras Dashan, Ethiopia	4533

Europe

Mt.Blanc, France-Italy	4807

North America

McKinley, USA	6194
Logan, Canada	6050
Citalalepet, Mexico	5700
St.Elias, USA-Canada	5489

South America

Aconcagua, Argentina	6980
Ojos del salado, Argentina-Chile	6863
Boneto, Argentina	6872
Tupungato, Argentina-Chile	6800

Australia – New Zealand

Cook, New Zealand	3764
Aspring, New Zealand	3035
Tupuaenkuku, New Zealand	2885
Kosclusko, Australia	2330

MAJOR ISLANDS (Area in sq km)

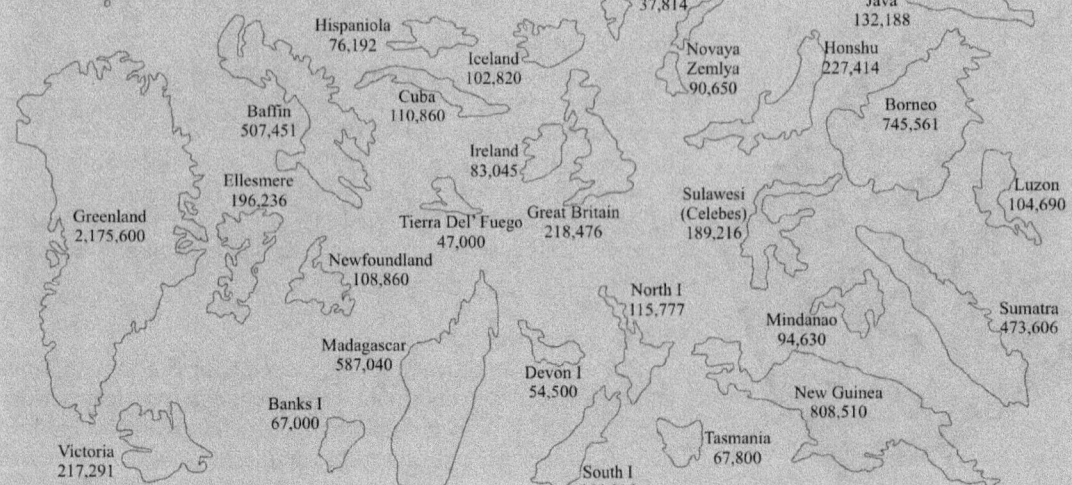

Spitsbergen 37,814
Java 132,188
Hispaniola 76,192
Iceland 102,820
Novaya Zemlya 90,650
Honshu 227,414
Cuba 110,860
Baffin 507,451
Borneo 745,561
Ireland 83,045
Ellesmere 196,236
Sulawesi (Celebes) 189,216
Luzon 104,690
Greenland 2,175,600
Tierra Del Fuego 47,000
Great Britain 218,476
Newfoundland 108,860
North I 115,777
Sumatra 473,606
Madagascar 587,040
Devon I 54,500
Mindanao 94,630
Banks I 67,000
New Guinea 808,510
Victoria 217,291
Tasmania 67,800
South I 151,215

SYMBOLS

BOUNDARIES
International Boundary ....
State/Province/Union Territory.........

COMMUNICATIONS
National Highway..........}
Other Road.....................
Major Road....................
Railway.........................
Sea Route......................

HYDROGRAPHY
Coastline..
Canal..
River: perennial; seasonal.................
Lake/Reservoir: perennial; seasonal
Marsh/Swamp.................................
Waterfall..
Dam..
Reef..
Permanent Ice Cap............................
Ocean Depth (metres)....................... ▼10920

SETTLEMENTS

Altitude Scale

m
6000
4500
3000
1800
1350
900
600
300
150
0 — 0
200
2000
4000
6000
8000
m

POPULATION	Country Capital	Dependent Territory Capital	State/UT Headquarter	District Headquarter	Other Town
Over 1,000,000...........................	▣	▣	▢	▢	▢
500,000-1,000,000:....................	◉	◉	◎	○	○
100,000-500,000:.......................	●	●	◦	◦	◦
50,000-100,000:.........................	•	•	•	•	•
10,000-50,000:...........................	·	·	·	·	·
Under 10,000.............................	·	·	·	·	·

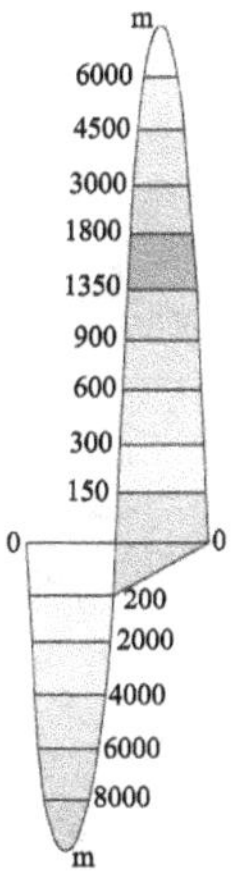

RELIEF
Peak Height (metres)... ....   ▲10920
Pass...   ⋈
Depression (metres).......................   ▼411

ADMINISTRATIVE NAMES
Continent Name...............................   A S I A
Country Name...................................   I N D I A
State/Union Territory/
Province Name...................................   G U J A R A T
Dependent Territory Name..............   GREENLAND(DENMARK)
Country/Dependent Territory
Capital/State/UT Headquarters........   Delhi Torshavn Mumbai Silvassa
District headquarters/Other
Town...   Kurnool Jagtial

HYDROGRAPHY FEATURES
Ocean Name......................   P A C I F I C O C E A N
Bay/Sea Name...................................   B A Y O F B E N G A L
Gulf/Strait/Passage/Channel
Mouths/Delta/Lake/Reservoir/
Waterfall/River Name........................   Gulf of Mannar   Palk Strait
Dam Name...   Gudha Dam

PHYSICAL FEATURES
Range/Mountains/Hills....................   G r e a t H i m a l a y a
Plain/Plateau/Peninsula/Region/
Trench/Coast/Desert.........................   PLAIN OF THE GANGA DECCAN
Cape/Point..   Cape Comorin   Indira Point
Islands/Archipelago/Ref.................   Baffin I.   Mergui Arch. Cherbaniani Reef
Peak/Deep/Pass...............................   Mt. Everest   Mergui Arch.

GEOGRAPHIC EXTREMES OF THE WORLD

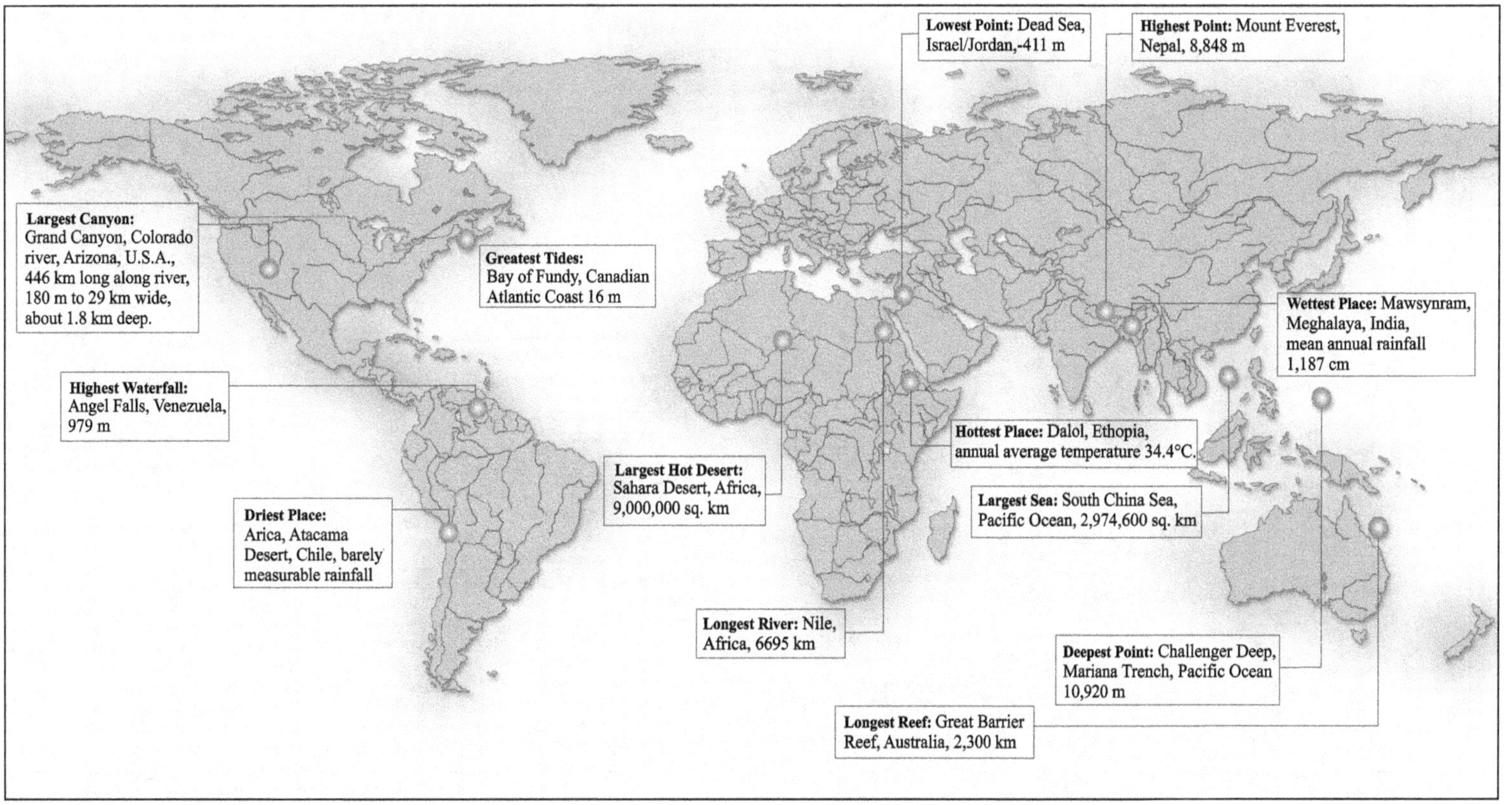

Lowest Point: Dead Sea, Israel/Jordan,-411 m

Highest Point: Mount Everest, Nepal, 8,848 m

Largest Canyon: Grand Canyon, Colorado river, Arizona, U.S.A., 446 km long along river, 180 m to 29 km wide, about 1.8 km deep.

Greatest Tides: Bay of Fundy, Canadian Atlantic Coast 16 m

Wettest Place: Mawsynram, Meghalaya, India, mean annual rainfall 1,187 cm

Highest Waterfall: Angel Falls, Venezuela, 979 m

Hottest Place: Dalol, Ethopia, annual average temperature 34.4°C.

Driest Place: Arica, Atacama Desert, Chile, barely measurable rainfall

Largest Hot Desert: Sahara Desert, Africa, 9,000,000 sq. km

Largest Sea: South China Sea, Pacific Ocean, 2,974,600 sq. km

Longest River: Nile, Africa, 6695 km

Deepest Point: Challenger Deep, Mariana Trench, Pacific Ocean 10,920 m

Longest Reef: Great Barrier Reef, Australia, 2,300 km

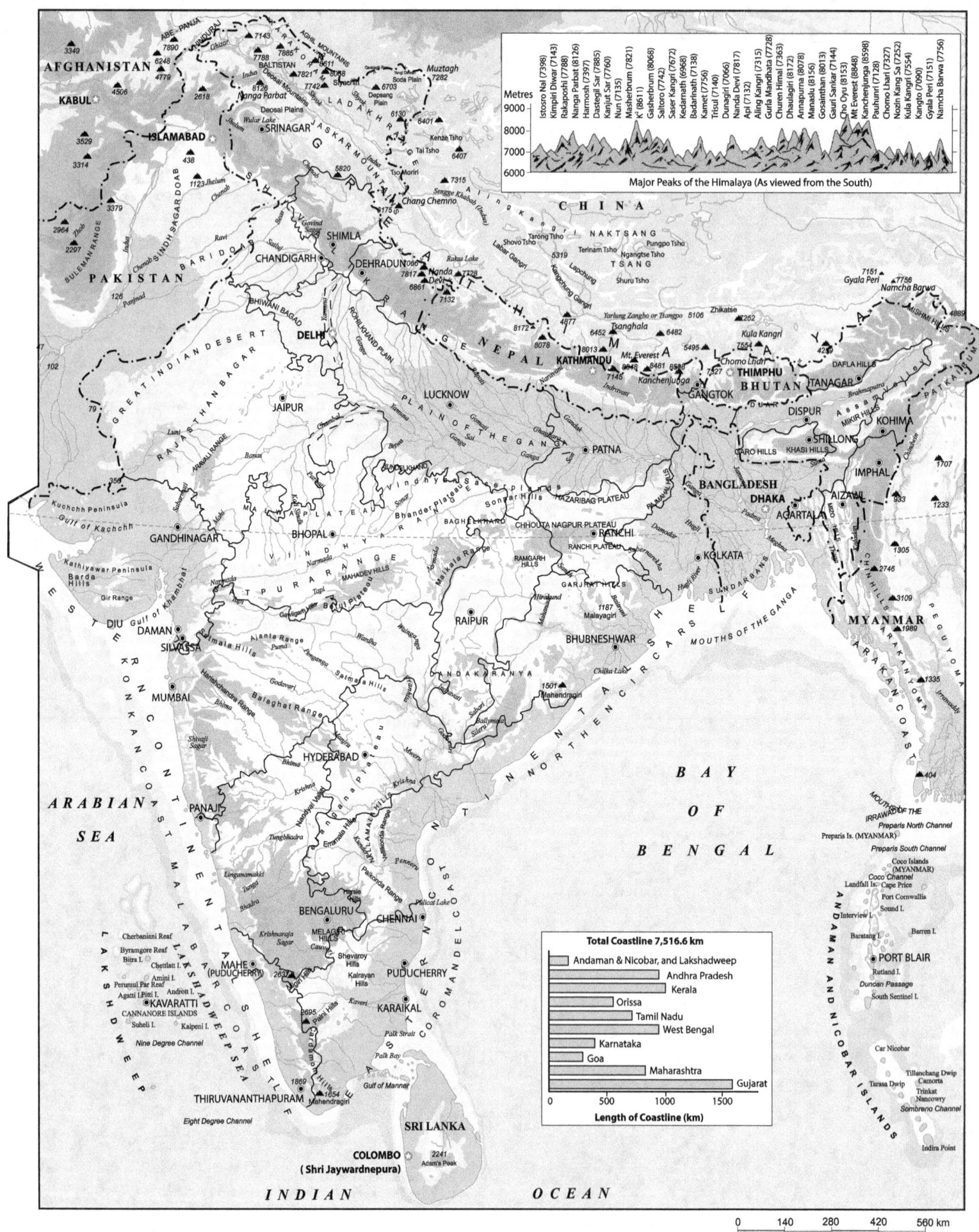

Major Peaks of the Himalaya (As viewed from the South)

Total Coastline 7,516.6 km

Length of Coastline (km)

SCALE 1:14,000,000

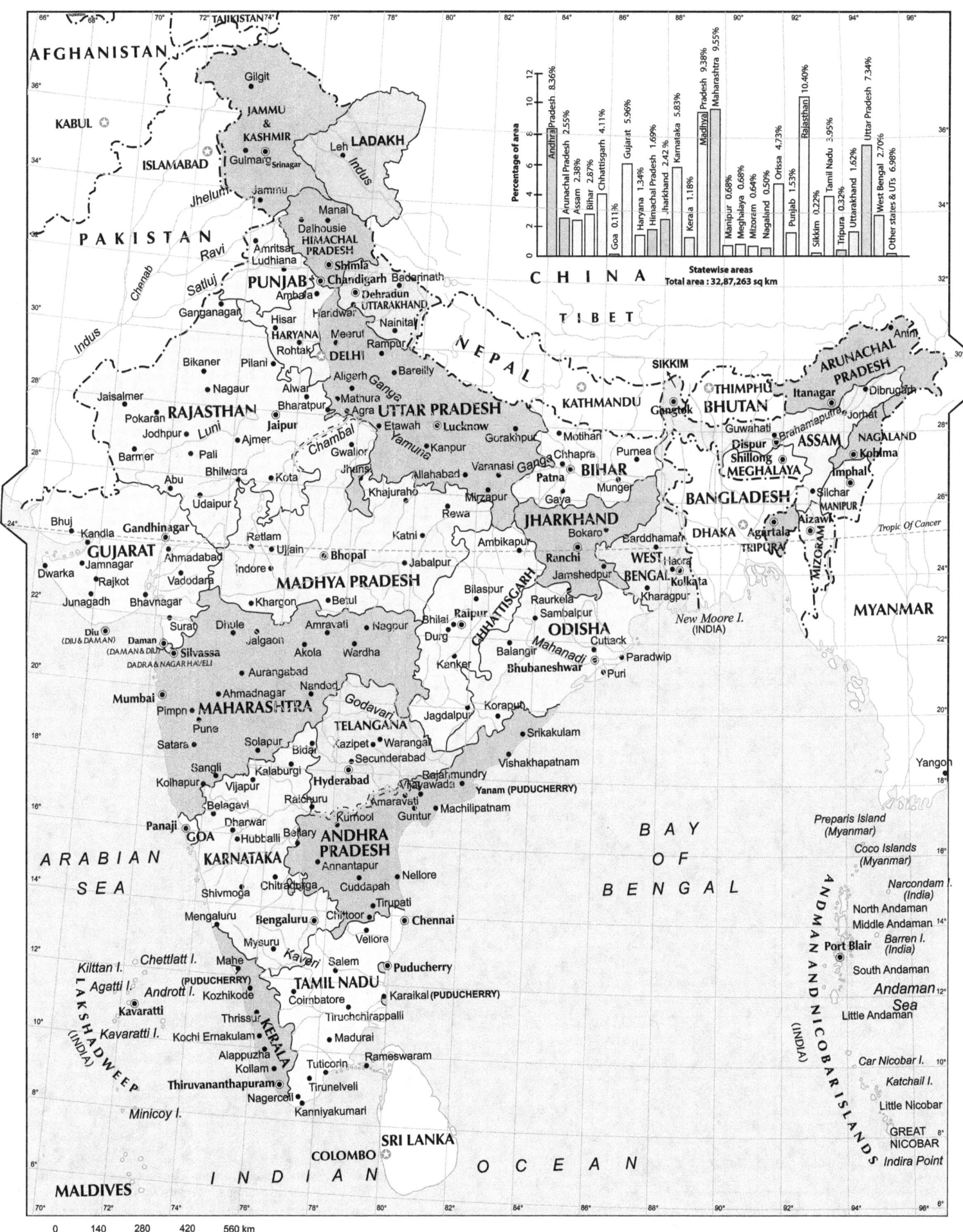

Statewise areas
Total area : 32,87,263 sq km

SCALE : 1:14,000,000

0   140   280   420   560 km

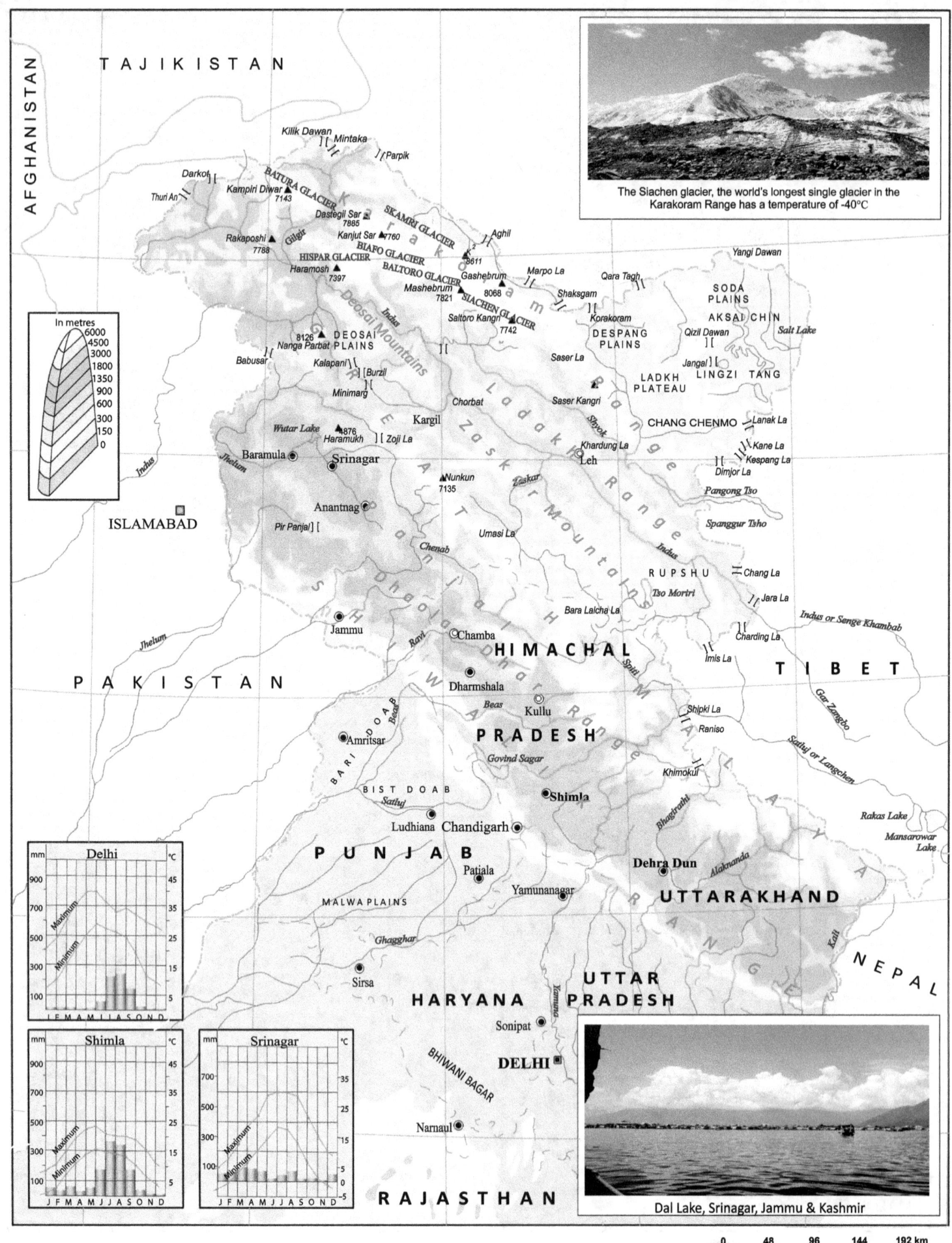

The Siachen glacier, the world's longest single glacier in the Karakoram Range has a temperature of -40°C

Dal Lake, Srinagar, Jammu & Kashmir

SCALE 1:4,850,000 (Approx)

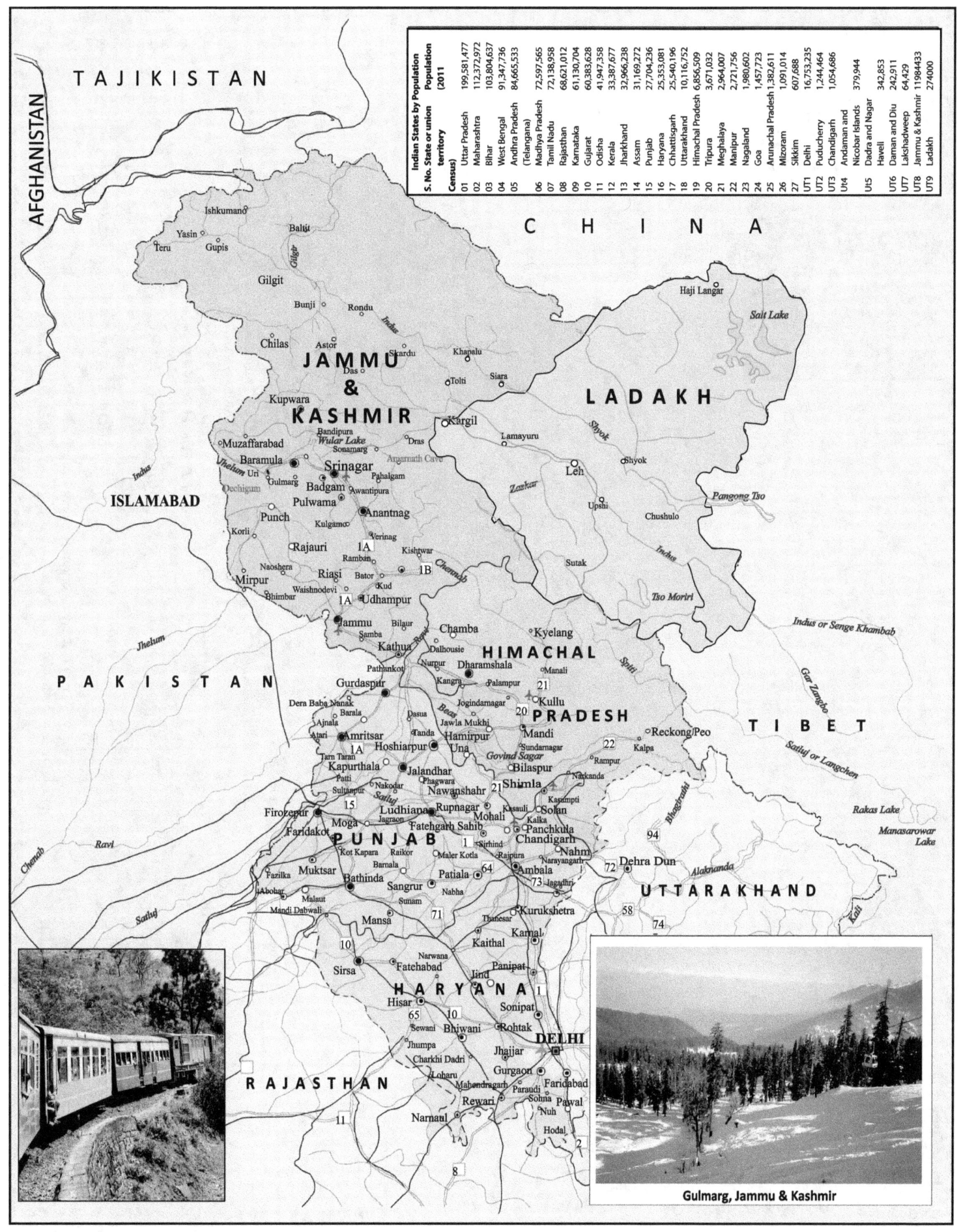

Gulmarg, Jammu & Kashmir

SCALE 1:4,850,000 (Approx)

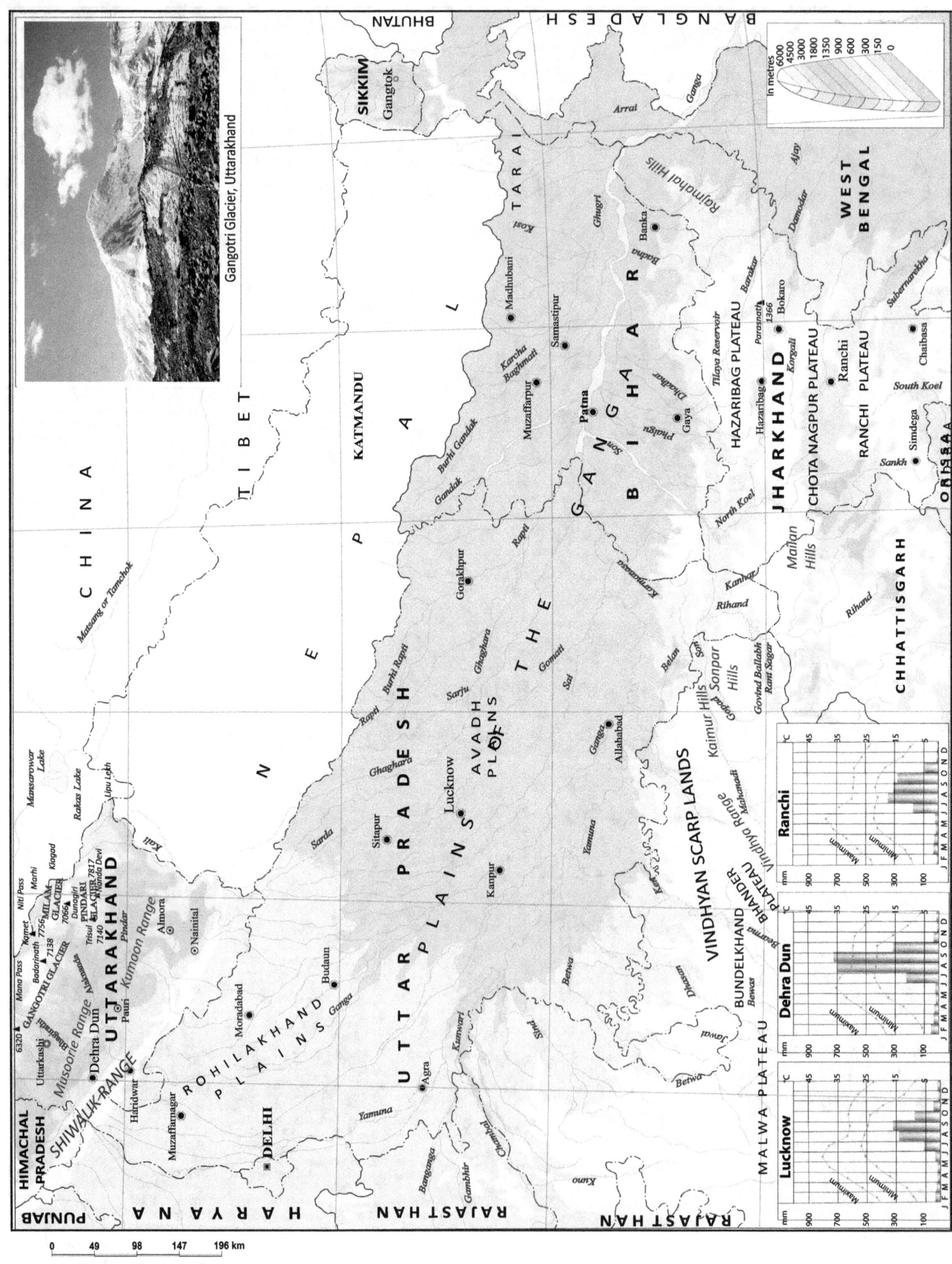

Gangotri Glacier, Uttarakhand

In metres
6000
4500
3000
1800
1350
900
600
300
150
0

BHUTAN
BANGLADESH
SIKKIM
Gangtok
Rajmahal Hills
WEST BENGAL
Arral
Ganga
TARAI
Kosi
Ghugri
Ajay
Banka
Damodar
Baghmati
Madhubani
Samastipur
Tilaya Reservoir
HAZARIBAG PLATEAU
Karcha
Baghmati
Parasnath 1366
Bokaro
Subernarekha
JHARKHAND
Korgali
Ranchi
Chaibasa
Muzaffarpur
Patna
BIHAR
Dhakur
Phalgu
Gaya
Hazaribag
CHOTA NAGPUR PLATEAU
RANCHI PLATEAU
South Koel
Son
North Koel
Simdega
Sankh
ORISSA
KATMANDU
Burhi Gandak
Gandak
Maltan Hills
N
E
P
A
L
Rapti
THE GANGA
Kanhar
Rihand
Rihand
CHHATTISGARH
Gorakhpur
Ghaghara
Gomati
Karmanasa
Sai
Belan
Son
Sonpar Hills
Govind Ballabh
Rani Sagar

TIBET
CHINA
Matsang or Tamchok
Ghaghara
Rapti
Burhi Rapti
Sarju
AVADH PLAINS
Lucknow
UTTAR PRADESH PLAINS
Sitapur
Ganga
Allahabad
Kaimur Hills
Godavari
VINDHYAN SCARP LANDS
Vindhya Range
Mahanadi
Kampur
Yamuna
Ken
BUNDELKHAND PLATEAU
Betwa
Dhasan
Son
MALWA PLATEAU

Mansarowar Lake
Rakas Lake
Lipu Lekh
Kali
Kingad
Marhi
Niti Pass
Kamet
7756 MILAM GLACIER
Mana Pass
Badrinath 7138
PINDARI GLACIER
7066
Trisul 7817
Nanda Devi
7140
GANGOTRI GLACIER
6320
Uttarkashi
Bhagirathi
Musoorie Range
Alaknanda
UTTARAKHAND
Pindar
Kumaon Range
Almora
Nainital
Dehra Dun
Pauri
SHIWALIK RANGE
Haridwar
HIMACHAL PRADESH
Muzaffarnagar
ROHILAKHAND PLAINS
Moradabad
Budaun
Ganga
Agra
Yamuna
DELHI
Betwa
PUNJAB
HARYANA
Bangaga
Gambhir
Kuno
Chambal
Parbati
RAJASTHAN

Ranchi
°C 45 35 25 15 5
mm 900 700 500 300 100
Maximum
Minimum
J F M A M J J A S O N D

Dehra Dun
°C 45 35 25 15 5
mm 900 700 500 300 100
Maximum
Minimum
J F M A M J J A S O N D

Lucknow
°C 45 35 25 15 5
mm 900 700 500 300 100
Maximum
Minimum
J F M A M J J A S O N D

0   49   98   147   196 km

SCALE 1:4,900,000 (Approx)

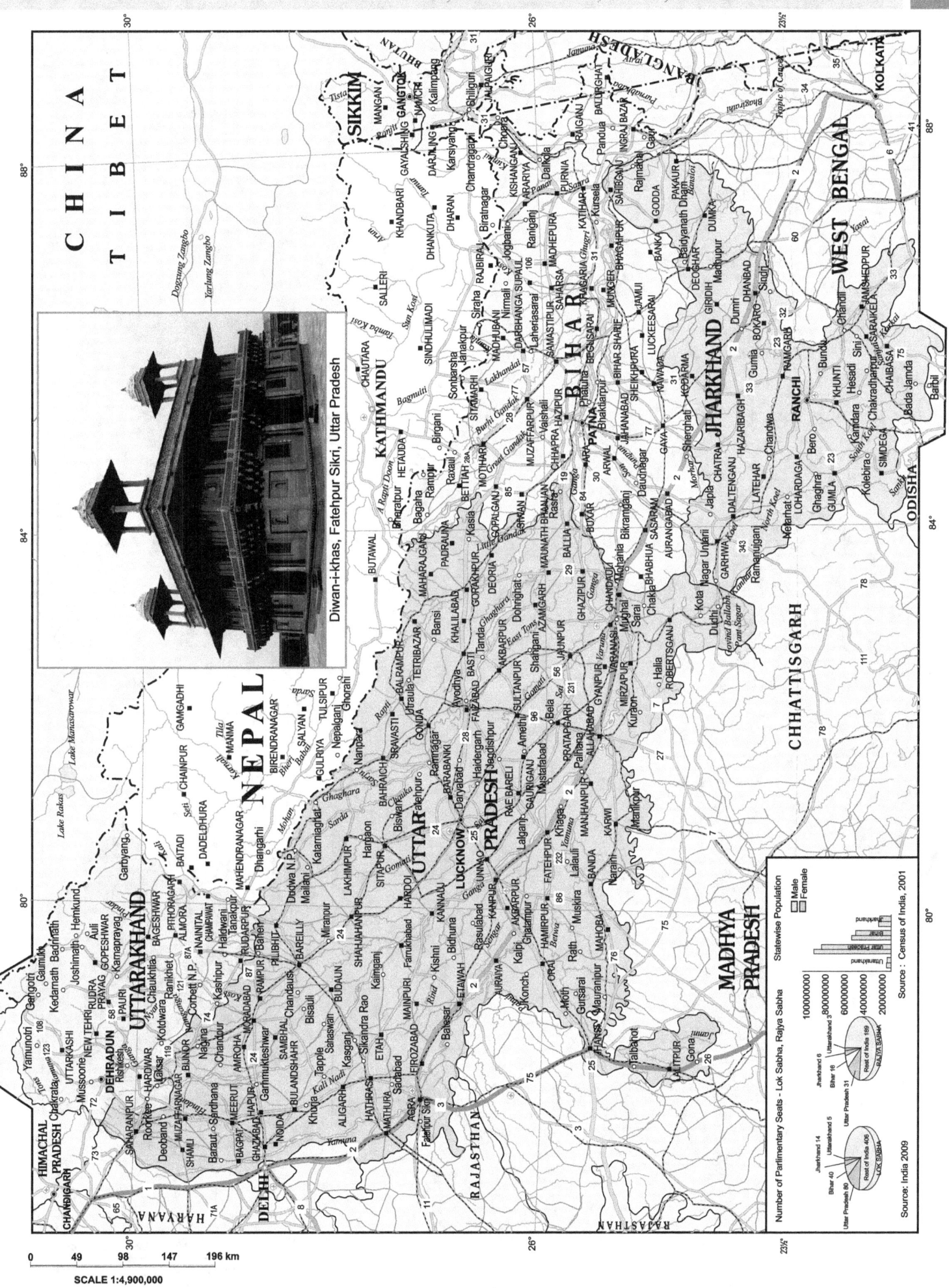

Diwan-i-khas, Fatehpur Sikri, Uttar Pradesh

SCALE 1:4,900,000

0   49   98   147   196 km

Source : Census of India, 2001

Source: India 2009

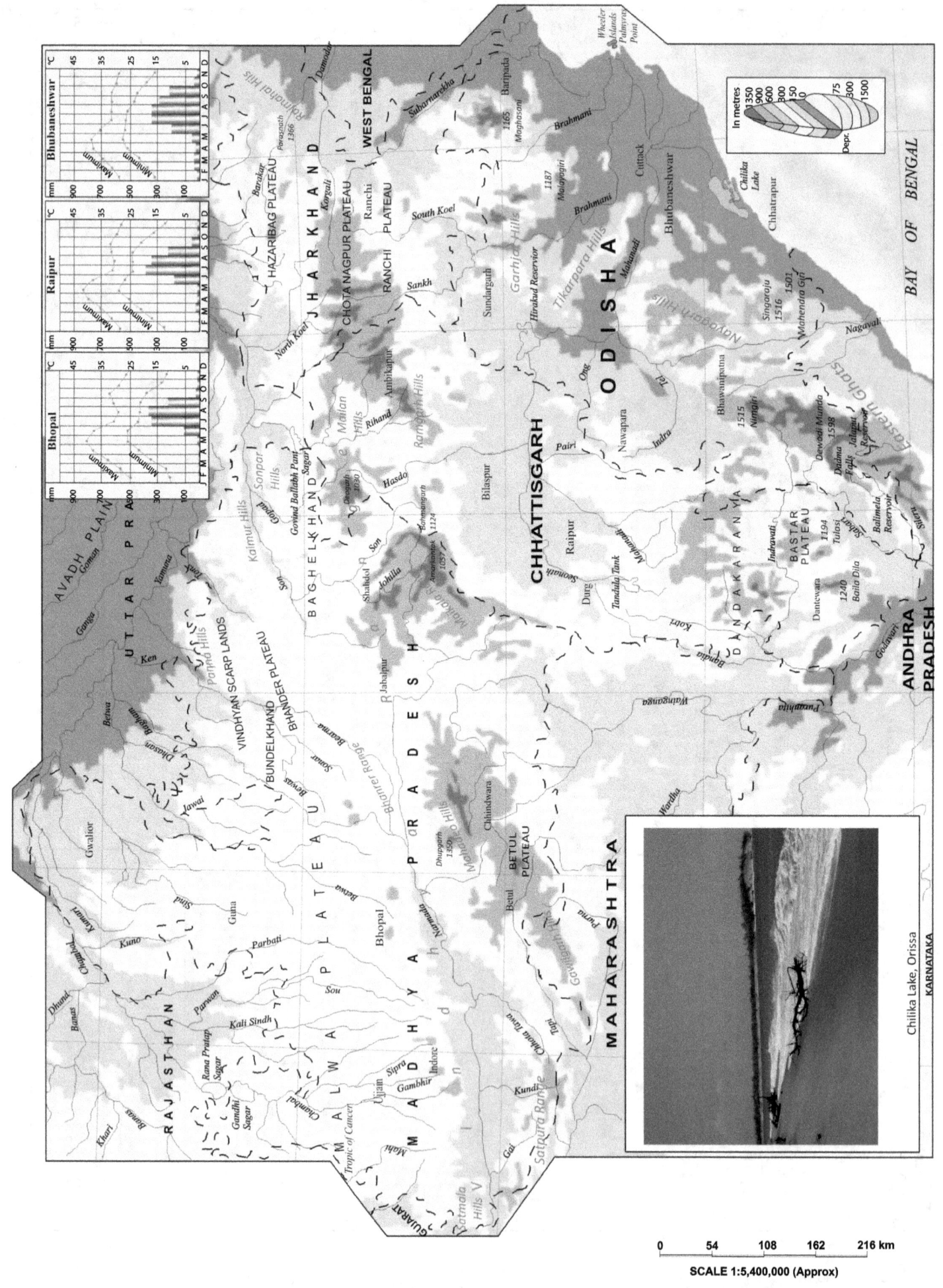

Chilika Lake, Orissa

SCALE 1:5,400,000 (Approx)

| 0 | 54 | 108 | 162 | 216 km |

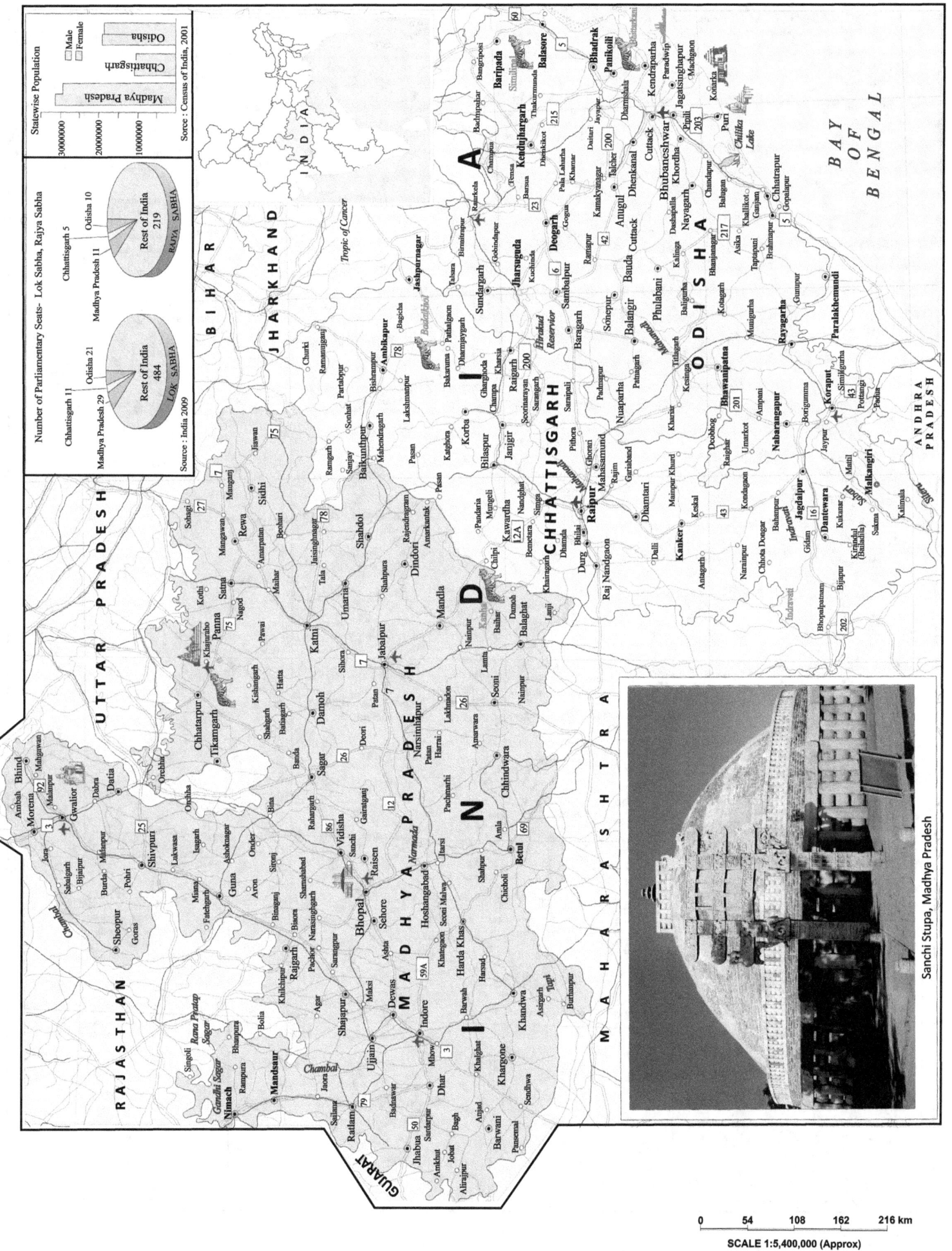

Statewise Population

Male
Female

Odisha

Chhattisgarh

Madhya Pradesh

30000000
20000000
10000000

Sorce : Census of India, 2001

Number of Parliamentary Seats– Lok Sabha, Rajya Sabha

RAJYA SABHA

Chhattisgarh 5
Odisha 10
Madhya Pradesh 11
Rest of India 219

LOK SABHA

Chhattisgarh 11
Odisha 21
Madhya Pradesh 29
Rest of India 484

Source : India 2009

BAY OF BENGAL

INDIA

Tropic of Cancer

BIHAR

JHARKHAND

UTTAR PRADESH

RAJASTHAN

GUJARAT

MADHYA PRADESH

CHHATTISGARH

ODISHA

ANDHRA PRADESH

MAHARASHTRA

Sanchi Stupa, Madhya Pradesh

0   54   108   162   216 km

SCALE 1:5,400,000 (Approx)

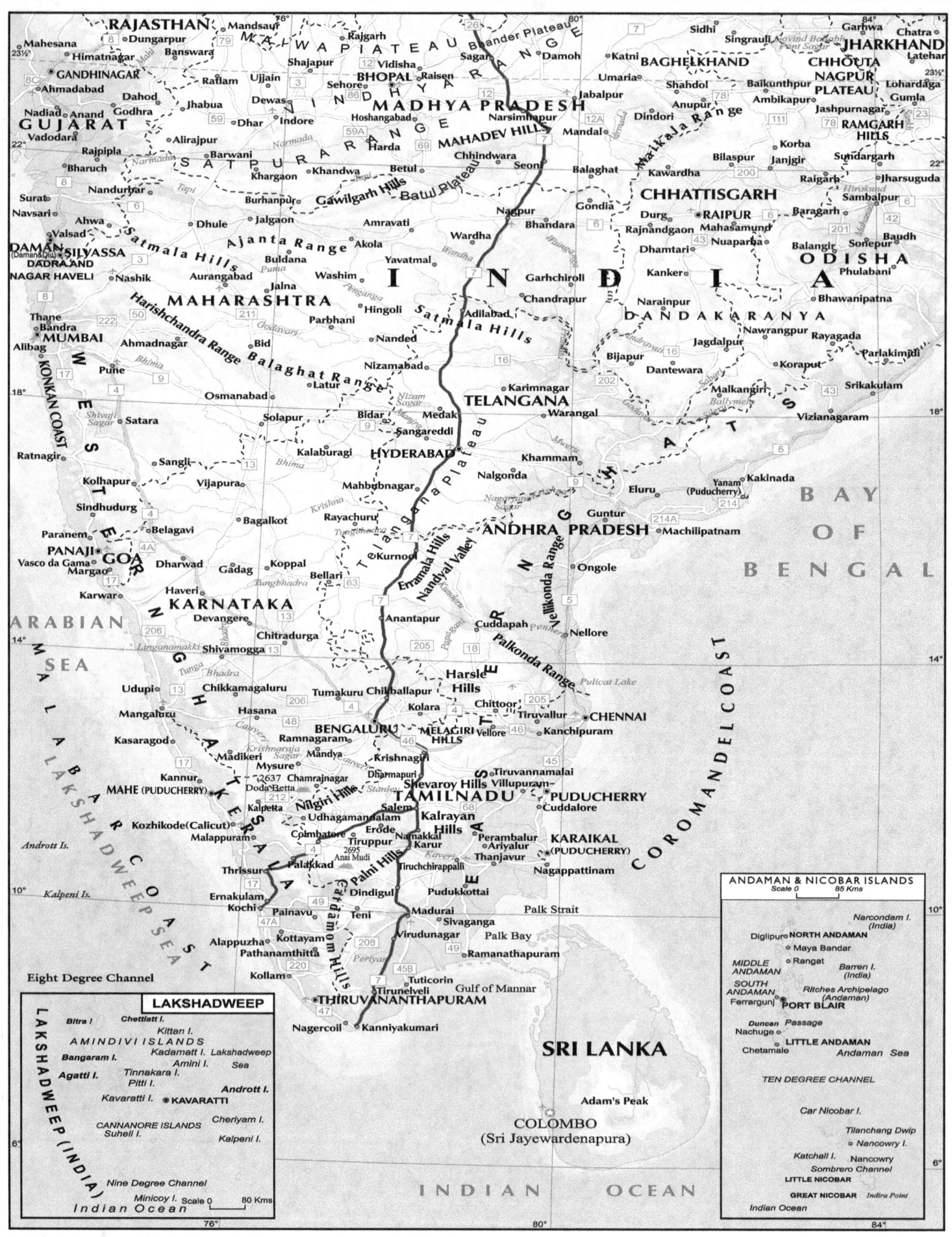

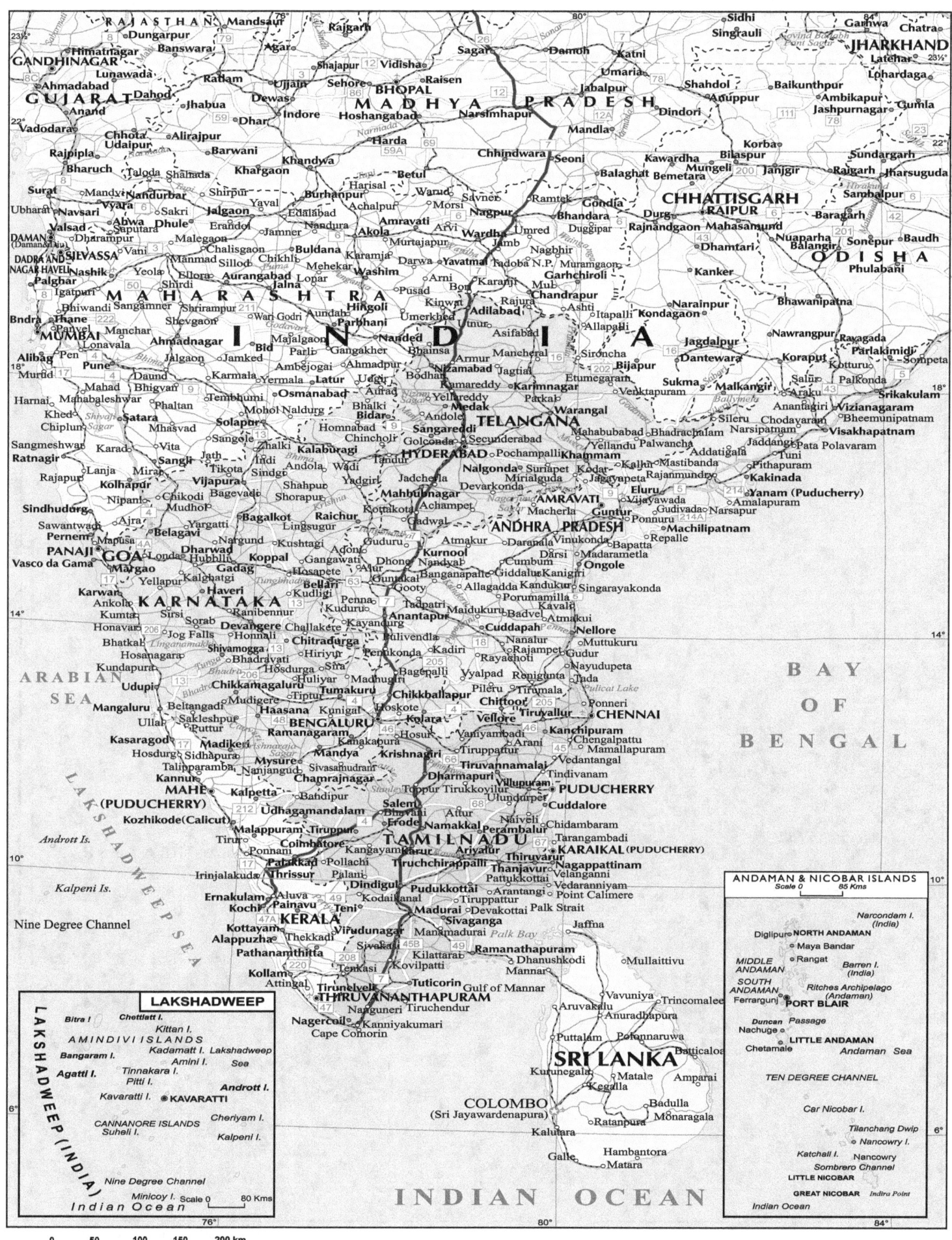

ANDAMAN & NICOBAR ISLANDS
Scale 0   85 Kms

Narcondam I.
(India)
Diglipur   NORTH ANDAMAN
• Maya Bandar
MIDDLE   • Rangat   Barren I.
ANDAMAN   (India)
SOUTH   Ritches Archipelago
ANDAMAN   Ferrargunj   (Andaman)
          • PORT BLAIR
Duncan Passage
Nachuge
Chetamale • LITTLE ANDAMAN
                  Andaman Sea

TEN DEGREE CHANNEL

Car Nicobar I.

Tilanchang Dwip
• Nancowry I.
Katchall I.   Nancowry
          Sombrero Channel
LITTLE NICOBAR
  GREAT NICOBAR Indira Point
  Indian Ocean

LAKSHADWEEP

Bitra I.   Chettlatt I.
          Kittan I.
AMINDIVI ISLANDS
          Kadamatt I. Lakshadweep
Bangaram I.   Amini I.   Sea
Agatti I.   Tinnakara I.
          Pitti I.   Andrott I.
  Kavaratti I. ★ KAVARATTI
CANNANORE ISLANDS   Cheriyam I.
Suheli I.   Kalpeni I.

Nine Degree Channel
Minicoy I. Scale 0   80 Kms
          Indian Ocean

SCALE 1:5,000,000 (Approx)

0   50   100   150   200 km

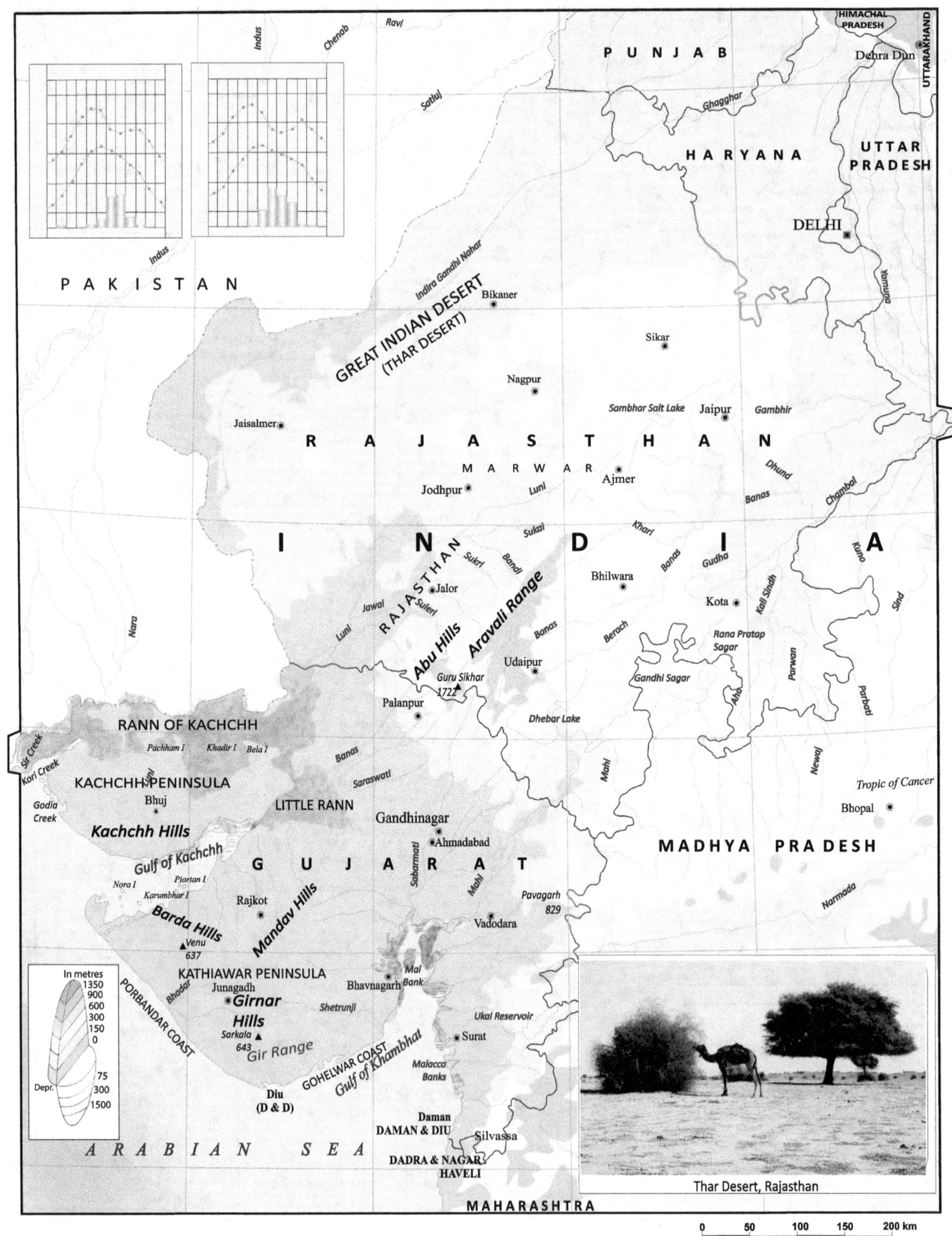

Thar Desert, Rajasthan

SCALE 1:4,700,000 (Approx)

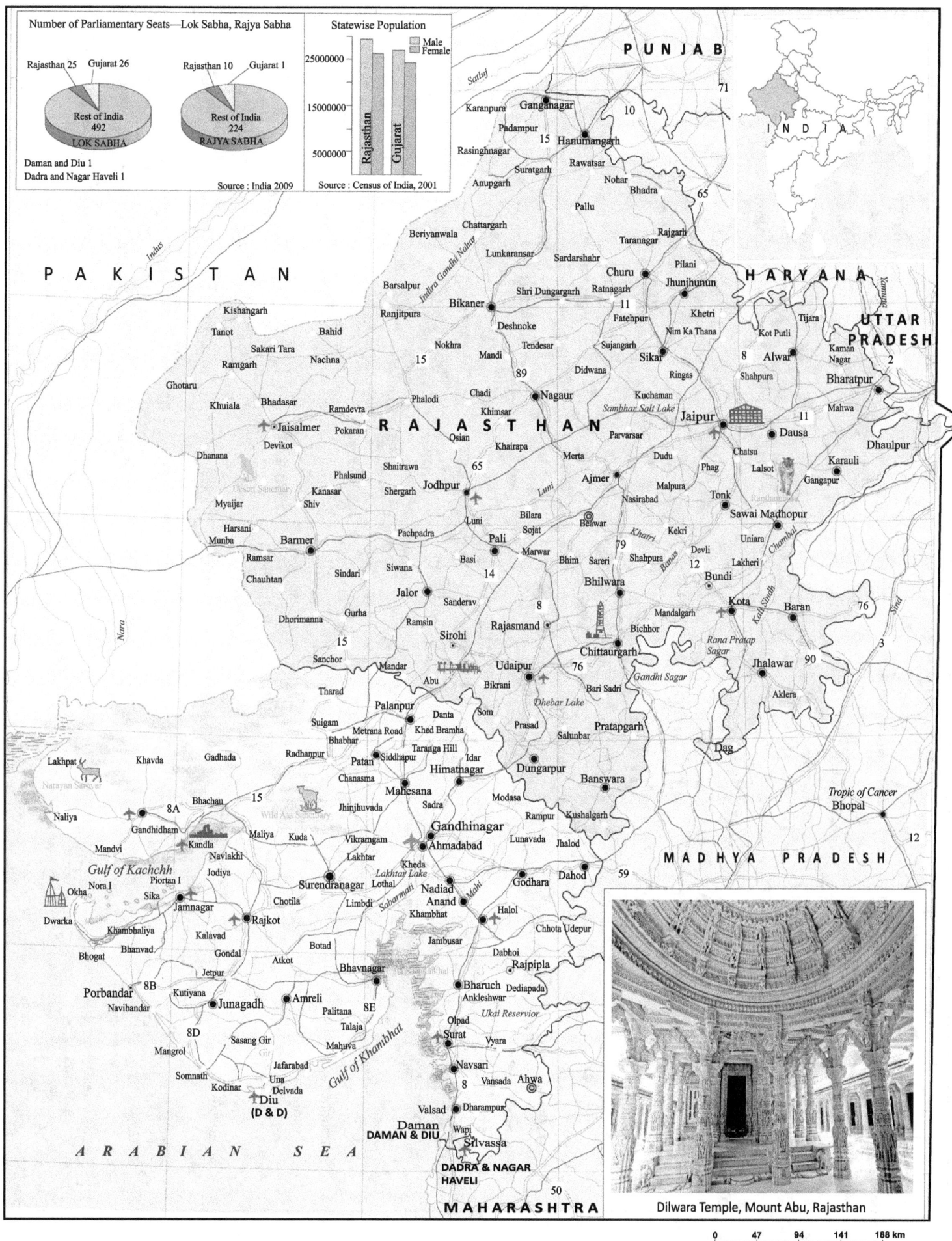

Number of Parliamentary Seats—Lok Sabha, Rajya Sabha

Rajasthan 25   Gujarat 26   Rajasthan 10   Gujarat 1

Rest of India 492   LOK SABHA
Rest of India 224   RAJYA SABHA

Daman and Diu 1
Dadra and Nagar Haveli 1

Source : India 2009

Statewise Population

Male
Female

25000000
15000000
5000000

Rajasthan
Gujarat

Source : Census of India, 2001

PUNJAB
Satluj
Karanpura   Ganganagar   10   71
Padampur   15   Hanumangarh
Rasinghnagar   Rawatsar
Suratgarh   Nohar
Anupgarh   Bhadra   65
Pallu

PAKISTAN
Indus
Chattargarh
Beriyanwala
Lunkaransar   Sardarshahr
Barsalpur   Shri Dungargarh   Churu   Jhunjhunun   HARYANA   Yamuna
Ranjitpura   Ratnagarh   11   Khetri   Tijara   UTTAR
Kishangarh   Bikaner   Deshnoke   Fatehpur   Nim Ka Thana   Kot Putli   PRADESH
Tanot   Bahid   Nokhra   Tendesar   Sujangarh   Sikar   Ringas   8   Alwar   Kaman Nagar   2
Sakari Tara   Nachna   Mandi   Didwana   Shahpura   Bharatpur
Ramgarh   Chadi   89   Nagaur   Kuchaman   Jaipur   11   Mahwa
Ghotaru   Phalodi   Khimsar   Sambhar Salt Lake   Dausa   Dhaulpur
Khuiala   Bhadasar   Ramdevra   Qsian   Parvarsar   Chatsu   Karauli
Jaisalmer   Pokaran   Khairapa   Merta   Dudu   Lalsot   Gangapur
Dhanana   Devikot   Shaitrawa   65   Ajmer   Phag   Ranthambhor
Phalsund   Jodhpur   Luni   Nasirabad   Malpura   Tonk   Sawai Madhopur
Myaijar   Kanasar   Shergarh   Luni   Bilara   Beawar   Khatri   Kekri   Uniara   Chambal
Harsani   Shiv   Pachpadra   Sojat   Bhim   Sareri   Devli   Lakheri   76
Munba   Barmer   Pali   Marwar   79   Shahpura   Banas   12   Bundi   Baran   Sind
Ramsar   Sindari   Basi   Bhilwara   Mandalgarh   Kota
Chauhtan   Siwana   14   Bichhor   Bichhor   3
Dhorimanna   Gurha   Jalor   Sanderav   8   Rajsamand   Chittaurgarh   Rana Pratap Sagar   Jhalawar   90
Nara   Ramsin   Sirohi   Udaipur   76   Gandhi Sagar   Aklera
15   Sanchor   Mandar   Abu   Bikrani   Bari Sadri   Dhebar Lake   Dag
Tharad   Danta   Som   Pratapgarh
Palanpur   Khed Bramha   Prasad   Salunbar
Suigam   Metrana Road   Taranga Hill
Bhabhar   Patan   Siddhapur   Idar   Himatnagar   Dungarpur   Banswara   Tropic of Cancer
Radhanpur   Chanasma   Mahesana   Sadra   Modasa   Bhopal
Lakhpat   Khavda   Gadhada   Jhinjhuvada   Rampur   Kushalgarh   MADHYA PRADESH   12
Narayan Sarovar   Bhachau   15   Wild Ass Sanctuary   Gandhinagar   Lunavada   Jhalod   59
Naliya   8A   Maliya   Kuda   Vikramgam   Ahmadabad   Godhara   Dahod
Mandvi   Gandhidham   Kandla   Navlakhi   Lakhtar   Kheda   Dahod
Okha   Nora I   Sika   Jodiya   Surendranagar   Nadiad   Halol
Dwarka   Jamnagar   Chotila   Limbdi   Lothal   Khambhat   Chhota Udepur
Khambhaliya   Rajkot   Botad   Jambusar   Dabhoi
Bhanvad   Kalavad   Atkot   Bhavnagar   Bharuch   Rajpipla
Bhogat   Gondal   Dediapada
Jetpur   Palitana   Ankleshwar
Porbandar   8B   Kutiyana   Junagadh   Amreli   8E   Olpad   Ukai Reservoir
Navibandar   8D   Talaja   Surat   Vyara
Mangrol   Sasang Gir   Mahuva   Navsari
Somnath   Una   Vansada   Ahwa
Kodinar   Delvada   Gulf of Khambhat   8   Dharampur
Diu (D & D)   Valsad   Daman & Diu   Wapi
DAMAN & DIU   Silvassa
ARABIAN SEA   DADRA & NAGAR HAVELI   50
MAHARASHTRA

Dilwara Temple, Mount Abu, Rajasthan

0   47   94   141   188 km

SCALE 1:4,700,000 (Approx)

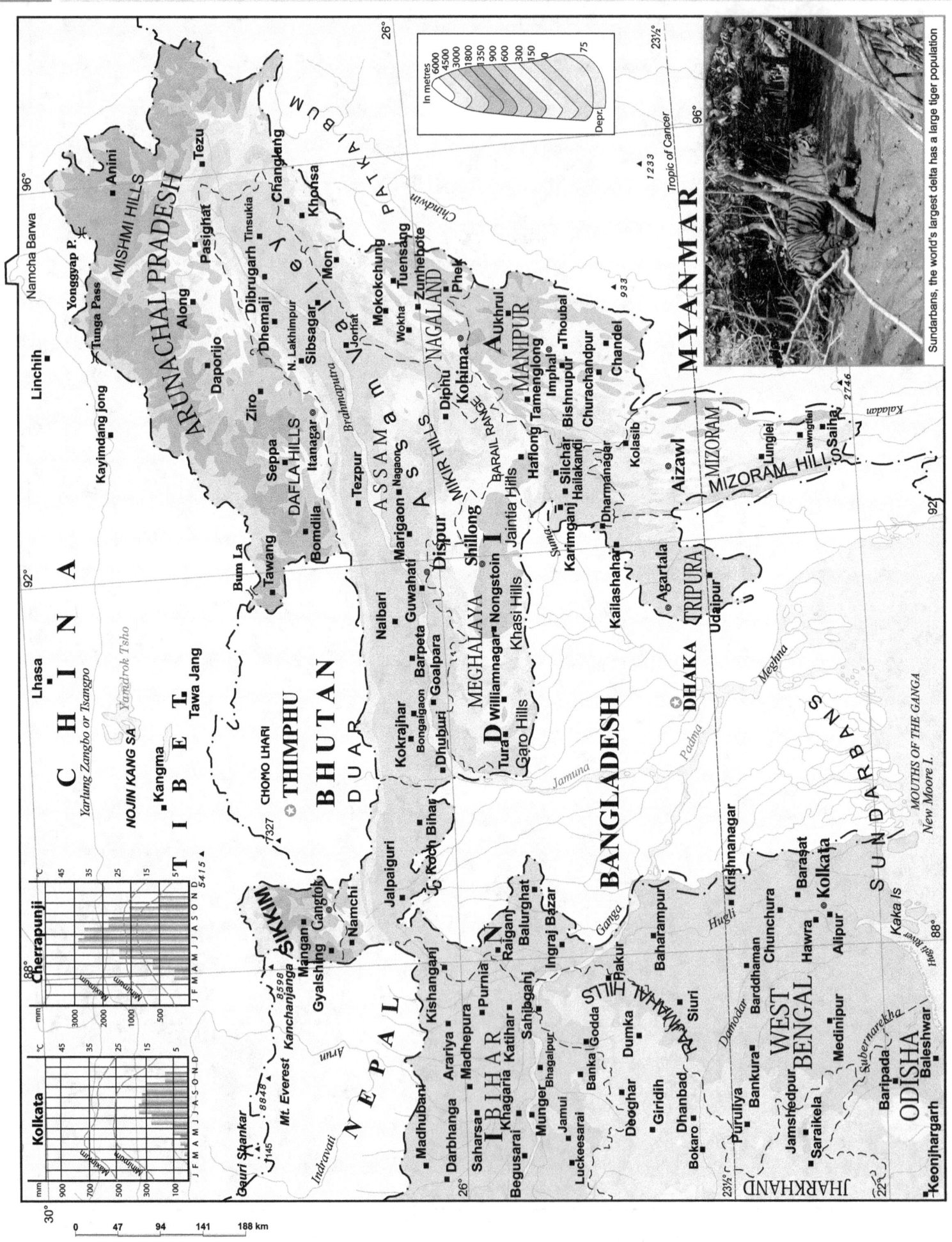

SCALE 1:4,800,000 (Approx)

0   47   94   141   188 km

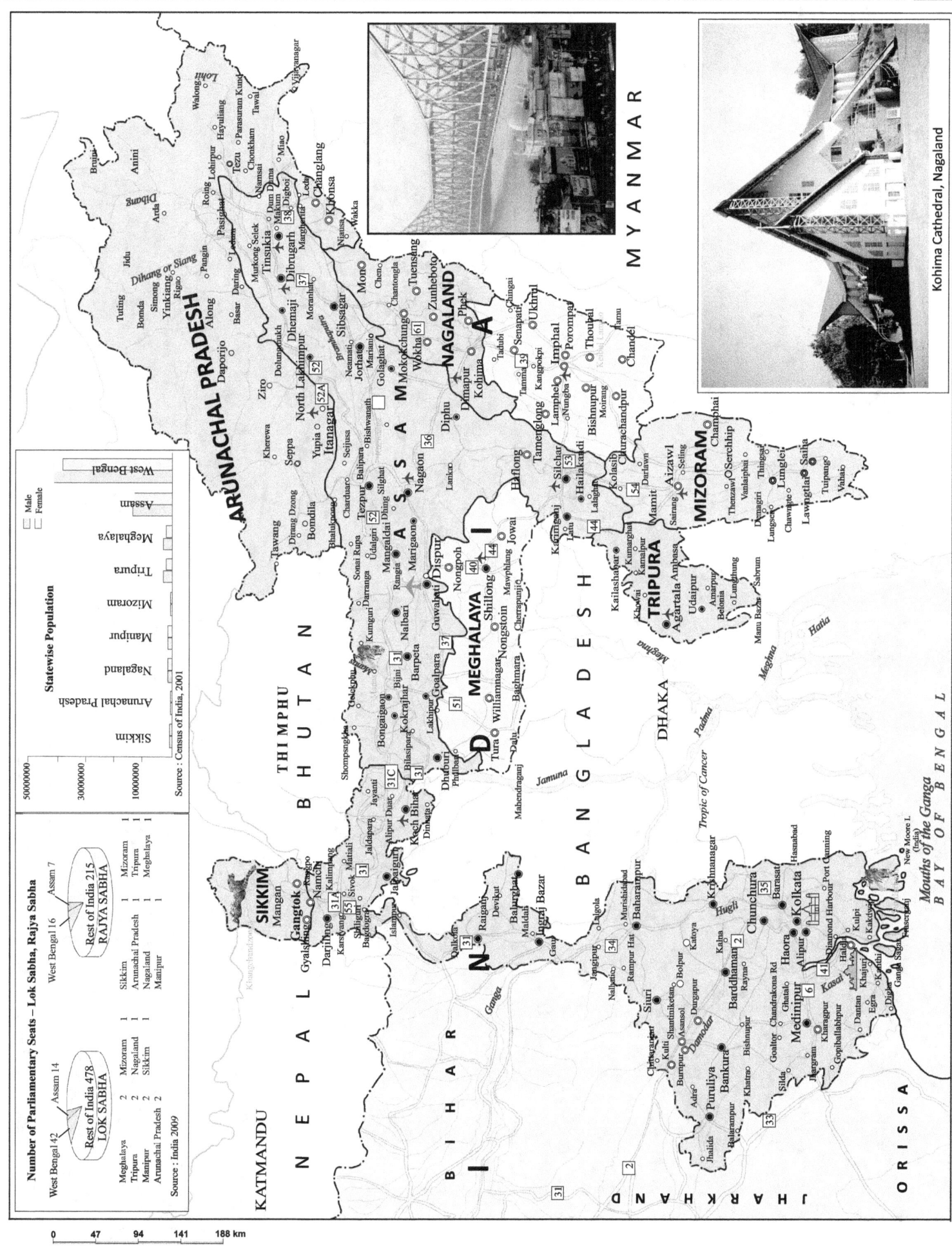

Kohima Cathedral, Nagaland

Number of Parliamentary Seats – Lok Sabha, Rajya Sabha

LOK SABHA

Rest of India 478

West Bengal 42   Assam 14

Meghalaya	2
Tripura	2
Manipur	2
Arunachal Pradesh	2

Mizoram	1
Nagaland	1
Sikkim	1

Source : India 2009

RAJYA SABHA

Rest of India 215

West Bengal 16   Assam 7

Sikkim	1
Arunachal Pradesh	1
Nagaland	1
Manipur	1

Mizoram	1
Tripura	1
Meghalaya	1

Statewise Population

Source : Census of India, 2001

- Male
- Female

Sikkim, Arunachal Pradesh, Nagaland, Manipur, Mizoram, Tripura, Meghalaya, Assam, West Bengal

50000000 — 30000000 — 10000000

SCALE 1:4,700,000

0   47   94   141   188 km

ARUNACHAL PRADESH

ASSAM

NAGALAND

MANIPUR

MEGHALAYA

MIZORAM

TRIPURA

SIKKIM

WEST BENGAL

NEPAL

BHUTAN

BANGLADESH

MYANMAR

BIHAR

JHARKHAND

ORISSA

KATMANDU

THIMPHU

DHAKA

BAY OF BENGAL

Mouths of the Ganga

Tropic of Cancer

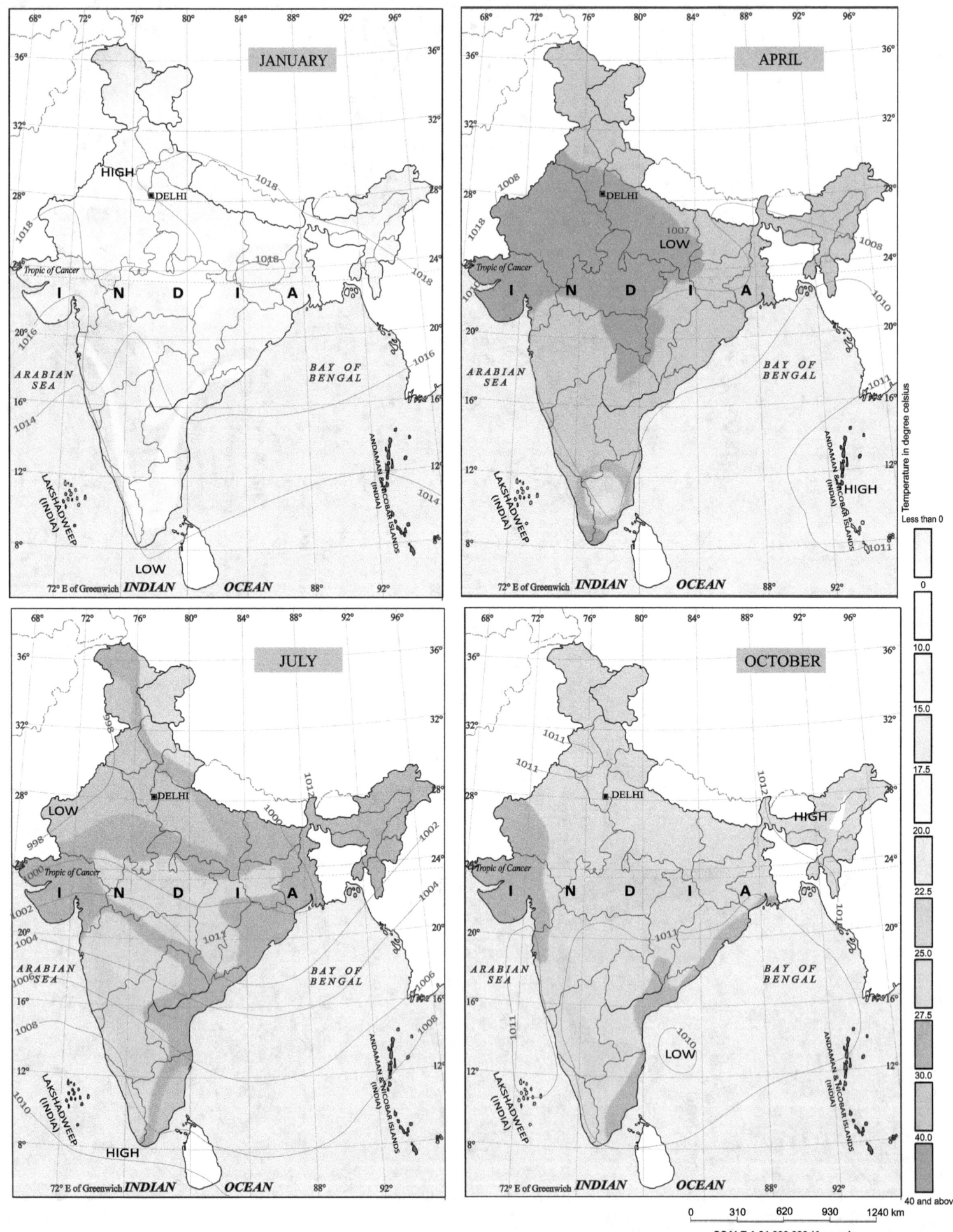

SCALE 1:31,000,000 (Approx)

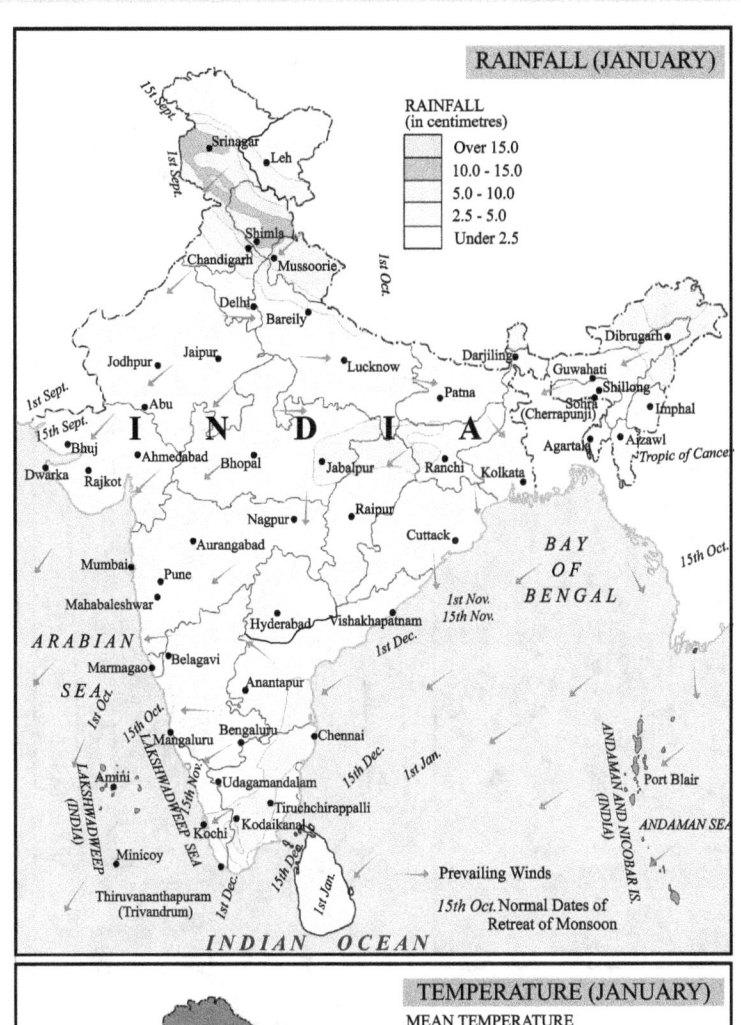

RAINFALL (JANUARY)

RAINFALL
(in centimetres)

Over 15.0
10.0 - 15.0
5.0 - 10.0
2.5 - 5.0
Under 2.5

→ Prevailing Winds

15th Oct. Normal Dates of
Retreat of Monsoon

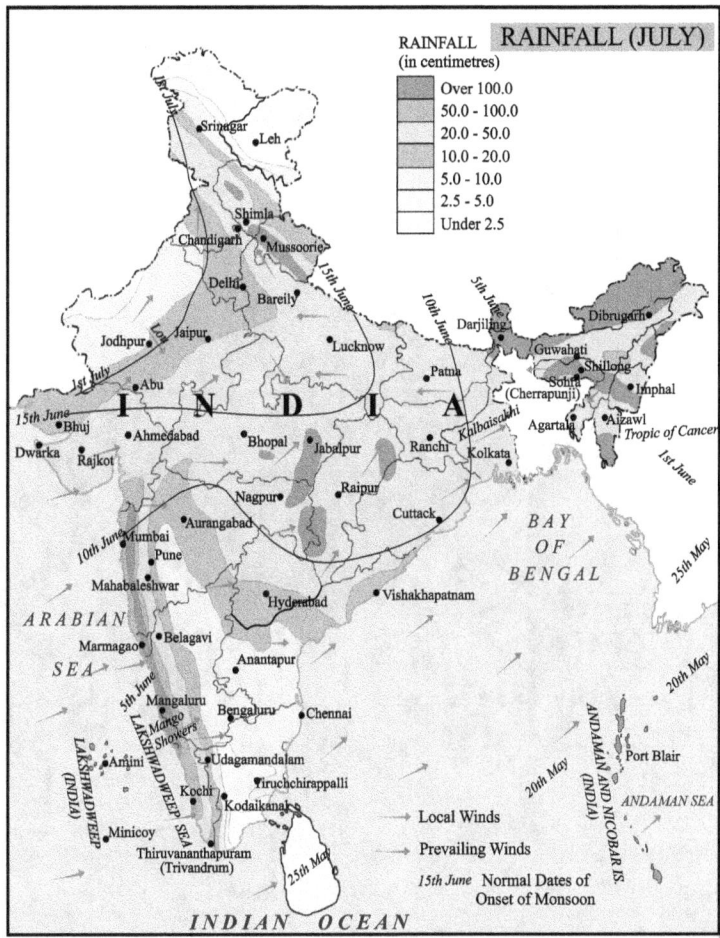

RAINFALL (JULY)

RAINFALL
(in centimetres)

Over 100.0
50.0 - 100.0
20.0 - 50.0
10.0 - 20.0
5.0 - 10.0
2.5 - 5.0
Under 2.5

→ Local Winds

→ Prevailing Winds

15th June Normal Dates of
Onset of Monsoon

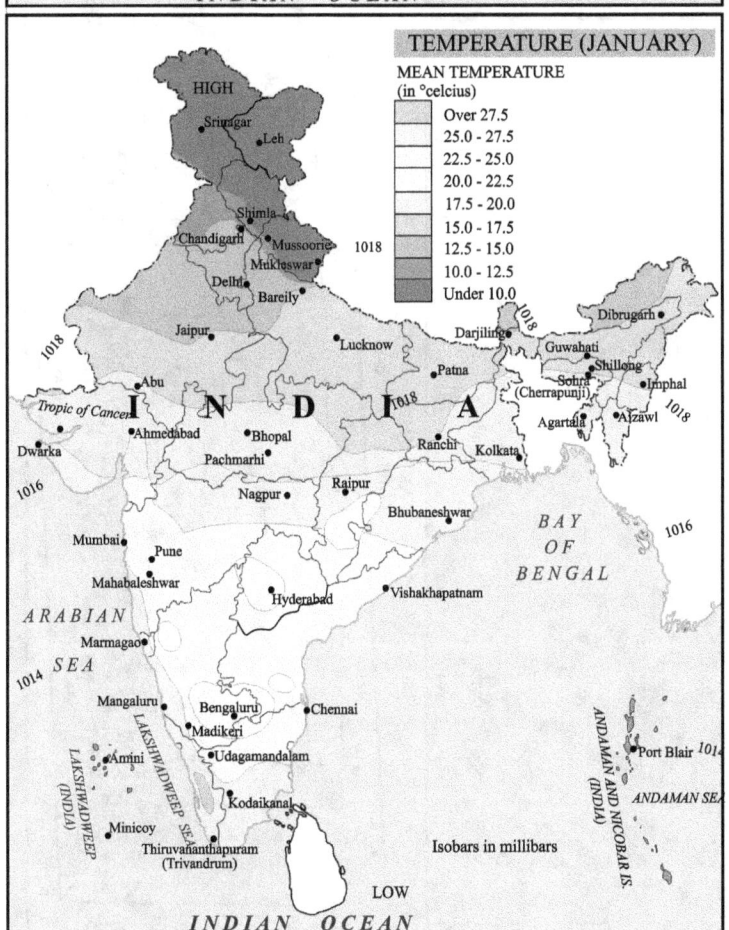

TEMPERATURE (JANUARY)

MEAN TEMPERATURE
(in °celcius)

Over 27.5
25.0 - 27.5
22.5 - 25.0
20.0 - 22.5
17.5 - 20.0
15.0 - 17.5
12.5 - 15.0
10.0 - 12.5
Under 10.0

Isobars in millibars

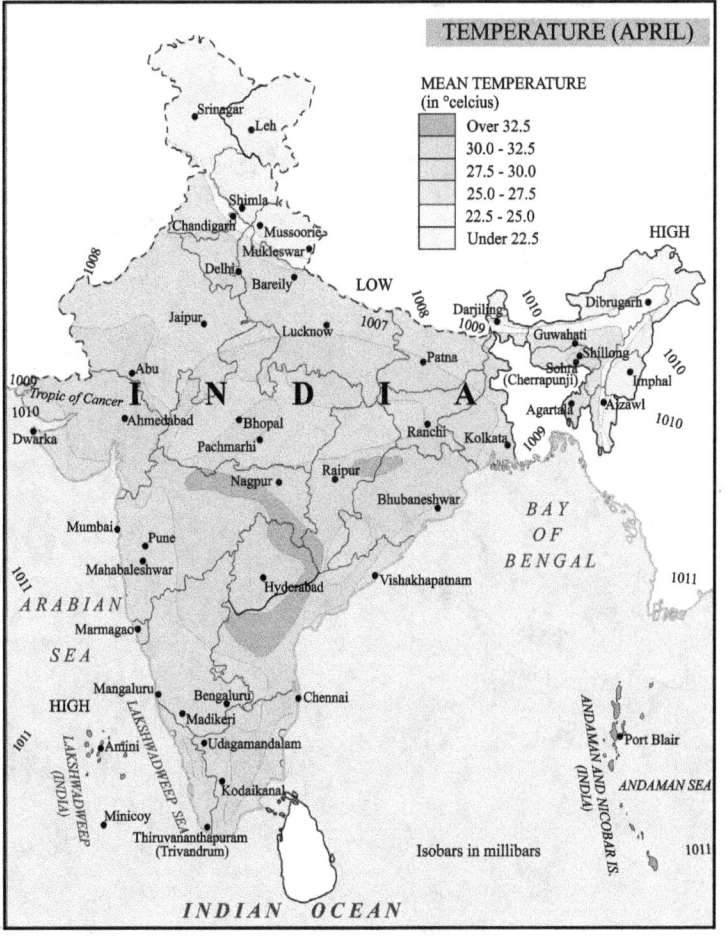

TEMPERATURE (APRIL)

MEAN TEMPERATURE
(in °celcius)

Over 32.5
30.0 - 32.5
27.5 - 30.0
25.0 - 27.5
22.5 - 25.0
Under 22.5

Isobars in millibars

0   290   58   870   1160 km

SCALE 1:29,000,000

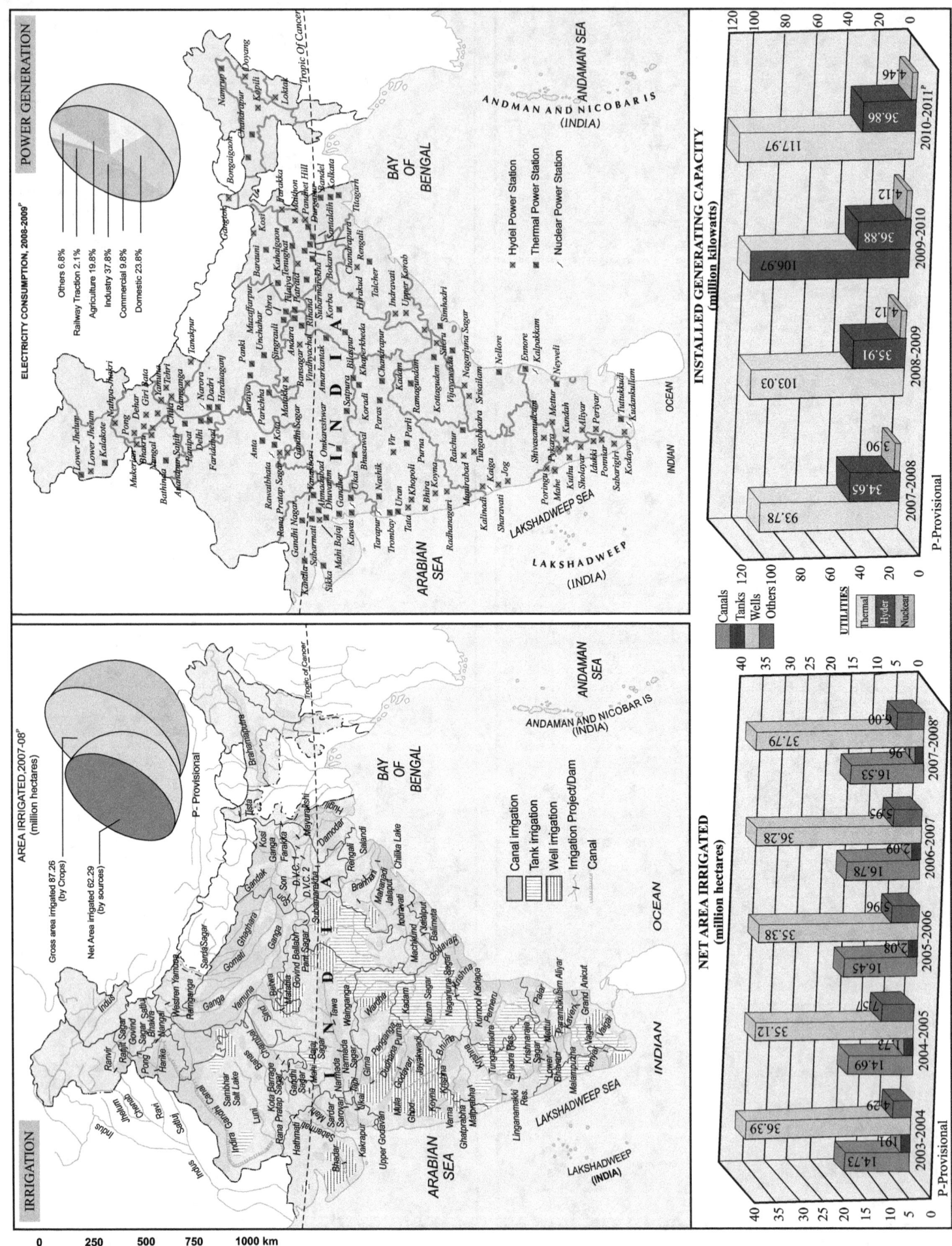

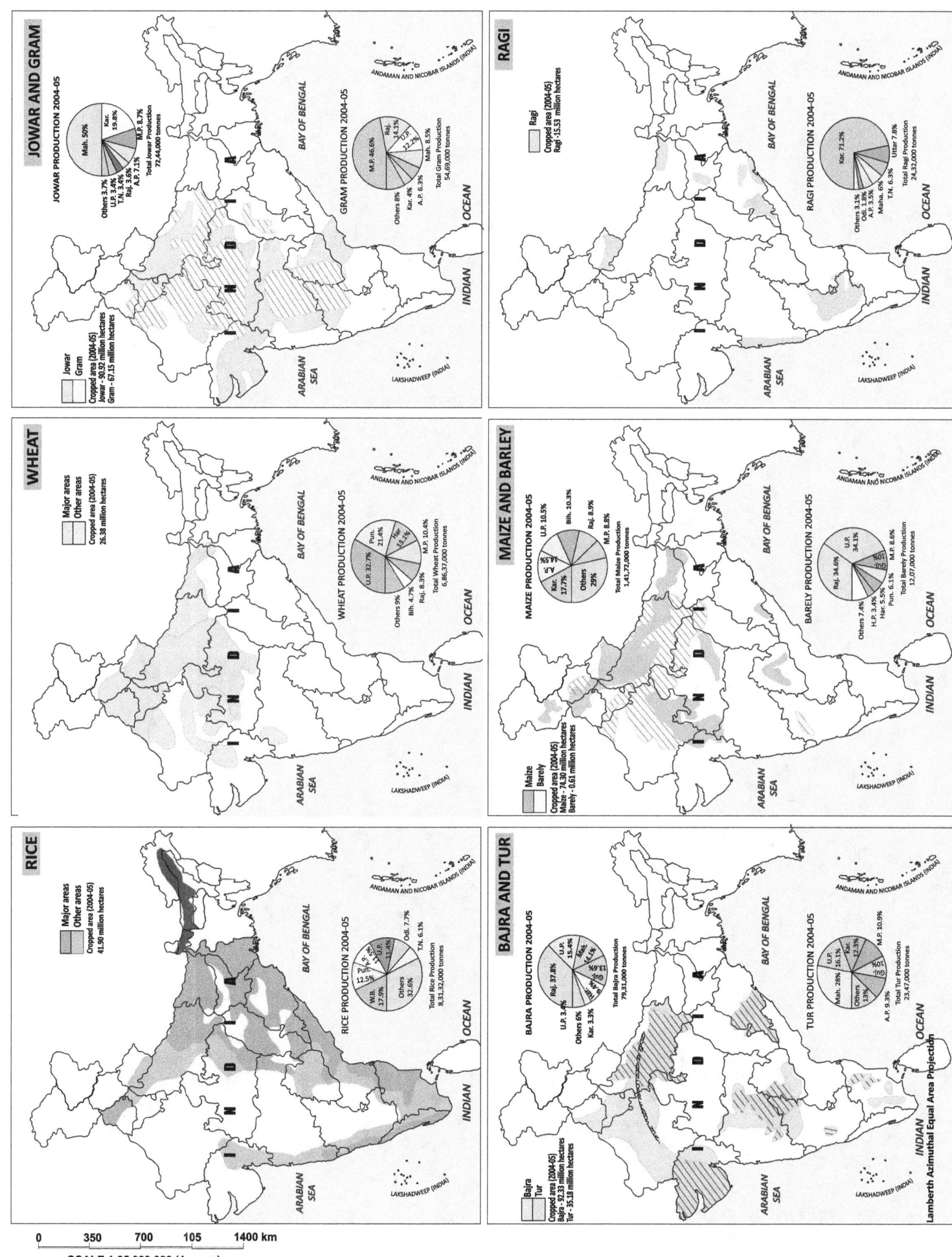

JOWAR AND GRAM

Jowar
Gram
Cropped area (2004-05)
Jowar - 90.52 million hectares
Gram - 67.15 million hectares

JOWAR PRODUCTION 2004-05
Mah. 50%
Kar. 19.8%
M.P. 8.7%
A.P. 7.1%
Raj. 3.6%
T.N. 3.4%
U.P. 3.4%
Others 3.7%
Total Jowar Production
72,44,000 tonnes

GRAM PRODUCTION 2004-05
M.P. 46.6%
Raj. 14.1%
U.P. 12.2%
Mah. 8.5%
A.P. 6.3%
Kar. 4%
Others 8%
Total Gram Production
54,69,000 tonnes

RAGI

Ragi
Cropped area (2004-05)
Ragi -15.53 million hectares

RAGI PRODUCTION 2004-05
Kar. 71.2%
Uttar 7.8%
T.N. 6.3%
Maha. 6%
A.P. 3.5%
Odi. 1.8%
Others 3.1%
Total Ragi Production
24,32,000 tonnes

WHEAT

Major areas
Other areas
Cropped area (2004-05)
26.38 million hectares

WHEAT PRODUCTION 2004-05
U.P. 32.7%
Pun. 21.4%
Har. 13.5%
M.P. 10.4%
Raj. 8.3%
Bih. 4.7%
Others 9%
Total Wheat Production
6,86,37,000 tonnes

MAIZE AND BARLEY

Maize
Barley
Cropped area (2004-05)
Maize - 74.30 million hectares
Barley - 0.61 million hectares

MAIZE PRODUCTION 2004-05
U.P. 10.5%
Bih. 10.3%
M.P. 8.9%
Kar. 17.7%
A.P. 9.5%
Others 29%
Total Maize Production
1,41,72,000 tonnes

BARLEY PRODUCTION 2004-05
U.P. 34.1%
Raj. 34.6%
M.P. 8.6%
Bih. 10%
Pun. 5.5%
Har. 3.4%
H.P. 3.4%
Others 7.4%
Total Barley Production
12,07,000 tonnes

RICE

Major areas
Other areas
Cropped area (2004-05)
41.90 million hectares

RICE PRODUCTION 2004-05
U.P. 11.4%
Pun. 12.5%
W.B. 17.9%
Odi. 7.7%
T.N. 6.1%
Others 32.6%
Total Rice Production
8,31,32,000 tonnes

BAJRA AND TUR

Bajra
Tur
Cropped area (2004-05)
Bajra - 92.39 million hectares
Tur - 35.18 million hectares

BAJRA PRODUCTION 2004-05
U.P. 37.8%
Mah. 15.4%
Guj. 13.6%
Kar. 4.5%
Raj. 13%
U.P. 3.4%
Kar. 3.3%
Others 6%
Total Bajra Production
79,31,000 tonnes

TUR PRODUCTION 2004-05
M.P. 10.9%
Kar. 12.3%
U.P. 16.1%
Mah. 28%
Others 13%
Guj. 10%
A.P. 9.3%
Total Tur Production
23,47,000 tonnes

BAY OF BENGAL
ARABIAN SEA
INDIAN OCEAN
ANDAMAN AND NICOBAR ISLANDS (INDIA)
LAKSHADWEEP (INDIA)
INDIA

Lamberth Azimuthal Equal Area Projection

0 350 700 105 1400 km
SCALE 1:35,000,000 (Approx)

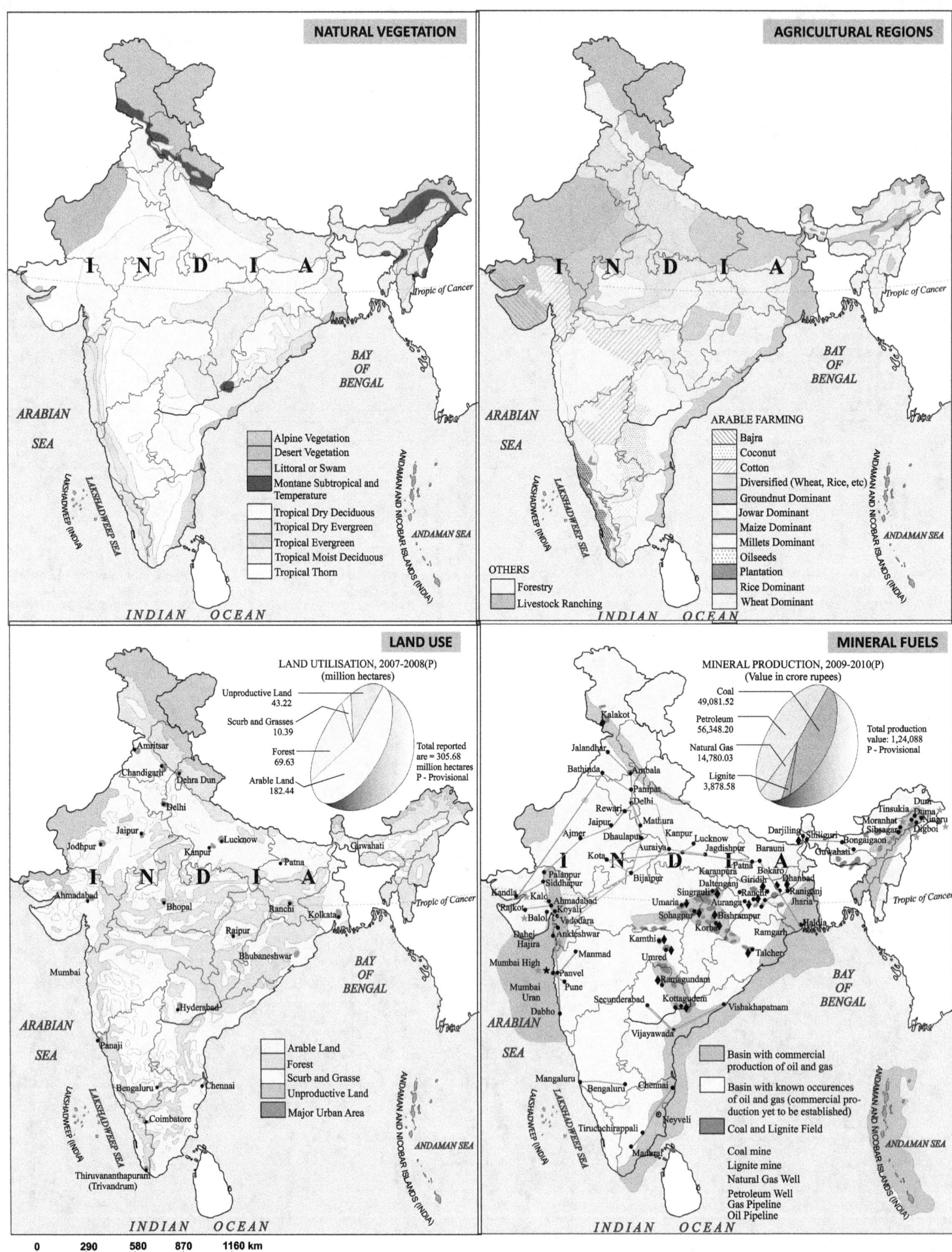

NATURAL VEGETATION

BAY OF BENGAL

ARABIAN SEA

ANDAMAN SEA

LAKSHADWEEP (INDIA)

ANDAMAN AND NICOBAR ISLANDS (INDIA)

INDIAN OCEAN

Tropic of Cancer

- Alpine Vegetation
- Desert Vegetation
- Littoral or Swam
- Montane Subtropical and Temperature
- Tropical Dry Deciduous
- Tropical Dry Evergreen
- Tropical Evergreen
- Tropical Moist Deciduous
- Tropical Thorn

AGRICULTURAL REGIONS

BAY OF BENGAL

ARABIAN SEA

ANDAMAN SEA

LAKSHADWEEP (INDIA)

ANDAMAN AND NICOBAR ISLANDS (INDIA)

INDIAN OCEAN

Tropic of Cancer

ARABLE FARMING
- Bajra
- Coconut
- Cotton
- Diversified (Wheat, Rice, etc)
- Groundnut Dominant
- Jowar Dominant
- Maize Dominant
- Millets Dominant
- Oilseeds
- Plantation
- Rice Dominant
- Wheat Dominant

OTHERS
- Forestry
- Livestock Ranching

LAND USE

LAND UTILISATION, 2007-2008(P)
(million hectares)

Unproductive Land 43.22
Scurb and Grasses 10.39
Forest 69.63
Arable Land 182.44

Total reported are = 305.68 million hectares
P - Provisional

Amritsar, Chandigarh, Dehra Dun, Delhi, Jaipur, Jodhpur, Kanpur, Lucknow, Ahmadabad, Bhopal, Patna, Ranchi, Kolkata, Raipur, Bhubaneshwar, Mumbai, Panaji, Hyderabad, Bengaluru, Chennai, Coimbatore, Guwahati, Thiruvananthapuram (Trivandrum)

BAY OF BENGAL

ARABIAN SEA

ANDAMAN SEA

LAKSHADWEEP (INDIA)

ANDAMAN AND NICOBAR ISLANDS (INDIA)

INDIAN OCEAN

Tropic of Cancer

- Arable Land
- Forest
- Scurb and Grasse
- Unproductive Land
- Major Urban Area

MINERAL FUELS

MINERAL PRODUCTION, 2009-2010(P)
(Value in crore rupees)

Coal 49,081.52
Petroleum 56,348.20
Natural Gas 14,780.03
Lignite 3,878.58

Total production value: 1,24,088
P - Provisional

Kalakot, Jalandhar, Bathinda, Ambala, Panipat, Rewari, Delhi, Mathura, Jaipur, Ajmer, Dhaulapur, Kanpur, Lucknow, Auraiya, Jagdishpur, Barauni, Kota, Bijaipur, Patna, Bokaro, Dhanbad, Karanpura, Giridih, Kandla, Palanpur, Siddhapur, Daltenganj, Raniganj, Rajkot, Kalol, Ahmadabad, Singrauli, Jharia, Balol, Koyali, Umaria, Aurang, Ranchi, Vadodara, Sohagpur, Bishrampur, Haldia, Dahej, Ankleshwar, Korba, Ramgarh, Hajira, Kamthi, Talcher, Mumbai High, Manmad, Umred, Panvel, Ramagundam, Mumbai, Uran, Pune, Secunderabad, Kottagudem, Vishakhapatnam, Dabho, Vijayawada, Mangaluru, Bengaluru, Chennai, Tiruchchirappali, Neyveli, Madurai, Darjiling, Shiliguri, Bongaigaon, Guwahati, Tinsukia, Moranhat, Sibsagar, Digboi, Duma, Ningru, Dum

BAY OF BENGAL

ARABIAN SEA

ANDAMAN SEA

LAKSHADWEEP (INDIA)

ANDAMAN AND NICOBAR ISLANDS (INDIA)

INDIAN OCEAN

Tropic of Cancer

- Basin with commercial production of oil and gas
- Basin with known occurences of oil and gas (commercial production yet to be established)
- Coal and Lignite Field
- Coal mine
- Lignite mine
- Natural Gas Well
- Petroleum Well
- Gas Pipeline
- Oil Pipeline

0   290   580   870   1160 km

SCALE 1:29,000,000 (Approx)

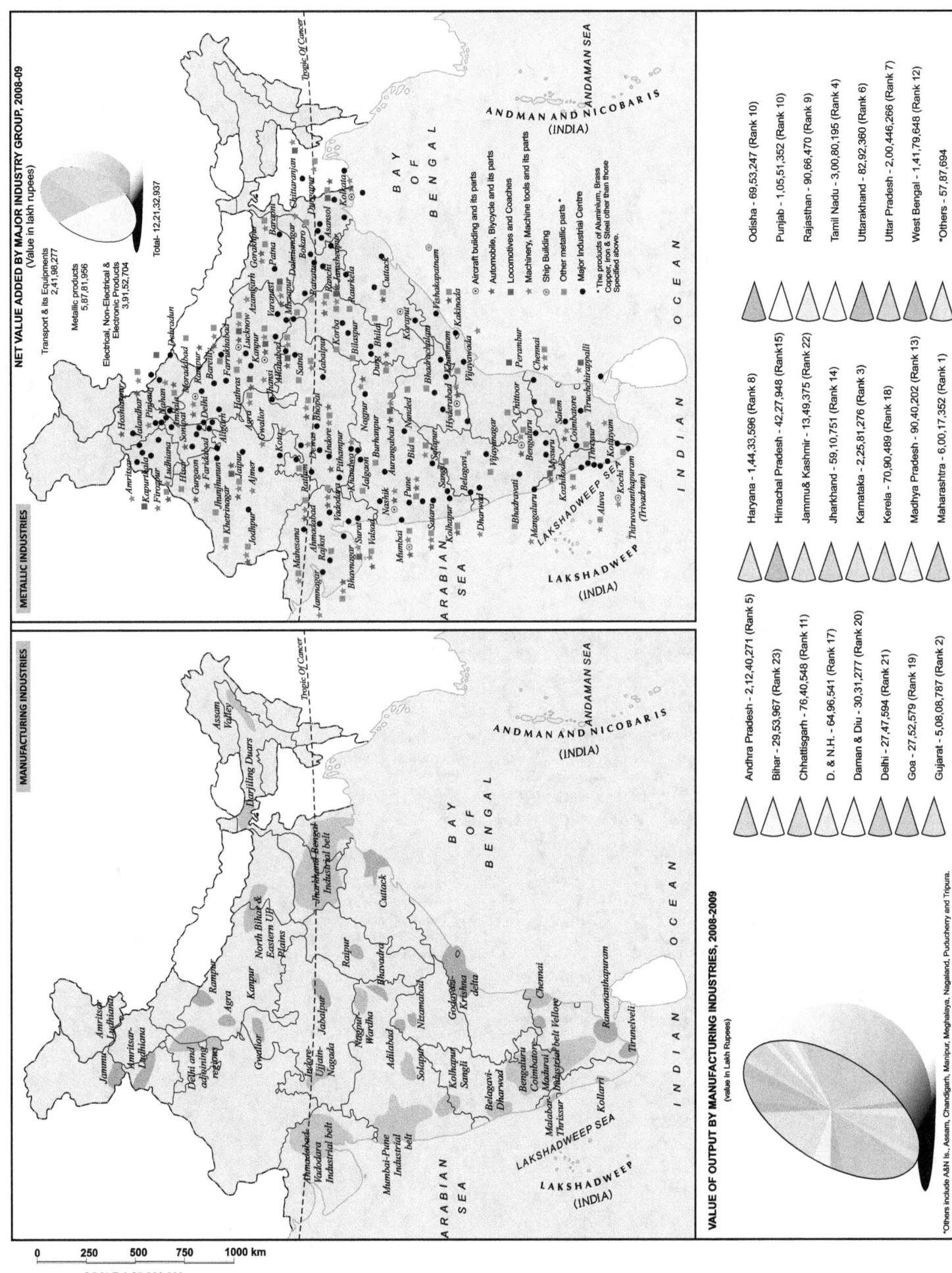

METALLIC INDUSTRIES

NET VALUE ADDED BY MAJOR INDUSTRY GROUP, 2008-09
(Value in lakh rupees)

Transport & Its Equipments 2,41,98,277

Metallic products 5,87,81,956

Electrical, Non-Electrical & Electronic Products 3,91,52,704

Total- 12,21,32,937

⊙ Aircraft building and its parts
★ Automobile, Bicycle and its parts
■ Locomotives and Coaches
★ Machinery, Machine tools and its parts
⊙ Ship Building
■ Other metallic parts
● Major Industrial Centre

* The products of Aluminium, Brass Copper, Iron & Steel other than those Specified above.

MANUFACTURING INDUSTRIES

Odisha - 69,53,247 (Rank 10)
Punjab - 1,05,51,352 (Rank 10)
Rajasthan - 90,66,470 (Rank 9)
Tamil Nadu - 3,00,80,195 (Rank 4)
Uttarakhand - 82,92,360 (Rank 6)
Uttar Pradesh - 2,00,446,266 (Rank 7)
West Bengal - 1,41,79,648 (Rank 12)
*Others - 57,87,694

Haryana - 1,44,33,596 (Rank 8)
Himachal Pradesh - 42,27,948 (Rank15)
Jammu& Kashmir - 13,49,375 (Rank 22)
Jharkhand - 59,10,751 (Rank 14)
Karnataka - 2,25,81,276 (Rank 3)
Kerela - 70,90,489 (Rank 18)
Madhya Pradesh - 90,40,202 (Rank 13)
Maharashtra - 6,00,17,352 (Rank 1)

Andhra Pradesh - 2,12,40,271 (Rank 5)
Bihar - 29,53,967 (Rank 23)
Chhattisgarh - 76,40,548 (Rank 11)
D. & N.H. - 64,96,541 (Rank 17)
Daman & Diu - 30,31,277 (Rank 20)
Delhi - 27,47,594 (Rank 21)
Goa - 27,52,579 (Rank 19)
Gujarat - 5,08,08,787 (Rank 2)

VALUE OF OUTPUT BY MANUFACTURING INDUSTRIES, 2008-2009
(value in Lakh Rupees)

*Others include A&N Is., Assam, Chandigarh, Manipur, Meghalaya, Nagaland, Puducherry and Tripura.

0   250   500   750   1000 km

SCALE 1:25,000,000

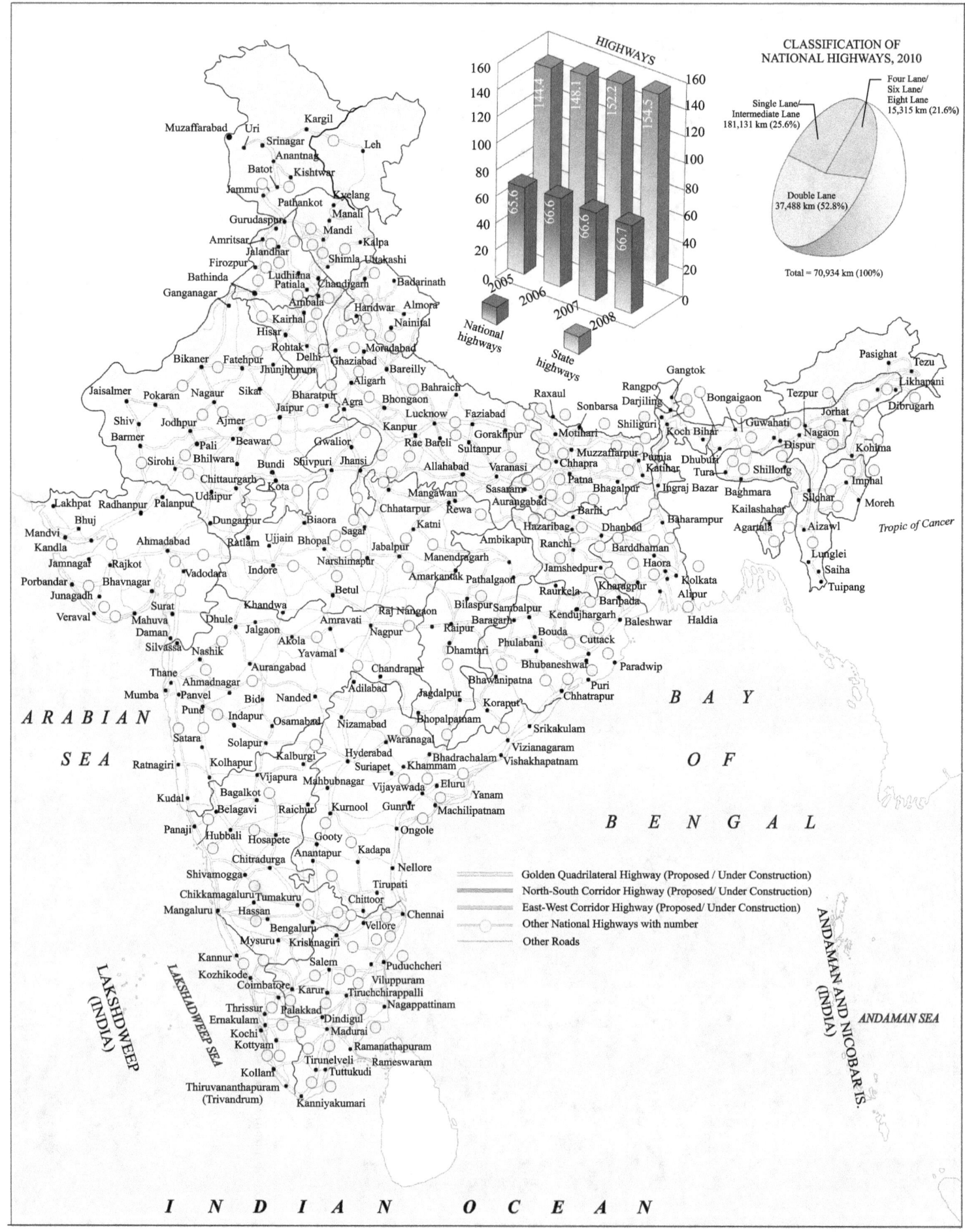

HIGHWAYS

CLASSIFICATION OF
NATIONAL HIGHWAYS, 2010

Four Lane/
Six Lane/
Eight Lane
15,315 km (21.6%)

Single Lane/
Intermediate Lane
181,131 km (25.6%)

Double Lane
37,488 km (52.8%)

Total = 70,934 km (100%)

National
highways

State
highways

Golden Quadrilateral Highway (Proposed / Under Construction)
North-South Corridor Highway (Proposed/ Under Construction)
East-West Corridor Highway (Proposed/ Under Construction)
Other National Highways with number
Other Roads

A R A B I A N

S E A

B A Y

O F

B E N G A L

Tropic of Cancer

LAKSHDWEEP
(INDIA)

LAKSHADWEEP SEA

ANDAMAN AND NICOBAR IS.
(INDIA)

ANDAMAN SEA

I N D I A N   O C E A N

0   145   290   435   580 km

SCALE : 1:14,500,000 (Approx)

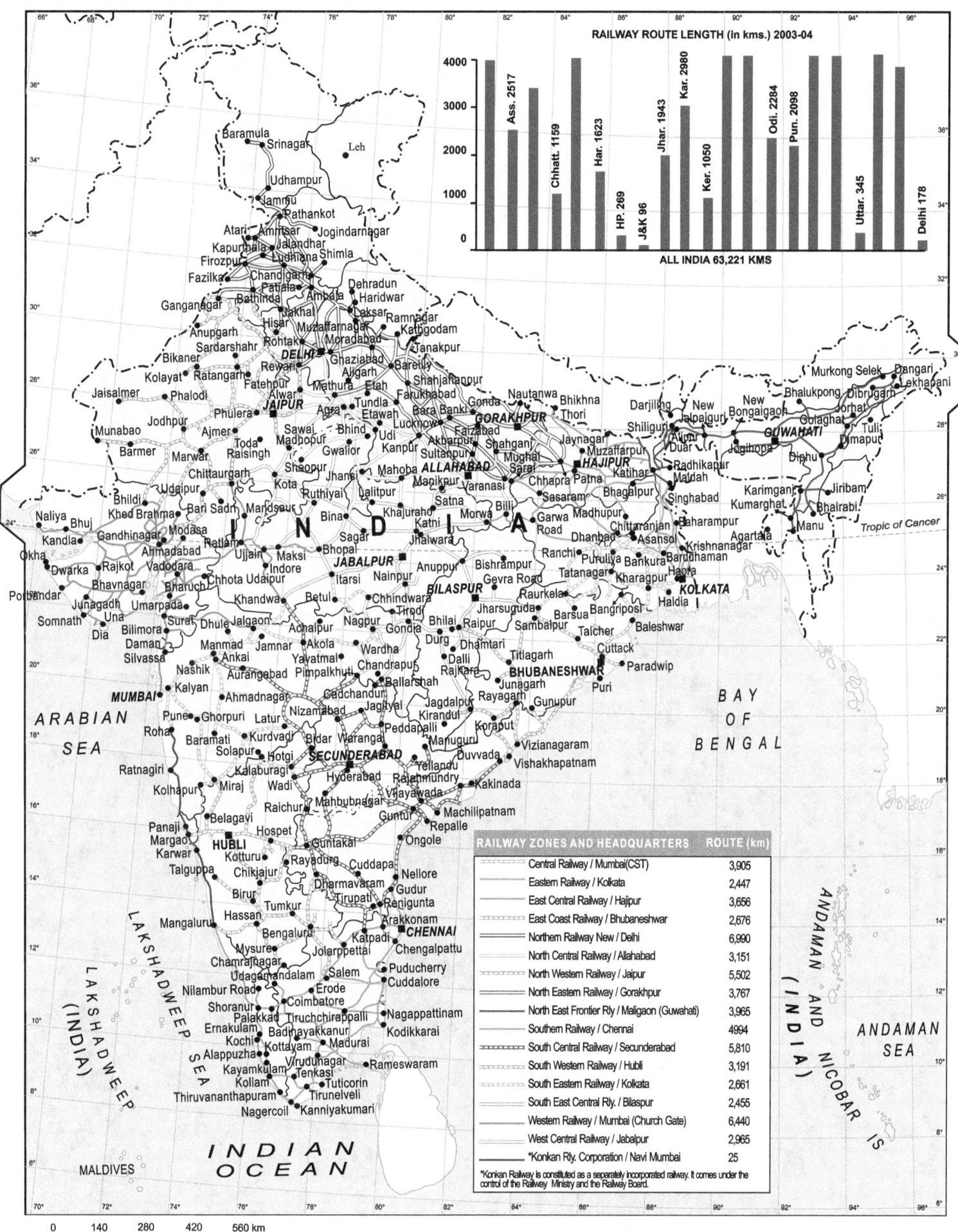

RAILWAY ROUTE LENGTH (in kms.) 2003-04

Ass. 2517, Chhatt. 1159, Har. 1623, HP. 269, J&K 96, Jhar. 1943, Kar. 2980, Ker. 1050, Odi. 2284, Pun. 2098, Uttar. 345, Delhi 178

ALL INDIA 63,221 KMS

RAILWAY ZONES AND HEADQUARTERS	ROUTE (km)
Central Railway / Mumbai(CST)	3,905
Eastern Railway / Kolkata	2,447
East Central Railway / Hajipur	3,656
East Coast Railway / Bhubaneshwar	2,676
Northern Railway New / Delhi	6,990
North Central Railway / Allahabad	3,151
North Western Railway / Jaipur	5,502
North Eastern Railway / Gorakhpur	3,767
North East Frontier Rly / Maligaon (Guwahati)	3,965
Southern Railway / Chennai	4994
South Central Railway / Secunderabad	5,810
South Western Railway / Hubli	3,191
South Eastern Railway / Kolkata	2,661
South East Central Rly. / Bilaspur	2,455
Western Railway / Mumbai (Church Gate)	6,440
West Central Railway / Jabalpur	2,965
*Konkan Rly. Corporation / Navi Mumbai	25

*Konkan Railway is constituted as a separately incorporated railway. It comes under the control of the Railway Ministry and the Railway Board.

SCALE : 1:14,500,000

0   140   280   420   560 km

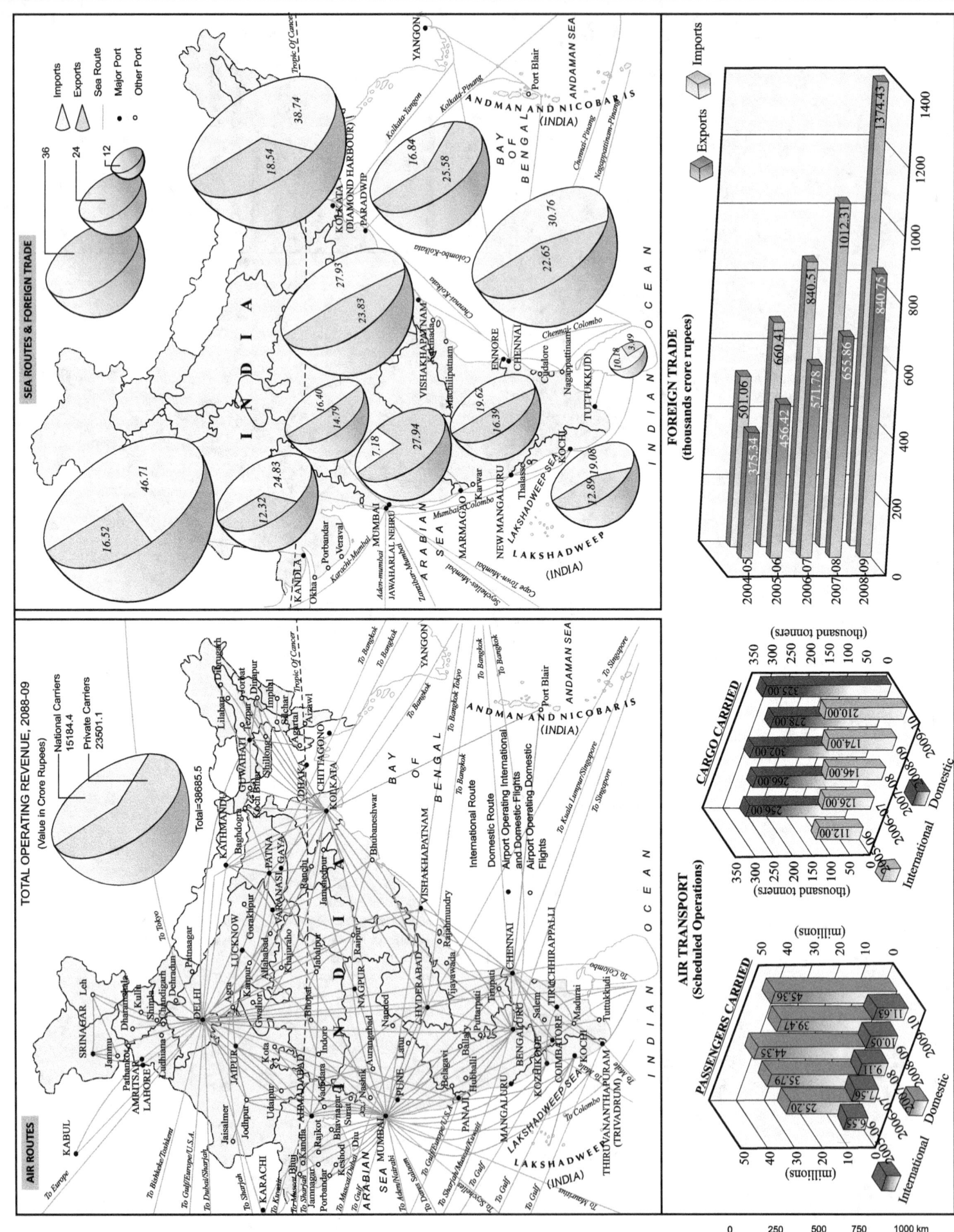

SEA ROUTES & FOREIGN TRADE

Imports
Exports
Sea Route
Major Port
Other Port

36 24 12

FOREIGN TRADE
(thousands crore rupees)

	Exports	Imports
2004-05	375.34	501.06
2005-06	456.42	660.41
2006-07	571.78	840.51
2007-08	655.86	1012.31
2008-09	840.75	1374.43

AIR ROUTES

TOTAL OPERATING REVENUE, 2008-09
(Value in Crore Rupees)
National Carriers 15184.4
Private Carriers 23501.1
Total=38685.5

International Route
Domestic Route
Airport Operating International
and Domestic Flights
Airport Operating Domestic
Flights

CARGO CARRIED
(thousand tonners)

AIR TRANSPORT
(Scheduled Operations)

PASSENGERS CARRIED
(millions)

SCALE 1:25,000,000 (Approx)
0   250   500   750   1000 km

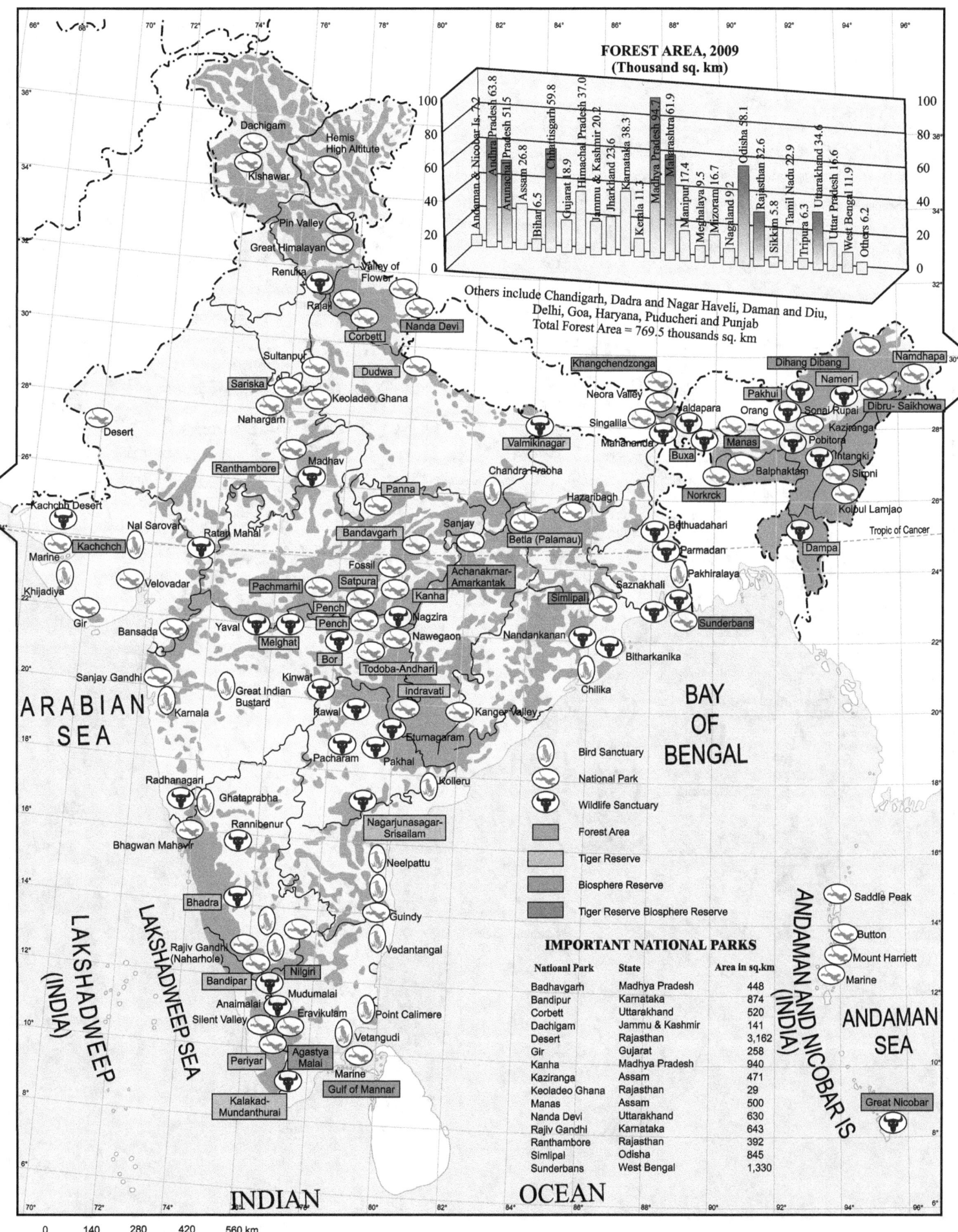

FOREST AREA, 2009
(Thousand sq. km)

Andaman & Nicobar Is. 7.2
Andhra Pradesh 63.8
Arunachal Pradesh 51.5
Assam 26.8
Bihar 6.5
Chhattisgarh 59.8
Gujarat 18.9
Himachal Pradesh 37.0
Jammu & Kashmir 20.2
Jharkhand 23.6
Karnataka 38.3
Kerala 11.3
Madhya Pradesh 94.7
Maharashtra 61.9
Manipur 17.4
Meghalaya 9.5
Mizoram 16.7
Nagaland 9.2
Odisha 58.1
Rajasthan 32.6
Sikkim 5.8
Tamil Nadu 22.9
Tripura 6.3
Uttarakhand 34.6
Uttar Pradesh 16.6
West Bengal 11.9
Others 6.2

Others include Chandigarh, Dadra and Nagar Haveli, Daman and Diu,
Delhi, Goa, Haryana, Puducheri and Punjab
Total Forest Area = 769.5 thousands sq. km

Legend:

- Bird Sanctuary
- National Park
- Wildlife Sanctuary
- Forest Area
- Tiger Reserve
- Biosphere Reserve
- Tiger Reserve Biosphere Reserve

IMPORTANT NATIONAL PARKS

Natioanl Park	State	Area in sq.km
Badhavgarh	Madhya Pradesh	448
Bandipur	Karnataka	874
Corbett	Uttarakhand	520
Dachigam	Jammu & Kashmir	141
Desert	Rajasthan	3,162
Gir	Gujarat	258
Kanha	Madhya Pradesh	940
Kaziranga	Assam	471
Keoladeo Ghana	Rajasthan	29
Manas	Assam	500
Nanda Devi	Uttarakhand	630
Rajiv Gandhi	Karnataka	643
Ranthambore	Rajasthan	392
Simlipal	Odisha	845
Sunderbans	West Bengal	1,330

ARABIAN SEA

BAY OF BENGAL

ANDAMAN SEA

INDIAN OCEAN

LAKSHADWEEP (INDIA)

LAKSHADWEEP SEA

ANDAMAN AND NICOBAR IS (INDIA)

Tropic of Cancer

SCALE : 1:14,500,000

0   140   280   420   560 km

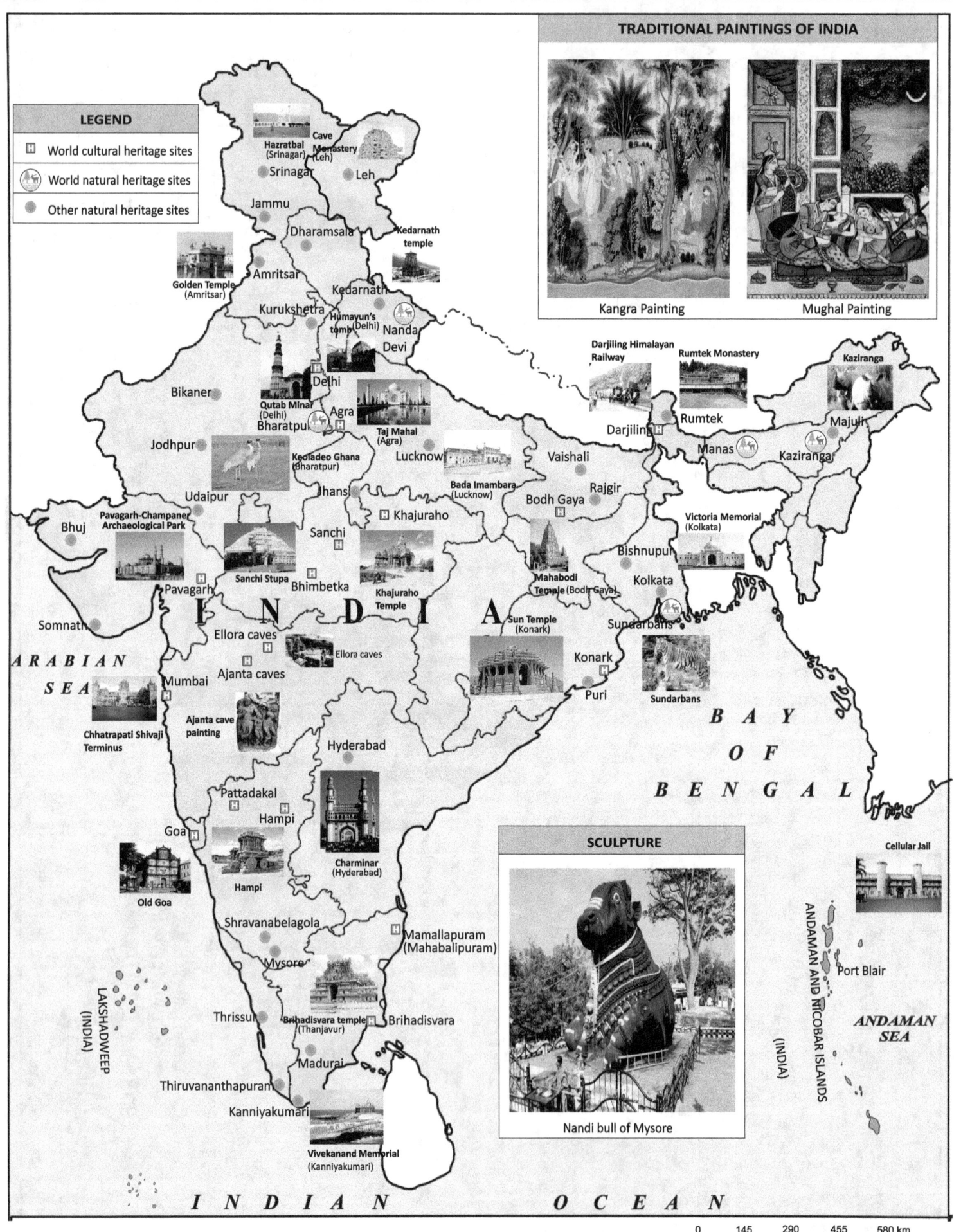

TRADITIONAL PAINTINGS OF INDIA

Kangra Painting

Mughal Painting

LEGEND

World cultural heritage sites

World natural heritage sites

Other natural heritage sites

Hazratbal (Srinagar)
Cave Monastery (Leh)
Srinagar
Leh
Jammu
Dharamsala
Kedarnath temple
Golden Temple (Amritsar)
Amritsar
Kedarnath
Kurukshetra
Humayun's tomb (Delhi)
Nanda Devi
Bikaner
Delhi
Qutab Minar (Delhi)
Agra
Bharatpur
Taj Mahal (Agra)
Jodhpur
Keoladeo Ghana (Bharatpur)
Lucknow
Vaishali
Udaipur
Jhansi
Bada Imambara (Lucknow)
Rajgir
Bodh Gaya
Bhuj
Pavagarh-Champaner Archaeological Park
Khajuraho
Sanchi
Victoria Memorial (Kolkata)
Somnath
Pavagarh
Sanchi Stupa
Bhimbetka
Khajuraho Temple
Bishnupur
Mahabodi Temple (Bodh Gaya)
Kolkata
Ellora caves
Sun Temple (Konark)
Sundarbans
Mumbai
Ajanta caves
Ellora caves
Konark
Chhatrapati Shivaji Terminus
Ajanta cave painting
Puri
Sundarbans
Hyderabad
Pattadakal
Hampi
Goa
Charminar (Hyderabad)
Old Goa
Hampi
Shravanabelagola
Mysore
Mamallapuram (Mahabalipuram)
Thrissur
Brihadisvara temple (Thanjavur)
Brihadisvara
Madurai
Thiruvananthapuram
Kanniyakumari
Vivekanand Memorial (Kanniyakumari)

Darjiling Himalayan Railway
Rumtek Monastery
Kaziranga
Darjiling
Rumtek
Manas
Majuli
Kaziranga

ARABIAN SEA

INDIA

BAY OF BENGAL

Cellular Jail
ANDAMAN AND NICOBAR ISLANDS (INDIA)
Port Blair
ANDAMAN SEA

LAKSHADWEEP (INDIA)

SCULPTURE

Nandi bull of Mysore

INDIAN OCEAN

0   145   290   455   580 km

SCALE : 1:14,500,000 (Approx)

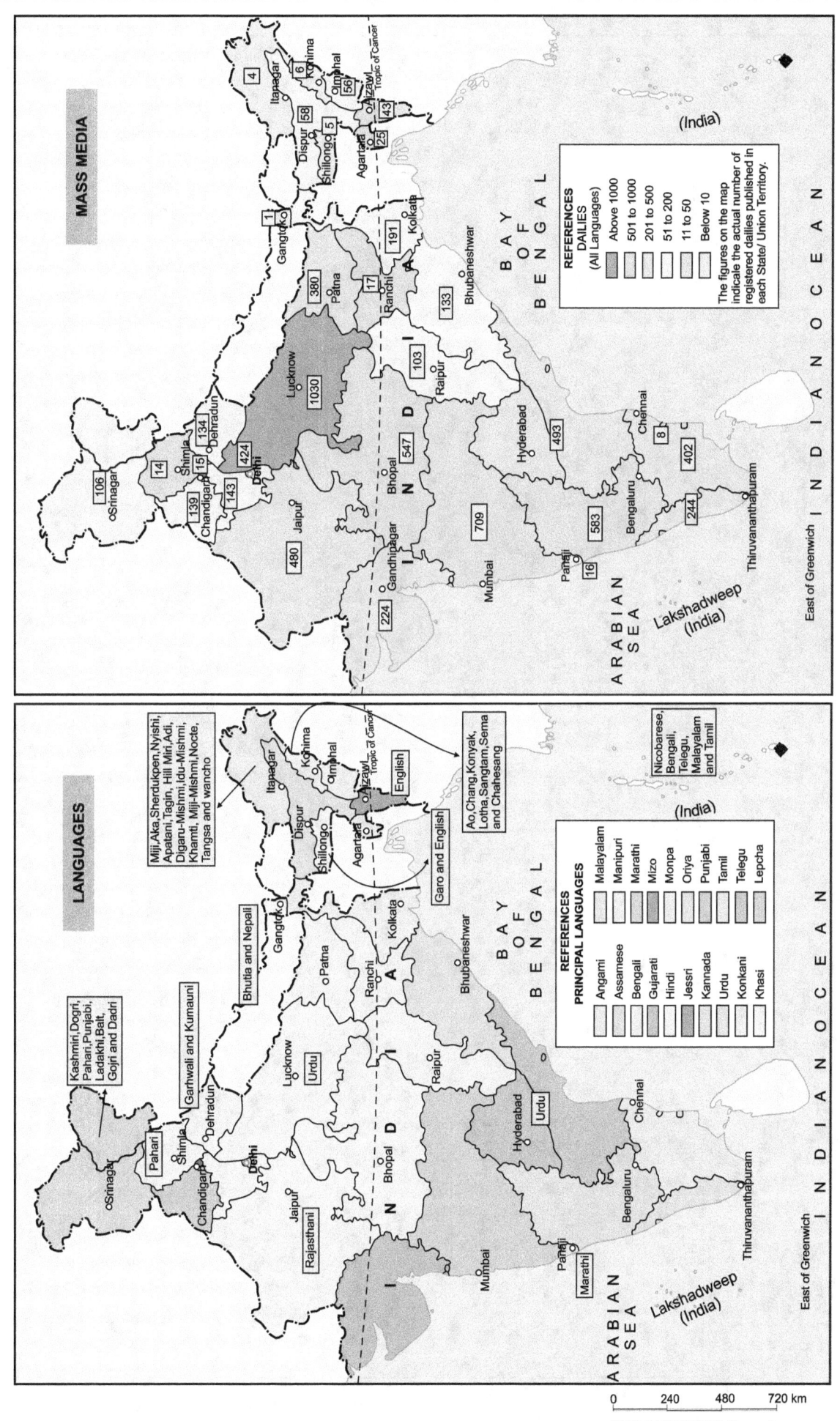

MASS MEDIA

Itanagar 4
Kohima 6
Imphal
Aizawl 56
Agartala 43
25
Dispur 58
Shillong 5
Gangtok 1
Patna 380
Ranchi 17
191 Kolkata
133
Bhubaneshwar
103 Raipur
Lucknow 1030
Dehradun 134
Shimla 15
Delhi 424
Srinagar 106
Shimla 14
Chandigarh 139
143
Jaipur 480
Bhopal 547
709 Mumbai
Hyderabad 493
Chennai 8
Bengaluru 583
402
244
Panaji 16
Gandhinagar 224
Thiruvananthapuram

BAY OF BENGAL
ARABIAN SEA
INDIAN OCEAN
Lakshadweep (India)
(India)
INDIA
East of Greenwich
Tropic of Cancer

LANGUAGES

Miji,Aka,Sherdukpen,Nyishi,
Apatani,Tagin, Hill Miri,Adi,
Digaru-Mishmi,Idu-Mishmi,
Khamti, Miji-Mishmi,Nocte,
Tangsa and wancho

Ao,Chang,Konyak,
Lotha,Sangtam,Sema
and Chahesang

English
Garo and Eng1ish

Nicobarese,
Bengali,
Telegu,
Malayalam
and Tamil

Itanagar
Kohima
Imphal
Aizawl
Agartala
Dispur
Shillong
Gangtok

Kashmiri,Dogri,
Pahari,Punjabi,
Ladakhi,Balt,
Gojri and Dadri

Bhutia and Nepali

Garhwali and Kumauni

Pahari
Shimla
Chandigarh
Dehradun
Delhi

Srinagar

Urdu
Lucknow
Patna
Ranchi
Kolkata
Bhubaneshwar
Raipur

Rajasthani
Jaipur
Bhopal

Urdu
Hyderabad

Mumbai
Marathi

Bengaluru
Chennai
Panaji
Thiruvananthapuram

BAY OF BENGAL
ARABIAN SEA
INDIAN OCEAN
Lakshadweep (India)
(India)
INDIA
East of Greenwich
Tropic of Cancer

0   240   480   720 km

SCALE 1:24,000,000 (Approx)

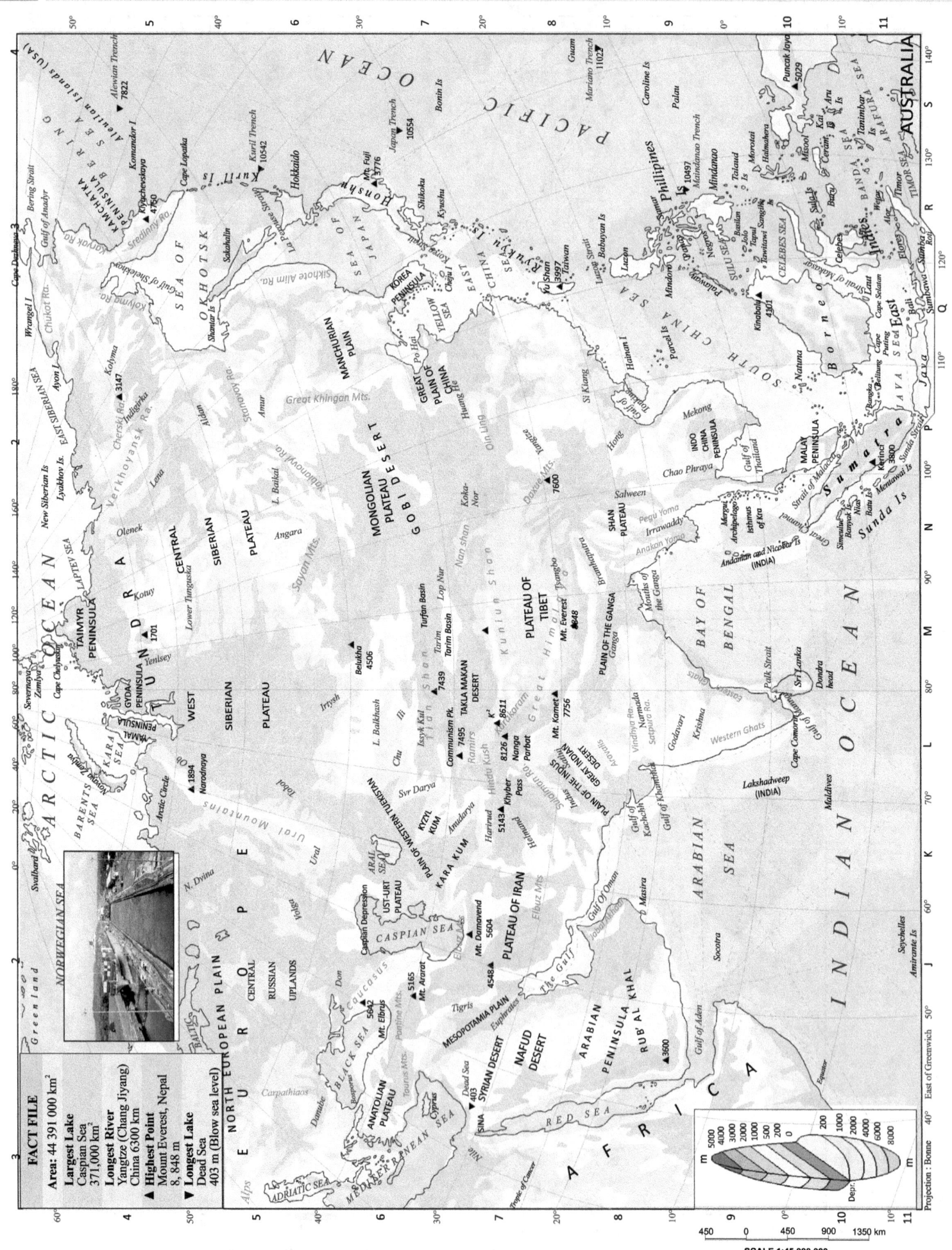

FACT FILE

Area: 44 391 000 km²

Largest Lake Caspian Sea 371,000 km²

Longest River Yangtze (Chang Jiyang) China 6300 km

▲ **Highest Point** Mount Everest, Nepal 8, 848 m

▼ **Longest Lake** Dead Sea 403 m (Blow sea level)

Projection : Bonne

East of Greenwich

450   0   450   900   1350 km

SCALE 1:45,000,000

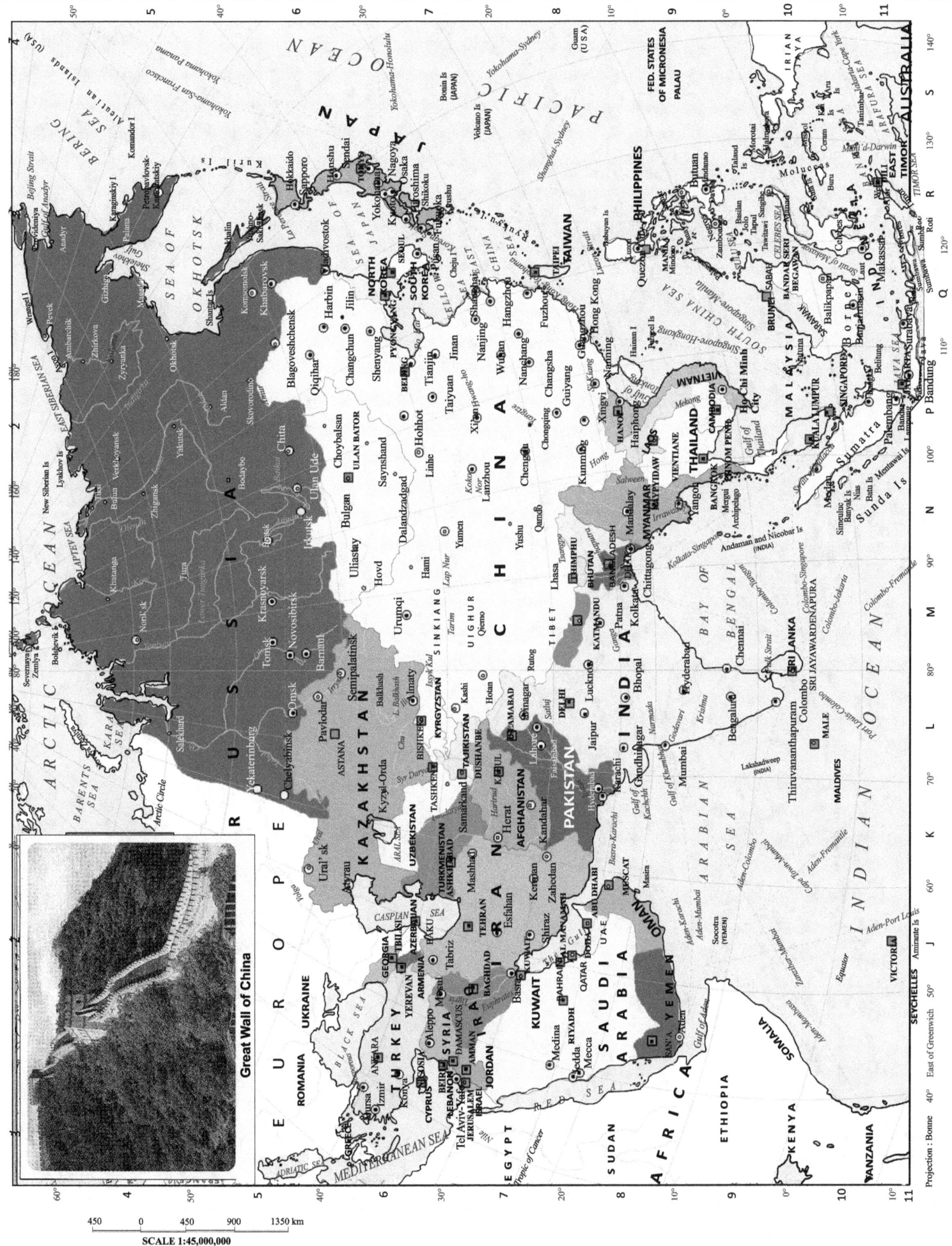

Great Wall of China

SCALE 1:45,000,000

450 0 450 900 1350 km

Projection : Bonne

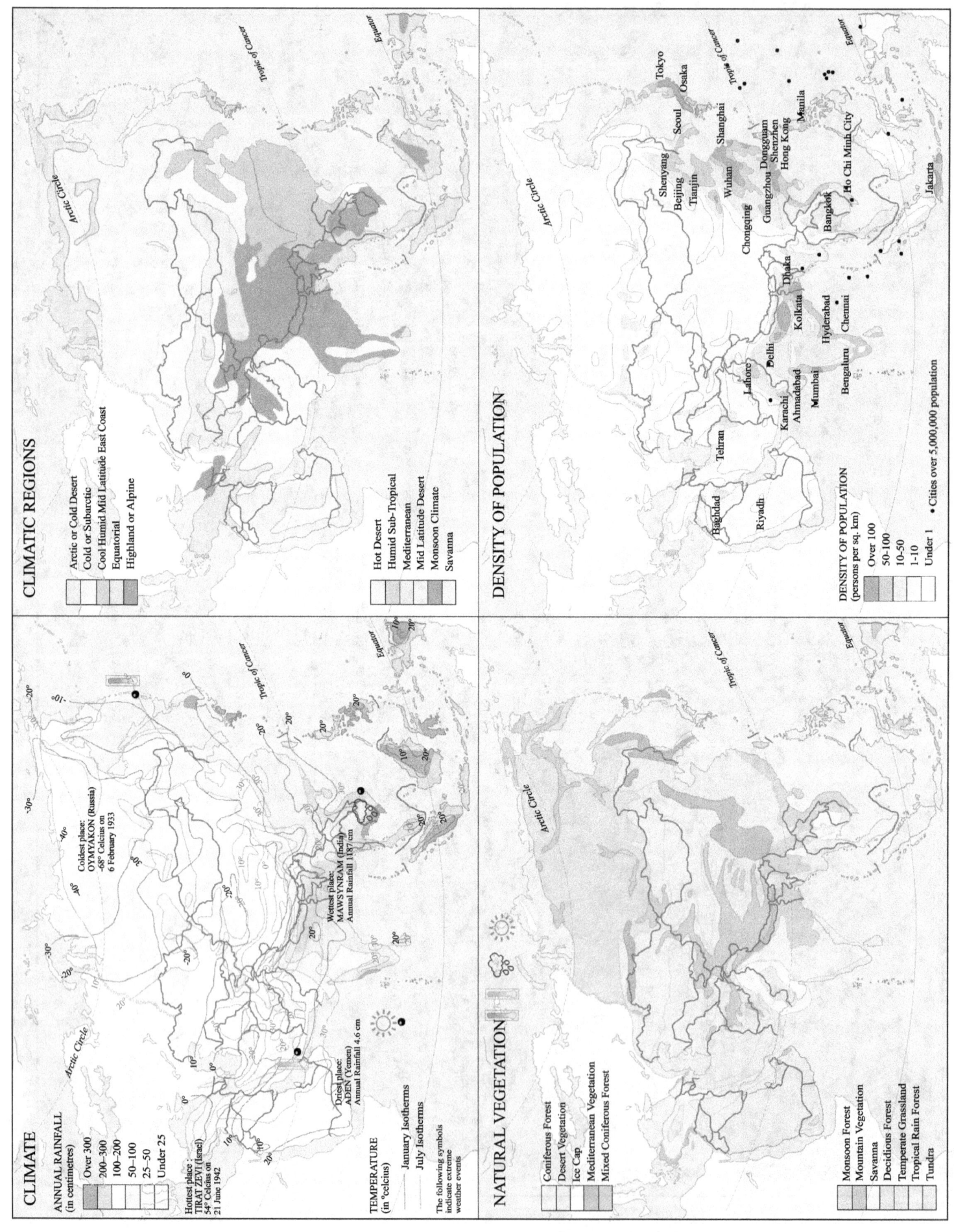

CLIMATIC REGIONS

Arctic or Cold Desert
Cold or Subarctic
Cool Humid Mid Latitude East Coast
Equatorial
Highland or Alpine

Hot Desert
Humid Sub-Tropical
Mediterranean
Mid Latitude Desert
Monsoon Climate
Savanna

DENSITY OF POPULATION

Tokyo
Osaka
Seoul
Shenyang
Shanghai
Beijing
Tianjin
Wuhan
Chongqing
Guangzhou
Dongguan
Shenzhen
Hong Kong
Manila
Ho Chi Minh City
Jakarta
Bangkok
Dhaka
Kolkata
Hyderabad
Chennai
Delhi
Lahore
Karachi
Ahmadabad
Mumbai
Bengaluru
Tehran
Baghdad
Riyadh

DENSITY OF POPULATION
(persons per sq. km)
Over 100
50–100
10–50
1–10
Under 1
• Cities over 5,000,000 population

CLIMATE

ANNUAL RAINFALL
(in centimetres)
Over 300
200–300
100–200
50–100
25–50
Under 25

Hottest place :
TIRAT ZEVI (Israel)
54° Celcius on
21 June 1942

Coldest place:
OYMYAKON (Russia)
-68° Celcius on
6 February 1933

Wettest place:
MAWSYNRAM (India)
Annual Rainfall 1187 cm

Driest place:
ADEN (Yemen)
Annual Rainfall 4.6 cm

TEMPERATURE
(in °celcius)
— January Isotherms
— July Isotherms

The following symbols
indicate extreme
weather events

NATURAL VEGETATION

Coniferous Forest
Desert Vegetation
Ice Cap
Mediterranean Vegetation
Mixed Coniferous Forest

Monsoon Forest
Mountain Vegetation
Savanna
Decidious Forest
Temperate Grassland
Tropical Rain Forest
Tundra

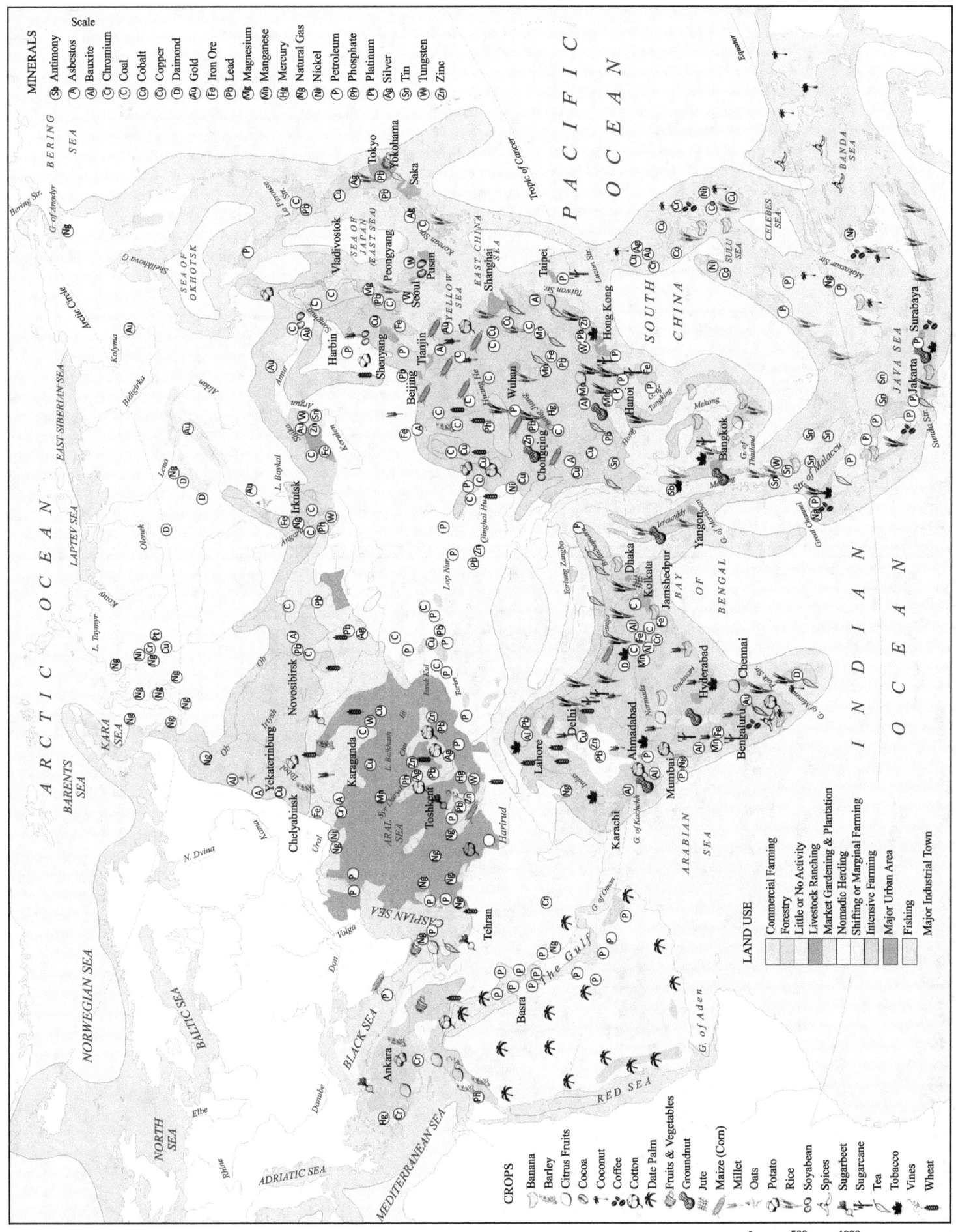

MINERALS

(Sb)	Antimony
(A)	Asbestos
(A)	Bauxite
(Cr)	Chromium
(C)	Coal
(G)	Cobalt
(Cu)	Copper
(D)	Diamond
(Au)	Gold
(Fe)	Iron Ore
(Pb)	Lead
(Mg)	Magnesium
(Mn)	Manganese
(Hg)	Mercury
(Ng)	Natural Gas
(Ni)	Nickel
(P)	Petroleum
(Ph)	Phosphate
(Pt)	Platinum
(Ag)	Silver
(Sn)	Tin
(W)	Tungsten
(Zn)	Zinc

Scale

LAND USE

- Commercial Farming
- Forestry
- Little or No Activity
- Livestock Ranching
- Market Gardening & Plantation
- Nomadic Herding
- Shifting or Marginal Farming
- Intensive Farming
- Major Urban Area
- Fishing

Major Industrial Town

CROPS

- Banana
- Barley
- Citrus Fruits
- Cocoa
- Coconut
- Coffee
- Cotton
- Date Palm
- Fruits & Vegetables
- Groundnut
- Jute
- Maize (Corn)
- Millet
- Oats
- Potato
- Rice
- Soyabean
- Spices
- Sugarbeet
- Sugarcane
- Tea
- Tobacco
- Vines
- Wheat

SCALE 1:50,000,000 (1 cm to 500 km)

0   500   1000

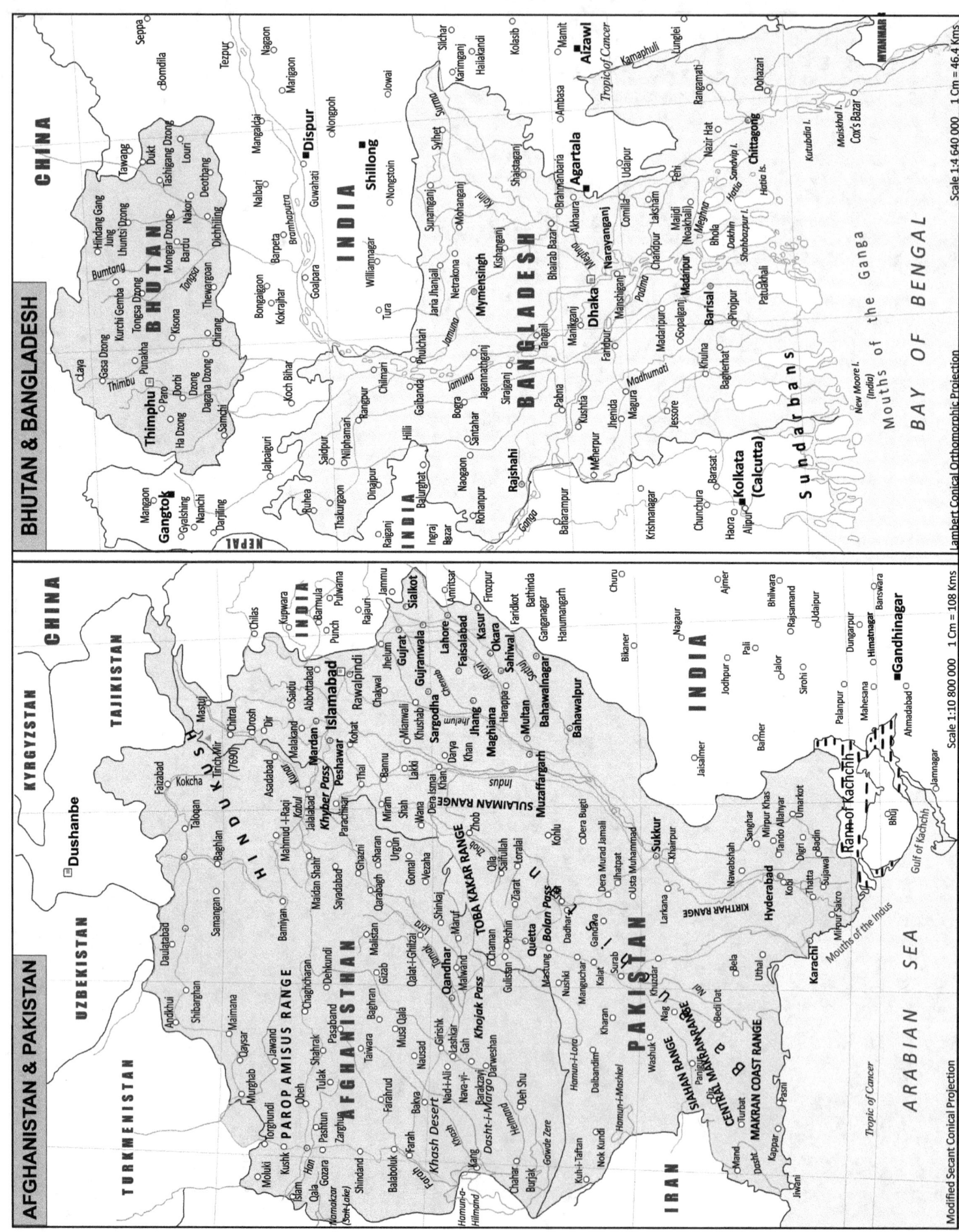

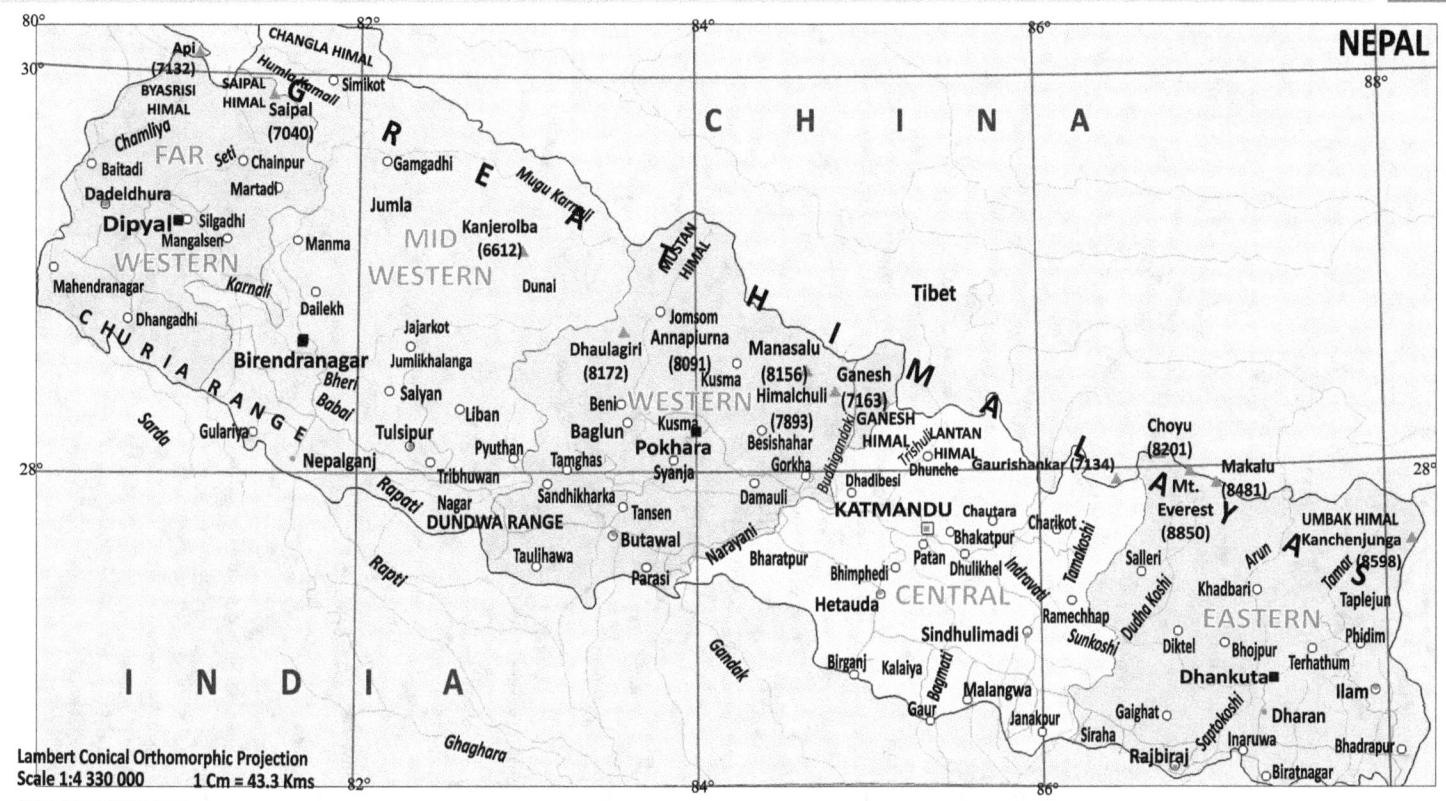

NEPAL

80°   82°   84°   86°   88°

30°

CHANGLA HIMAL

Api
(7132)
BYASRISI
HIMAL
SAIPAL
HIMAL
Saipal
(7040)

Humla Karnali

Simikot

C H I N A

Chamliya

Baitadi

Gamgadhi

Seti

Chainpur

FAR

Martadi

Dadeldhura

Jumla

Dipyal Silgadhi

Mangalsen

G

R

E

Kanjerolba
(6612)

E

MID

WESTERN

WESTERN

Manma

Tibet

Mahendranagar

Dailekh

Karnali

Dunai

MUSTAN
HIMAL

Dhangadhi

Jajarkot

Jomsom

Annapurna
(8091)

Jumlikhalanga

Dhaulagiri
(8172)

Manasalu
(8156)

Ganesh
(7163)

Choyu
(8201)

Makalu
(8481)

Birendranagar

Salyan

Kusma

Himalchuli
(7893)

GANESH
HIMAL

Mt.
Everest
(8850)

Kanchenjunga
(8598)

Bheri

Babai

Liban

Beni

WESTERN

Besishahar

LANTAN
HIMAL

Gaurishankar (7134)

A

UMBAK HIMAL

CHURIA RANGE

Tulsipur

Baglun

Pokhara

Gorkha

Trishuli

Dhunche

L

Arun

Salleri

Tamor

Sarda

Gulariya

Pyuthan

Tamghas

Syanja

Dhadibesi

Gaurishankar

Y

Khadbari

Taplejun

Nepalganj

Tribhuwan

Rapati

Nagar

Sandhikharka

Tansen

Damauli

KATMANDU

Chautara

Charikot

Tamakoshi

A

S

Phidim

Rapti

DUNDWA RANGE

Butawal

Bharatpur

Dhadikhel

Patan

Bhaktapur

Dudho Koshi

Ramechhap

Diktel

Bhojpur

Terhathum

Taulihawa

Parasi

Narayani

Damauli

Bhimphedi

Indravati

Sunkoshi

Ilam

Sindhulimadi

Saptokoshi

Gandak

Hetauda

Birganj

Kalaiya

Malangwa

Bagmati

Gaighat

Dhankuta

Dharan

I N D I A

Ghaghara

Gaur

Janakpur

Siraha

Inaruwa

Rajbiraj

Bhadrapur

Biratnagar

Lambert Conical Orthomorphic Projection
Scale 1:4 330 000   1 Cm = 43.3 Kms

28°

MALDIVES

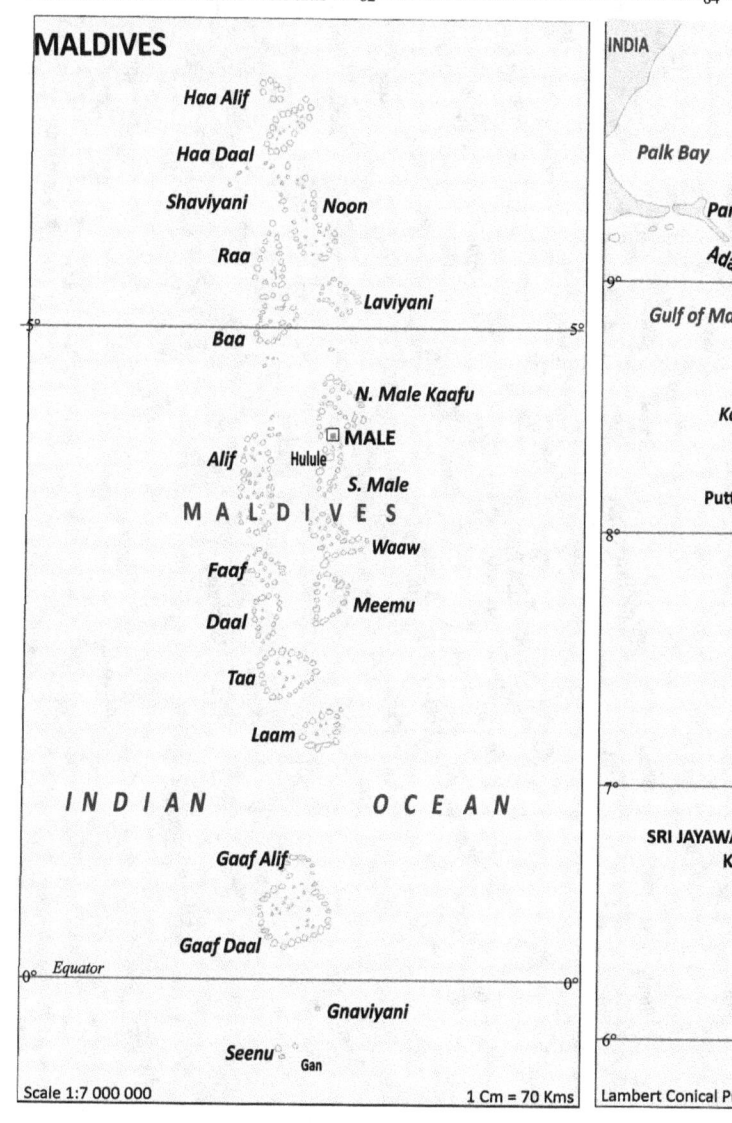

Haa Alif

Haa Daal

Shaviyani

Noon

Raa

Laviyani

Baa

N. Male Kaafu

□ **MALE**

Alif   Hulule

S. Male

M A L D I V E S

Waaw

Faaf

Meemu

Daal

Taa

Laam

I N D I A N   O C E A N

Gaaf Alif

Gaaf Daal

Equator

Gnaviyani

Seenu   Gan

Scale 1:7 000 000   1 Cm = 70 Kms

SRI LANKA

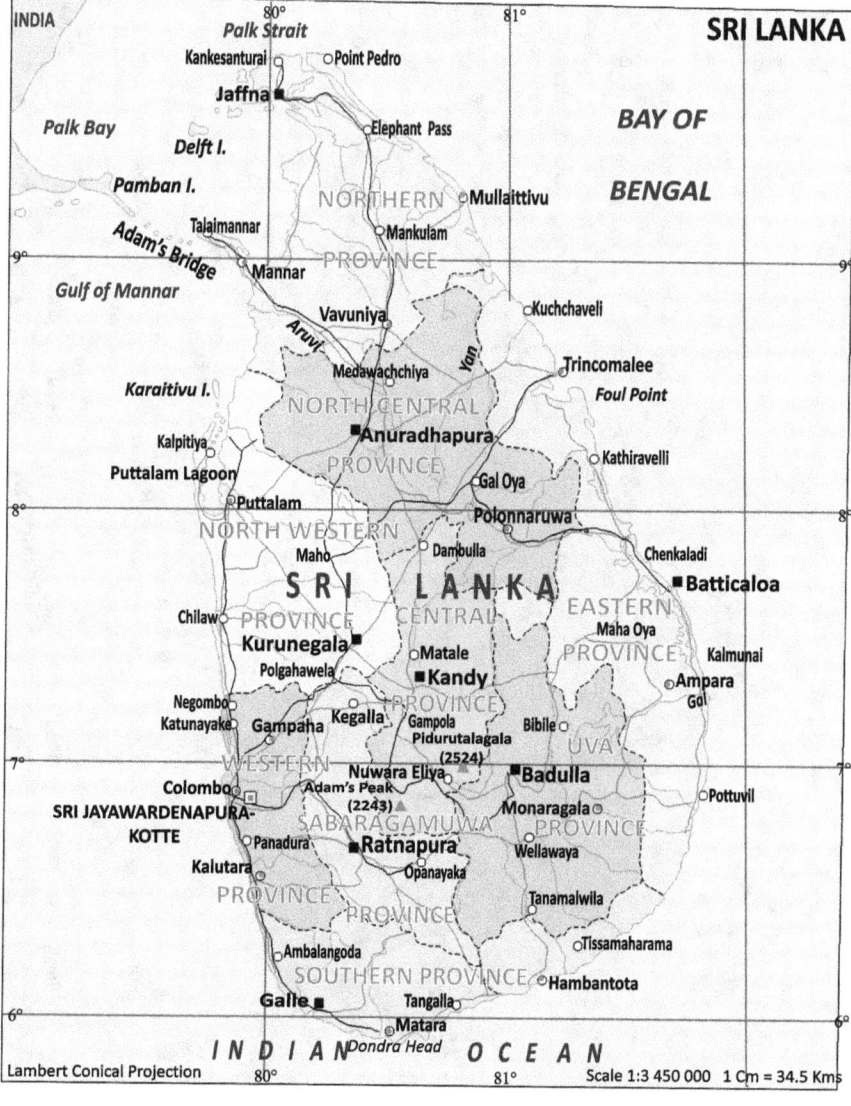

INDIA

Palk Strait

80°   81°

Kankesanturai   ○ Point Pedro

Jaffna■

Palk Bay

○ Elephant Pass

BAY OF

Delft I.

Delft I.

NORTHERN

BENGAL

Pamban I.

○ Mullaittivu

Talaimannar

PROVINCE

Mankulam

Adam's Bridge

Mannar

Vavuniya

○ Kuchchaveli

Gulf of Mannar

Medawachchiya

Aruvi

Yan

Trincomalee

Karaitivu I.

NORTH CENTRAL

Foul Point

Kalpitiya

■**Anuradhapura**

○ Kathiraveli

Puttalam Lagoon

PROVINCE

Gal Oya

■ Puttalam

Polonnaruwa

NORTH WESTERN

Maho

Dambulla

Chenkaladi

S R I   L A N K A

Chilaw

PROVINCE

CENTRAL

EASTERN

Batticaloa■

Kurunegala■

Matale

Maha Oya

PROVINCE

Kalmunai

Negombo

Polgahawela

Kandy■

Gampola

Ampara
○ Gal

Katunayake

Kegalla

Pidurutalagala
(2524)

UVA

Gampaha

Bibile

Nuwara Eliya

Badulla■

Colombo

Adam's Peak
(2243)

Pottuvil

SABARAGAMUWA

SRI JAYAWARDENAPURA-KOTTE

Monaragala

PROVINCE

Ratnapura■

Wellawaya

Kalutara

Panadura

Opanayaka

Tanamalwila

PROVINCE

Ambalangoda

Tissamaharama

SOUTHERN PROVINCE

Hambantota

Galle■

Tangalla

Matara

Dondra Head

I N D I A N   O C E A N

Lambert Conical Projection   80°   81°   Scale 1:3 450 000   1 Cm = 34.5 Kms

9°

8°

7°

6°

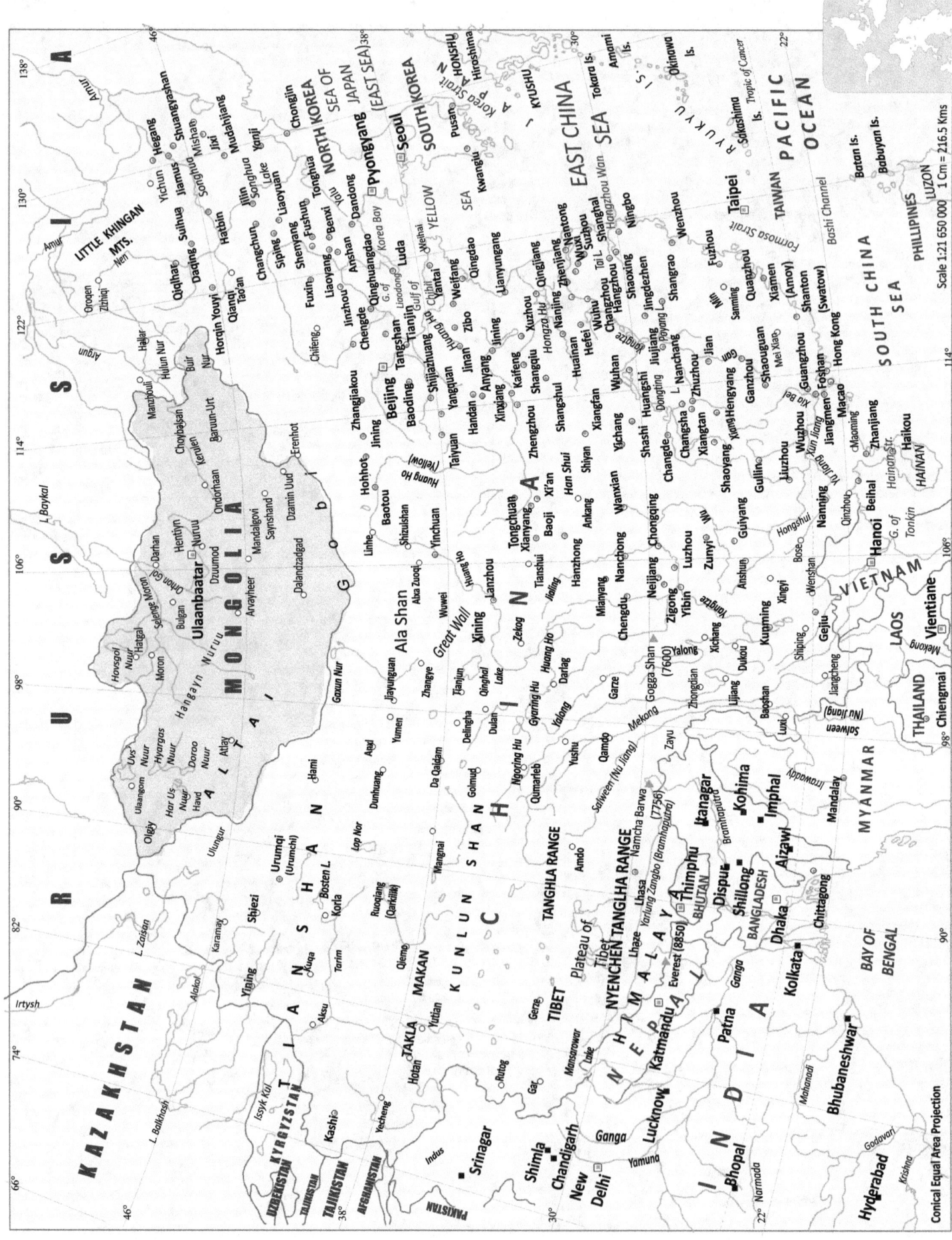

Scale 1:21 650 000   1 Cm = 216.5 Kms

Conical Equal Area Projection

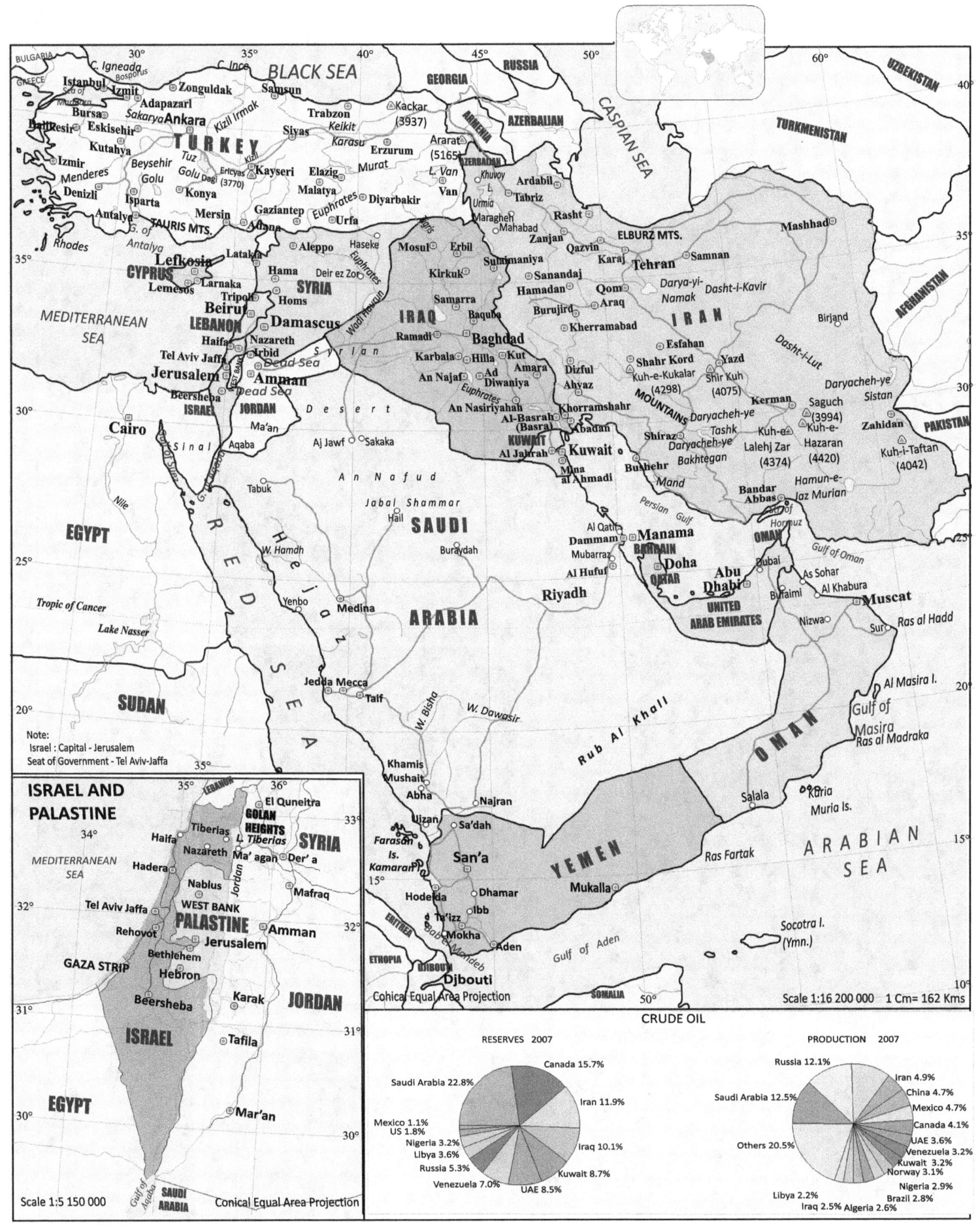

ISRAEL AND PALESTINE

Note:
Israel : Capital - Jerusalem
Seat of Government - Tel Aviv-Jaffa

Scale 1:5 150 000   Conical Equal Area Projection

Conical Equal Area Projection

Scale 1:16 200 000   1 Cm= 162 Kms

CRUDE OIL

RESERVES 2007

Canada 15.7%
Saudi Arabia 22.8%
Iran 11.9%
Mexico 1.1%
US 1.8%
Nigeria 3.2%
Libya 3.6%
Iraq 10.1%
Russia 5.3%
Venezuela 7.0%
UAE 8.5%
Kuwait 8.7%

PRODUCTION 2007

Russia 12.1%
Iran 4.9%
China 4.7%
Saudi Arabia 12.5%
Mexico 4.7%
Canada 4.1%
Others 20.5%
UAE 3.6%
Venezuela 3.2%
Kuwait 3.2%
Norway 3.1%
Libya 2.2%
Nigeria 2.9%
Iraq 2.5%
Brazil 2.8%
Algeria 2.6%

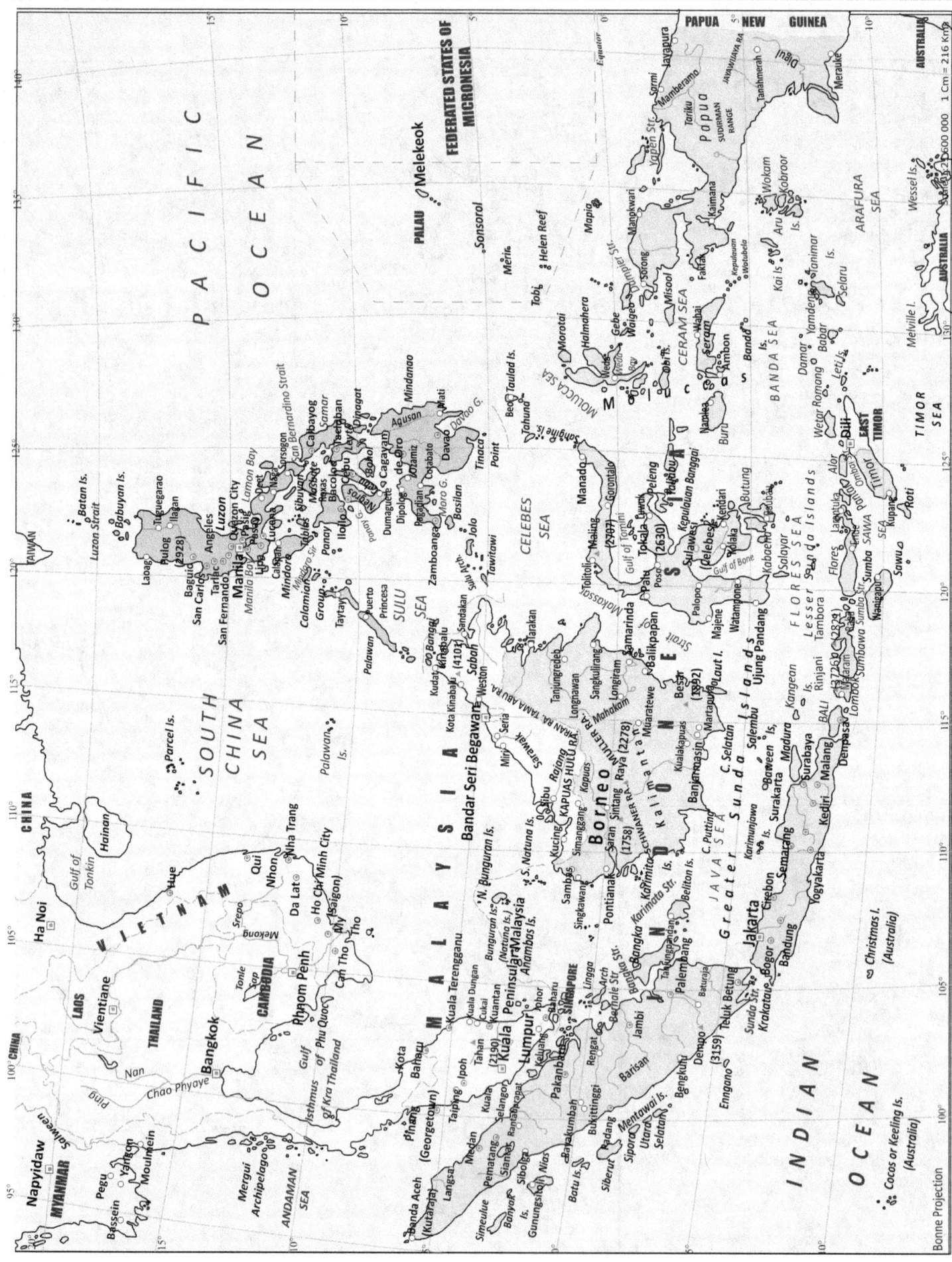

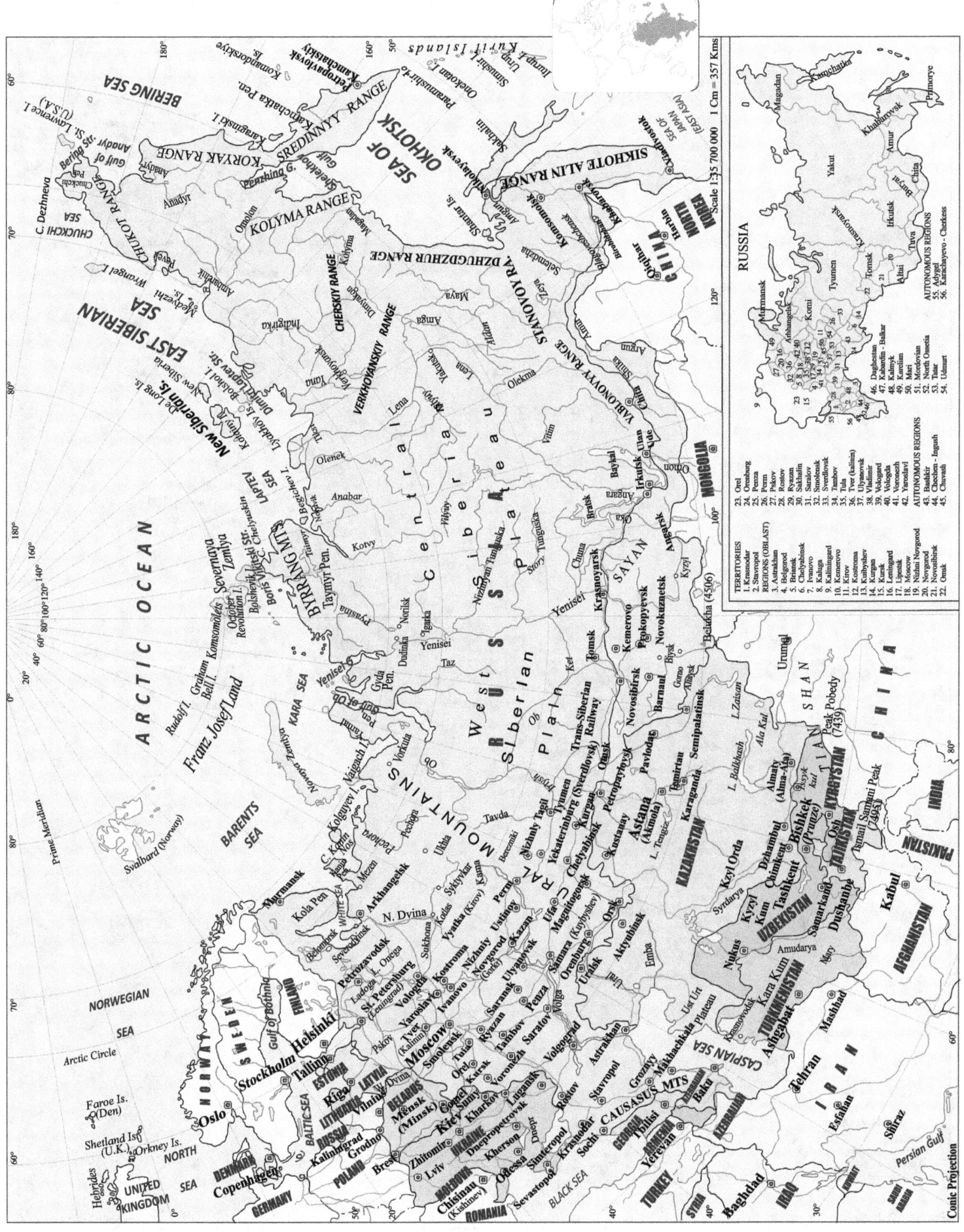

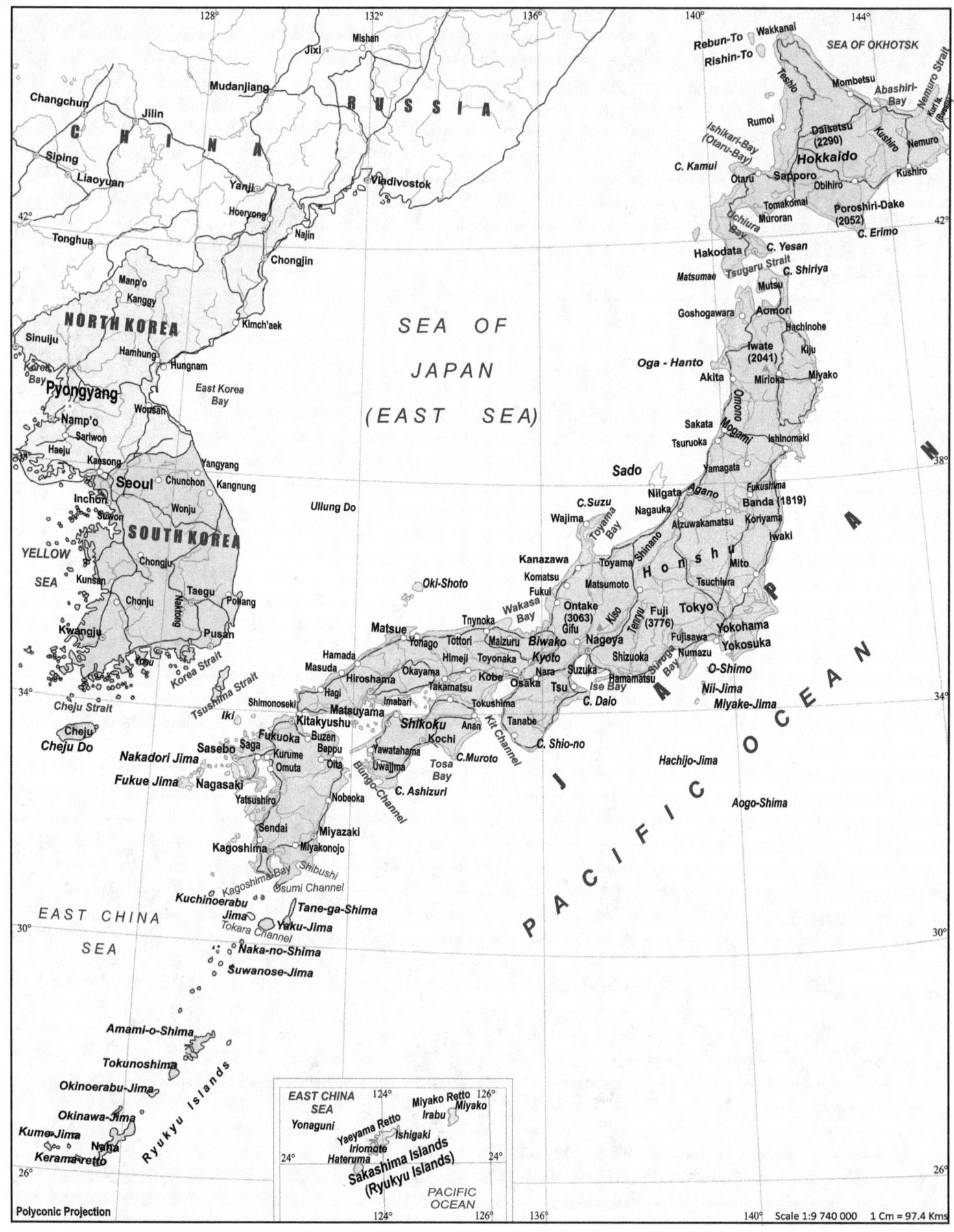

SEA OF
JAPAN
(EAST SEA)

YELLOW
SEA

EAST CHINA
SEA

PACIFIC OCEAN

Polyconic Projection

Scale 1:9 740 000   1 Cm = 97.4 Kms

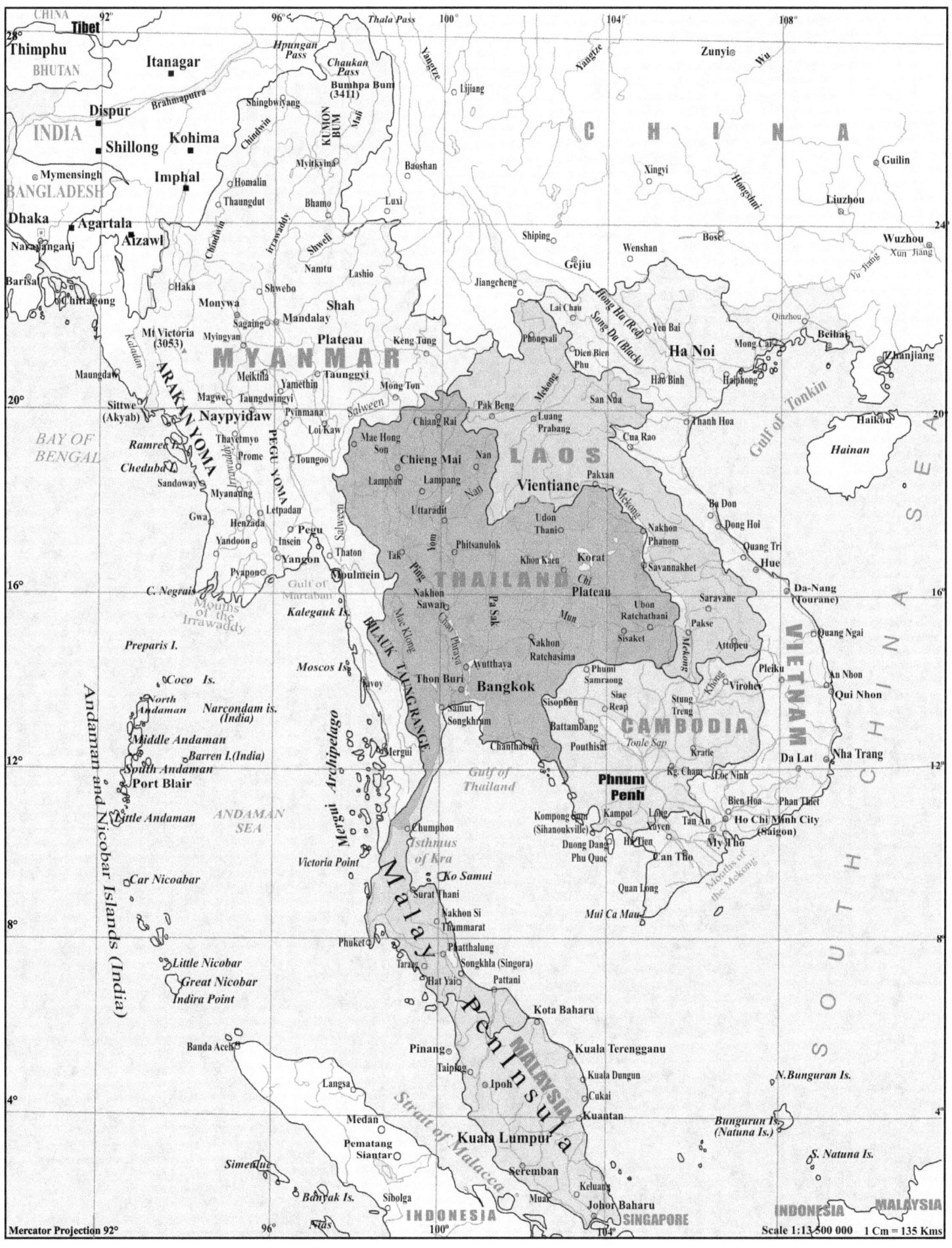

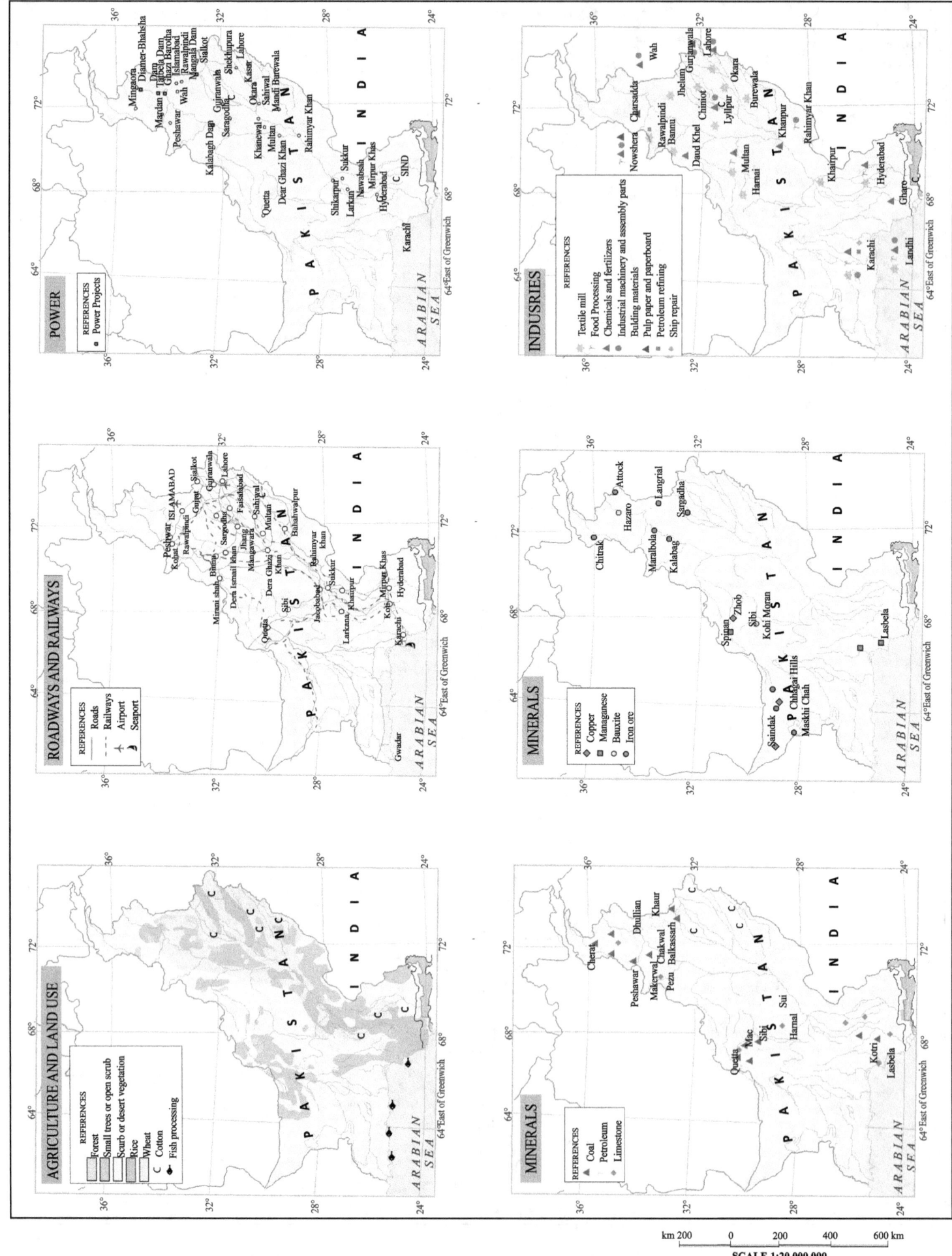

SCALE 1:20,000,000

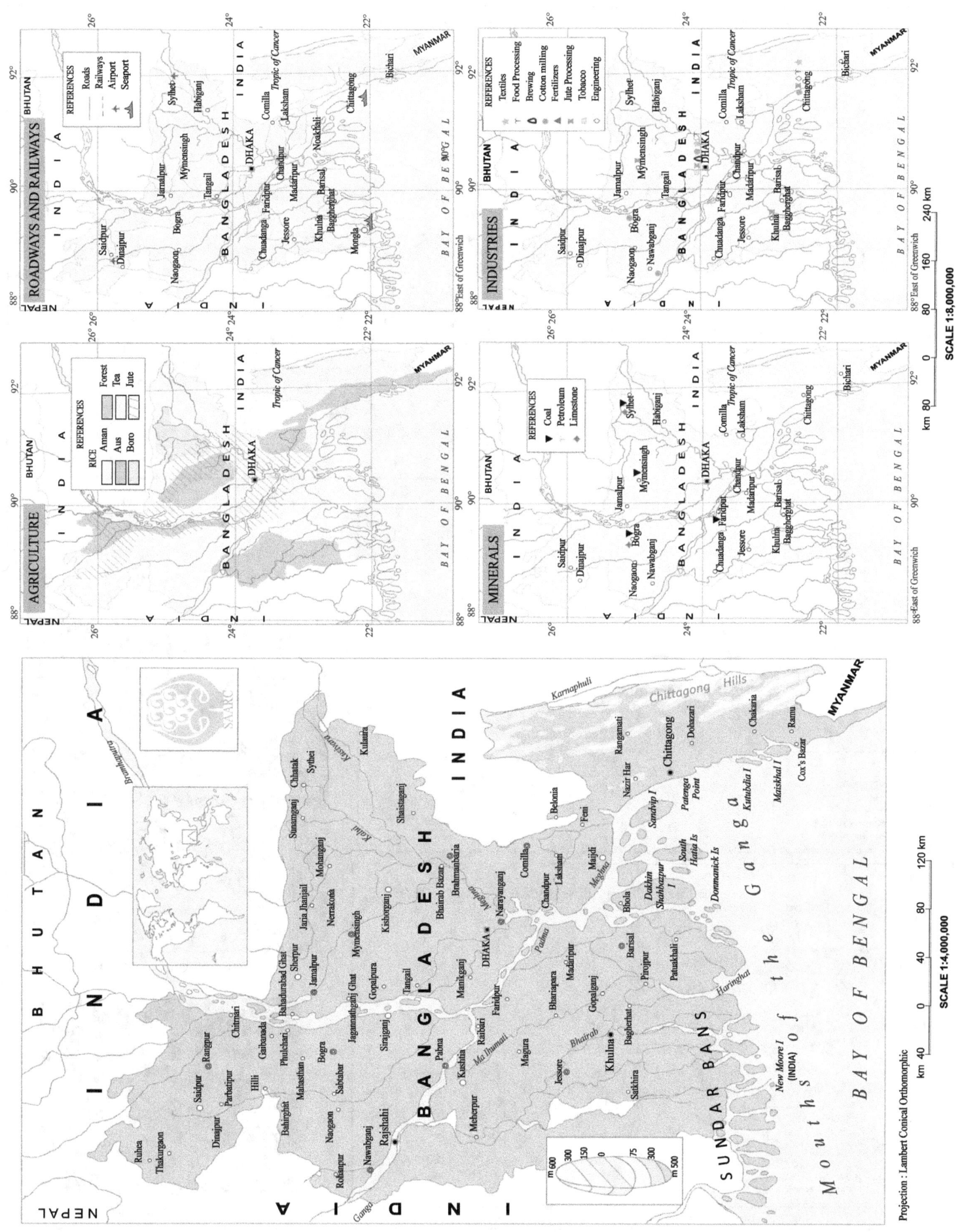

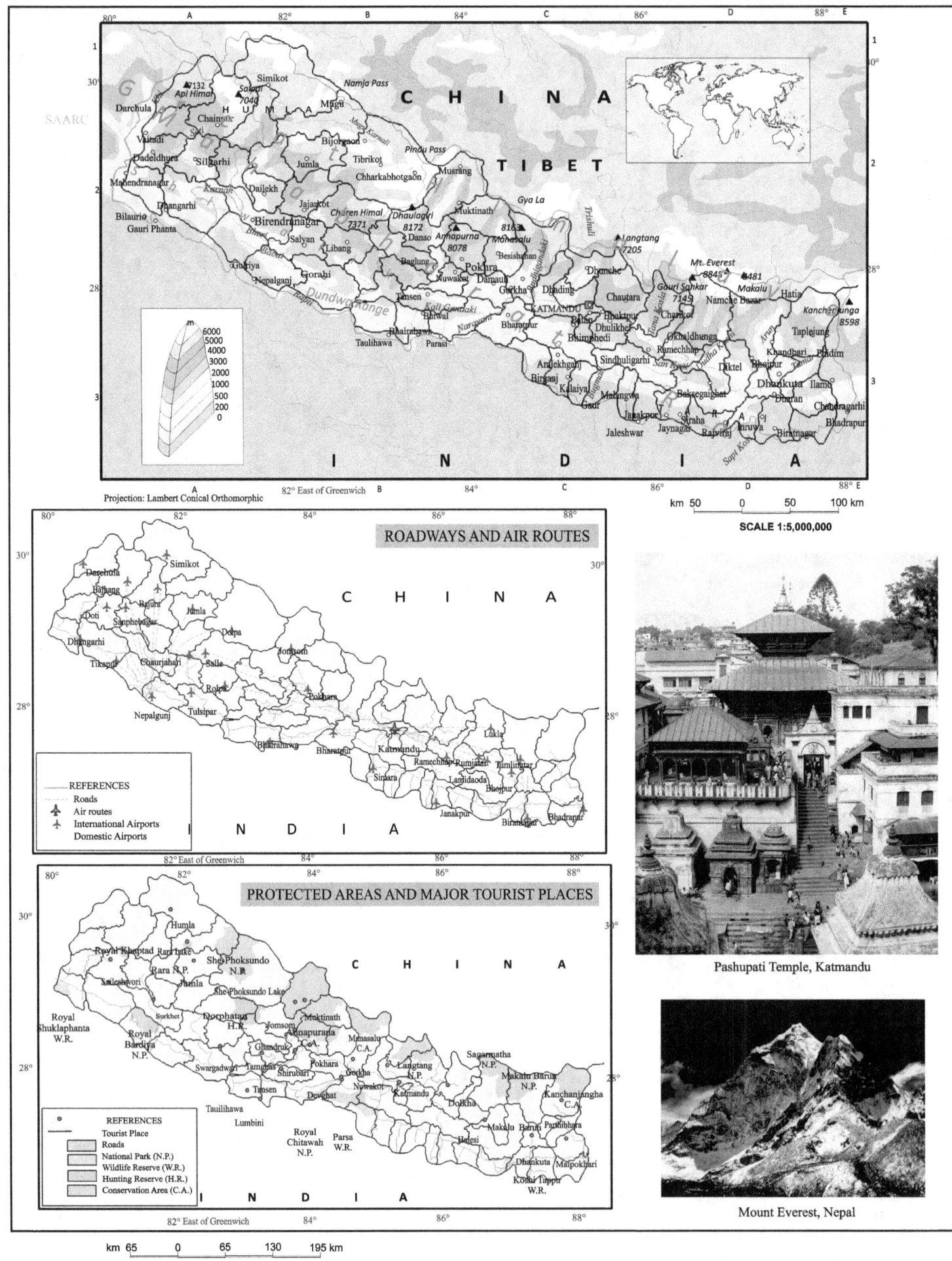

ROADWAYS AND AIR ROUTES

CHINA

INDIA

REFERENCES
Roads
Air routes
International Airports
Domestic Airports

82° East of Greenwich

PROTECTED AREAS AND MAJOR TOURIST PLACES

CHINA

Royal Khaptad
Rara Lake
She Phoksundo N.P.
Rara N.P.
She Phoksundo Lake
Sailesh wori
Humla
Jumla
Royal
Shuklaphanta
W.R.
Surkhet
Dorphatan H.R.
Muktinath
Jomsom
Annapurna C.A.
Royal
Bardiya
N.P.
Ghandruk
Manaslu C.A.
Langtang N.P.
Sagarmatha N.P.
Makalu Barun N.P.
Swargadwari
Tamghas
Shirubari
Pokhara
Gorkha
Nuwakot
Kanchanjangha C.A.
Timsen
Deoghat
Katmandu
Dolkha
Tauilihawa
Lumbini
Royal
Chitawah
N.P.
Parsa
W.R.
Makalu Barun
Pashubhara
Helesi
Dhankuta
Maipokhari
Makalu Barun
Koshi Tappu
W.R.

INDIA

REFERENCES
Tourist Place
Roads
National Park (N.P.)
Wildlife Reserve (W.R.)
Hunting Reserve (H.R.)
Conservation Area (C.A.)

82° East of Greenwich   84°   86°   88°

km 65   0   65   130   195 km

SCALE 1:6,500,000

CHINA

TIBET

SAARC

Pashupati Temple, Katmandu

Mount Everest, Nepal

Projection: Lambert Conical Orthomorphic

82° East of Greenwich

km 50   0   50   100 km

SCALE 1:5,000,000

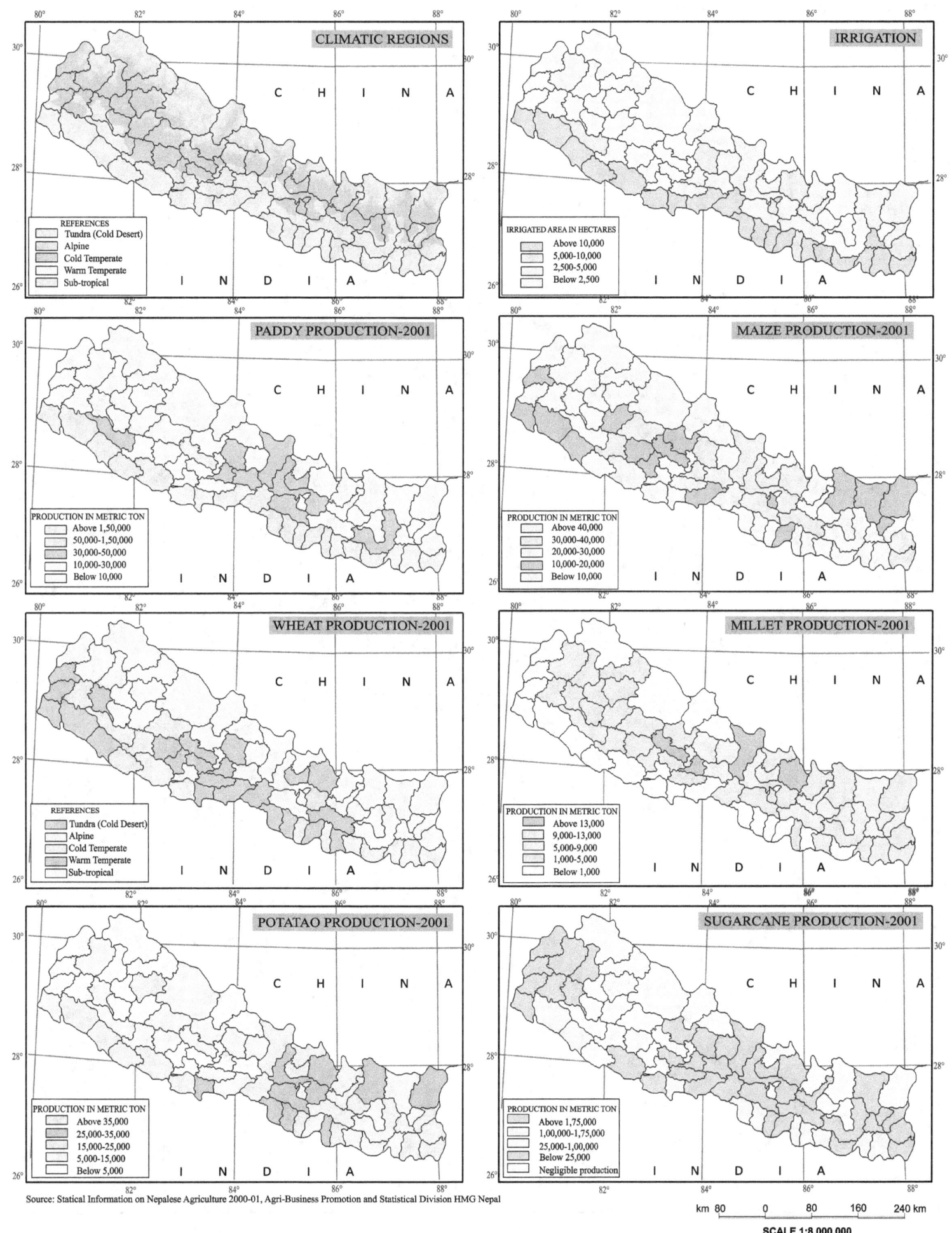

CLIMATIC REGIONS

REFERENCES
- Tundra (Cold Desert)
- Alpine
- Cold Temperate
- Warm Temperate
- Sub-tropical

IRRIGATION

IRRIGATED AREA IN HECTARES
- Above 10,000
- 5,000-10,000
- 2,500-5,000
- Below 2,500

PADDY PRODUCTION-2001

PRODUCTION IN METRIC TON
- Above 1,50,000
- 50,000-1,50,000
- 30,000-50,000
- 10,000-30,000
- Below 10,000

MAIZE PRODUCTION-2001

PRODUCTION IN METRIC TON
- Above 40,000
- 30,000-40,000
- 20,000-30,000
- 10,000-20,000
- Below 10,000

WHEAT PRODUCTION-2001

REFERENCES
- Tundra (Cold Desert)
- Alpine
- Cold Temperate
- Warm Temperate
- Sub-tropical

MILLET PRODUCTION-2001

PRODUCTION IN METRIC TON
- Above 13,000
- 9,000-13,000
- 5,000-9,000
- 1,000-5,000
- Below 1,000

POTATAO PRODUCTION-2001

PRODUCTION IN METRIC TON
- Above 35,000
- 25,000-35,000
- 15,000-25,000
- 5,000-15,000
- Below 5,000

SUGARCANE PRODUCTION-2001

PRODUCTION IN METRIC TON
- Above 1,75,000
- 1,00,000-1,75,000
- 25,000-1,00,000
- Below 25,000
- Negligible production

Source: Statical Information on Nepalese Agriculture 2000-01, Agri-Business Promotion and Statistical Division HMG Nepal

km 80   0   80   160   240 km

SCALE 1:8,000,000

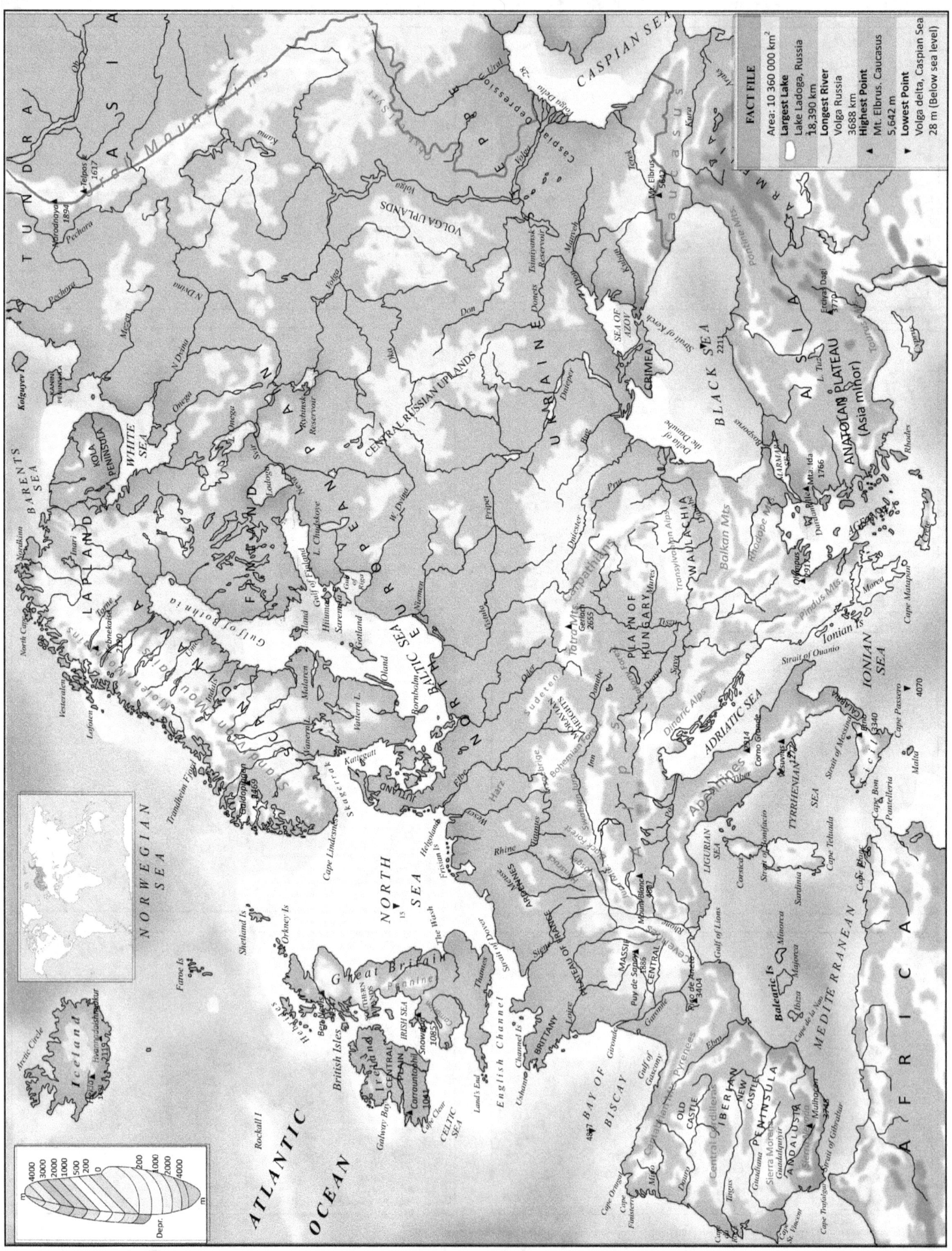

FACT FILE

Area: 10 360 000 km²

Largest Lake
Lake Ladoga, Russia
18,390 km²

Longest River
Volga Russia
3688 km

Highest Point
Mt. Elbrus, Caucasus
5,642 m

Lowest Point
Volga delta, Caspian Sea
28 m (Below sea level)

ATLANTIC OCEAN

NORWEGIAN SEA

NORTH SEA

BALTIC SEA

BARENTS SEA

WHITE SEA

CASPIAN SEA

BLACK SEA

SEA OF AZOV

ADRIATIC SEA

TYRRHENIAN SEA

IONIAN SEA

LIGURIAN SEA

MEDITERRANEAN SEA

CELTIC SEA

IRISH SEA

ATLANTIC OCEAN

AFRICA

ASIA

A S I A

TUNDRA

LAPLAND

Iceland

Great Britain

Ireland

English Channel

BAY OF BISCAY

IBERIAN PENINSULA

PLAIN OF HUNGARY

CRIMEA

UKRAINE

CAUCASUS

ANATOLIAN PLATEAU
(Asia minor)

VOLGA UPLANDS

CENTRAL RUSSIAN UPLANDS

Caspian Depression

Scandinavian Mountains

Ural Mountains

Carpathians

Apennines

Pyrenees

Alps

Pindus Mts

Balkan Mts

Dinaric Alps

Transylvanian Alps

Pontine Mts

Volga

Don

Dnieper

Danube

Rhine

Loire

Ebro

Vistula

Oder

Elbe

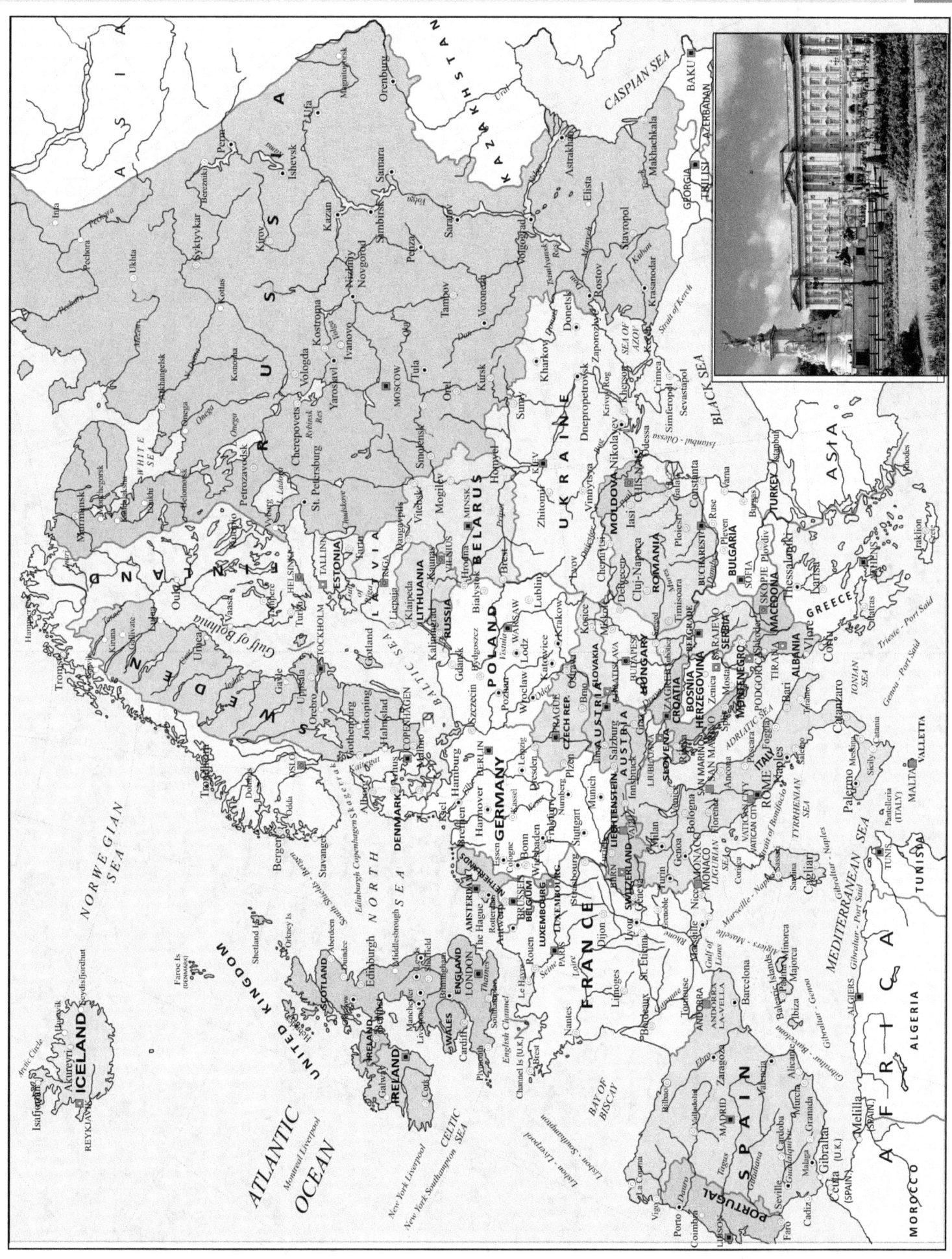

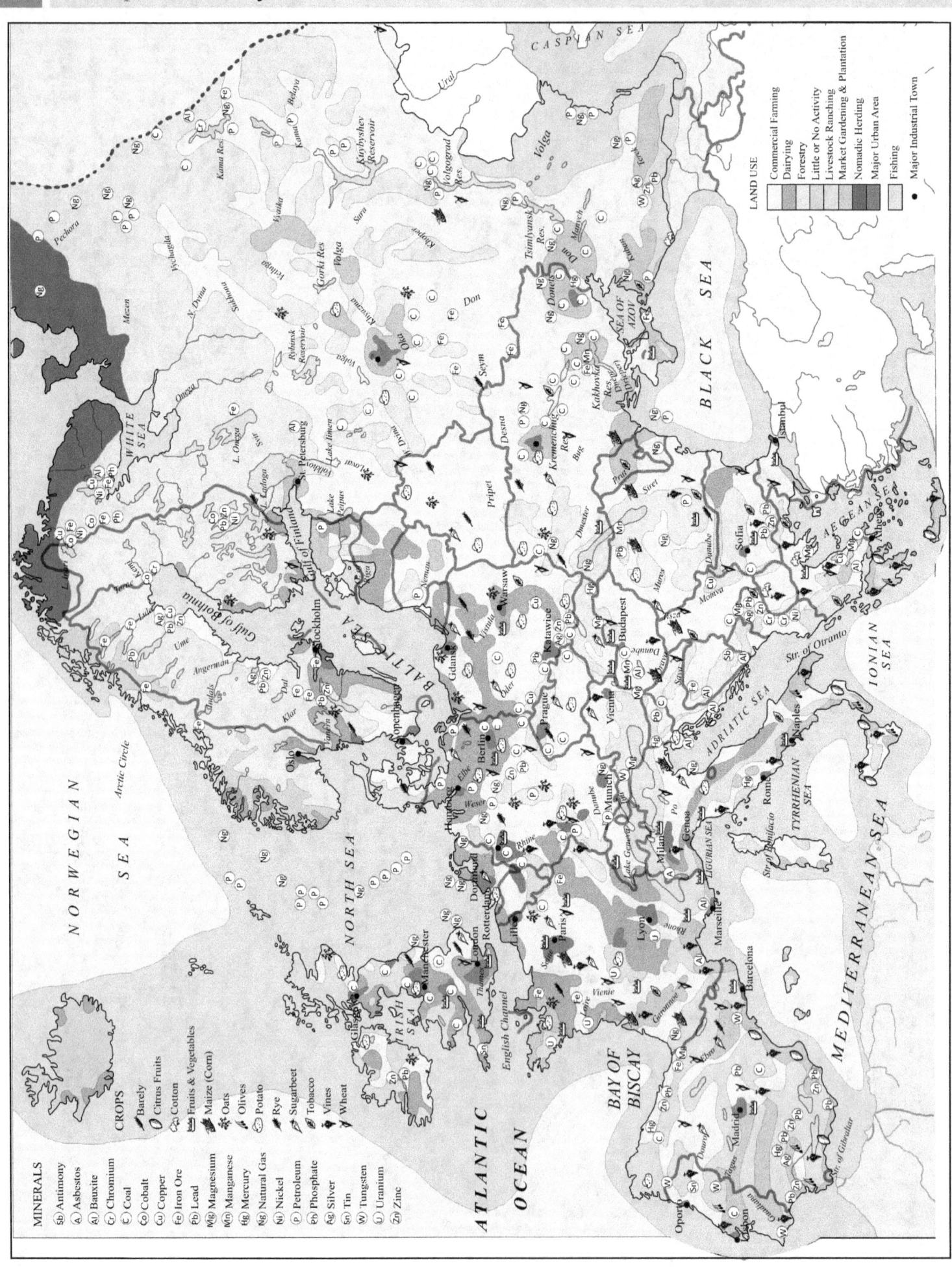

LAND USE

Commercial Farming
Dairying
Forestry
Little or No Activity
Livestock Ranching
Market Gardening & Plantation
Nomadic Herding
Major Urban Area
Fishing
● Major Industrial Town

MINERALS
Sb Antimony
A Asbestos
Al Bauxite
Cr Chromium
C Coal
Co Cobalt
Cu Copper
Fe Iron Ore
Pb Lead
Mg Magnesium
Mn Manganese
Hg Mercury
Ng Natural Gas
Ni Nickel
P Petroleum
Ph Phosphate
Ag Silver
Sn Tin
W Tungsten
U Uranium
Zn Zinc

CROPS
Barely
Citrus Fruits
Cotton
Fruits & Vegetables
Maize (Corn)
Oats
Olives
Potato
Rye
Sugarbeet
Tobacco
Vines
Wheat

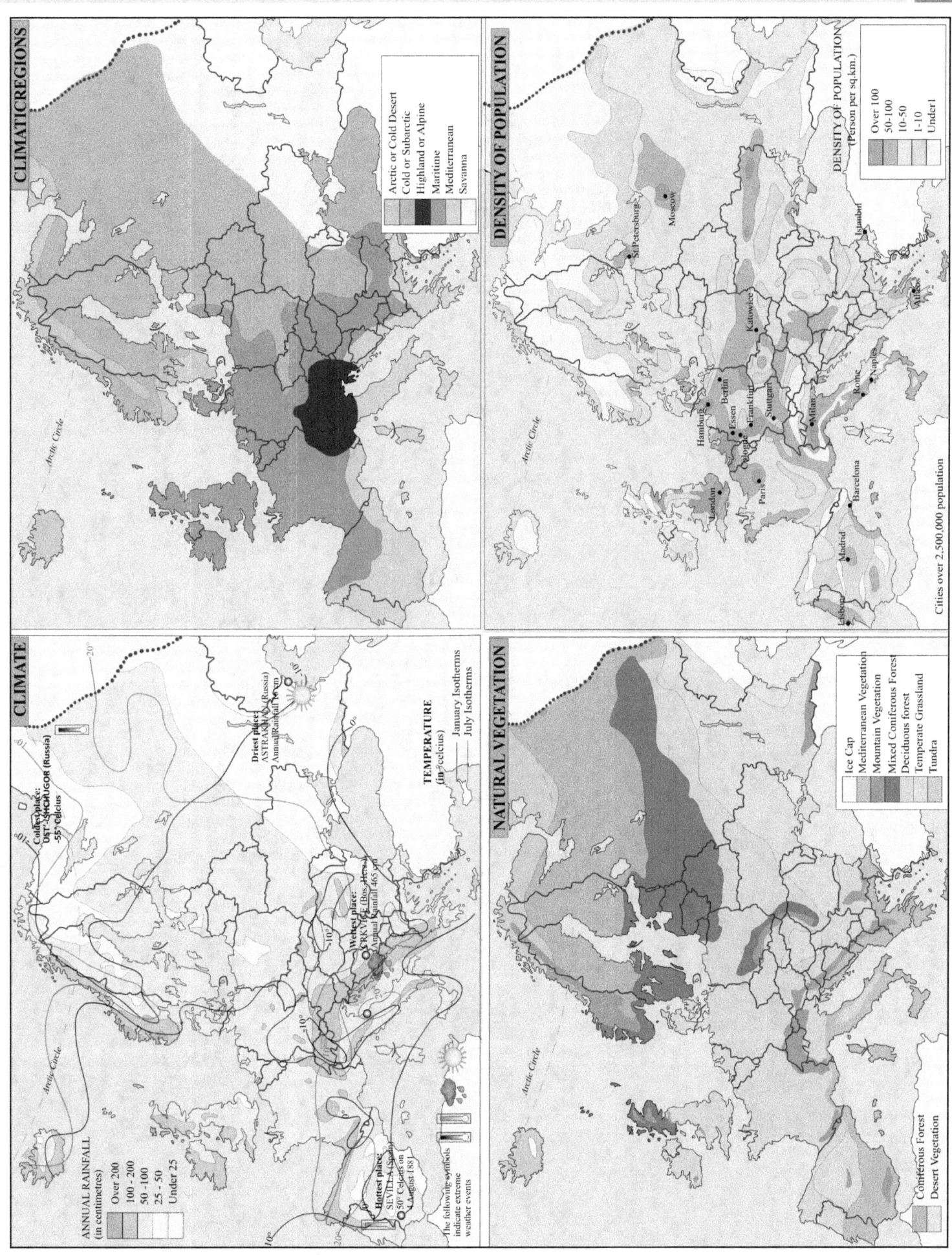

CLIMATICREGIONS

Arctic or Cold Desert
Cold or Subarctic
Highland or Alpine
Maritime
Mediterranean
Savanna

Arctic Circle

DENSITY OF POPULATION

DENSITY OF POPULATION
(Person per sq.km.)

Over 100
50 -100
10 -50
1 -10
Under1

St.Petersburg
Moscow

Istanbul

Athens

Kattowice

Berlin
Frankfurt
Hamburg
Essen
Stuttgart
Cologne
Milan
Rome
Naples

London
Paris
Barcelona

Arctic Circle

Madrid

Lisbon

Cities over 2,500,000 population

CLIMATE

20°

Coldest place:
UST'-SHUGUOR (Russia)
-55°Celcius

Driest place:
ASTRAKHAN (Russia)
Annual Rainfall 160 cm

10°

0°

Wettest place:
CRKVICE (Bos. Herz.)
Annual Rainfall 465 cm

Arctic Circle

ANNUAL RAINFALL
(in centimetres)

Over 200
100 - 200
50 - 100
25 - 50
Under 25

TEMPERATURE
(in °celcius)

—— January Isotherms
—— July Isotherms

Hottest place:
SEVILLE (Spain)
50°Celcius on
4 August 1881

The following symbols
indicate extreme
weather events

NATURAL VEGETATION

Ice Cap
Mediterranean Vegetation
Mountain Vegetation
Mixed Coniferous Forest
Deciduous forest
Temperate Grassland
Tundra

Arctic Circle

Coniferous Forest
Desert Vegetation

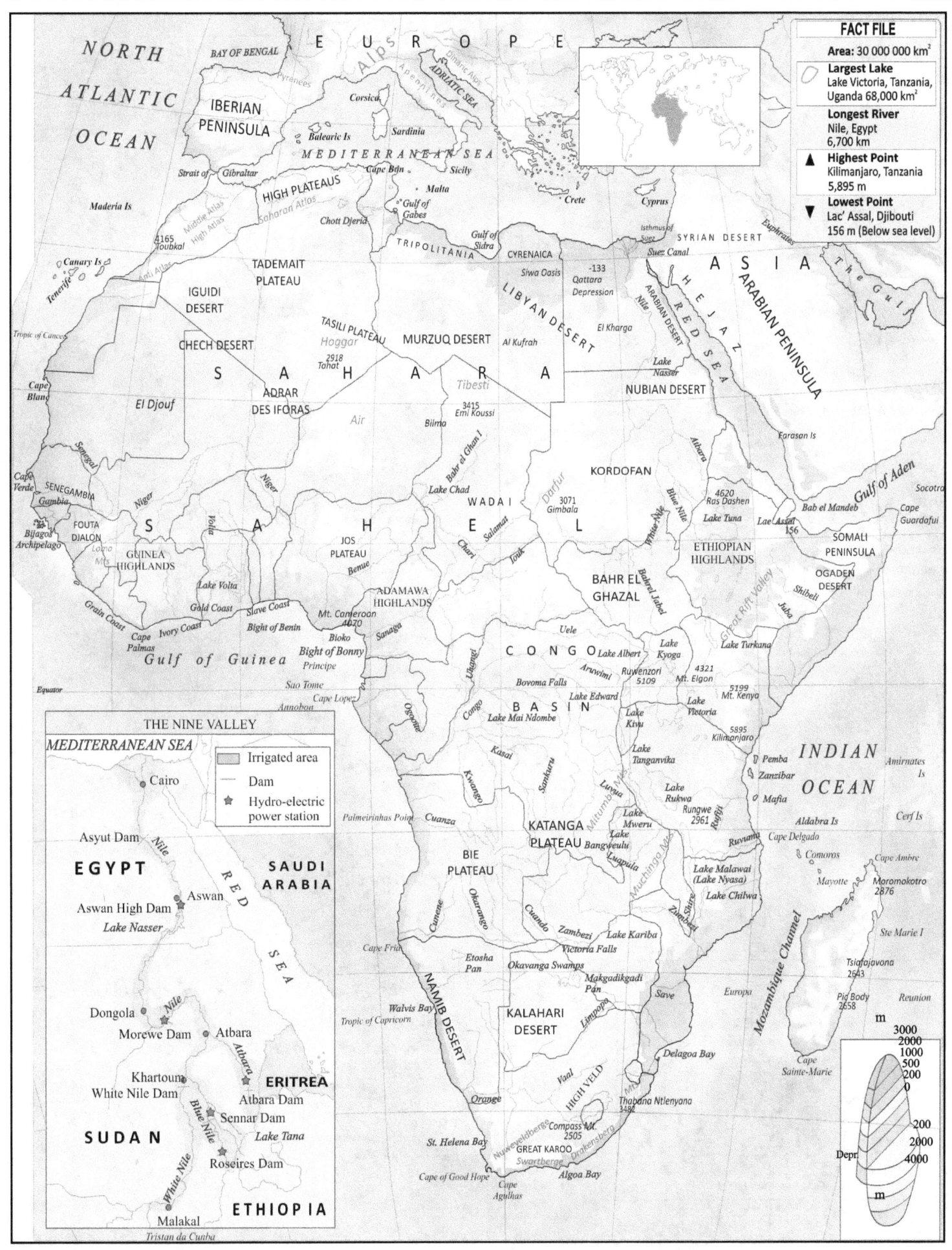

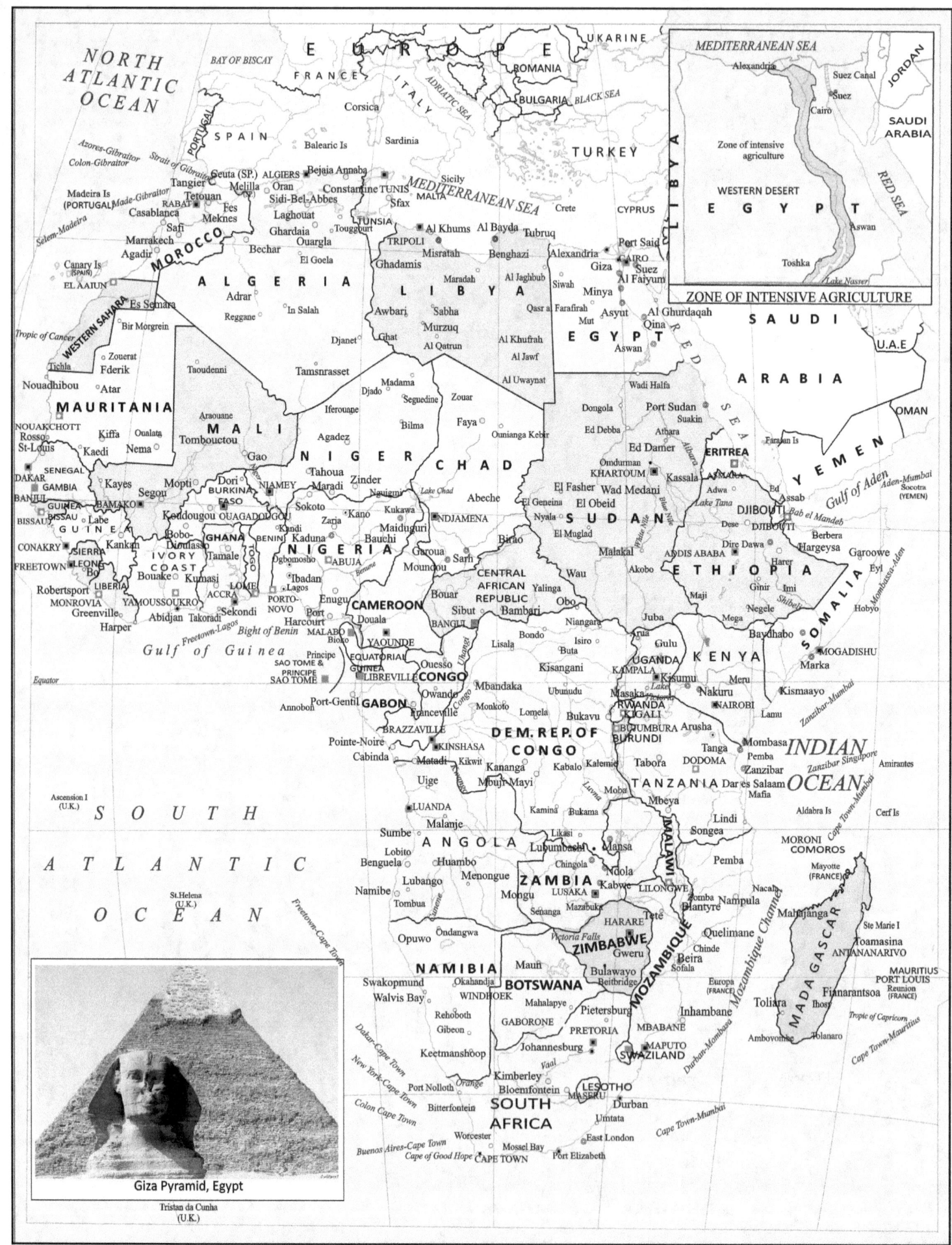

Giza Pyramid, Egypt

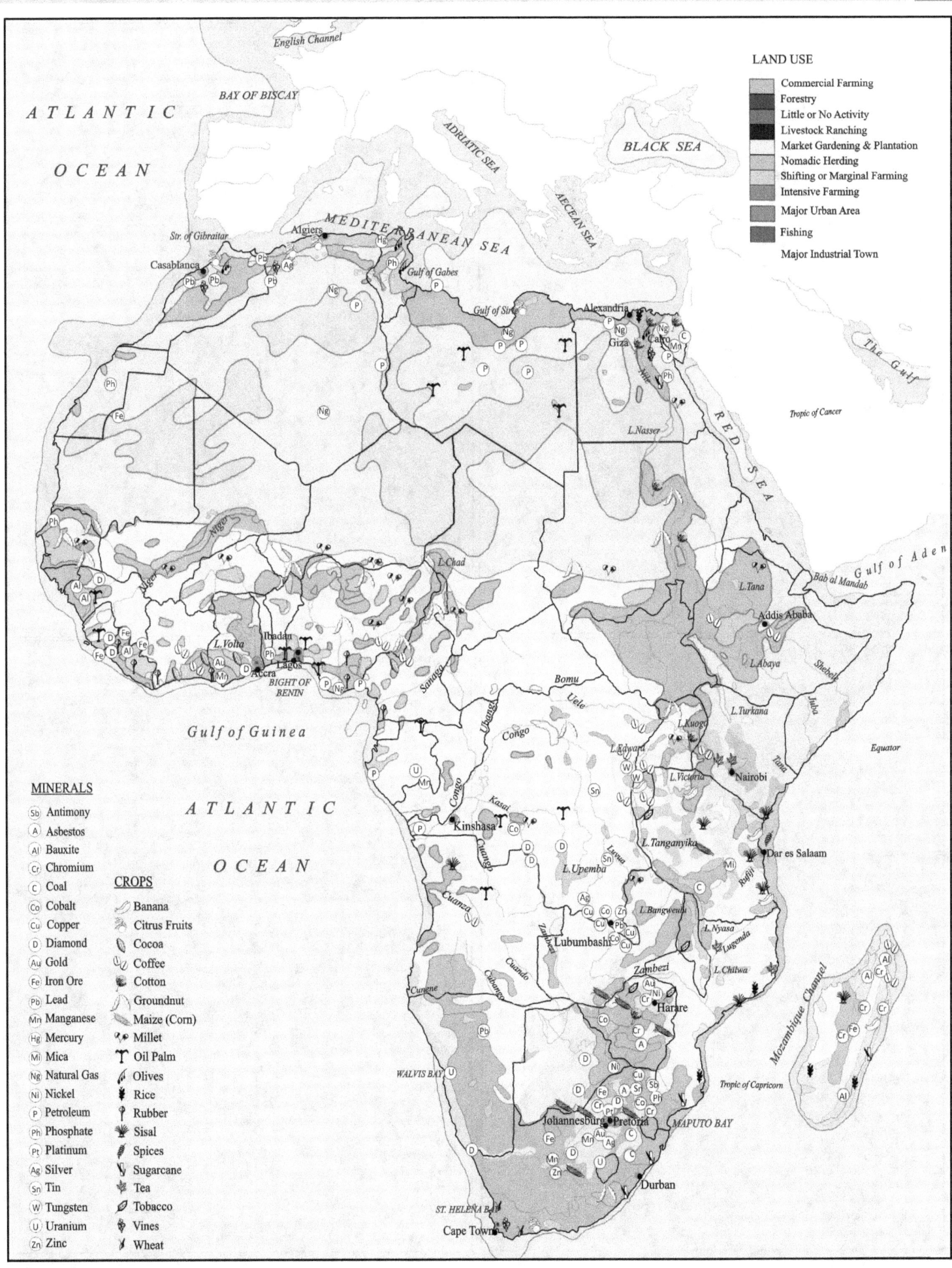

LAND USE

- Commercial Farming
- Forestry
- Little or No Activity
- Livestock Ranching
- Market Gardening & Plantation
- Nomadic Herding
- Shifting or Marginal Farming
- Intensive Farming
- Major Urban Area
- Fishing
- Major Industrial Town

MINERALS

- Sb Antimony
- A Asbestos
- Al Bauxite
- Cr Chromium
- C Coal
- Co Cobalt
- Cu Copper
- D Diamond
- Au Gold
- Fe Iron Ore
- Pb Lead
- Mn Manganese
- Hg Mercury
- Mi Mica
- Ng Natural Gas
- Ni Nickel
- P Petroleum
- Ph Phosphate
- Pt Platinum
- Ag Silver
- Sn Tin
- W Tungsten
- U Uranium
- Zn Zinc

CROPS

- Banana
- Citrus Fruits
- Cocoa
- Coffee
- Cotton
- Groundnut
- Maize (Corn)
- Millet
- Oil Palm
- Olives
- Rice
- Rubber
- Sisal
- Spices
- Sugarcane
- Tea
- Tobacco
- Vines
- Wheat

ATLANTIC OCEAN

MEDITERRANEAN SEA

BLACK SEA

ADRIATIC SEA

AEGEAN SEA

BAY OF BISCAY

English Channel

Str. of Gibraltar

Algiers

Casablanca

Gulf of Gabes

Gulf of Sirte

Alexandria

Giza Cairo

L.Nasser

RED SEA

Tropic of Cancer

The Gulf

Gulf of Aden

Bab al Mandab

L.Tana

Addis Ababa

L.Abaya

Shebeli

L.Turkana

Juba

Equator

Niger

L.Chad

Sanaga

Bomu

Uele

Congo

Ubangi

L.Kyoga

L.Edward

L.Victoria

Nairobi

Tana

Ibadan

Lagos

Accra

BIGHT OF BENIN

L.Volta

Gulf of Guinea

ATLANTIC OCEAN

Kasai

Kwango

Kwilu

Cuanza

Kinshasa

Lomani

L.Tanganyika

Dar es Salaam

Rufiji

Lubumbashi

L.Upemba

L.Bangweulu

L.Nyasa

Lugenda

L.Chilwa

Zambezi

Cuando

Cubango

Cunene

Harare

WALVIS BAY

Zambezi

Johannesburg Pretoria

MAPUTO BAY

Durban

Tropic of Capricorn

Mozambique Channel

ST. HELENA BAY

Cape Town

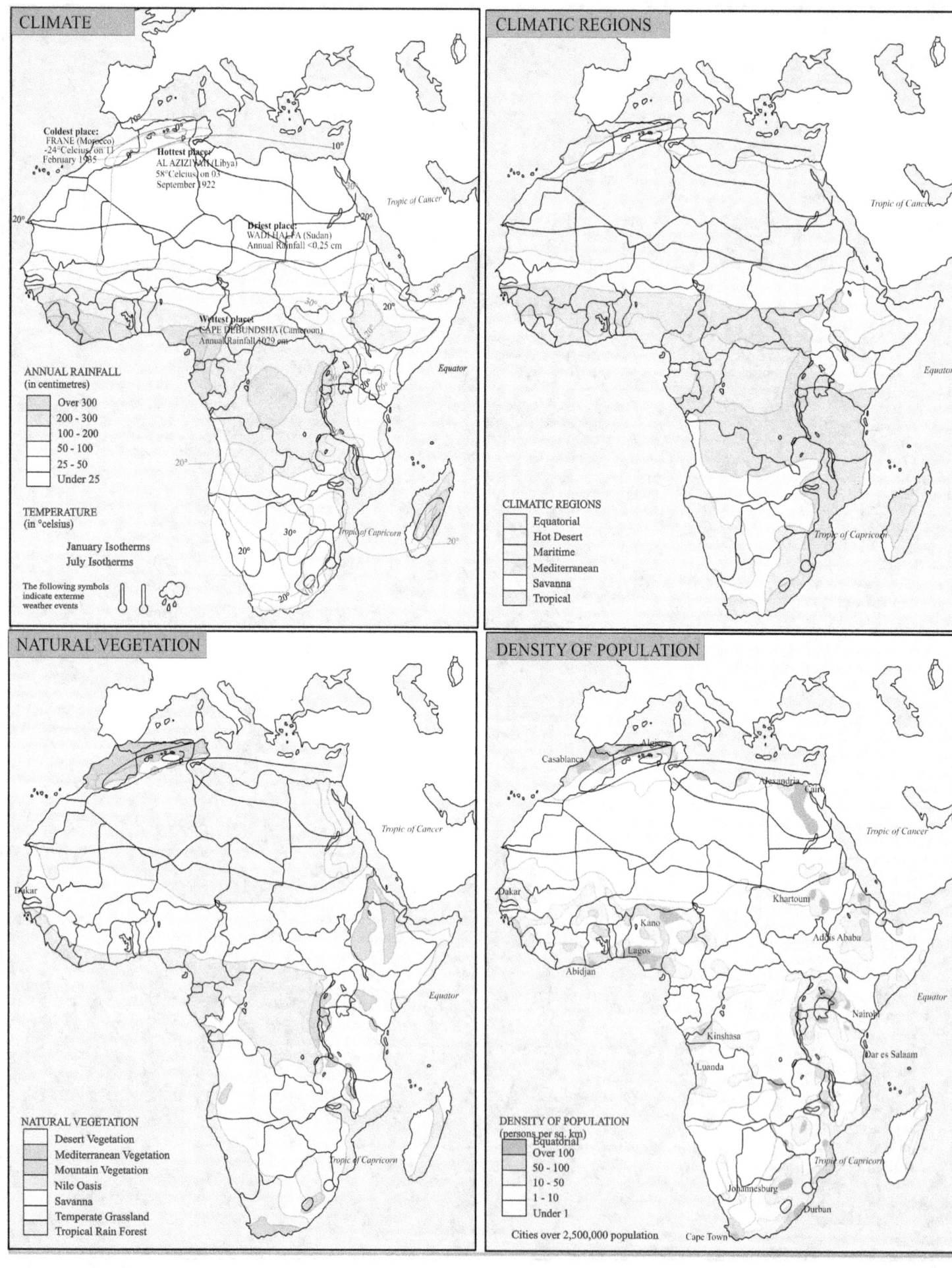

CLIMATE

Coldest place:
FRANE (Morocco)
-24°Celcius on 11
February 1935

Hottest place:
AL AZIZIYAH (Libya)
58°Celcius on 03
September 1922

Driest place:
WADI HALFA (Sudan)
Annual Rainfall <0.25 cm

Wettest place:
CAPE DEBUNDSHA (Cameroon)
Annual Rainfall 1029 cm

Tropic of Cancer

Equator

Tropic of Capricorn

ANNUAL RAINFALL
(in centimetres)

Over 300
200 - 300
100 - 200
50 - 100
25 - 50
Under 25

TEMPERATURE
(in °celsius)

January Isotherms
July Isotherms

The following symbols
indicate exterme
weather events

CLIMATIC REGIONS

Tropic of Cancer

Equator

Tropic of Capricorn

CLIMATIC REGIONS

Equatorial
Hot Desert
Maritime
Mediterranean
Savanna
Tropical

NATURAL VEGETATION

Tropic of Cancer

Dakar

Equator

Tropic of Capricorn

NATURAL VEGETATION

Desert Vegetation
Mediterranean Vegetation
Mountain Vegetation
Nile Oasis
Savanna
Temperate Grassland
Tropical Rain Forest

DENSITY OF POPULATION

Casablanca
Algiers
Alexandria
Cairo

Tropic of Cancer

Dakar
Khartoum
Kano
Addis Ababa
Lagos
Abidjan

Equator

Nairobi
Kinshasa
Dar es Salaam
Luanda

Tropic of Capricorn

Johannesburg
Durban
Cape Town

DENSITY OF POPULATION
(persons per sq. km)

Equatorial
Over 100
50 - 100
10 - 50
1 - 10
Under 1

Cities over 2,500,000 population

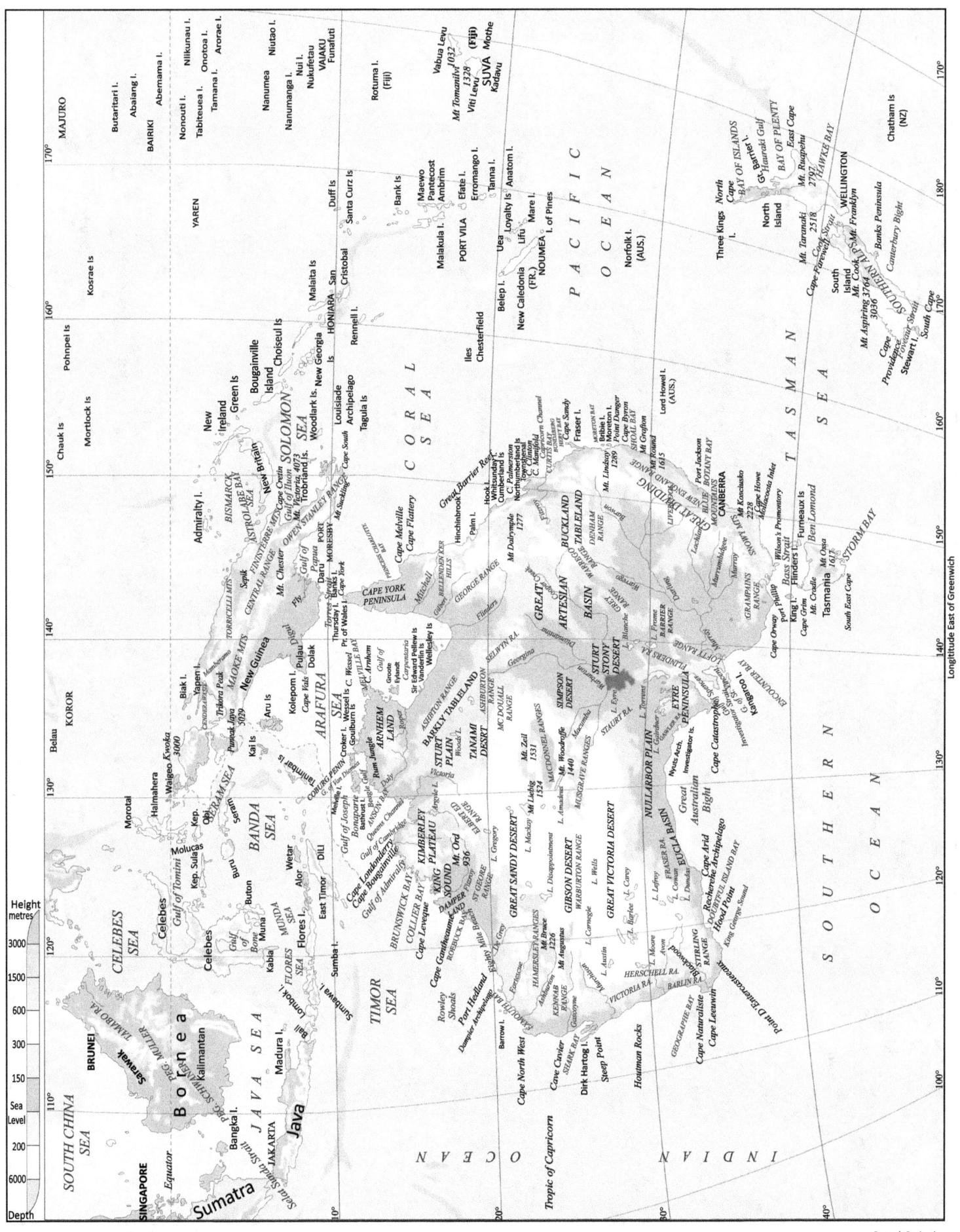

Height
metres

3000
1500
600
300
150
Sea Level
200
6000
Depth

| 0 | 345 | 690 | 1035 | 1380 km |

SCALE 1:34,500,000

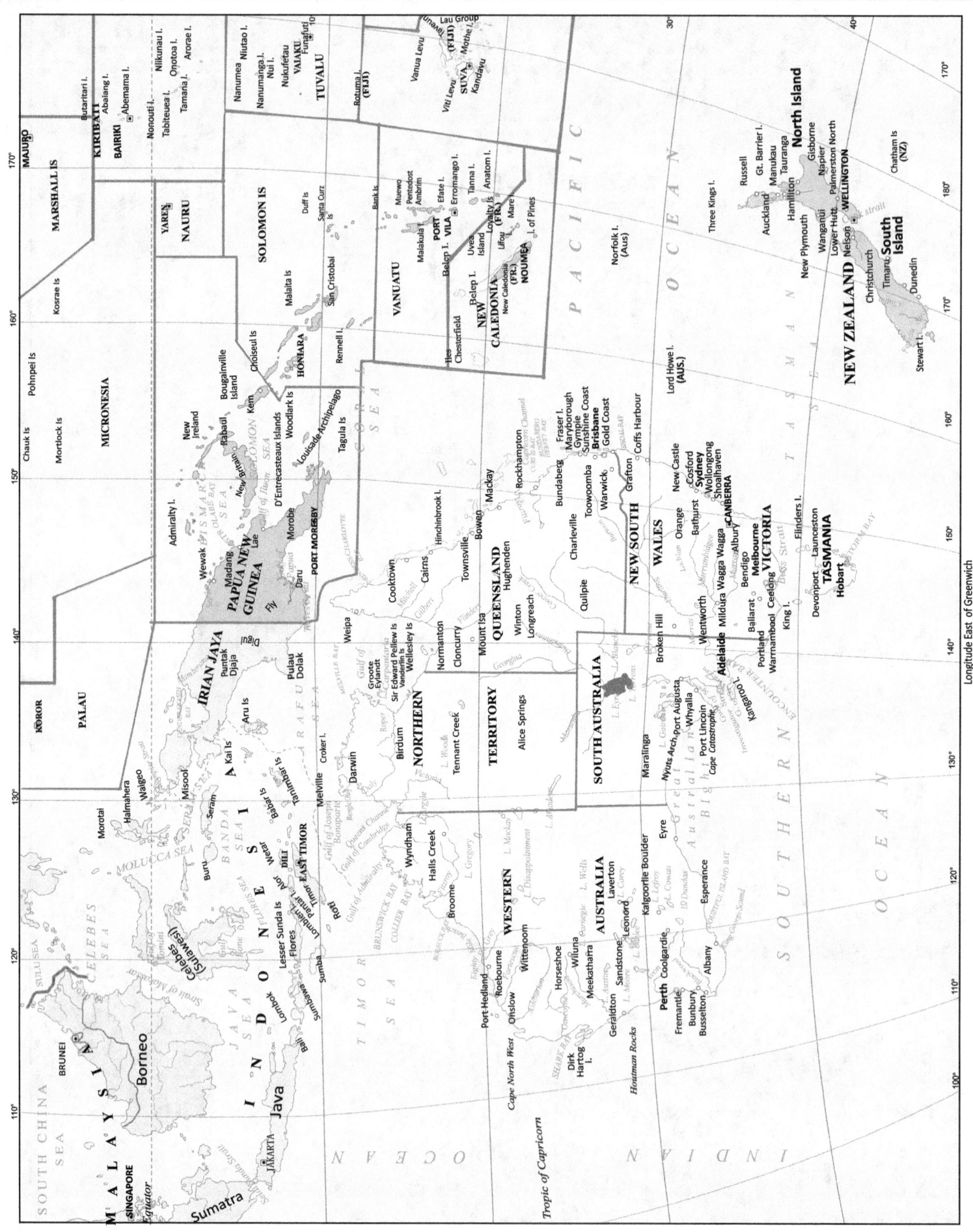

Longitude East of Greenwich

| 0 | 345 | 690 | 1035 | 1380 km |

SCALE 1:34,500,000

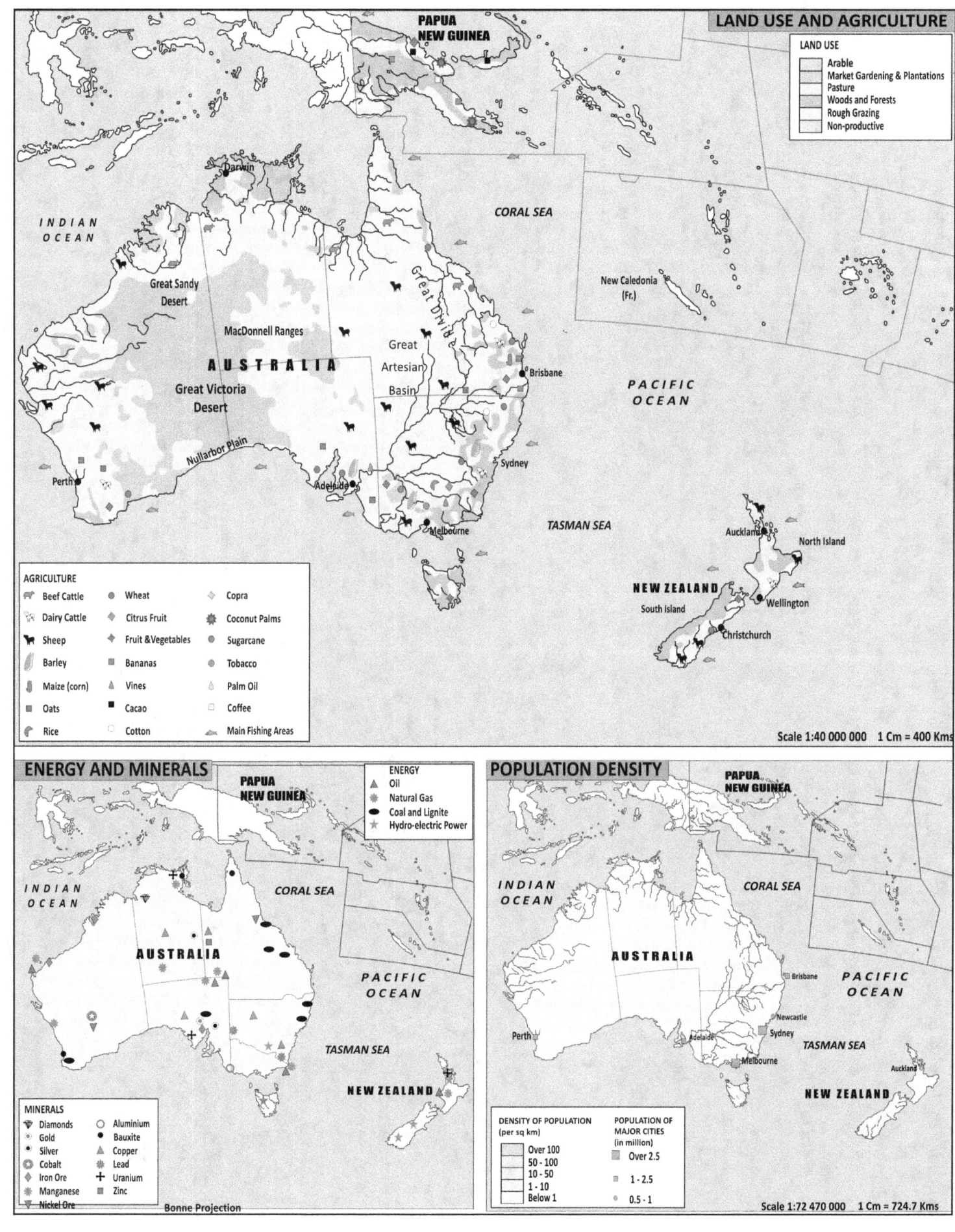

LAND USE AND AGRICULTURE

LAND USE
- Arable
- Market Gardening & Plantations
- Pasture
- Woods and Forests
- Rough Grazing
- Non-productive

PAPUA NEW GUINEA

Darwin

INDIAN OCEAN

CORAL SEA

Great Sandy Desert

MacDonnell Ranges

AUSTRALIA

Great Artesian Basin

Great Victoria Desert

Great Dividing

New Caledonia (Fr.)

Brisbane

PACIFIC OCEAN

Nullarbor Plain

Perth

Adelaide

Sydney

Melbourne

TASMAN SEA

Auckland

North Island

NEW ZEALAND

South Island

Wellington

Christchurch

AGRICULTURE

Beef Cattle	Wheat	Copra
Dairy Cattle	Citrus Fruit	Coconut Palms
Sheep	Fruit &Vegetables	Sugarcane
Barley	Bananas	Tobacco
Maize (corn)	Vines	Palm Oil
Oats	Cacao	Coffee
Rice	Cotton	Main Fishing Areas

Scale 1:40 000 000   1 Cm = 400 Kms

ENERGY AND MINERALS

PAPUA NEW GUINEA

ENERGY
- Oil
- Natural Gas
- Coal and Lignite
- Hydro-electric Power

INDIAN OCEAN

CORAL SEA

AUSTRALIA

PACIFIC OCEAN

TASMAN SEA

NEW ZEALAND

MINERALS

Diamonds	Aluminium
Gold	Bauxite
Silver	Copper
Cobalt	Lead
Iron Ore	Uranium
Manganese	Zinc
Nickel Ore	

Bonne Projection

POPULATION DENSITY

PAPUA NEW GUINEA

INDIAN OCEAN

CORAL SEA

AUSTRALIA

Brisbane

PACIFIC OCEAN

Newcastle

Perth

Adelaide

Sydney

TASMAN SEA

Melbourne

Auckland

NEW ZEALAND

DENSITY OF POPULATION (per sq km)	POPULATION OF MAJOR CITIES (in million)
Over 100	Over 2.5
50 - 100	
10 - 50	1 - 2.5
1 - 10	
Below 1	0.5 - 1

Scale 1:72 470 000   1 Cm = 724.7 Kms

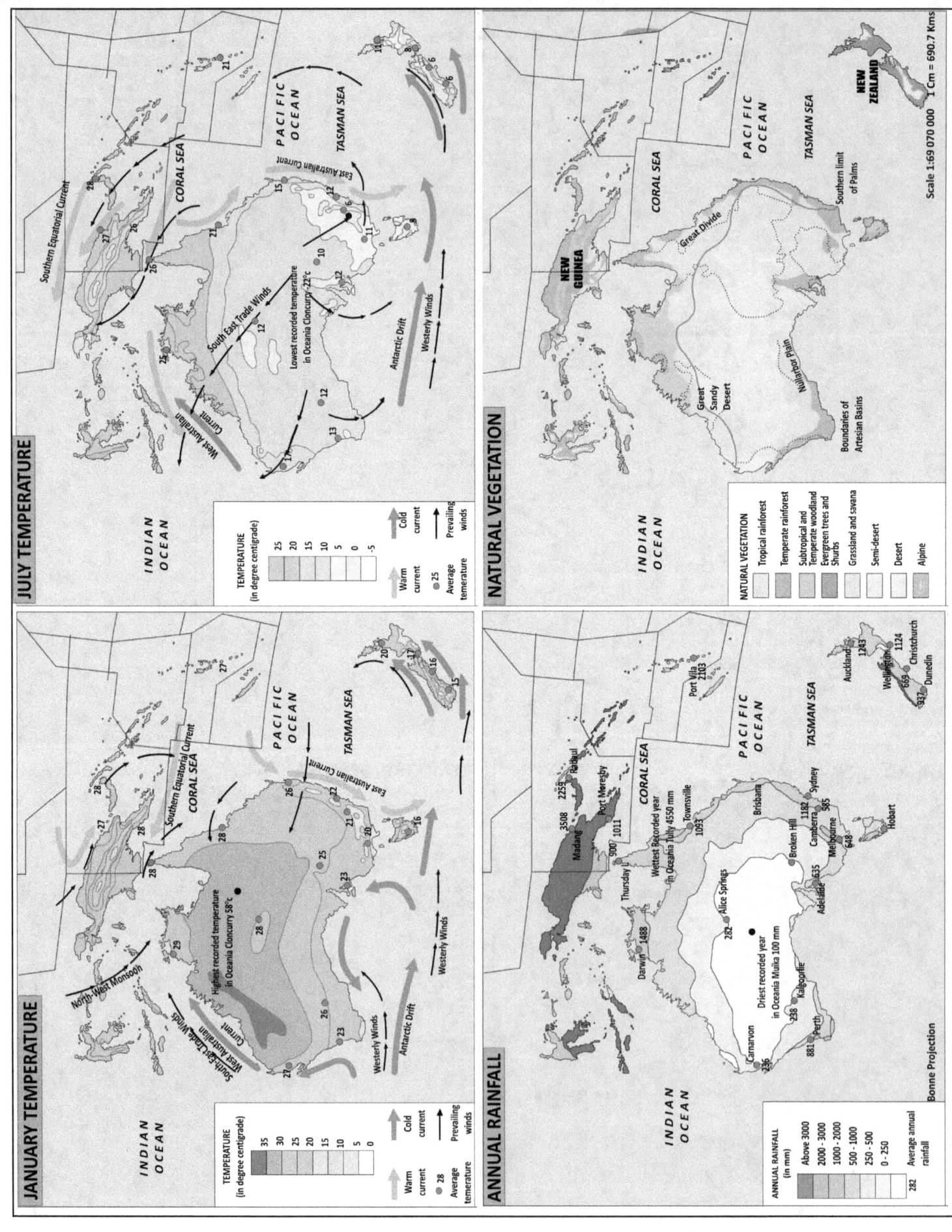

ASIA

ARCTIC OCEAN

60° 3 70° 2 80° 1 80° 2 70° 3

St. Lawrence I.

BERING SEA

Bering Strait Hope Point

Cape Prince of Wales

Nunivak I.

Barrow Point

BEAUFORT SEA

Greenland

Petermann's Peak 2940

Denmark Strait

Iceland

Mt. Forel 3360

Yukon

Porcupine

Brooks Ra.

M'Clure Strait

Axel Heiberg I.

Ellesmere I.

Queen Elizabeth Is.

Melville I.

Bathurst I.

Devon I.

Baffin Bay

Mt. Mckinley 6194

ALASKA PENINSULA

Alaska Ra.

Mackenzie Mts.

Cape Bathurst

Amundsen Gulf

Banks I.

Prince of Wales I.

Somerset I.

Gulf of Boothia

Prince Charles I.

Disko I.

Davis Strait

Cape Farewell

Mt. Sanford 4949

Kodiak I.

Mt. St. Elias 5489

Gulf of Alaska

Mt. Logan 5959

YUKON PLATEAU

Liard

Great Bear Lake

Victoria I.

BOOTHIA PEN.

MELVILLE PEN.

Fox Basin

Foxe Channel

Southampton I.

Cumberland Sound

Frobisher Bay

Cape Chidley

LABRADOR SEA

Alexander Archipelago

Churchill Peak 3200

Great Slave Lake

Dupuwni Lake

Back

Baffin Island

Hudson Strait

Mansel I.

Coats I.

C. Wolstenholme

UNGAVA PENINSULA

Ungava Bay

Hamilton Inlet

Belle Isle

Queen Charlotte Is.

Peace

Athabasca

Athabaska Lake

Reindeer Lake

Hudson Bay

COAST OF LABRADOR

Churchill Falls

Cape Bauld

Queen Charlotte Strait

Coast Mts.

Fraser

Mt. Robson 3954

Mt. Columbia 3747

Saskatchewan

CANADIAN SHIELD

Churchill

Nelson

Severn

Winisk

Eastmain

James Bay

Belcher Is.

Cape Henrietta Maria

Gros Morne 806

Newfoundland

Vancouver I.

Mt. Washington 3994

Selkirk Mts.

Rocky Mountains

Mt. Cleveland 3185

Lake Winnipegosis

Lake Winnipeg

Lake Manitoba

Albany

Lake Mistassini

LAURENTIAN PLATEAU

Gulf of St. Lawrence

Prince Edward I.

Cape Race

Cape Breton I.

Juan de Fuca Strait

Cape Flattery

Mt. Rainier 4392

Columbia

Missouri

Yellowstone

Lake Superior

Great Lakes

Onawa

St. Lawrence

Mt. Washington 1917

NOVA SCOTIA

Sable I.

Cape Blanco

Snake

Great Salt Lake

4207 Gannett Peak

Platte

Great Ontario

Lake Huron

B. of Fundy

Cape Sable

Cape Mendocino

Mt. Shasta 4317

Sierra Nevada

Wasatch Ra.

GREAT BASIN

4399 Mt. Elbert

Pikes Peak 4301

Lake Michigan

Lake Erie

Niagara Falls

Cape Cod

Nantucket I.

Long I.

Mt. Whitney 4418

Death Valley -86

Grand Canyon

COLORADO PLATEAU

Humphreys Peak 3851

Mt. Taylor 3471

Ozark PLATEAU

Ohio

Wabash

Mississippi

Tennessee

CUMBERLAND PLATEAU

Allegheny Mts.

Appalachian Mts.

Blue Ridge Mts.

Mt. Mitchell 2037

Cape Charles

Chesapeake Bay

Cape Hatteras

Bermuda

MOJAVE DESERT

LLANO ESTACADO

Red

Brazos

Colorado

Pecos

EDWARDS PLATEAU

Rio Grande

COASTAL PLAIN

FLORIDA

NORTH

Guadalupe I.

Eugenia Point

LOWER CALIFORNIA

Gulf of California

Western Sierra Madre

MEXICAN

Eastern Sierra Madre

Mississippi River Delta

Cape Canaveral

Grand Bahama

Great Abaco

ATLANTIC

OCEAN

SARGASSO SEA

PACIFIC OCEAN

Tropic of Cancer

BAJA PENINSULA

Cape San Lucas

Revilla Gigedo Is.

PLATEAU

Santiago

Southern Sierra Madre

Popocatepetl 5452

Balsas

Citlaltepetl 5700

Gulf of Campeche

YUCATAN PENINSULA

Yucatan Channel

Gulf of Mexico

Florida Strait

Andros

Great Inagua

West Indies

Cuba

Greater

Jamaica

Cayman Trough

Yucatan Basin

Hispaniola

Windward Passage

Antilles

Puerto Rico

Cape Corrientes

Gulf of Tehuantepec

Isthmus of Tehuantepec

Gulf of Honduras

Colombian Basin

CARIBBEAN SEA

Point Gallinas

Gulf of Venezuela

Gulf of Fonseca

Cape Gracias a Dios

Gulf of Panama

Isthmus of Panama

Panama Canal

Lake Nicaragua

Gualemala

Chirripo Grande 3819

Middle America Trench

Lake Maracaibo

Andes

m
3000
2000
1000
500
200
0

200
2000
4000

Dept.

m

Projection : Azimuthal Equal Area Projection

120° West of Greenwich 110° 100° 90° 80° 70°

G J K L M

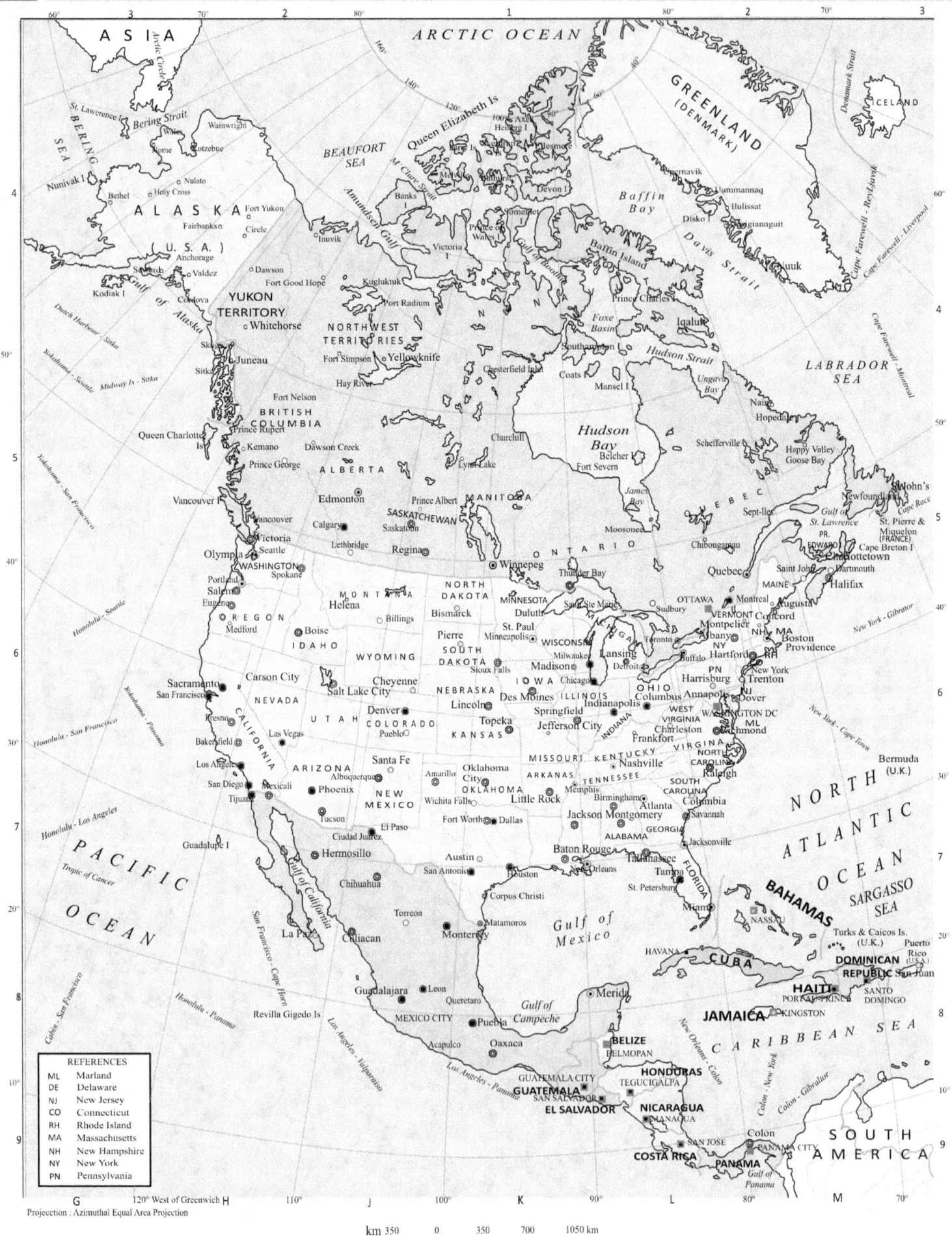

REFERENCES

ML	Marland
DE	Delaware
NJ	New Jersey
CO	Connecticut
RH	Rhode Island
MA	Massachusetts
NH	New Hampshire
NY	New York
PN	Pennsylvania

km 350   0   350   700   1050 km

1 : 35 000 000

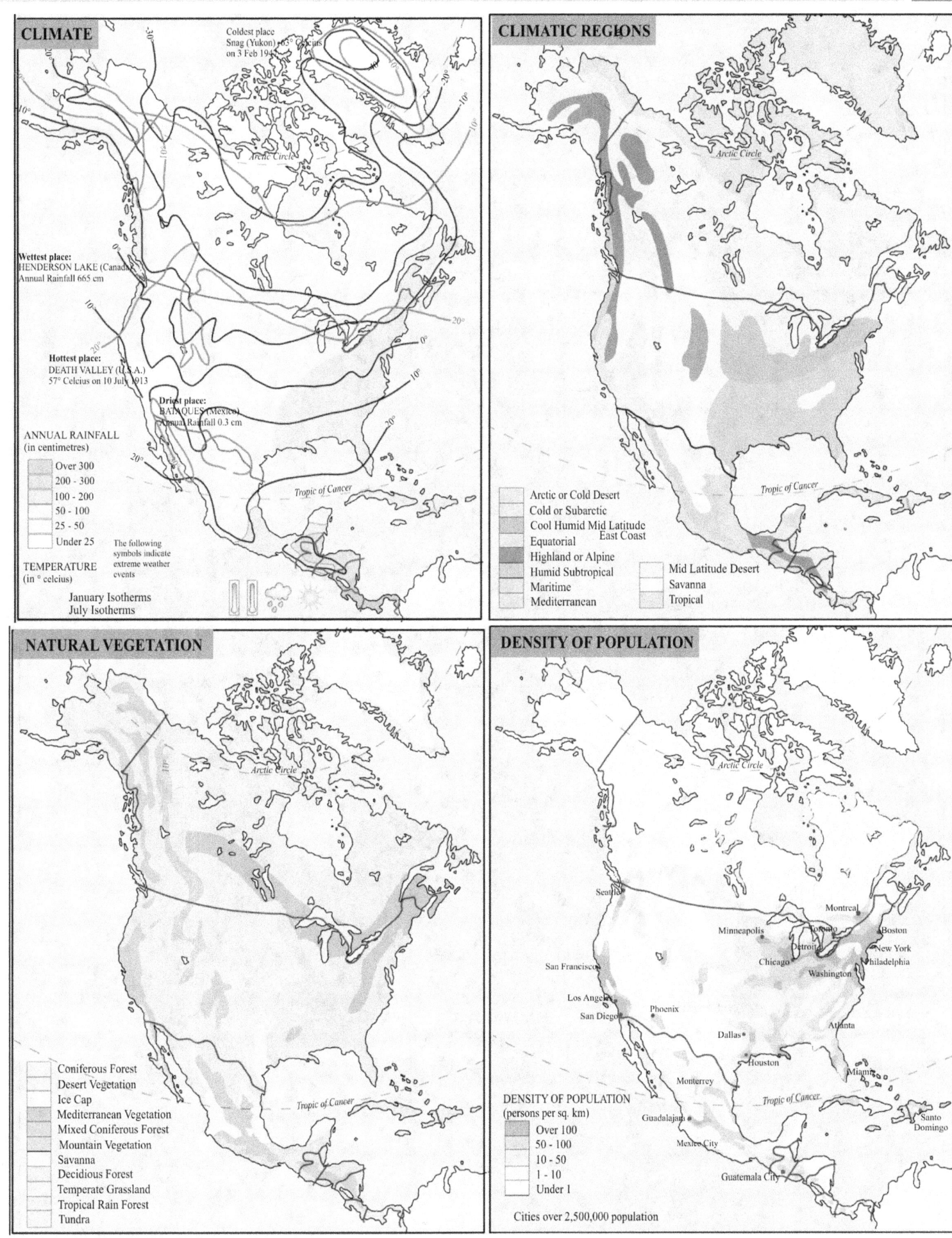

CLIMATE

Coldest place
Snag (Yukon) 63° Celcius
on 3 Feb 1947

Wettest place:
HENDERSON LAKE (Canada)
Annual Rainfall 665 cm

Hottest place:
DEATH VALLEY (U.S.A.)
57° Celcius on 10 July 1913

Driest place:
BATAQUES (Mexico)
Annual Rainfall 0.3 cm

ANNUAL RAINFALL
(in centimetres)

- Over 300
- 200 - 300
- 100 - 200
- 50 - 100
- 25 - 50
- Under 25

The following
symbols indicate
extreme weather
events

TEMPERATURE
(in ° celcius)

January Isotherms
July Isotherms

CLIMATIC REGIONS

- Arctic or Cold Desert
- Cold or Subarctic
- Cool Humid Mid Latitude
- Equatorial East Coast
- Highland or Alpine
- Humid Subtropical
- Maritime
- Mediterranean
- Mid Latitude Desert
- Savanna
- Tropical

Arctic Circle
Tropic of Cancer

NATURAL VEGETATION

- Coniferous Forest
- Desert Vegetation
- Ice Cap
- Mediterranean Vegetation
- Mixed Coniferous Forest
- Mountain Vegetation
- Savanna
- Decidious Forest
- Temperate Grassland
- Tropical Rain Forest
- Tundra

Arctic Circle
Tropic of Cancer

DENSITY OF POPULATION

Seattle
Montreal
Minneapolis
Toronto   Boston
Detroit   New York
San Francisco   Chicago   Philadelphia
Washington
Los Angeles
San Diego   Phoenix
Dallas   Atlanta
Houston   Miami
Monterrey
Guadalajara   Santo Domingo
Mexico City
Guatemala City

Arctic Circle
Tropic of Cancer

DENSITY OF POPULATION
(persons per sq. km)

- Over 100
- 50 - 100
- 10 - 50
- 1 - 10
- Under 1

Cities over 2,500,000 population

MINERALS

- (Sb) Antimony
- (A) Asbestos
- (Al) Bauxite
- (C) Coal
- (Co) Cobalt
- (Cu) Copper
- (Au) Gold
- (Fe) Iron Ore
- (Pb) Lead
- (Mn) Manganese
- (Hg) Mercury
- (Mo) Molybdenum
- (Ng) Natural Gas
- (Ni) Nickel
- (P) Petroleum
- (Ph) Phosphate
- (Pt) Platinum
- (K) Potassium
- (Na) Salt
- (Ag) Silver
- (W) Tungsten
- (U) Uranium
- (Zn) Zinc

CROPS

- Banana
- Barley
- Citrus Fruits
- Cocoa
- Coffee
- Cotton
- Fruits & Vegetables
- Groundnut
- Maize (Corn)
- Millet
- Oats
- Potato
- Rice
- Sisal
- Soyabean
- Sugarbeet
- Sugarcane
- Tobacco
- Vines
- Wheat

LAND USE

Commercial Farming
Dairying
Forestry
Little or No Activity
Livestock Ranching
Market Gardening & Plantation
Nomadic Herding
Shifting or Marginal Farming
Intensive Farming
Major Urban Area
Fishing
Major Indistrial Town

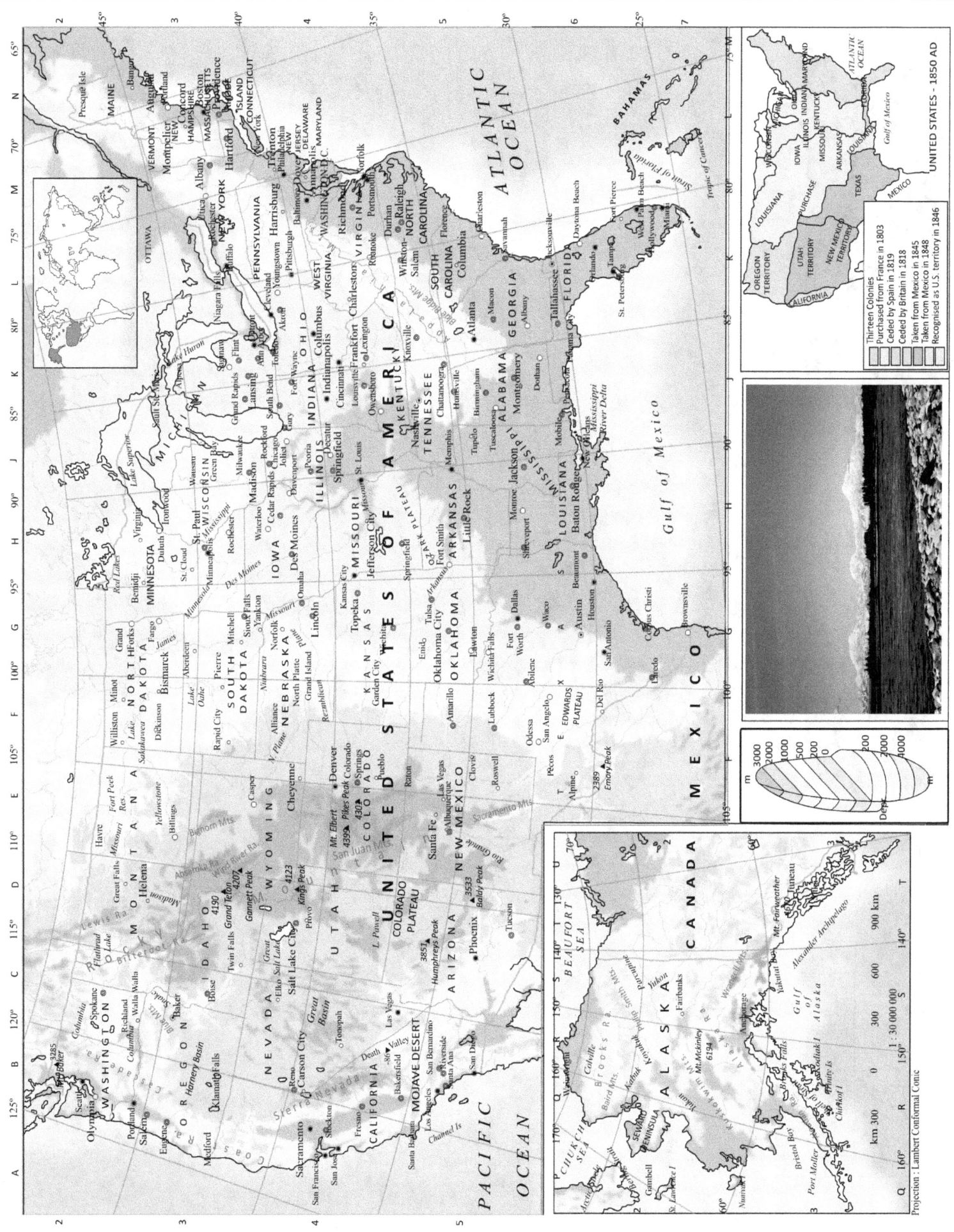

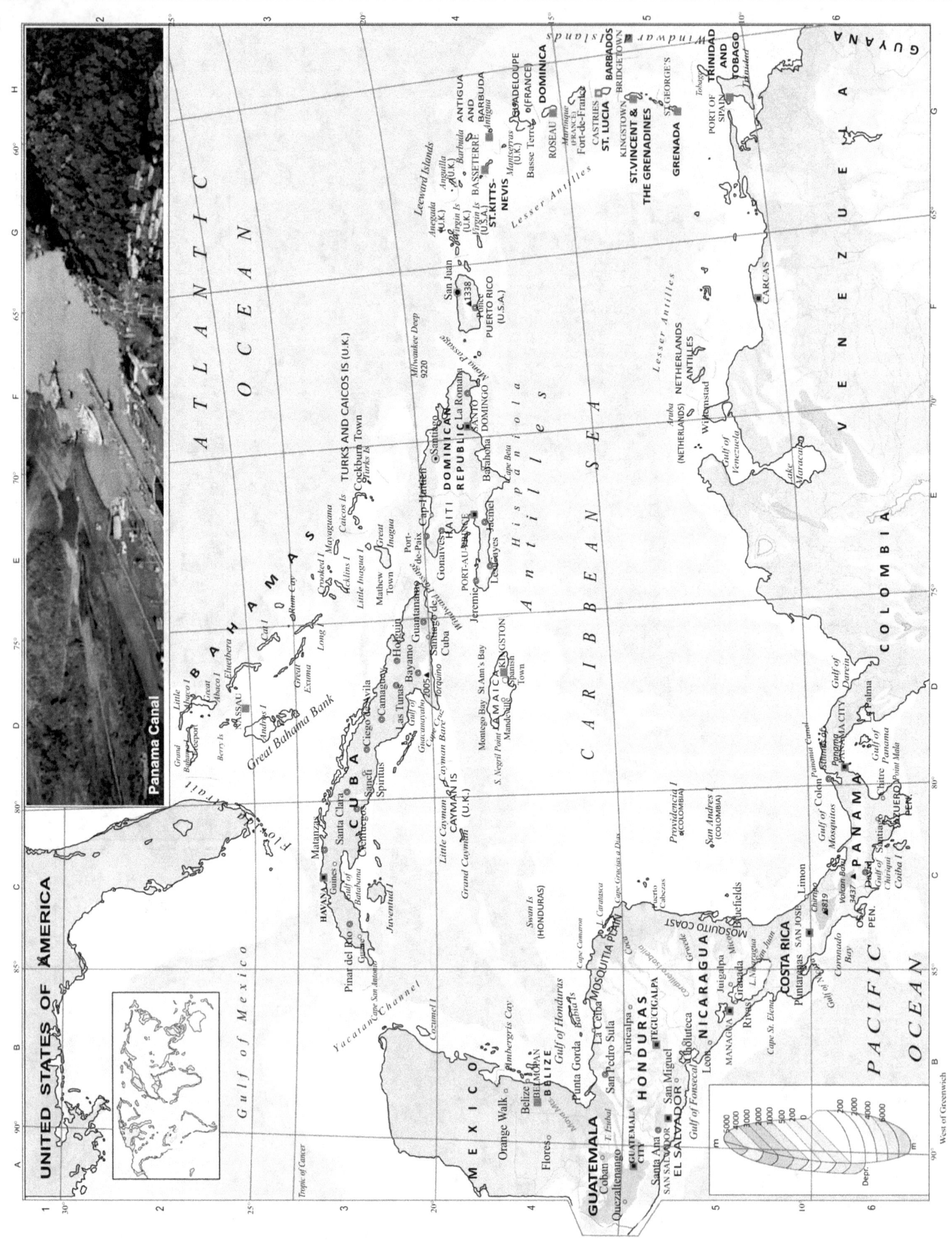

Panama Canal

ATLANTIC OCEAN

CARIBBEAN SEA

PACIFIC OCEAN

UNITED STATES OF AMERICA

Gulf of Mexico

Tropic of Cancer

B A H A M A S

Great Bahama Bank

Little Abaco I
Great Abaco I
Berry Is
Grand Bahama I
NASSAU
Andros I
Eleuthera
Cat I
Rum Cay
San Salvador I
Long I
Great Exuma
Little Exuma
Crooked I
Acklins I
Mayaguana
Great Inagua
Little Inagua

TURKS AND CAICOS IS (U.K.)
Caicos Is
Cockburn Town
Turks Is

Milwaukee Deep
9220

MEXICO

Cozumel I
Yucatan Channel
Cape Catoche
Cape San Antonio

C U B A
HAVANA
Guines
Gulf of Batabanó
Pinar del Rio
Matanzas
Santa Clara
Cienfuegos
Sancti Spíritus
Ciego de Avila
Camagüey
Guacanayabo
Gulf of
Las Tunas
Bayamo
Holguín
Santiago de Cuba
Guantánamo 2005
Torquino

Juventud I

Swan Is
(HONDURAS)

CAYMAN IS (U.K.)
Little Cayman
Cayman Brac
Grand Cayman

J A M A I C A
Montego Bay
S. Negril Point
St Ann's Bay
KINGSTON
Spanish Town
Mandeville

Florida Strait

H A I T I
Port-de-Paix
Gonaïves
PORT-AU-PRINCE
Jérémie
Les Cayes
Cape Tiburon

Cap-Haïtien
Santiago
DOMINICAN REPUBLIC
La Romana
SANTO DOMINGO N
Barahona
Cape Beata

Mona Passage

H i s p a n i o l a

PUERTO RICO (U.S.A.)
San Juan
1338

Virgin Is
(U.K.)
Virgin Is
(U.S.A.)
Anegada (U.K.)

Leeward Islands
Anguilla (U.K.)
Barbuda
BASSETERRE
ST KITTS-NEVIS
Antigua
ANTIGUA AND BARBUDA
GUADELOUPE (FRANCE)
Basse-Terre
DOMINICA
ROSEAU
Fort-de-France
Martinique (FRANCE)
CASTRIES
ST. LUCIA
KINGSTOWN
ST. VINCENT & THE GRENADINES
BRIDGETOWN
BARBADOS
GRENADA
ST GEORGE'S

Windward Islands

L e s s e r   A n t i l l e s

PORT OF SPAIN
TRINIDAD AND TOBAGO
Tobago
Trinidad

GUYANA

VENEZUELA
CARACAS
Gulf of Venezuela
Lake Maracaibo

NETHERLANDS ANTILLES
Aruba (NETHERLANDS)
Curaçao
Bonaire
Willemstad

COLOMBIA

A n t i l l e s

BELIZE
Orange Walk
Belize City
BELMOPAN
Turneffe Is
Ambergris Cay
Punta Gorda

GUATEMALA
Flores
Cobán
El Est_al
GUATEMALA CITY
Quezaltenango
Santa Ana

EL SALVADOR
SAN SALVADOR
San Miguel
Gulf of Fonseca

HONDURAS
San Pedro Sula
La Ceiba
TEGUCIGALPA
Juticalpa
Cholúteca
Maya Mts
Gulf of Honduras
Bahía Is
Cape Camarón
Cape Gracias a Dios

MOSQUITIA PLAIN
MOSQUITO COAST
Caratasca
Coco

NICARAGUA
León
MANAGUA
L. Managua
L. Nicaragua
Granada
Rivas
Puerto Cabezas
Bluefields
Juigalpa
San Juan

COSTA RICA
Puntarenas
SAN JOSE
Limón
Cape St. Elena

Coronado Bay
Cordillera Isabelia
Gulf of Coiba
Cape Gracias a Dios

PANAMA
PANAMA CITY
Panama Canal
Colón
David
Chiriquí
3437
Santiago
Chitré
Gulf of Santiago
Coiba I
AZUERO PEN.
Point Mala
Gulf of Panama
Gulf of Chiriquí
Chiriquí

Providencia I (COLOMBIA)
San Andrés I (COLOMBIA)

Gulf of Urabá
Gulf of Darién
PALMA

90° West of Greenwich

Projection : Lambert Azimuthal Equal Area

m
5000 4000 3000 2000 1000 500 200
200 2000 3000 4000 6000
Dept.

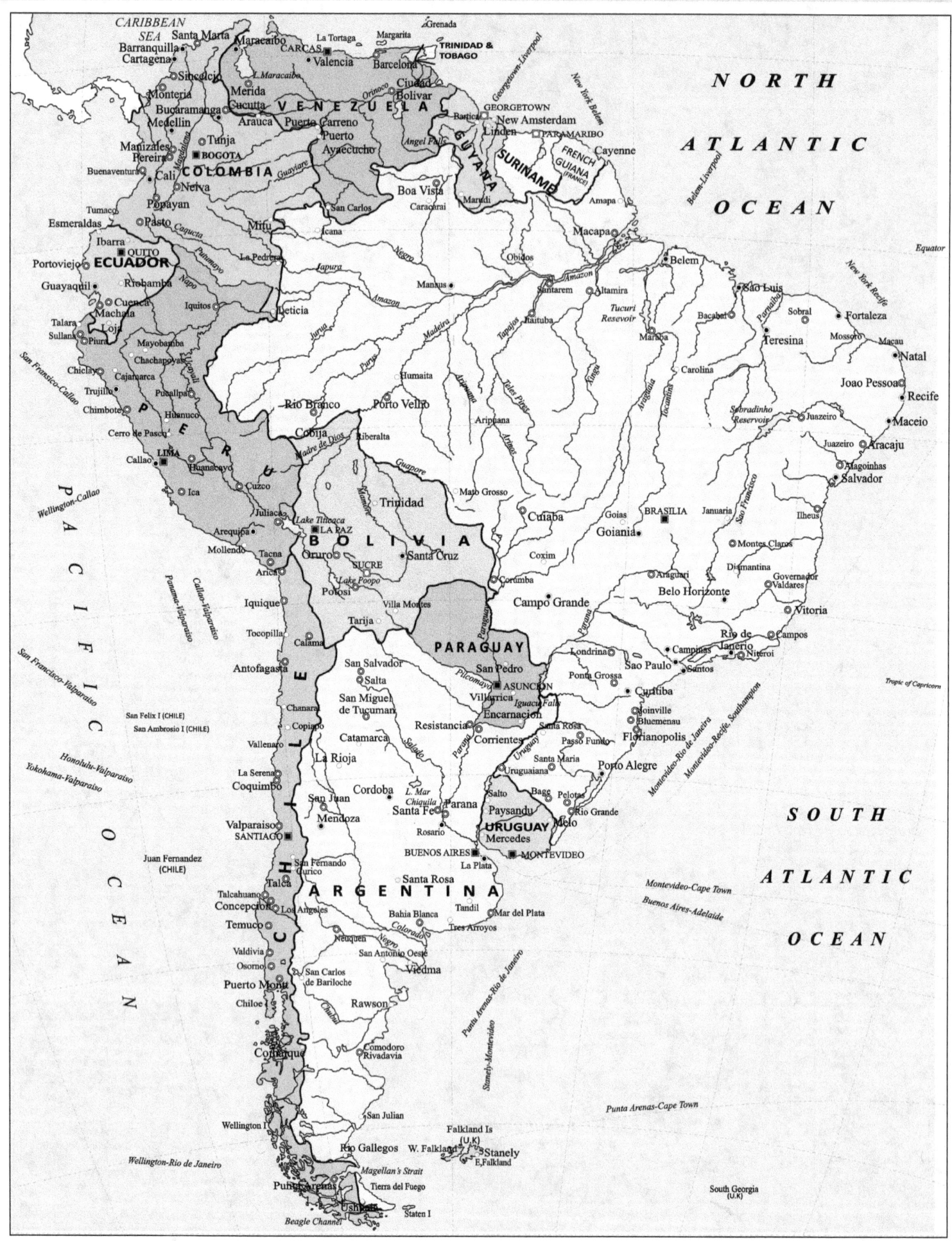

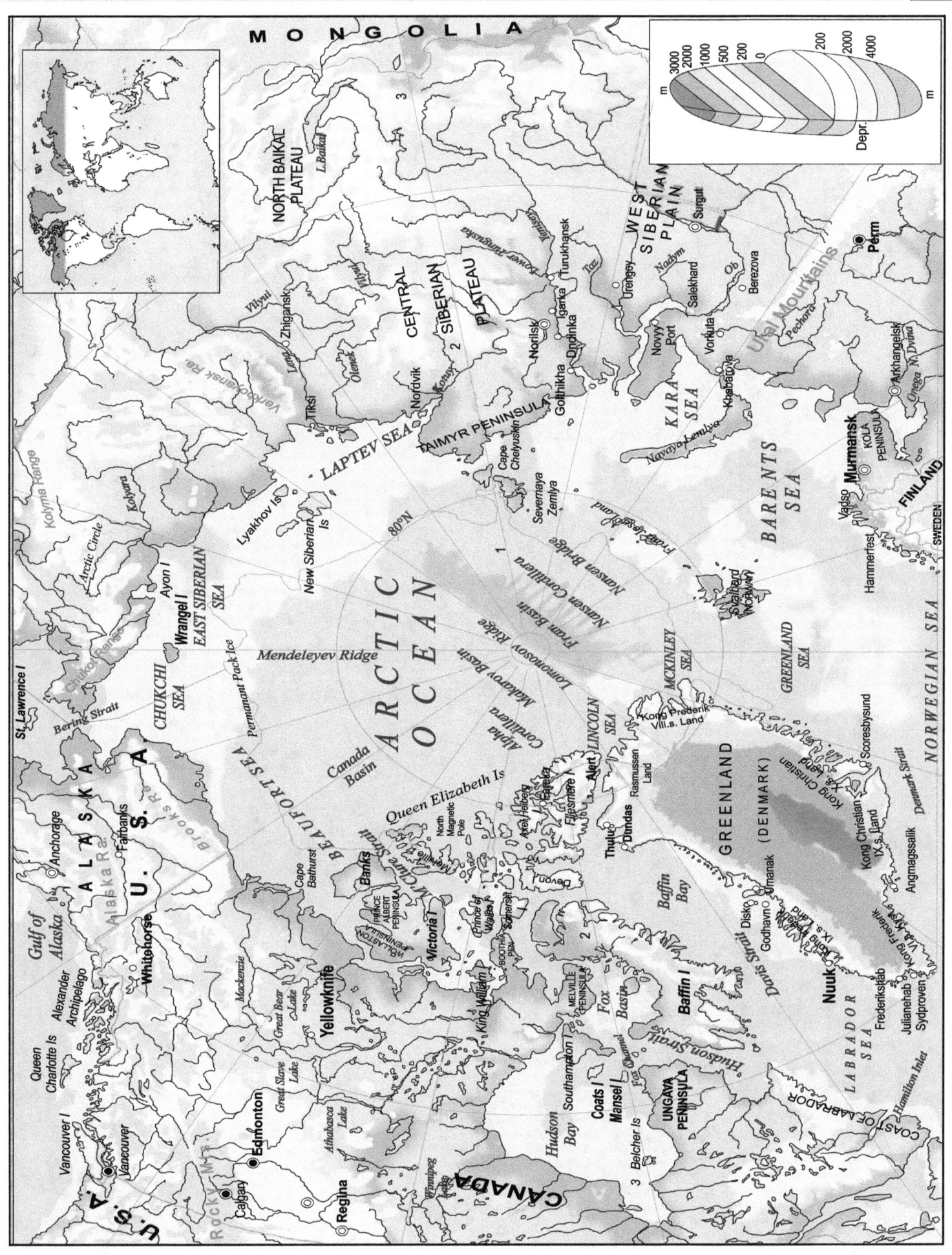

MONGOLIA

NORTH BAIKAL PLATEAU

L.Baikal

WEST SIBERIAN PLAIN

Surgut

Perm

Drengey
Nadym
Salekhard
Ob
Berezova

Upper Tunguska

CENTRAL SIBERIAN PLATEAU

Turukhansk
Igarka
Dudinka
Golthikha

Novy Port
Vorkuta
Pechora

Ural Mountains

Vilyui
Leng Zhigansk

Norilsk

KARA SEA

Khabatova

Arkhangelsk
Onega N. Dvina

Vilyui
Olenek
Kotuy

Nordvik
Tiksi

Cape Chelyuskin

TAIMYR PENINSULA

Severnaya Zemlya

Navaya Zemlya

Murmansk
KOLA PENINSULA

Vadso
FINLAND

Verkhoyansk Ra.

LAPTEV SEA

Franz Josef Land

BARENTS SEA

Hammerfest
SWEDEN

Kolyma Range
Kolyma

Lyakhov Is

New Siberian Is

80°N

Nansen Cordillera
Nansen Bridge

Arctic Circle

ARCTIC OCEAN

Fram Basin

Spitsbergen
Svalbard (NORWAY)

GREENLAND SEA

NORWEGIAN SEA

Ayon I
Wrangel I
EAST SIBERIAN SEA

Permanent Pack Ice
Mendeleyev Ridge

Makarov Basin

Lomonosov Ridge

MCKINLEY SEA

Chukot Range

CHUKCHI SEA

Bering Strait

St. Lawrence I

Canada Basin

Alpha Cordillera

LINCOLN SEA

Rasmussen Land

Kong Frederik VIII.s. Land

GREENLAND (DENMARK)

Scoresbysund

Kong Christian IX.s. Land

Denmark Strait

ALASKA
Alaska Ra.
Anchorage
Fairbanks

U. S. A.

BEAUFORT SEA

Queen Elizabeth Is

North Magnetic Pole

Axel Heiberg
Eureka
Ellesmere I
Alert

Thule
Dundas

Baffin Bay

Kong Christian

Angmagssalik

Gulf of Alaska

Whitehorse

BROOKS

Cape Bathurst

Banks I

PRINCE ALBERT PENINSULA
WOLLASTON PENINSULA

Victoria I

Prince of Wales I
Somerset I
BOOTHIA PEN.

Devon I

Nuuk

Fredenikshåb

Alexander Archipelago

Mackenzie

Great Bear Lake

Yellowknife

King William I

MELVILLE PENINSULA

Fox Basin

Baffin I

Davis Strait
Disko
Godhavn
Umanak

Julianehab
Sydproven

Queen Charlotte Is

Great Slave Lake

Athabasca Lake

Coats I
Mansel I

UNGAVA PENINSULA

LABRADOR SEA

Vancouver I

Edmonton

Hudson Bay

Southampton I
Belcher Is

Hudson Strait

COAST OF LABRADOR

Hamilton Inlet

Vancouver

Calgary

Regina

ROCK M TS

CANADA

Winnipeg

U. S. A.

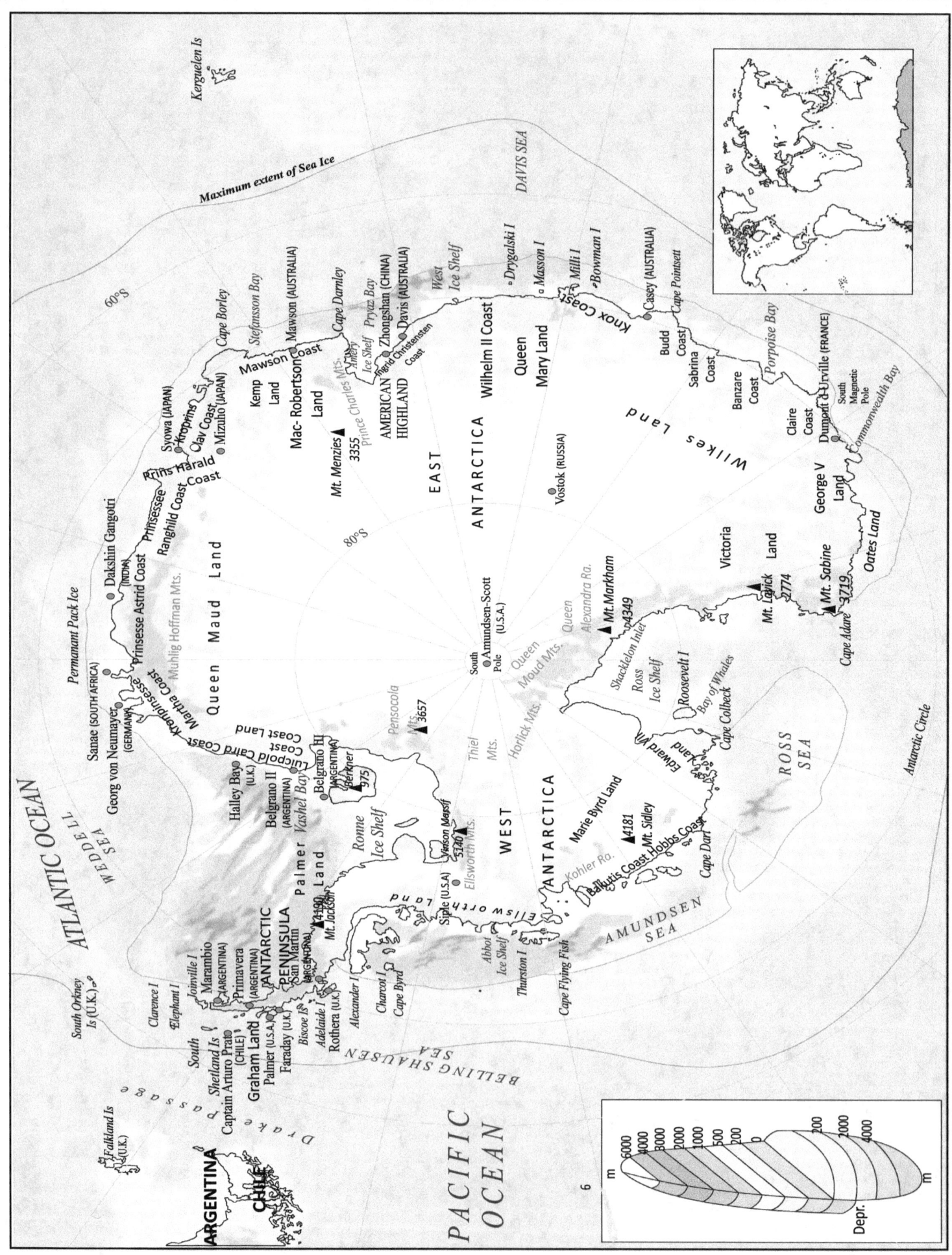

ARGENTINA
CHILE

PACIFIC OCEAN

6

ATLANTIC OCEAN

Kerguelen Is

Maximum extent of Sea Ice

DAVIS SEA

60°S

Cape Borley
Stefansson Bay
Mawson (AUSTRALIA)
Cape Darnley
West Ice Shelf
Drygalski I
Masson I
Milli I
Bowman I
Casey (AUSTRALIA)
Cape Poinsett

Kemp Land
Mawson Coast
Mac-Robertson Land
Amery Ice Shelf
Pryuz Bay
Zhongshan (CHINA)
Davis (AUSTRALIA)
Ingrid Christensen Coast
AMERICAN HIGHLAND
Wilhelm II Coast
Queen Mary Land
Budd Coast
Sabrina Coast
Banzare Coast

Syowa (JAPAN)
Kronprins
Olav Coast
Mizuho (JAPAN)
Prince Charles Mts.
Mt. Menzies 3355
EAST
ANTARCTICA
Vostok (RUSSIA)
Wilkes Land
Claire Coast
Dumont d'Urville (FRANCE)
South Magnetic Pole
Commonwealth Bay

Prins Harald Coast
Prinsessee Ranghild Coast
Dakshin Gangotri (INDIA)
Muhlig Hoffman Mts.
Queen Maud Land

Permanent Pack Ice
Sanae (SOUTH AFRICA)
Georg von Neumayer (GERMANY)
Prinsesse Astrid Coast

South Orkney Is (U.K.)

WEDDELL SEA

Kronprinsesse Martha Coast
Luitpold Coast Land
Caird Coast
Halley Bay (U.K.)
Belgrano II (ARGENTINA)
Belgrano II (ARGENTINA)
Vashel Bay
Berkner I
975
Filchner Ice Shelf

Clarence I
Elephant I
Toinville I
Marambio (ARGENTINA)
Primavera (ARGENTINA)
ANTARCTIC
San Martin (ARGENTINA)
PENINSULA
Palmer Land
Graham Land
Faraday (U.K.)
Palmer (U.S.A.)
Biscoe Is
Adelaide I
Rothera (U.K.)
Alexander I
Charcot I
Cape Byrd

South Shetland Is
Captain Arturo Prat (CHILE)
Mt. Jackson 4190

Ronne Ice Shelf
Pensacola Mts. 3657
Thiel Mts.
Horlick Mts.
WEST ANTARCTICA
Vinson Massif 5140
Ellsworth Mts.
Siple (U.S.A)
Ellsworth Land

BELLINGSHAUSEN SEA

Abbot Ice Shelf
Thurston I
Cape Flying Fish

Marie Byrd Land
4181
Kohler Ra.
Bakutis Coast Mt. Sidley Hobbs Coast
Cape Dart

AMUNDSEN SEA

South Pole
Amundsen-Scott (U.S.A.)
Queen Maud Mts.
Queen Alexandra Ra.
Mt. Markham 4349
Shackleton Inlet
Ross Ice Shelf
Roosevelt I
Bay of Whales
Cape Colbeck

Edward VII Land

ROSS SEA

Victoria Land
George V Land
Oates Land
Mt. Lavick 2774
Mt. Sabine 3719
Cape Adare

Antarctic Circle

m 6000 4000 3000 2000 1000 500 200 0 200 1000 4000 m
Depr.

Falkland Is (U.K.)
Drake Passage

ARCTIC OCEAN
BEAUFORT SEA
Parry Is
Queen Elizabeth Is
Ellesmere I
Baffin
Bay
Greenland
Victoria I
North
Magnetic Pole
Iceland
Great Bear
Lake
Hudson
Bay
Baffin
I
Davis Strait
Cape Farewell
British Isles
Arctic Circle
Bering St
Yukon
Great Slave
Lake
Hudson Strait
BERING
SEA
Alaska Ra
Coasts Mts
COAST OF
LABRADOR
West European
Basin
Bay of
Biscay
Mt. Mckinely(Denali)
6194
Gulf of
Alaska
Kodiak I
Lake
Winnipeg
St. Lawrence
Newfoundland
Aleutian Is
Vancouver I
Missouri
Great
Lakes
Lake
Superior
Lake
Huron
Lake
Ontario
Cape Race
IBERIAN
PENINSULA
Cascade Ra
Sierra Nevada
Lake
Michigan
Lake Eric
Mt. Mitchell
2037
Azores
Strait of Gibraltar
Madeira Is
Toubkal
4165
Mt. Whitney
4418
Mt. Elbert
4399
GREAT PLAINS
Ohio
Arkansas
Mississippi
Appalachian Mts
NORTH
Cape Hatteras
North American Basin
Mid Atlantic Ridge
Death Valley
86
AMERICA
Colorado
Rio Grande
Bermuda
ATLANTIC
Canary Is
Oahu
Hawai 4205
Mauna Kea
Midway Is
Tropic of Cancer
Hawaiian Is
LOWER CALIFORNIA
Sierra Madre
Gulf of
Mexico
Florida Strait
Bahamas
Cuba
West
Hispaniola
Milwaukee Deep
Indies
OCEAN
Cape Verde Is
Cape Verde
Popacatepetl
5452
Citlatepeti
5700
YUCATAN
PENINSULA
Greater
Antilles
Greater
Jamaica
CARIBBEAN
SEA
Lesser
Antilles
Cape Verde Basin
Niger
PACIFIC
Palmyra Is
Kiritimati
Isthmus
of Panama
LLANOS
Orinoco
Mt. Roraima
GUINA HIGHLANDS
2810
Guiana
Basin
Cape Palmas
Equator
OCEAN
Galapagos Is
6267
Chimboraza
Negro
Amazon
Sao Paulo
Fernando de Noronba
Mid Atlantic Ridge
Phoenix Is
SELVAS
SOUTH
Cape de Sao Roque
Ascension
Takelau Is
Marquesas Is
Madeira
Tocantins
Samoa Is
Society Is
Tahiti
Tuamotu Is
PLATEAU OF
MATO GROSSO
AMERICA
BRAZILIAN HIGHLANDS
Brazil Basin
St. Hele
Lake
Titicaca
ANDES
PERU CHILE TRENCH
Peru Basin
Cook Is
Tonga Is
Tropic of Capricorn
Tubuai Is
Pitcairn I
Easter I
ATACAMA DESERT
GRAN CHACO
Paraguay
Parana
Trindade
Cape Frio
Kermadec Is
Southwest
Pacific Basin
Rapa
6863
Ojos del Salado
7020
Aconcagua
PAMPAS
Rio de la Plaza
SOUTH
ATLANTIC
Negro
Tristan da Cunch
Gough I
Chatham Is
Argentine
Basin
OCEAN
PATAGONIA
Magellan's Strait
Falkland Is
(U.K.)
Easter I
SCOTIA
SEA
South
Georgia
South
Sandwich Is
Tierra del Fuego
Cape Horn
Drake Passage
South
Shetland Is
South
Orkney Is
Southeast
Pacific Basin
ANTARCTIC
PENINSULA
BELLINGSHAUSEN SEA
Palmer Land
Caird Coast
WEDDELL
SEA
Coasts Land
Antarctic Circle
ROSS SEA
AMUNDSEN SEA
Byrd Land
Ellsworth Land

m Ice-cap
5000
3000
2000
1000
500
200
0
200
2000
Depr.
4000
m

Projection : Ecket IV

West of Greenw

ARCTIC OCEAN

lbard
RWEGIAN North Cape
SEA
Svalbard
Novaya Severnaya
Zemlya Zemlya
LAPTEV SEA New Siberian Is EAST SIBERIAN
SEA

BARENTS KARA
SEA SEA
Yenisey
Lena

Lower Tunguska
Scandinavia Aldan

NORTH
SEA
North Cape Lake
Ladoga Ob WEST
SIBERIAN CENTRAL
SIBERIAN
PLATEAU
Stanovoy Ra. SEA OF
OKHOTSK
KAMCHATKA

BALTIC SEA NORTH EUROPEAN PLAIN
PLAIN Irtysh
Sayan Mts Lake
Baikal
Kuril Is

EUROPE Dnieper Volga Lake Balkash Altai ASIA ASIA Sukhalin Hokkaido
SEA OF
JAPAN

Alps Carpathians Syr Darya GOBI
DESERT Honshu Japan

807 Mt. Elbrus ARAL SEA Tien Shan NORTH CHINA PLAIN Mt. Fuji
Blanc 5642 Amudarya Tarim 3776
Apennines Caucasus Pamirs Basin Huang He KOREA Shikoku Japan Trench
BLACK SEA ASIA MINOR 5165 Kuntun Shan Kyushu 10554
d' Aneto BALKAN PEN. (ANATOLIA) Mt. Ararat Qilian Shan Ryukyu Is
404 Taurus Mts. Hindu Kush K² EAST
Damavend 8611 Karakoram CHINA
MEDITERRANEAN SEA 5604 PLATEAU OF Yangtze SEA
Euphrates IRAN PLATEAU OF Gongga Shan
Dead Sea Tigris TIBET 7556 Taiwan
Isthmus -40.3 Great Himalaya
LIBYAN of Suez SYRIAN DESERT Indus Mt. Everest 8598 St. Kiang PACIFIC OCEAN
DESERT NAFUD 8848 Kanchenjunga
Nile DESERT The Gulf Ganga Hainan Wake
ARABIAN Gulf of Oman GREAT INDIAN DESERT Mariana Is
HARA PENINSULA Godavari DECCAN INDO-CHINA Philippines Guam
AFRICA RUB' AL KHALI ARABIAN BAY OF PENINSULA Is Mariana Trench
H E L SEA BENGAL Mekong SOUTH CHINA SEA Marshall Is
N E A Gulf of Aden Socotra Lakshadweep Brahmaputra Ghats Andaman and Nicobar Is Caroline Is
4070 Cape Guardafui (INDIA) Palk Strait (INDIA) SULU Gilbert Is
Mt. Cameroon ETHIOPIAN SOMALI Cape Sri Lanka Strait of Malacca Gulf of SEA 4101 Nauru
ulf of HIGHLANDS PENINSULA Comorin Thailand MALAY Kinabalu CELEBES
inea Lake Tukana Maldives PENINSULA SEA Bismark
CONGO Mt. Kenya Borneo Archipelago
BASIN 5199 Kerinci Sumatra Celebes Puncak Jaya
Lake Victoria 3800 JAVA SEA 5029 New Guinea Solomon Is
Congo Kilimanjaro Seychelles BANDA SEA Ellice Is
5895 Chago Java Trench Timor Torres Strait
Lake Archipelago Cocos Cape CORAL SEA New
Tanganyika INDIAN OCEAN York Hebrides
Kasai Comoros West Arnhem Fiji Is
Angola Lake Mozambique Channel Australian Land Barkly
Basin Malawi Basin Tableland Great Barrier Reef
Zanbezi Mauritius New
KALAHARI Madagascar Pic Boby Reunion GREAT SANDY Caledonia
DESERT Limpopo 2658 DESERT Hamersley Ra. Macdonnel Ra.
Orange AUSTRALIA
Drakensberg GREAT VICTORIA Darling
Cape of DESERT Mt. Kosciuszko North I
Good Hope Amsterdam I St. Paul Great 2237 Mt. Ruapehu
Australian Bass Strait TASMAN SEA 2797
Bight Cape Leeuwin 40°
Prince Crozet Is South I Mt. Cook
Edward Is Kerguelen Tasmania 3753
Bouvet I McDonalds Is Heard I Stewart I Bounty Is
SOUTHERN OCEAN Auckland Is Antipodes Is
Macquarie Is Campbell I

Queen Maud Land Enderby Land Queen Mary Land Wilkes South
ANTARCTICA Land Victoria Magnetic Pole
Land ROSS SEA

of Greenwich

km 800 0 800 1600 2400 km
1 : 80 000 000

COMPARATIVE AREAS OF
CONTINENTS AND OCEANS

LAND AREA 29%
EUROPE
N. AMERICA
S. AMERICA
AFRICA
ASIA
ARCTIC
INDIAN PACIFIC
ATLANTIC
WATER AREA 71%

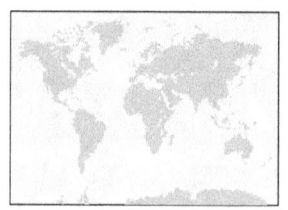

Fact File	Continents	No. of countries	Biggest country	Smallest country	Biggest city
	Asia	47	Russia	Maldives	Tokyo
	Europe	50	Russia	Vatican City	Paris
	Africa	54	Sudan	Seychelles	Cairo
	North America	23	Canada	St.Kitts and Nevis	Mexico
	South America	12	Brazil	Suriname	Sao Paulo
	Oceania	15	Australia	Nauru	Sydney

ARCTIC OCEAN

International Date Line

GREENLAND (DENMARK)

Jan Mayen (NORWAY)

Baffin Bay

Parry Is
Banks I
Victoria I
Queen Elizabeth I
Devon I
Ellesmere I
Godhavn
Qasigiannguit
Nuuk
Ammassalik
REYKJAVIK
ICELAND
Faroe Is (DENMARK)

Arctic Circle
Fairbanks
ALASKA (U.S.A)
Inuvik
Chesterfield Inlet
Baffin
Qaqortoq

UNITED KINGDOM
DUBLIN
IRELAND
LONDON

BERING SEA
St. Lawrence I
Anchorage
Whitehorse
Yellowknife
Dawson

Hudson Bay
Churchill

CANADA
Edmonton
Schefferville
Sept-Iles

Gulf of Alaska
Juneau
Kodiak I
Queen Charlotte Is
Vancouver I
Victoria
Vancouver
Calgary
Seattle
Portland
Williston
Billings
St. Paul
Minneapolis
Winnipeg
Moonsonee
Quebec
Montreal
Newfoundland
St. John's

Bay of Biscay

Aleutian Is (U.S.A.)

Salt Lake City
Sacramento
Denver
Chicago
Detroit
Toronto
Boston
New York

PORTUGAL
LISBON
MADRID
SPAIN

San Francisco
UNITED STATES
OF AMERICA
Kansas City
St. Louis
Pittsburgh
Philadelphia
Washington D.C.

Azores (PORTUGAL)

Los Angeles
San Diego
Phoenix
El Paso
Dallas
Atlanta
Columbia
Charleston

Bermuda (U.K.)

Madeira (PORTUGAL)
RABAT
MOROCCO

Midway Is

Guadalupe I (MEXICO)
Chihuahua
Ciudad Juarez
Austin
Houston
New Orleans
Jacksonville

Canary Is (SPAIN)
EL AAIUN
WESTERN SAHARA

Hawaiin Is (U.S.A.)

Tropic of Cancer

Honolulu
Oahu
Hawaii

NORTH

Monterrey
La Paz
MEXICO
Tampico
Leon
NASSAU
BAHAMAS
HAVANA
CUBA
Miami
Gulf of Mexico

ATLANTIC

OCEAN

MAURITANIA
MALI
NOUAKCHOTT

Revilla Gigedo Is (MEXICO)
Guadalajara
MEXICO CITY
Oaxaca
Merida
Campeche
Turks & Caicos Is (U.K.)

Cape Verde Is

DAKAR
SENEGAL
GAMBIA BANJUL
BISSAU
GUINEA-BISSAU

Clippperton I (FRANCE)

GUATEMALA CITY
GUATEMALA
BELIZE
BELMOPAN
HONDURAS
TEGUCIGALPA
SAN SALVADOR
EL SALVADOR
NICARAGUA
MANAGUA
COSTA RICA
SAN JOSE
PANAMA CITY
PANAMA
PORT-AU-PRINCE
HAITI
DOMINICAN REP.
SANTO DOMINGO
KINGSTON
JAMAICA
Puerto Rico (U.S.A.)
Virgin Is (U.S.A.) & (U.K.)
ANTIGUA & BARBUDA
ST. KITTS & NEVIS
DOMINICA
ST.LUCIA
ST. VINCENT &
THE GRENADINES
BARBADOS
GRENEDA
PORT OF SPAIN
TRINIDAD & TOBAGO
CARIBBEAN SEA

CONAKRY
GUINEA
FREETOWN
SIERRA LEONE
BAMAKO
BURKINA FASO
OUAGADOUGOU
IVORY COAST
YAMOUSSOUKRO
MONROVIA
LIBERIA
ACCRA

Coco I (Costa Rica)
Malpelo I (COLUMBIA)
Cali
Medellin
BOGOTA
CARACAS
VENEZUELA
GEORGETOWN
GUYANA
PARAMARIBO
SURINAME
Cayenne
FRENCH GUIANA (FRANCE)

Palmyra I (U.S.A.)
Kiritimati

COLOMBIA

Howland I
Baker I (U.S.A)
Jarvis I (U.S.A.)
Equator

Galapagos Is (ECUADOR)
ECUADOR
QUITO
Guayaquil

Sao Paulo (BRAZIL)

Abariringa

Malden I
Starbuck I

Manaus
Iquitos
Altamira
Belem
Fortaleza
Fernando de Noronha (BRAZIL)

Phoenix Is

Tokelau Is (N.Z.)
Penrhyn Is
Manihiki
Flint I
Marquesas Is

PERU

BRAZIL
Maraba
Natal
Recife

Ascension (U.K.)

WALLIS FUTUNA (FRANCE)
WESTERN SAMOA
AMERICAN SAMOA

FRENCH POLYNESIA
Society Is
Tahiti
Tuamotu Is

Callao
LIMA
Porto Velho
Mato Grosso
Juazeiro
BRASILIA
Salvador

Cook Is (N.Z.)
Niue (N.Z.)
TONGA

Tropic of Capricon

Tubuai Is

Rapa

Pitcairn I (U.K.)
Ducie I
Adamstown

Arequipa
LA PAZ
BOLIVIA
SUCRE
Cuiaba
Belo Horizonte
St. Helena (U.K.)

Antofagasta
Sao Paulo
Rio de Janeiro
Trindade (BRAZIL)

Kermadec Is (N.Z.)

Easter I (CHILE)
Sala-y-Gomez
Sala Felix I (CHILE)
San Ambrosio I (CHILE)
Salta
Resistencia
ASUNCION
Curitiba
LAGOS

Porto Alegre

International Date Line

Valparaiso
Juan Fernandez (CHILE)
SANTIAGO
Cordoba
Rosario
Parana
URUGUAY
MONTEVIDEO
Rio Grande

SOUTH

Talcahuano
ARGENTINA
CHILE
BUENOS AIRES
Neuquen
Bahia Blanca

ATLANTIC

Tristan da Cunha (U.K.)
Gough I (U.K.)

Charham Is (N.Z.)

Chiloe I

OCEAN

Comodoro Rivadavia

Antarctic Circle

Rio Gallegos
Punta Arenas
Tierra del Fuego
Falkland Is (U.K.)
SCOTIA SEA
South Georgia (U.K.)
South Sandwich Is (U.K.)

South Shetland Is
South Orkney Is
Drake Passage
WEDDEL SEA

BELLINGSHAUSEN SEA

ROSS SEA
AMUNDEN SEA

ANTARCTICA

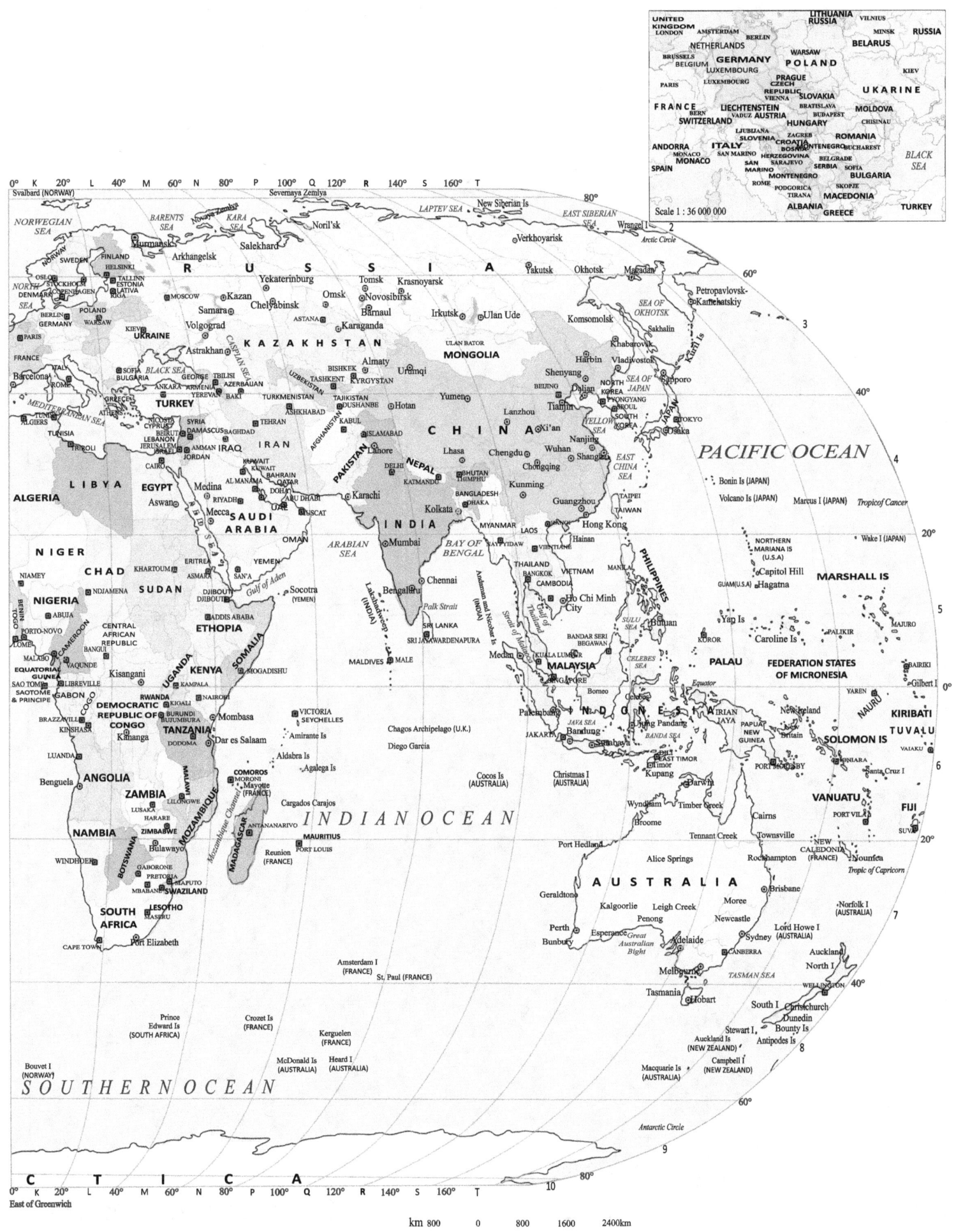

UNITED KINGDOM
LONDON
AMSTERDAM
NETHERLANDS
BRUSSELS
BELGIUM
LUXEMBOURG
PARIS
LUXEMBOURG
FRANCE
BERN
SWITZERLAND
ANDORRA
MONACO
SPAIN
BERLIN
GERMANY
PRAGUE
CZECH
REPUBLIC
VIENNA
LIECHTENSTEIN
VADUZ AUSTRIA
LJUBLJANA
SLOVENIA
ZAGREB
CROATIA
HERZEGOVINA
SAN MARINO
SAN MARINO
ROME
MONACO
ITALY
LITHUANIA
RUSSIA
VILNIUS
MINSK
WARSAW
POLAND
SLOVAKIA
BRATISLAVA
BUDAPEST
HUNGARY
BELGRADE
SARAJEVO
MONTENEGRO
PODGORICA
TIRANA
ALBANIA
RUSSIA
BELARUS
KIEV
UKARINE
MOLDOVA
CHISINAU
ROMANIA
BUCHAREST
SERBIA
SOFIA
BULGARIA
SKOPJE
MACEDONIA
GREECE
BLACK SEA
TURKEY

Scale 1 : 36 000 000

0° K 20° L 40° M 60° N 80° P 100° Q 120° R 140° S 160° T
Svalbard (NORWAY)
Severnaya Zemlya
New Siberian Is
80°

NORWEGIAN SEA
BARENTS SEA
Novaya Zemlya
KARA SEA
LAPTEV SEA
EAST SIBERIAN SEA
Wrangel I
2
Arctic Circle

Murmansk
Salekhard
Noril'sk
Verkhoyarsk
Yakutsk
Okhotsk
Magadan
60°

NORWAY
SWEDEN
FINLAND
Arkhangelsk
R U S S I A
Petropavlovsk-Kamchatskiy

OSLO
STOCKHOLM
HELSINKI
TALLINN
ESTONIA
LATVIA
RIGA
Yekaterinburg
Tomsk
Krasnoyarsk
SEA OF OKHOTSK
3

NORTH SEA
DENMARK
COPENHAGEN
MOSCOW
Kazan
Omsk
Novosibirsk
Irkutsk
Ulan Ude
Komsomolsk
Sakhalin

BERLIN
GERMANY
POLAND
WARSAW
KIEV
Samara
Chelyabinsk
Barnaul
Khabarovsk
Kuril Is

PARIS
UKRAINE
Volgograd
K A Z A K H S T A N
ULAN BATOR
Shenyang
Vladivostok
Sapporo
40°

FRANCE
Astrakhan
CASPIAN SEA
ASTANA
Karaganda
MONGOLIA
Harbin
Dalian
SEA OF JAPAN

Barcelona
ITALY
SOFIA
BULGARIA
GEORGE
TBILISI
ARMENIA
YEREVAN
AZERBAIJAN
BAKU
BISHKEK
KYRGYSTAN
TASHKENT
UZBEKISTAN
Almaty
Urumqi
ULAN BATOR
BEIJING
NORTH KOREA
PYONGYANG
SEOUL
SOUTH KOREA
TOKYO
OSAKA

ROME
Black Sea
ANKARA
TURKEY
TURKMENISTAN
TAJIKISTAN
DUSHANBE
Yumen
Lanzhou
Tianjin
Xi'an
YELLOW SEA
JAPAN

MEDITERRANEAN SEA
GREECE
ATHENS
CYPRUS
SYRIA
DAMASCUS
ASHKHABAD
Hotan
C H I N A
Nanjing
Shanghai
EAST CHINA SEA
PACIFIC OCEAN
4

TUNIS
TUNISIA
ALGIERS
NICOSIA
BEIRUT
LEBANON
JERUSALEM
AMMAN
JORDAN
IRAQ
BAGHDAD
TEHRAN
I R A N
AFGHANISTAN
KABUL
ISLAMABAD
DELHI
Lahore
Lhasa
Chengdu
Chongqing
Wuhan
Bonin Is (JAPAN)

TRIPOLI
KUWAIT
KUWAIT
PAKISTAN
NEPAL
KATMANDU
BHUTAN
THIMPHU
Kunming
Guangzhou
Volcano Is (JAPAN)
Marcus I (JAPAN)
Tropic of Cancer

LIBYA
EGYPT
Medina
AL MANAMA
BAHRAIN
QATAR
DOHA
ABU DHABI
Karachi
BANGLADESH
DHAKA
Kolkata
Guangzhou
TAIPEI
TAIWAN
Hong Kong

ALGERIA
Aswan
RIYADH
UAE
MUSCAT
I N D I A
MYANMAR
LAOS
Wake I (JAPAN)
20°

Mecca
SAUDI ARABIA
OMAN
ARABIAN SEA
Mumbai
BAY OF BENGAL
NAY PYI TAW
VIENTIANE
Hainan
NORTHERN MARIANA IS (U.S.A)

N I G E R
CHAD
SUDAN
KHARTOUM
YEMEN
SAN'A
Lakshadweep (INDIA)
Chennai
THAILAND
BANGKOK
VIETNAM
CAMBODIA
MANILA
GUAM(U.S.A)
Hagatna
Capitol Hill
MARSHALL IS
5

NIAMEY
NDJAMENA
ERITREA
ASMARA
DJIBOUTI
DJIBOUTI
Gulf of Aden
Socotra (YEMEN)
Palk Strait
SRI LANKA
Andaman and Nicobar Is (INDIA)
Ho Chi Minh City
PHILIPPINES
Yap Is
Caroline Is
PALIKIR

NIGERIA
ABUJA
CENTRAL AFRICAN REPUBLIC
ADDIS ABABA
ETHIOPIA
Bengaluru
SRI JAYAWARDENAPURA
Strait of Malacca
BANDAR SERI BEGAWAN
KOROR
MAJURO

BENIN
TOGO
PORTO-NOVO
LOME
CAMEROON
YAOUNDE
BANGUI
MALDIVES
MALE
Medan
KUALA LUMPUR
SULU SEA
Bruthan
Koror
PALAU
FEDERATION STATES OF MICRONESIA
BAIRIKI
Gilbert I

MALABO
EQUATORIAL GUINEA
SAO TOME & PRINCIPE
LIBREVILLE
Kisangani
UGANDA
KAMPALA
KENYA
NAIROBI
SOMALIA
MOGADISHU
MALAYSIA
SINGAPORE
Borneo
CELEBES SEA
YAREN
NAURU
0°

GABON
CONGO
BRAZZAVILLE
KINSHASA
RWANDA
KIGALI
BURUNDI
BUJUMBURA
VICTORIA
SEYCHELLES
Amirante Is
Chagos Archipelago (U.K.)
Palembang
JAVA SEA
JAKARTA
Bandung
I N D O N E S I A
Ujung Pandang
BANDA SEA
IRIAN JAYA
New Ireland
PAPUA NEW GUINEA
New Britain
KIRIBATI
TUVALU

DEMOCRATIC REPUBLIC OF CONGO
TANZANIA
Mombasa
Dar es Salaam
DODOMA
Diego Garcia
Surabaya
FLORES
EAST TIMOR
Kupang
Timor
PORT MORESBY
SOLOMON IS
HONIARA
Santa Cruz I
VAIAKU

LUANDA
Kananga
Aldabra Is
Agalega Is
Cocos Is (AUSTRALIA)
Christmas I (AUSTRALIA)
Darwin
6

ANGOLA
ZAMBIA
COMOROS
MORONI
Mayotte (FRANCE)
Cargados Carajos
I N D I A N   O C E A N
Wyndham
Timber Creek
VANUATU
PORT VILA
FIJI

Benguela
MALAWI
LILONGWE
MOZAMBIQUE
MADAGASCAR
ANTANANARIVO
Broome
Cairns
SUVA
20°

NAMBIA
ZIMBABWE
LUSAKA
HARARE
MAURITIUS
PORT LOUIS
Port Hedland
Alice Springs
Tennant Creek
Townsville
NEW CALEDONIA (FRANCE)
Noumea

WINDHOEK
Bulawayo
Reunion (FRANCE)
A U S T R A L I A
Rockhampton
Tropic of Capricorn

BOTSWANA
GABORONE
PRETORIA
MAPUTO
SWAZILAND
MBABANE
Geraldton
Kalgoorlie
Leigh Creek
Moree
Brisbane
Norfolk I (AUSTRALIA)
7

SOUTH AFRICA
LESOTHO
MASERU
Perth
Penong
Newcastle
Lord Howe I (AUSTRALIA)

CAPE TOWN
Port Elizabeth
Bunbury
Esperance
Great Australian Bight
Adelaide
Sydney
CANBERRA
Auckland
North I

Amsterdam I (FRANCE)
St. Paul (FRANCE)
Melbourne
TASMAN SEA
WELLINGTON
40°

Tasmania
Hobart
South I
Christchurch
Dunedin

Prince Edward Is (SOUTH AFRICA)
Crozet Is (FRANCE)
Kerguelen (FRANCE)
Stewart I
Bounty Is
Auckland Is (NEW ZEALAND)
Antipodes Is
8

Bouvet I (NORWAY)
McDonald Is (AUSTRALIA)
Heard I (AUSTRALIA)
Macquarie Is (AUSTRALIA)
Campbell I (NEW ZEALAND)

S O U T H E R N   O C E A N
60°

Antarctic Circle
9

C T I C A
80°

0° K 20° L 40° M 60° N 80° P 100° Q 120° R 140° S 160° T
10
East of Greenwich

km 800   0   800   1600   2400km
1 : 80 000 000

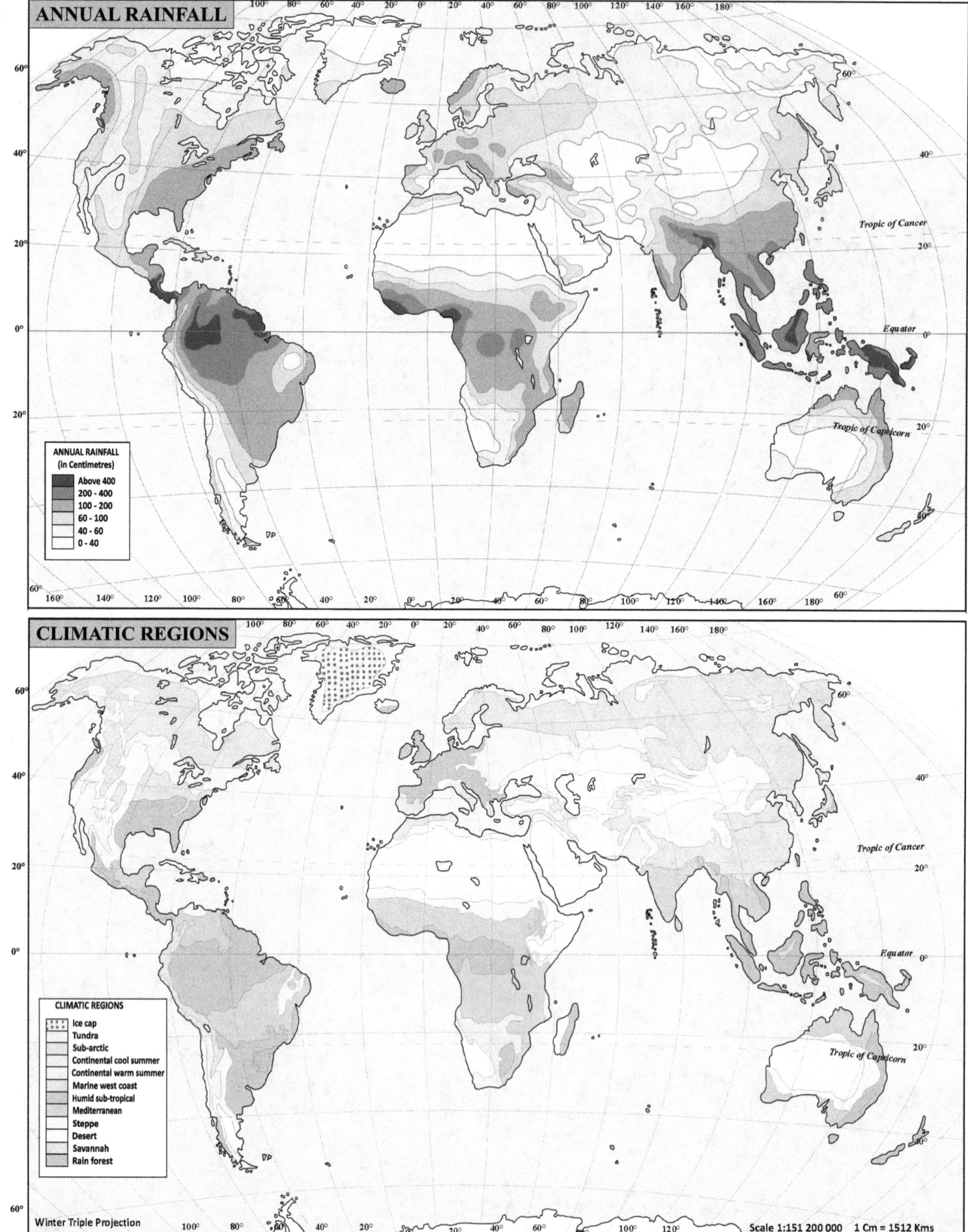

ANNUAL RAINFALL

ANNUAL RAINFALL
(in Centimetres)
- Above 400
- 200 - 400
- 100 - 200
- 60 - 100
- 40 - 60
- 0 - 40

Tropic of Cancer

Equator

Tropic of Capricorn

CLIMATIC REGIONS

CLIMATIC REGIONS
- Ice cap
- Tundra
- Sub-arctic
- Continental cool summer
- Continental warm summer
- Marine west coast
- Humid sub-tropical
- Mediterranean
- Steppe
- Desert
- Savannah
- Rain forest

Tropic of Cancer

Equator

Tropic of Capricorn

Winter Triple Projection

Scale 1:151 200 000   1 Cm = 1512 Kms

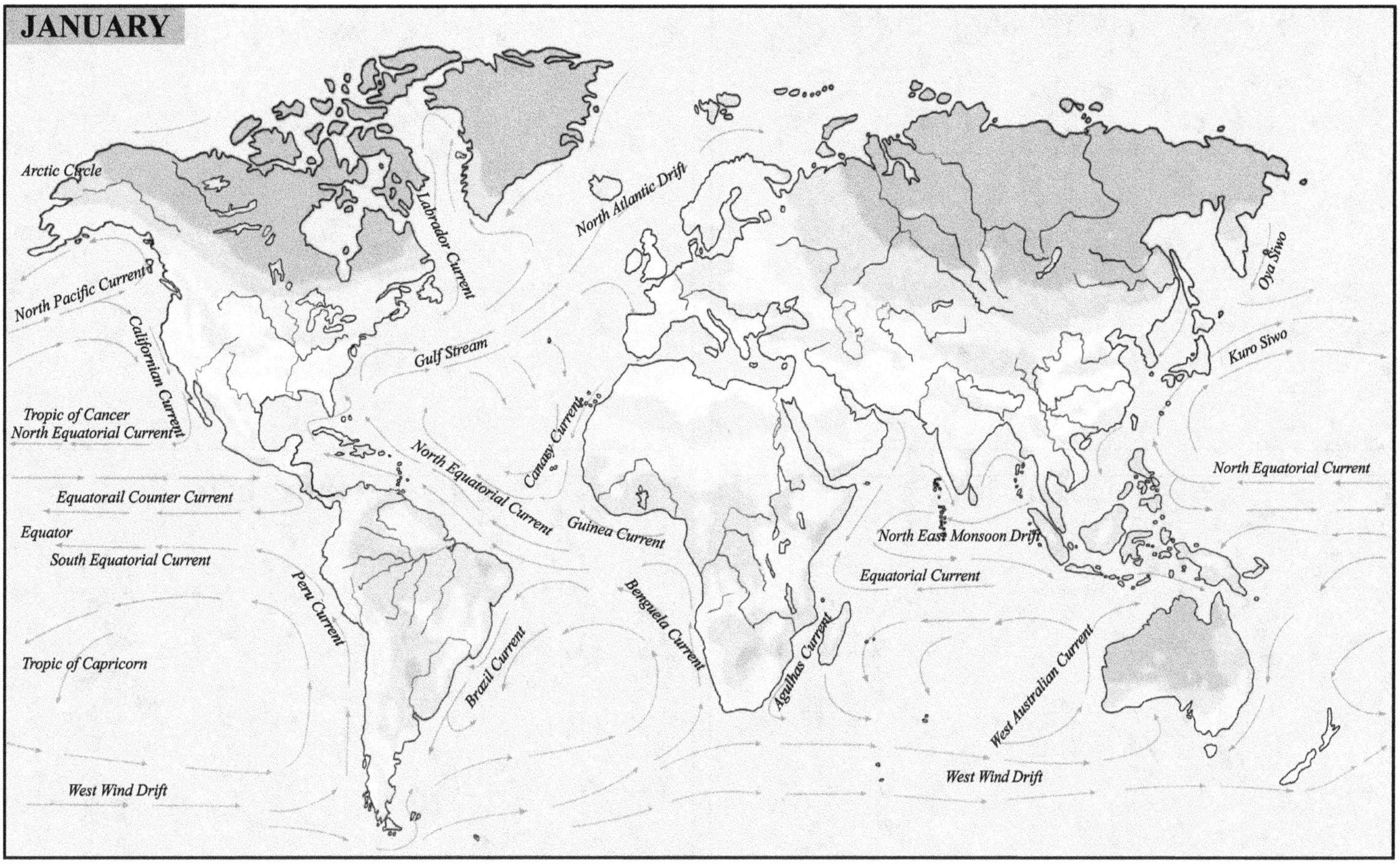

JANUARY

Arctic Circle

North Atlantic Drift

Labrador Current

North Pacific Current

Californian Current

Gulf Stream

Tropic of Cancer
North Equatorial Current

Canary Current

North Equatorial Current

Oya Siwo

Kuro Siwo

North Equatorial Current

Equatorail Counter Current

Equator

Guinea Current

North East Monsoon Drift

South Equatorial Current

Equatorial Current

Peru Current

Benguela Current

Agulhas Current

Tropic of Capricorn

Brazil Current

West Australian Current

West Wind Drift

West Wind Drift

AVERAGE SURFACE TEMPERATURE
(in °Celcius)

36	28	20	12	4	-4	-12	-20
32	24	16	8	0	-8	-16	

OCEAN CURRENTS

→ Warm current

→ Cold current

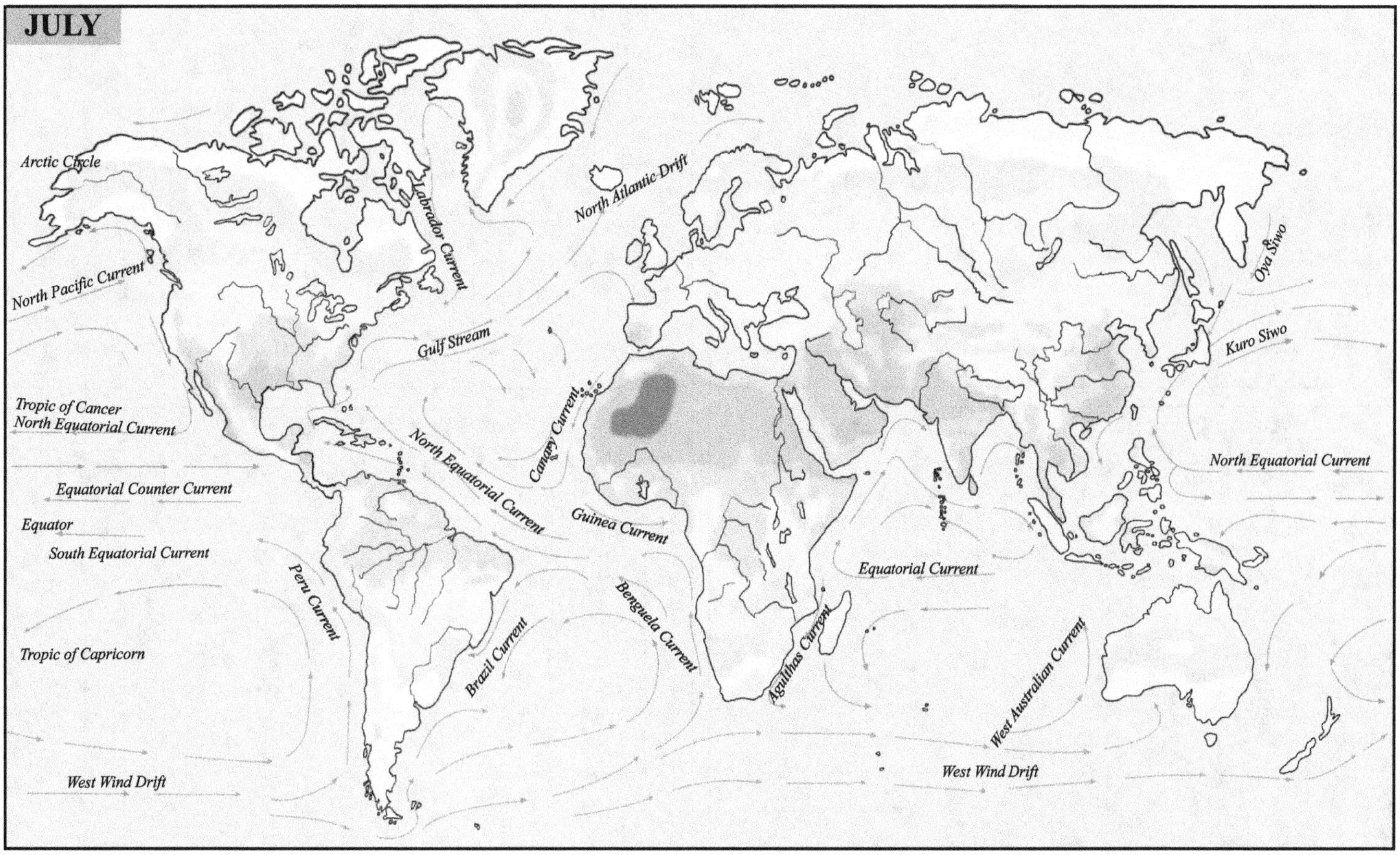

JULY

Arctic Circle

North Atlantic Drift

Labrador Current

North Pacific Current

Gulf Stream

Tropic of Cancer
North Equatorial Current

Canary Current

North Equatorial Current

Oya Siwo

Kuro Siwo

North Equatorial Current

Equatorial Counter Current

Equator

North Equatorial Current

Guinea Current

South Equatorial Current

Equatorial Current

Peru Current

Benguela Current

Agulhas Current

Tropic of Capricorn

Brazil Current

West Australian Current

West Wind Drift

West Wind Drift

HOT-WET EQUATORIAL REGIONS

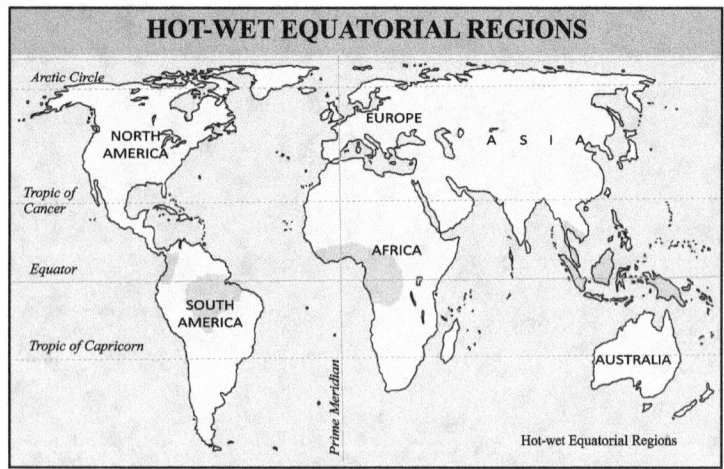

Hot-wet Equatorial Regions

TROPICAL MONSOON REGIONS

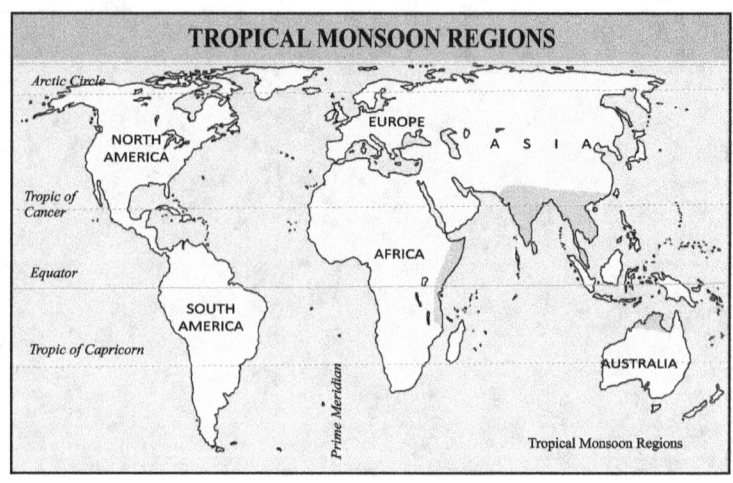

Tropical Monsoon Regions

TROPICAL RAINFORESTS

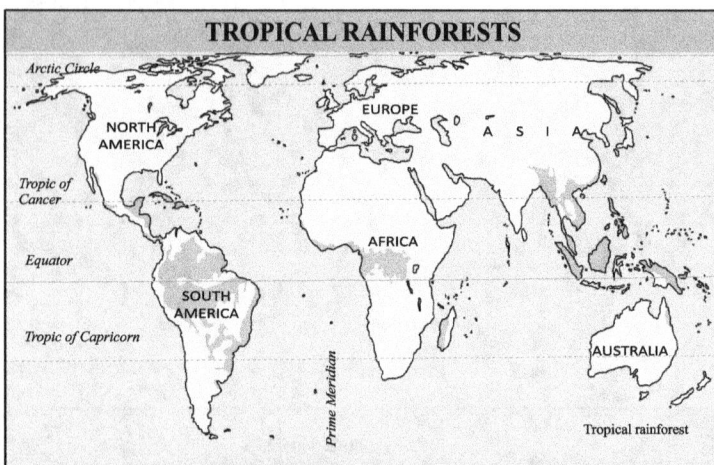

Tropical rainforest

MEDITERRANEAN REGIONS

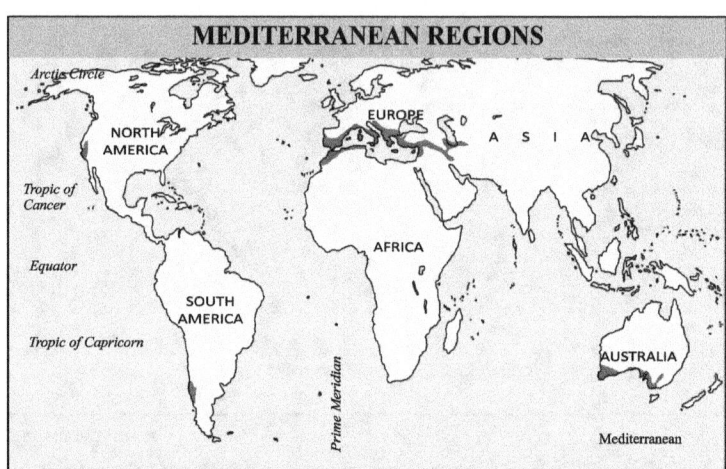

Mediterranean

TEMPERATE GRASSLANDS

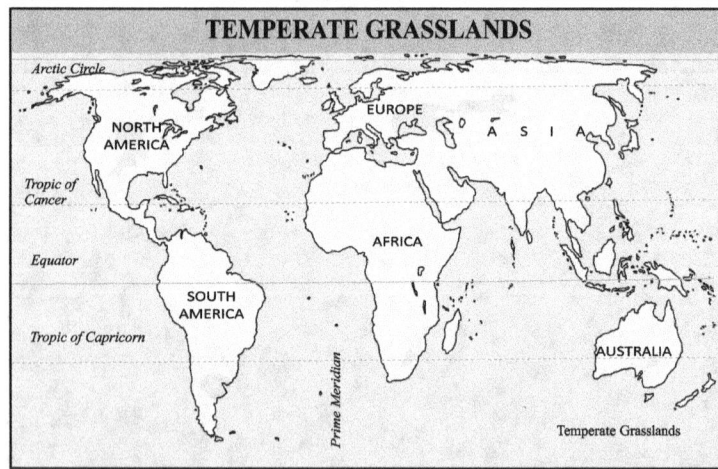

Temperate Grasslands

DESERTS

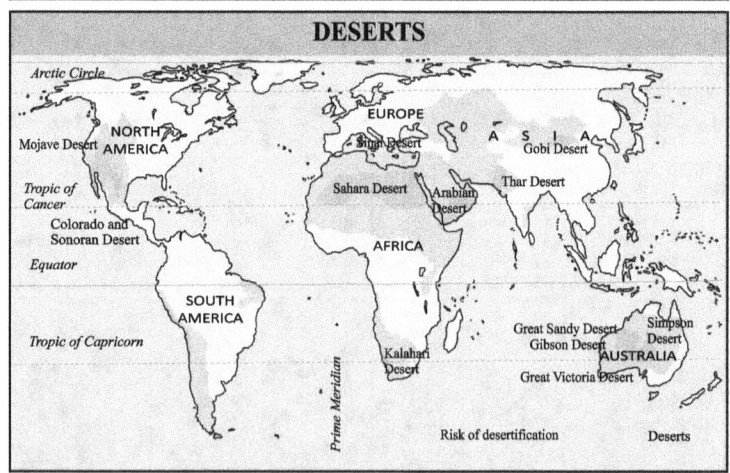

Risk of desertification   Deserts

CONTINENTAL TEMPERATE REGIONS

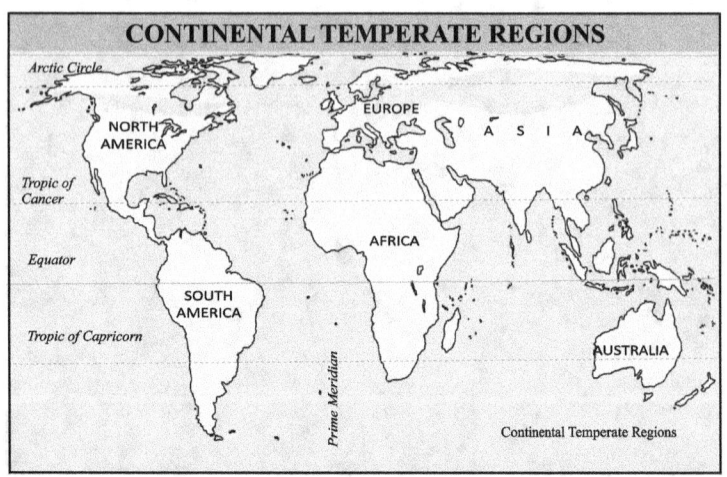

Continental Temperate Regions

TUNDRA REGIONS

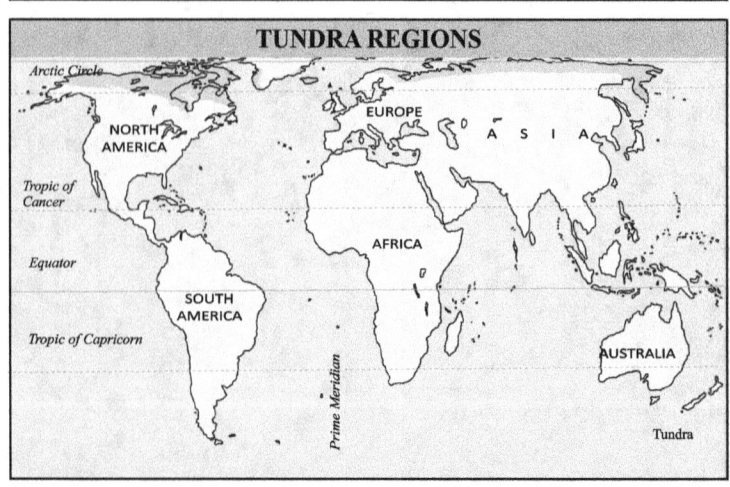

Tundra

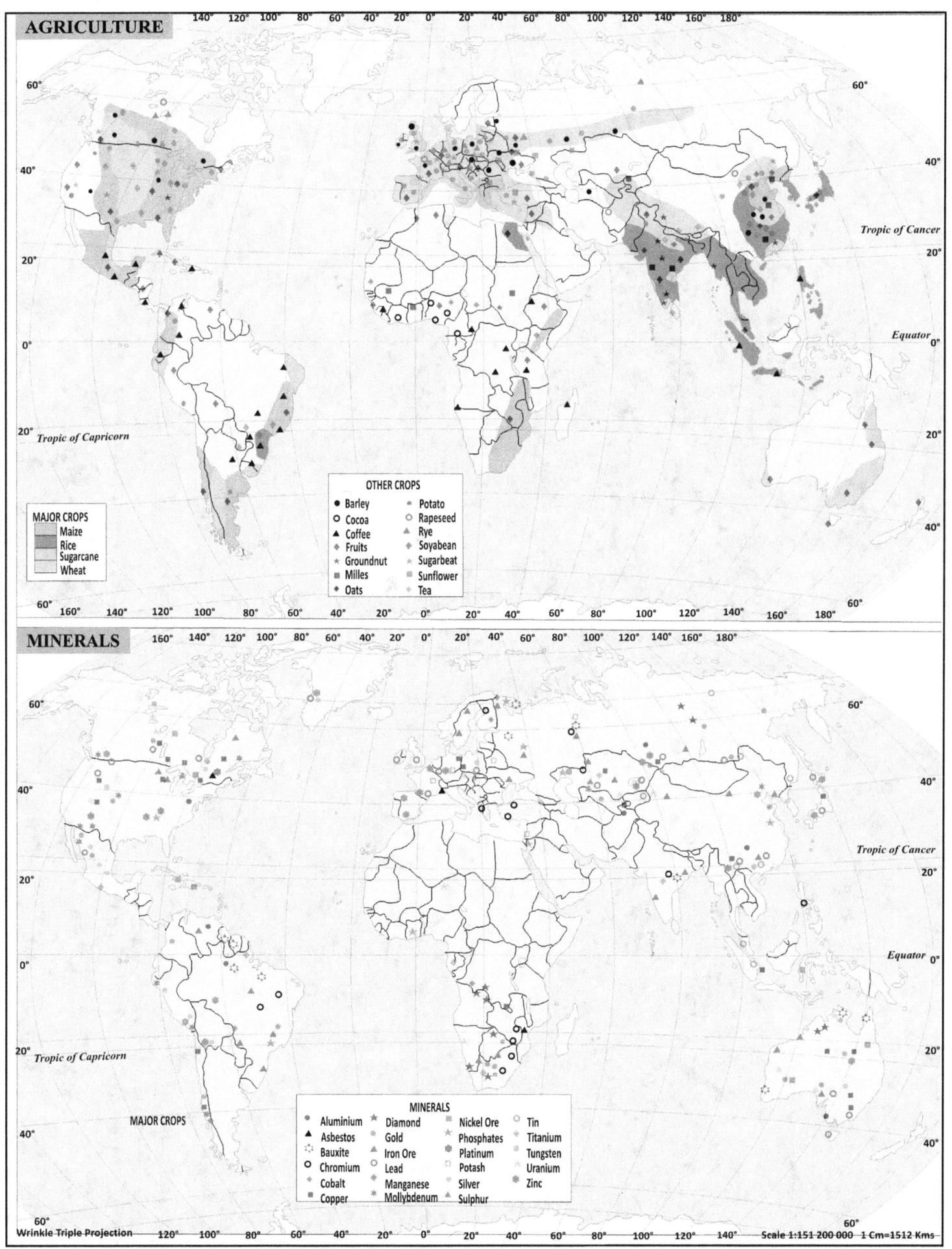

AGRICULTURE

MAJOR CROPS
- Maize
- Rice
- Sugarcane
- Wheat

OTHER CROPS
- ● Barley
- ○ Cocoa
- ▲ Coffee
- ◆ Fruits
- ★ Groundnut
- ▪ Milles
- ◆ Oats
- ▪ Potato
- ○ Rapeseed
- ▲ Rye
- ◆ Soyabean
- ▪ Sugarbeat
- ▪ Sunflower
- ◆ Tea

MINERALS

MAJOR CROPS

MINERALS
- ● Aluminium
- ▲ Asbestos
- ⋄ Bauxite
- ○ Chromium
- ◆ Cobalt
- ▪ Copper
- ★ Diamond
- ● Gold
- ▲ Iron Ore
- ○ Lead
- ◆ Manganese
- ✳ Mollybdenum
- ▪ Nickel Ore
- ★ Phosphates
- ⬡ Platinum
- ▫ Potash
- ◆ Silver
- ▲ Sulphur
- ○ Tin
- ◆ Titanium
- ▪ Tungsten
- ★ Uranium
- ✳ Zinc

Wrinkle Triple Projection   Scale 1:151 200 000   1 Cm=1512 Kms

GLOBAL WARMING

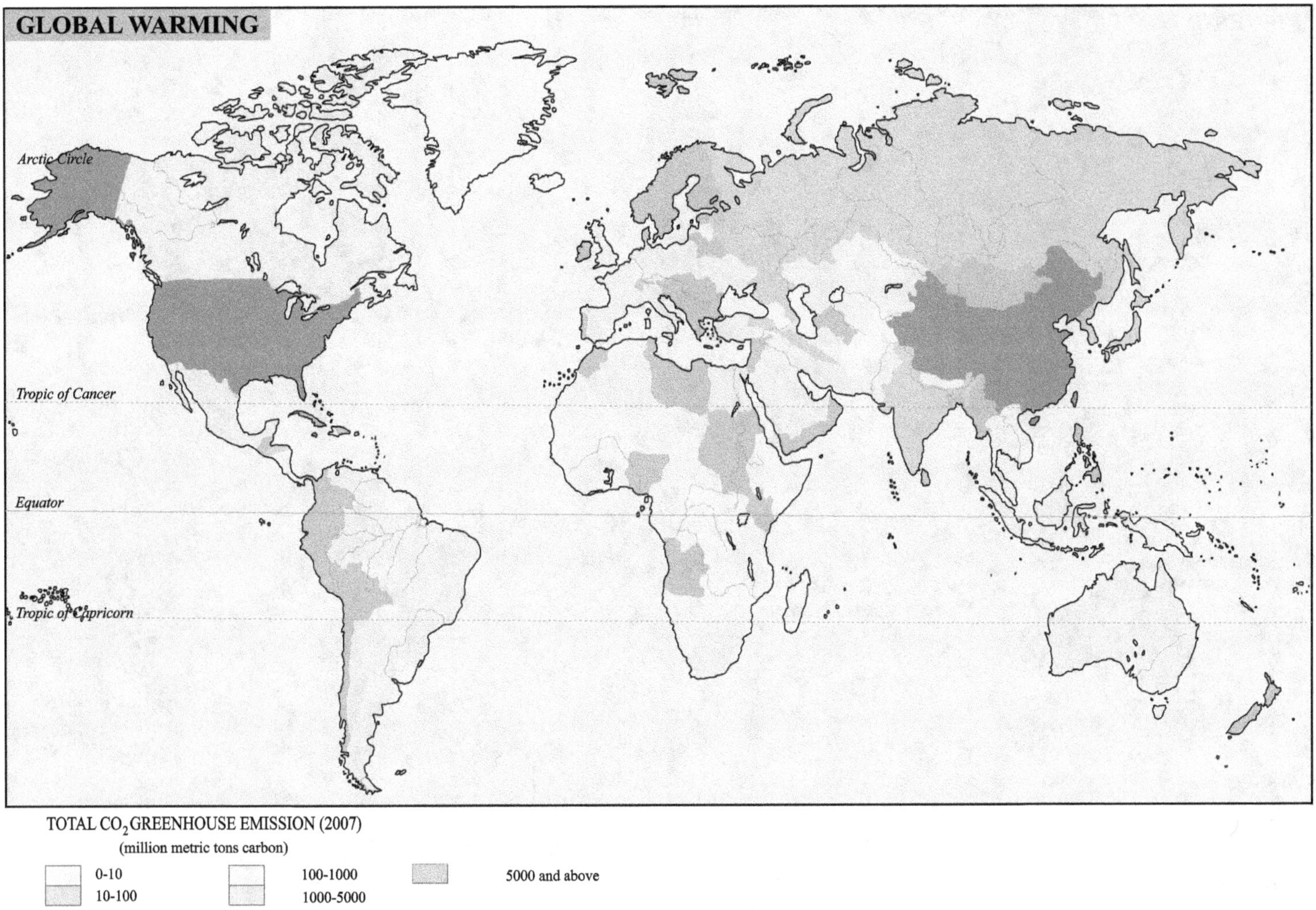

TOTAL CO$_2$ GREENHOUSE EMISSION (2007)
(million metric tons carbon)

0-10	100-1000
10-100	1000-5000

5000 and above

ACID RAIN

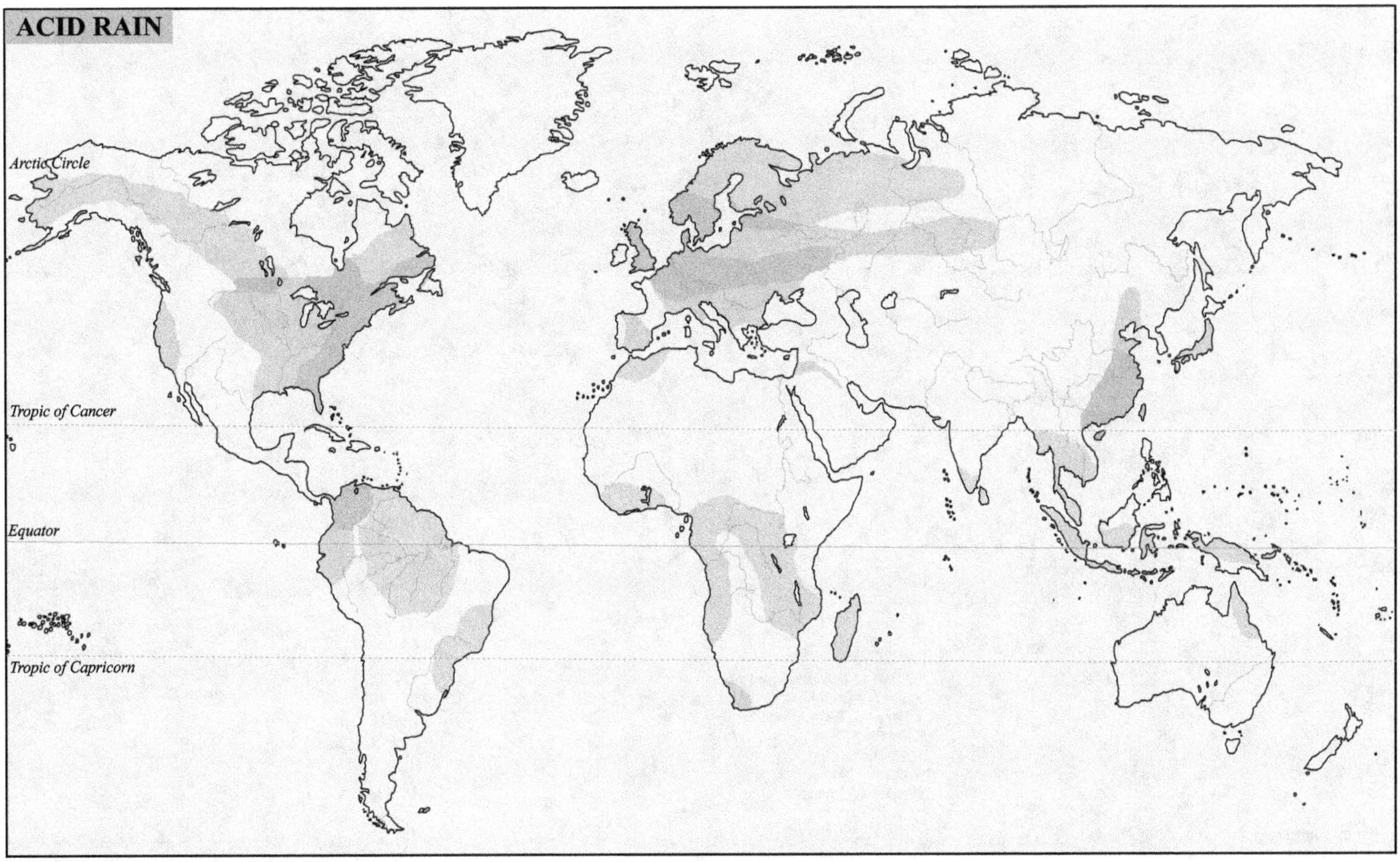

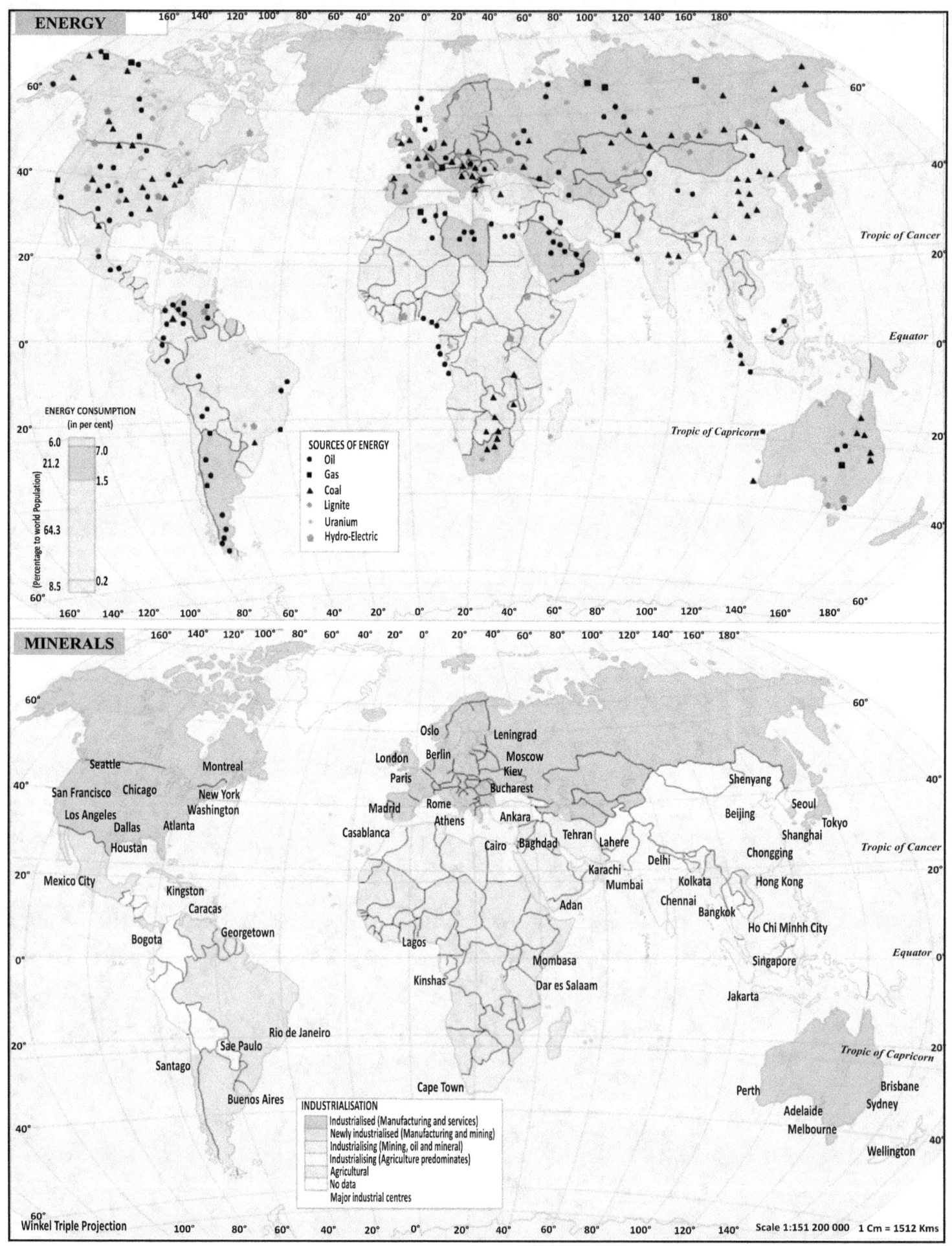

ENERGY

ENERGY CONSUMPTION
(in per cent)

6.0	7.0
21.2	1.5
64.3	
8.5	0.2

(Percentage to world Population)

SOURCES OF ENERGY
- ● Oil
- ■ Gas
- ▲ Coal
- ◆ Lignite
- ◆ Uranium
- ⬠ Hydro-Electric

Tropic of Cancer

Equator

Tropic of Capricorn

MINERALS

Seattle
San Francisco
Los Angeles
Dallas
Houstan
Chicago
Atlanta
Montreal
New York
Washington
Mexico City
Kingston
Caracas
Bogota
Georgetown
Lagos
Kinshas
Mombasa
Dar es Salaam
Cape Town

Oslo
London
Paris
Madrid
Berlin
Rome
Athens
Casablanca
Cairo
Leningrad
Moscow
Kiev
Bucharest
Ankara
Baghdad
Tehran
Lahere
Karachi
Mumbai
Adan
Delhi
Kolkata
Chennai

Shenyang
Beijing
Seoul
Tokyo
Shanghai
Chongging
Hong Kong
Bangkok
Ho Chi Minhh City
Singapore
Jakarta

Rio de Janeiro
Sae Paulo
Santago
Buenos Aires

Perth
Adelaide
Melbourne
Brisbane
Sydney
Wellington

Tropic of Cancer

Equator

Tropic of Capricorn

INDUSTRIALISATION
- Industrialised (Manufacturing and services)
- Newly industrialised (Manufacturing and mining)
- Industrialising (Mining, oil and mineral)
- Industrialising (Agriculture predominates)
- Agricultural
- No data
- Major industrial centres

Winkel Triple Projection

Scale 1:151 200 000   1 Cm = 1512 Kms

NATURAL WONDERS

Victoria Falls, Africa

Giant's Causeway, Antrim, Ireland

The Harbour at Rio de Janeiro, Brazil

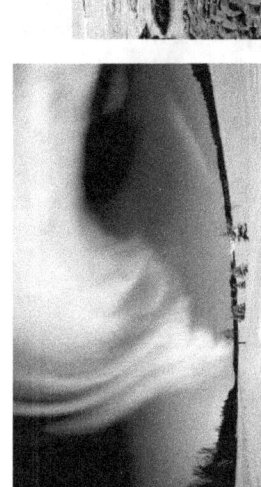

Aurora Borealis or the Northern Lights

Pauricutin Volcano, Mexico

Mount Everest, Nepal Himalayas

The Grand Canyon, Arizona, USA

The Great Barrier Reef, Pacific Ocean

MAN-MADE WONDERS

The Great Wall of China

Stone Giants of Easter Island, Pacific Ocean

The Taj Mahal, India

The Great Pyramid, Egypt

POPULATION DENSITY

Arctic Circle

Tropic of Cancer

Equator

Tropic of Capricorn

POPULATION DENSITY
Inhabitants per sq km

- Over 200
- 100-200
- 25-100
- 10-25
- Less than 10

CHILD MORTALITY

Arctic Circle

Tropic of Cancer

Equator

Tropic of Capricorn

CHILD DEATHS
Number of deaths of children under five per 1,000 children (2008)

- Over 200
- 150-199
- 100-149
- 50-99
- 10-49
- 1-9

Modified Times Projection

km 1450   0   1450   2900   4350 km

1 : 145 000 000

TIME ZONES

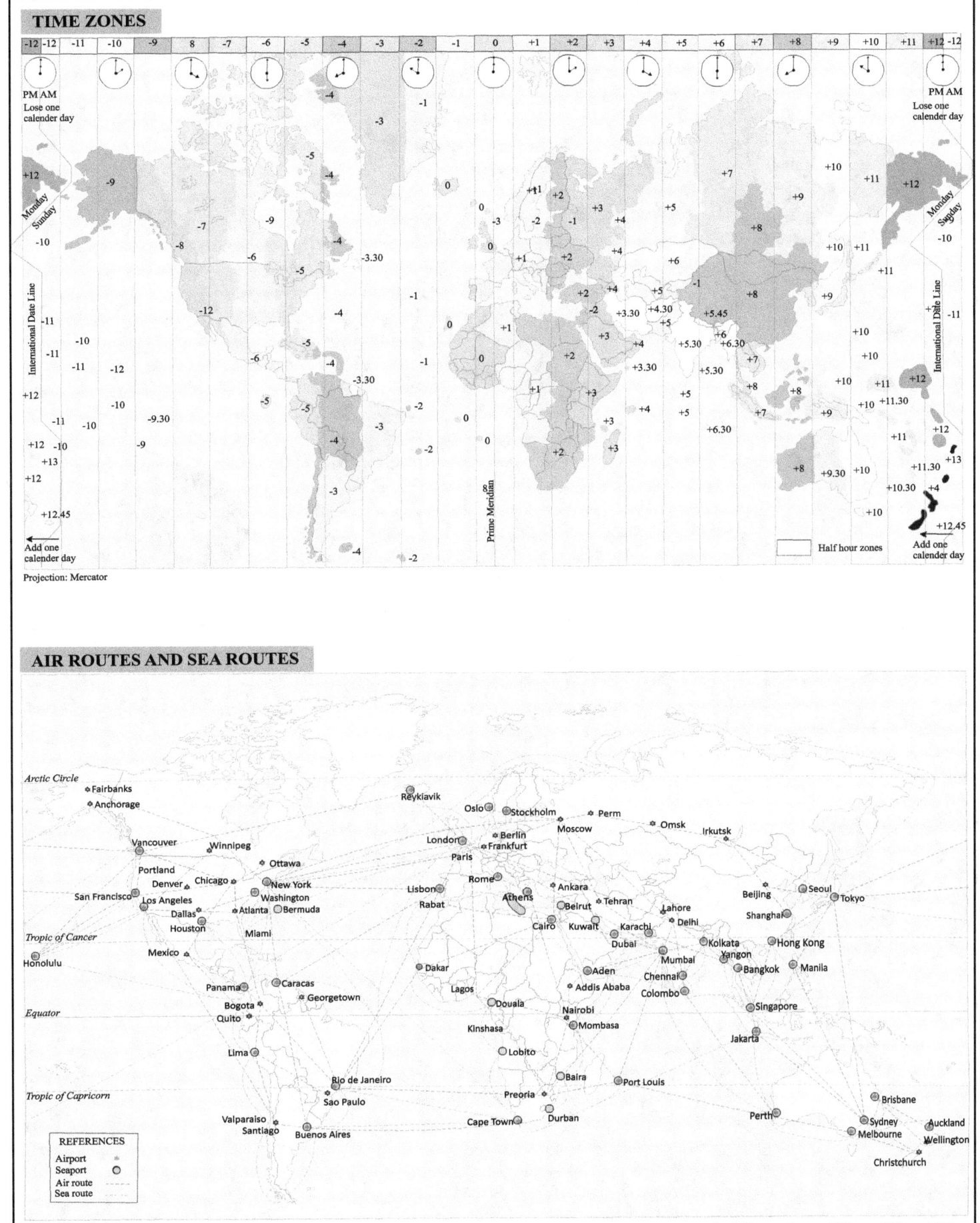

Projection: Mercator

AIR ROUTES AND SEA ROUTES

REFERENCES
Airport
Seaport
Air route
Sea route

Modified Times Projection

km 1450   0   1450   2900   4350 km

SCALE 1:145,000,000

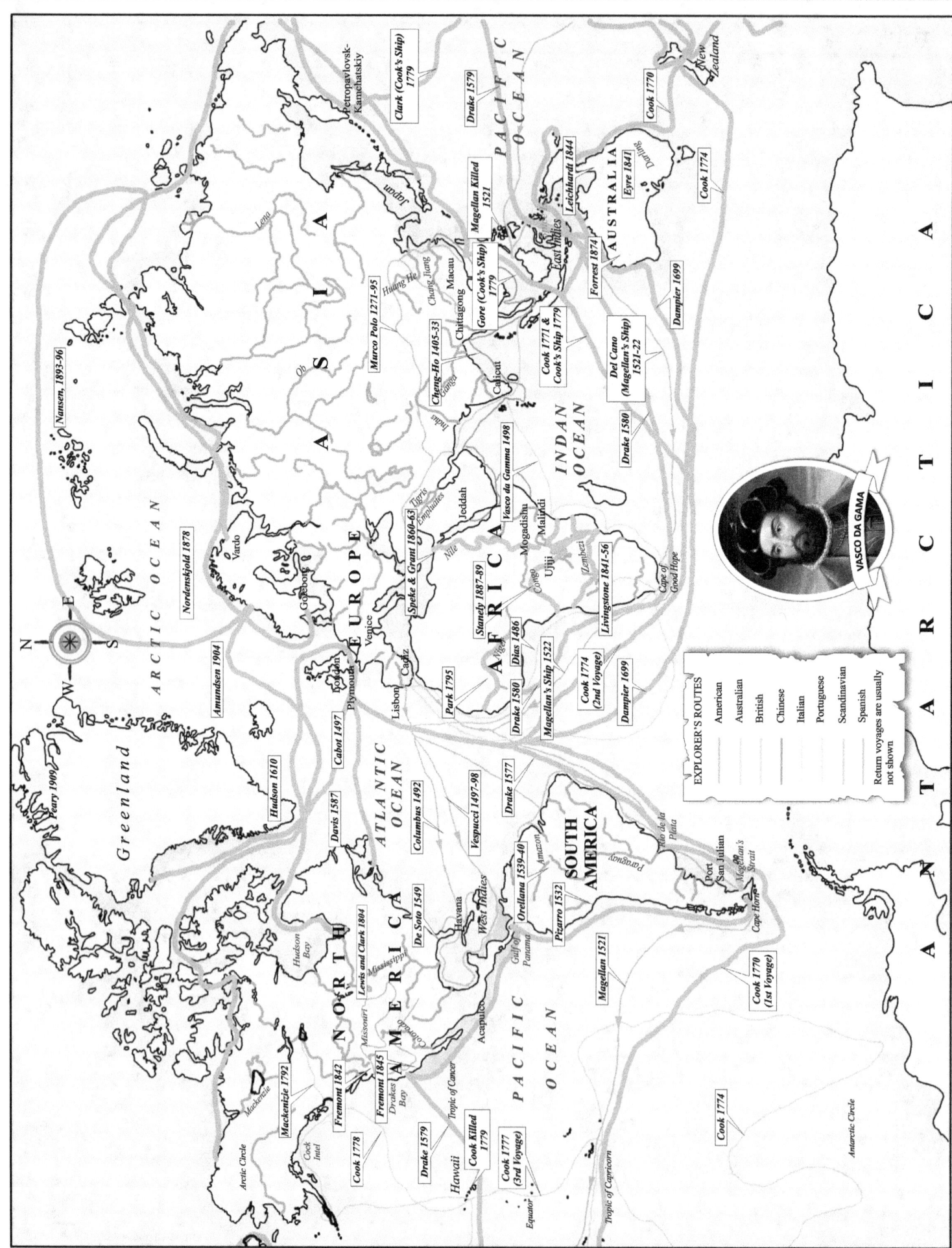

Nansen, 1893-96

Murco Polo 1271-95

Clark (Cook's Ship) 1779

Petropavlovsk-Kamchatskiy

Drake 1579

Cook 1770

New Zealand

PACIFIC OCEAN

Magellan Killed 1521

Leichhardt 1844

Eyre 1841

Darling

Cook 1774

AUSTRALIA

ASIA

Lena

Huang He

Chang Jiang

Gore (Cook's Ship) 1779

Macau

Chittagong

Cook 1771 & Cook's Ship 1779

Del Cano (Magellan's Ship) 1521-22

East Indies

Dampier 1699

Forrest 1874

Ob

Cheng-Ho 1405-33

Indus

Calicut

Vasco da Gamma 1498

Drake 1580

INDIAN OCEAN

Nordenskjold 1878

Vardo

Goteborg

Jeddah

Tigris Euphrates

Nile

Speke & Grant 1860-63

Mogadishu

Malindi

Uijij

Zambezi

Congo

VASCO DA GAMA

ARCTIC OCEAN

Amundsen 1904

EUROPE

Venice

London

Plymouth

Lisbon

Cadiz

Stanley 1887-89

Park 1795

AFRICA

Niger

Dias 1486

Drake 1580

Magellan's Ship 1522

Livingstone 1841-56

Cook 1774 (2nd Voyage)

Cape of Good Hope

Dampier 1699

N
W — E
S

Greenland

Peary 1909

Cabot 1497

ATLANTIC OCEAN

Davis 1587

Hudson 1610

EXPLORER'S ROUTES

American
Australian
British
Chinese
Italian
Portuguese
Scandinavian
Spanish
Return voyages are usually not shown

Columbus 1492

Vespucci 1497-98

Drake 1577

Arctic Circle

Mackenzie 1792

Cook Inlet

Fremont 1842

Fremont 1845

Drakes Bay

Hudson Bay

Lewis and Clark 1804

NORTH AMERICA

Missouri

Mississippi

De Soto 1549

Havana

West Indies

Orellana 1539-40

Pizarro 1532

SOUTH AMERICA

Amazon

Rio de la Plata

Paraguay

Orinoco

Port San Julian

Magellan's Strait

Cape Horn

Drake 1579

Cook Killed 1779

Hawaii

Cook 1777 (3rd Voyage)

Colorado

Tropic of Cancer

Acapulco

Gulf of Panama

Magellan 1521

PACIFIC OCEAN

Cook 1770 (1st Voyage)

Cook 1774

Equator

Tropic of Capricorn

Antarctic Circle

ANTARCTICA

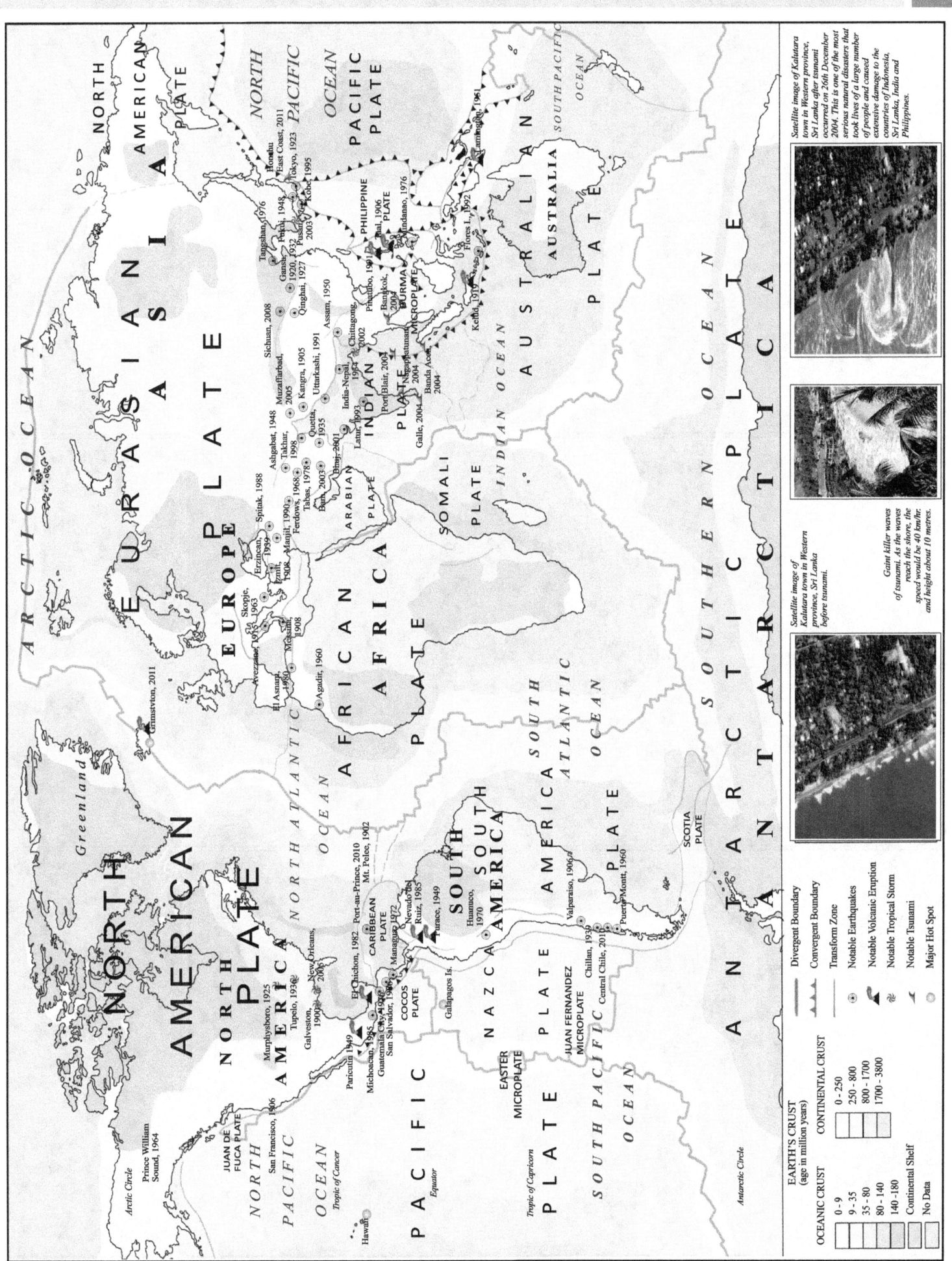

NORTH

NORTH AMERICAN PLATE

PACIFIC PLATE

NORTH PACIFIC OCEAN

PHILIPPINE PLATE

BURMA MICROPLATE

AUSTRALIAN PLATE

AUSTRALIA

SOUTH PACIFIC OCEAN

ARCTIC OCEAN

E U R A S I A

EUROPE PLATE

AFRICAN PLATE

AFRICA

SOMALI PLATE

ARABIAN PLATE

INDIAN OCEAN

SOUTHERN OCEAN

A N T A R C T I C A

ANTARCTIC PLATE

NORTH AMERICAN PLATE

NORTH AMERICA

AMERICA

Greenland

Arctic Circle

NORTH PACIFIC OCEAN

JUAN DE FUCA PLATE

Prince William Sound, 1964

San Francisco, 1906

Tropic of Cancer

Hawaii

Equator

PACIFIC OCEAN

SOUTH PACIFIC OCEAN

EASTER MICROPLATE

Tropic of Capricorn

Antarctic Circle

Galapagos Is.

COCOS PLATE

NAZCA PLATE

JUAN FERNANDEZ MICROPLATE

SOUTH AMERICA

SOUTH AMERICAN PLATE

NORTH ATLANTIC OCEAN

SOUTH ATLANTIC OCEAN

CARIBBEAN PLATE

SCOTIA PLATE

Mt. Pelee, 1902

Port-au-Prince, 2010

El Chichon, 1982

Managua, 1972

Guatemala City, 1976
San Salvador, 1986

Michoacan, 1985

Paricutin 1949

Murphysboro, 1925

Tupelo, 1936

Galveston, 1900
New Orleans, 2005

Nevado del Ruiz, 1985

Turace, 1949

Huanuco, 1970

Valparaiso, 1906

Chillan, 1939

Central Chile, 201

Puerto Montt, 1960

Tangshan, 1976

Homshu
East Coast, 2011

Tokyo, 1923
Kobe, 1995

Gansu, Pakil, 1948
1920, 1932

Qinghai, 1927

Sichuan, 2008

Muzaffarbad, 2005

Takhar, 1998

Kangra, 1905

Quetta, 1935

Ashgabat, 1948

Assam, 1950

Utarkashi, 1991

India-Nepal, 1964

Latur, 1993

Chittagong, 2002

Bhuj, 2001

Bam, 2003

Tabas, 1978

Ferdows, 1968

Manjil, 1990

Emit, 1908

Erzincan, 1939

Spitak, 1988

Skopje, 1963

Avezzano, 1915

Messina, 1908

El Asnam, 1980

Agadir, 1960

Bal, 1906

Pinatubo, 1991

Mindanao, 1976

Bangkok, 2003

Flores I, 1992

Kefid, 1976

North Sumatra, 2004

Port Blair, 2004

Banda Aceh, 2004

Galle, 2004

Grimsvotn, 2011

EARTH'S CRUST (age in million years)

OCEANIC CRUST | CONTINENTAL CRUST
0-9 | 0-250
9-35 | 250-800
35-80 | 800-1700
80-140 | 1700-3800
140-180 |
Continental Shelf
No Data

Divergent Boundary
Convergent Boundary
Transform Zone
Notable Earthquakes
Notable Volcanic Eruption
Notable Tropical Storm
Notable Tsunami
Major Hot Spot

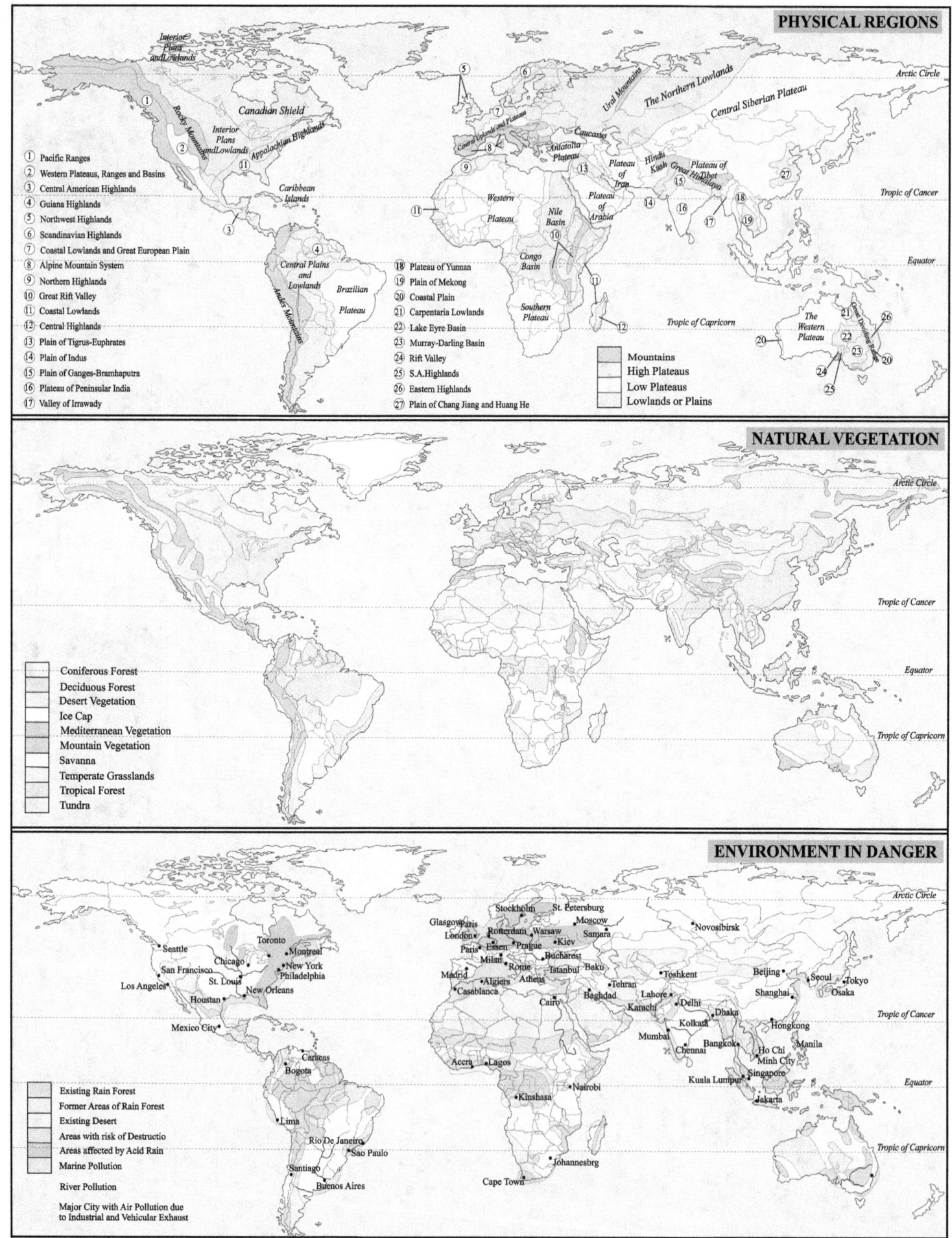

PHYSICAL REGIONS

Interior Plains and Lowlands
Rocky Mountains
Canadian Shield
Interior Plains and Lowlands
Appalachian Highlands
Caribbean Islands
Andes Mountains
Central Plains and Lowlands
Brazilian Plateau

Ural Mountains
The Northern Lowlands
Central Siberian Plateau
Central Uplands and Plateau
Caucasus
Anatolia Plateau
Plateau of Iran
Hindu Kush
Great Himalaya
Plateau of Tibet
Western Plateau
Nile Basin
Plateau of Arabia
Congo Basin
Southern Plateau
The Western Plateau
Great Dividing Range

Arctic Circle
Tropic of Cancer
Equator
Tropic of Capricorn

① Pacific Ranges
② Western Plateaus, Ranges and Basins
③ Central American Highlands
④ Guiana Highlands
⑤ Northwest Highlands
⑥ Scandinavian Highlands
⑦ Coastal Lowlands and Great European Plain
⑧ Alpine Mountain System
⑨ Northern Highlands
⑩ Great Rift Valley
⑪ Coastal Lowlands
⑫ Central Highlands
⑬ Plain of Tigris-Euphrates
⑭ Plain of Indus
⑮ Plain of Ganges-Bramhaputra
⑯ Plateau of Peninsular India
⑰ Valley of Irrawady

⑱ Plateau of Yunnan
⑲ Plain of Mekong
⑳ Coastal Plain
㉑ Carpentaria Lowlands
㉒ Lake Eyre Basin
㉓ Murray-Darling Basin
㉔ Rift Valley
㉕ S.A.Highlands
㉖ Eastern Highlands
㉗ Plain of Chang Jiang and Huang He

Mountains
High Plateaus
Low Plateaus
Lowlands or Plains

NATURAL VEGETATION

Arctic Circle
Tropic of Cancer
Equator
Tropic of Capricorn

Coniferous Forest
Deciduous Forest
Desert Vegetation
Ice Cap
Mediterranean Vegetation
Mountain Vegetation
Savanna
Temperate Grasslands
Tropical Forest
Tundra

ENVIRONMENT IN DANGER

Arctic Circle
Tropic of Cancer
Equator
Tropic of Capricorn

Seattle
San Francisco
Los Angeles
Houstan
Toronto
Montreal
Chicago
New York
Philadelphia
St. Louis
New Orleans
Mexico City
Caracas
Bogota
Lima
Rio De Janeiro
Santiago
Sao Paulo
Buenos Aires

Glasgow
London
Paris
Stockholm
St. Petersburg
Moscow
Rotterdam
Warsaw
Kiev
Samara
Novosibirsk
Essen
Prague
Paris
Milan
Rome
Bucharest
Istanbul
Baku
Madrid
Athens
Tehran
Toshkent
Beijing
Seoul
Tokyo
Algiers
Baghdad
Lahore
Shanghai
Osaka
Casablanca
Cairo
Karachi
Delhi
Dhaka
Kolkata
Hongkong
Mumbai
Bangkok
Manila
Chennai
Ho Chi Minh City
Accra
Lagos
Kuala Lumpur
Singapore
Nairobi
Jakarta
Kinshasa
Johannesbrg
Cape Town

Existing Rain Forest
Former Areas of Rain Forest
Existing Desert
Areas with risk of Destructio
Areas affected by Acid Rain
Marine Pollution

River Pollution

Major City with Air Pollution due to Industrial and Vehicular Exhaust

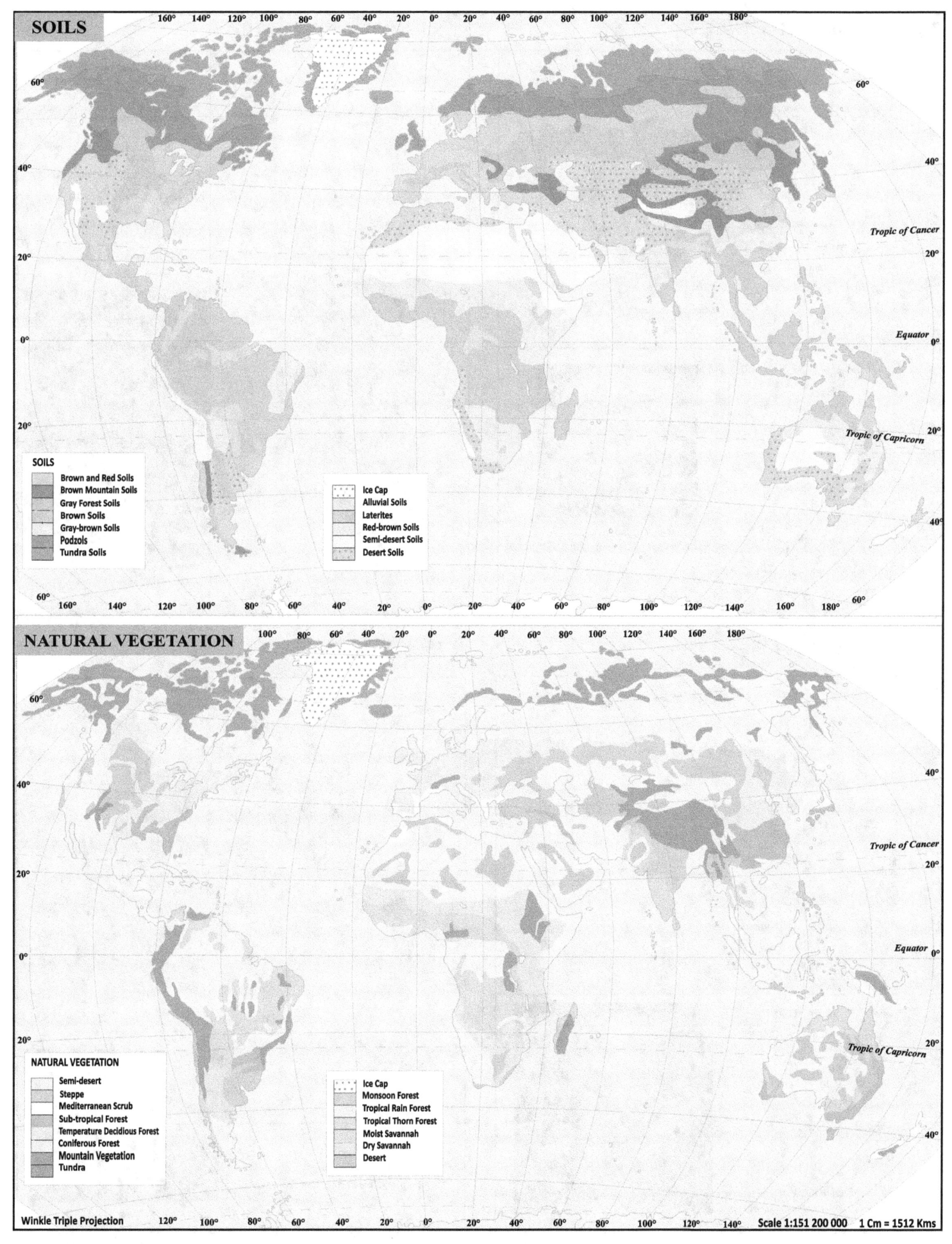

SOILS

160° 140° 120° 100° 80° 60° 40° 20° 0° 20° 40° 60° 80° 100° 120° 140° 160° 180°

60°   60°
40°   40°
20°   Tropic of Cancer   20°
0°   Equator   0°
20°   20°
Tropic of Capricorn   20°
40°

SOILS
- Brown and Red Soils
- Brown Mountain Soils
- Gray Forest Soils
- Brown Soils
- Gray-brown Soils
- Podzols
- Tundra Soils

- Ice Cap
- Alluvial Soils
- Laterites
- Red-brown Soils
- Semi-desert Soils
- Desert Soils

60° 160° 140° 120° 100° 80° 60° 40° 20° 0° 20° 40° 60° 80° 100° 120° 140° 160° 180° 60°

NATURAL VEGETATION

100° 80° 60° 40° 20° 0° 20° 40° 60° 80° 100° 120° 140° 160° 180°

60°   40°
40°   40°
20°   Tropic of Cancer   20°
0°   Equator   0°
20°   20°
Tropic of Capricorn   20°
40°

NATURAL VEGETATION
- Semi-desert
- Steppe
- Mediterranean Scrub
- Sub-tropical Forest
- Temperature Decidious Forest
- Coniferous Forest
- Mountain Vegetation
- Tundra

- Ice Cap
- Monsoon Forest
- Tropical Rain Forest
- Tropical Thorn Forest
- Moist Savannah
- Dry Savannah
- Desert

Winkle Triple Projection   120° 100° 80° 60° 40° 20° 0° 20° 40° 60° 80° 100° 120° 140°   Scale 1:151 200 000   1 Cm = 1512 Kms

MESOPOTAMIAN CIVILISATION

L. Van
CASPIAN SEA
L. Urmia
Carchemish
Nineveh
Tepe Gawra
Aleppo
Ashur
Hamazi
MESOPOTAMIA
ASSYRIA
SYRIAN DESERT
Mari
MEDITERRANEAN SEA
Damascus
Awan
Tyre
Sippar
Karkheh
Jerusalem
Agade Kish
AKKAD
Susa
Babylon
BABYLONIA
Gaza
Nippur SUMER
Shuruppak
Uruk
Lagash
Larsa
Eridu
Scale
0   208 km
The Gulf
RED SEA

Summer Civilisation
Babylonian Empire Under
Hammurabi, 1750 BC
Maximum Extent of the Middle
Assyrian Empire, 1243-1207 BC
Neo-Babylonian Empire Under
Nebuchadnezzar II, 604-562 BC
Site of Major Temple, Palace/ Royal Palace
Capital of Empire/ Capital City, Other city

*A copper cast of the head of
Akkadian King, the grandson of Sargon.*

NILE VALLEY CIVILISATION

Aleppo
Ugarit
Qadesh
MEDITERRANEAN SEA
Tyre
Joppa
Jerusalem
Gaza
LOWER EGYPT
Avaris
Giza
Heliopolis
Abusir
Memphis
Saqqara
Dahshur
SINAI
Herakleopolis
Asyut
EASTERN DESERT
WESTERN DESERT
Valley of the Kings
UPPER EGYPT
Thebes
RED SEA
Aniba
Qubán
Buhen
Kot
Amara West
Kumma
Amara East
Nile
Scale
0   180 km

Conjectural Borders of
Kingdom of Upper
Egypt, 3000 BC
Middle Kingdom (12th Dynasty,
1991-1783 BC)
Maximum Extent of New
Kingdom Under Tuthmosis I,
1504-1492 BC
Old Kingdom Pyramids,
2650-2040 BC
Royal Tomb for Middle and
New Kingdom
Fort or Garrison for Middle
and New Kingdom
Capital of Old Kingdom/
Royal Capital. with Dynasty
Other City

w mcindoo

Sphinx of Egypt

GREEK CIVILISATION

BLACK SEA
Scale
0   156 km
Thasos
Samothrace
Imroz
Lemnos
AEGEAN SEA
Lesbos
Orchomenos
Chios
Thebes
Andros
Athens
PELOPONNESE
Delos
Samos
Dendra
Mycenae
Ikaria
Miletos
Tiryns
Paros
Naxos
Karia
Pylos
Menelaion
Serraglia
Melos
Phylakopi
Kytera
Thera
Rhodes
Khania
Carpathos
Knossos
Phaistos
Kato Zakro
Cyprus
Enkomi
Crete
MEDITERRANEAN SEA

Minoan Civilisatin, 1600 BC
Mycenaean Civilisation, 1300 BC
Minoan City With Palace
Mycenaean City, With Palace
Capital City
Other Town

*Golden mask of Agamemnon
recovered at Mycenae*

CHINESE CIVILISATION

Long Wall of Zhao, built c300 BC
Long Wall of Yan, built c290 BC
SEA OF JAPAN
Yellow
Sangan
Anyang
Long Wall of Wei, built c353 BC
Xianyang
Zhengzhou
Qin
Hao
Changan
Luoyang
YELLOW SEA
L. Hongze
Han
Huai
L. Tai
L. Dongting
L. Pengli
EAST CHINA SEA
Scale
0   353 km

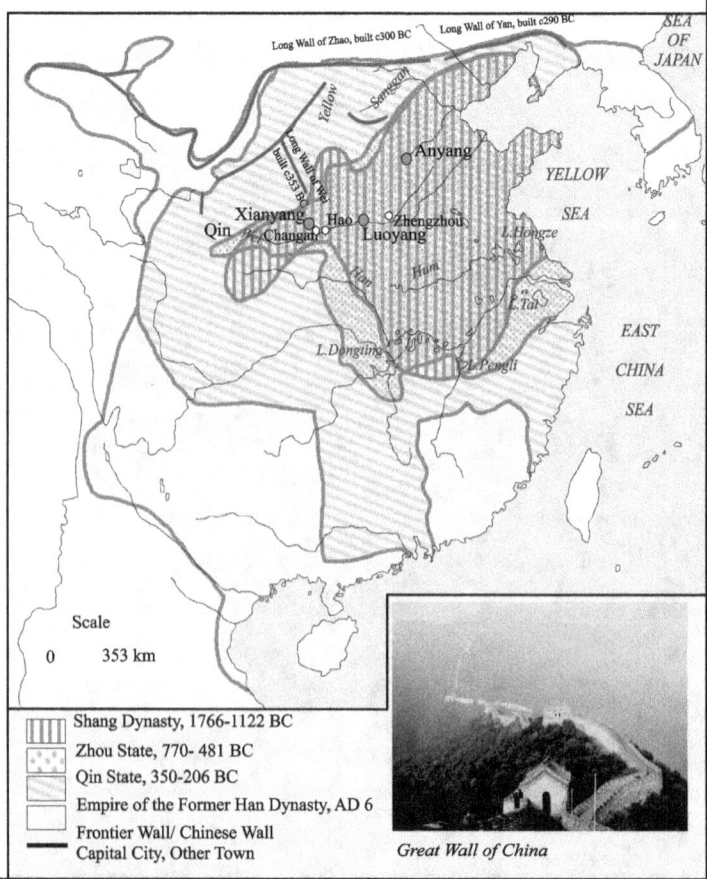

Shang Dynasty, 1766-1122 BC
Zhou State, 770- 481 BC
Qin State, 350-206 BC
Empire of the Former Han Dynasty, AD 6
Frontier Wall/ Chinese Wall
Capital City, Other Town

Great Wall of China

MAYAN CIVILISATION

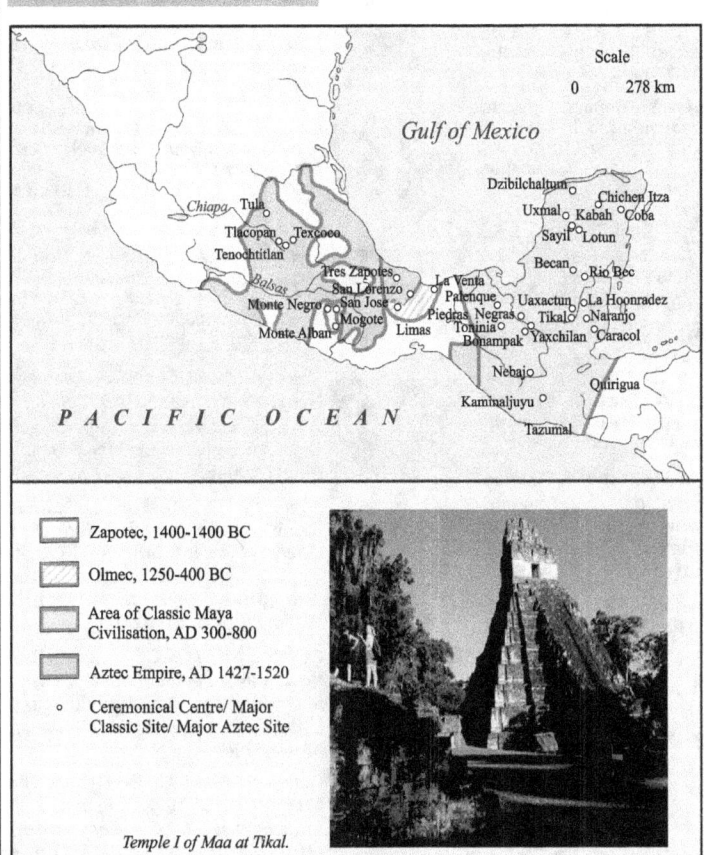

Scale
0   278 km

Gulf of Mexico

Chiapa Tula
Tlacopan Texcoco
Tenochtitlan
Balsas Tres Zapotes
San Lorenzo
Monte Negro San Jose
Mogote
Monte Alban Limas
Toninia
Bonampak
Piedras Negras
Yaxchilan

Dzibilchaltum
Uxmal Chichen Itza
Kabah Coba
Sayil Lotun
Becan
Rio Bec
La Venta
Uaxactun
Tikal Naranjo
Caracol

Nebaj

Kaminaljuyu

Quirigua

Tazumal

PACIFIC OCEAN

	Zapotec, 1400-1400 BC
	Olmec, 1250-400 BC
	Area of Classic Maya Civilisation, AD 300-800
	Aztec Empire, AD 1427-1520
○	Ceremonical Centre/ Major Classic Site/ Major Aztec Site

Temple I of Maa at Tikal.

IRANIAN EMPIRE

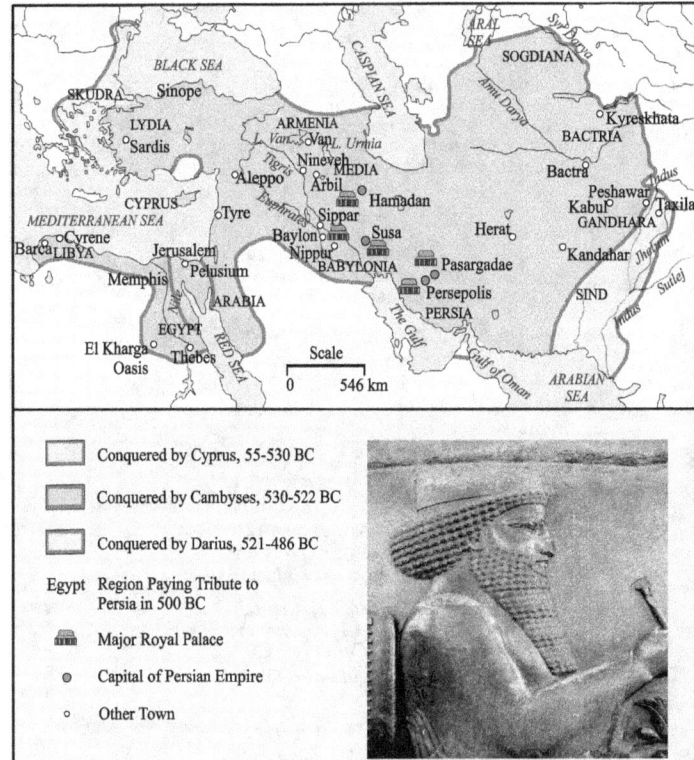

BLACK SEA
ARAL SEA
SOGDIANA
SKUDRA Sinope
LYDIA ARMENIA
Sardis *L. Van* Urmia BACTRIA
Kyreskhata
MEDITERRANEAN SEA
CYPRUS Nineveh MEDIA
Aleppo Arbil Bactra Peshawar
Tyre Hamadan Kabul Taxila
Cyrene Sippar Susa Herat GANDHARA
Barca LIBYA Baylon Kandahar
Jerusalem Nippur Pasargadae SIND
Memphis Pelusium Persepolis
ARABIA PERSIA
EGYPT
El Kharga Oasis Thebes RED SEA The Gulf Gulf of Oman ARABIAN SEA

Scale
0   546 km

	Conquered by Cyprus, 55-530 BC
	Conquered by Cambyses, 530-522 BC
	Conquered by Darius, 521-486 BC
Egypt	Region Paying Tribute to Persia in 500 BC
🏛	Major Royal Palace
●	Capital of Persian Empire
○	Other Town

A stone relef from Persepolis (ancient Persian city) showing Dauris.

GREEK IN THE AGE OF PERICLE

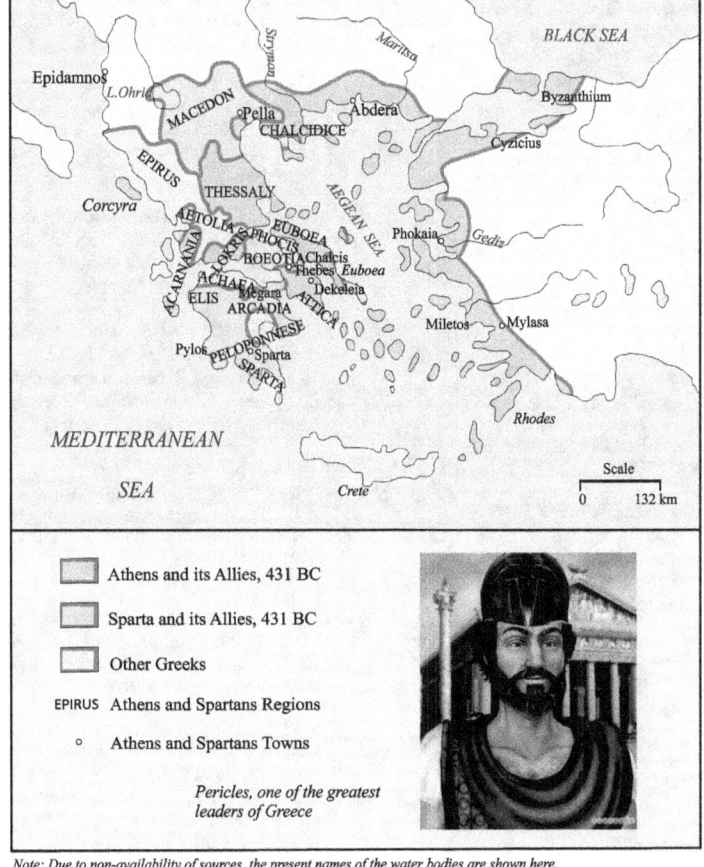

Epidamnos
L. Ohrid BLACK SEA
MACEDON *Marista*
Pella Abdera Byzanthium
EPIRUS CHALCIDICE
Cyzicus
Corcyra THESSALY
AEGEAN SEA
AETOLIA EUBOEA Phokaia *Gediz*
PHOCIS
ACARNANIA BOEOTIA Chalcis
Thebes *Euboea*
ACHAEA Megara Dekeleia
ELIS ARCADIA ATTICA
Pylos PELOPONNESE Miletos Mylasa
Sparta
SPARTA *Rhodes*

MEDITERRANEAN SEA *Crete*

Scale
0   132 km

	Athens and its Allies, 431 BC
	Sparta and its Allies, 431 BC
	Other Greeks
EPIRUS	Athens and Spartans Regions
○	Athens and Spartans Towns

Pericles, one of the greatest leaders of Greece

ALEXANDER'S EMPIRE

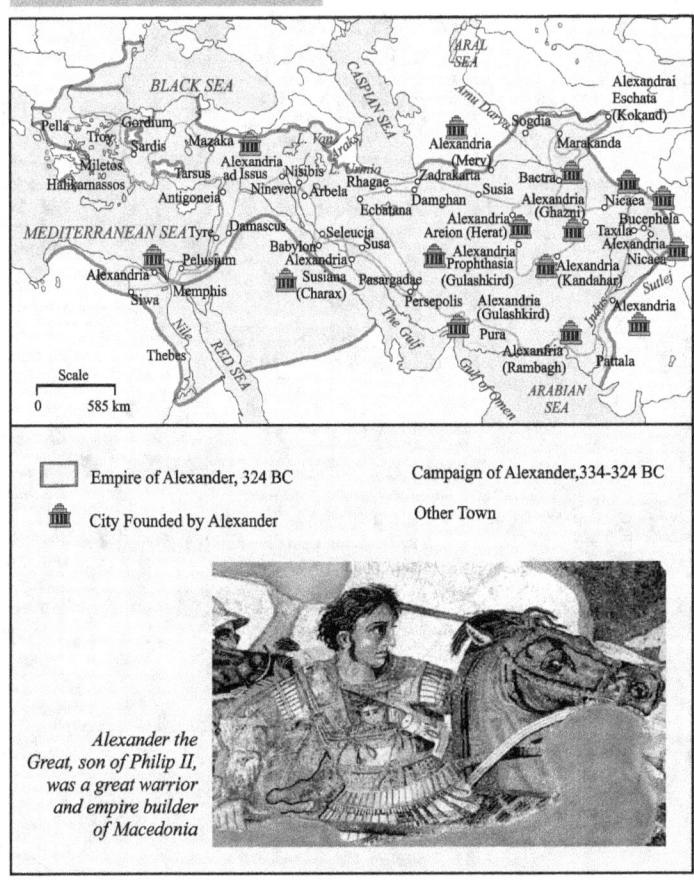

BLACK SEA
ARAL SEA
Alexandrai Eschata (Kokand)
Pella Gordium *Amu Darya* Sogdia
Troy Sardis Mazaka Marakanda
Miletos Alexandria *L. Van*
Halikarnassos ad Issus Nisibis Zadrakarta Bactra
Tarsus Nineveh Arbela Rhagae Alexandria (Ghazni)
Antigoneia Ecbatana Susia Nicaea
MEDITERRANEAN SEA Tyre Damascus Alexandria Taxila Bucephela
Seleucia Areion (Herat) Alexandria Nicaea
Damghan Alexandria (Kandahar)
Alexandria Babylon Alexandria Prophthasia
Memphis Susa (Gulashkird)
Siwa Susiana Pasargadae Alexandria
(Charax) Persepolis (Gulashkird)
Nile Pura Alexandria
Thebes RED SEA The Gulf (Rambagh) Pattala
Alexandria ARABIAN SEA
Gulf of Oman

Scale
0   585 km

	Empire of Alexander, 324 BC		Campaign of Alexander,334-324 BC
🏛	City Founded by Alexander		Other Town

Alexander the Great, son of Philip II, was a great warrior and empire builder of Macedonia

Note: Due to non-availability of sources, the present names of the water bodies are shown here.

AFRICA

Country: **ALGERIA,** *Capital:* **Algiers** *Area:* **2381.7,** *Population:* **35.0,** *Literacy:* **69.9,** *Currency:* **Algerian dinar,** ***Official*** *Language:* **Arabic,** *Nationality:* **Algerian(s)**

Country: **ANGOLA,** *Capital:* **Luanda** *Area:* **1246.7,** *Population:* **13.3,** *Literacy:* **67.4,** *Currency:* **Kwanza,** *Official Language:* **Portuguese,** *Nationality:* **Angolan(s)**

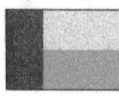

Country: **BENIN,** *Capital:* **Porto-Novo** *Area:* **112.6,** *Population:* **9.3,** *Literacy:* **34.7** *Currency:* **CFA franc,** *Official Language:* **French,** *Nationality:* **Beninese**

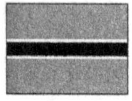

Country: **BOTSWANA,** *Capital:* **Gaborone,** *Area:* 581.7, *Population:* **2.1** *Literacy:* **81.2,** *Currency:* **Pulas,** *Official Language:* **Setswana, Kalanga Sekgalagadi & English,** *Nationality:* **Motswana (singular), Batswana (plural)**

Country: **BURKINA FASO,** *Capital:* **Ouagadougou,** *Area:* **274.2,** *Population:* **16.7,** *Literacy:* **21.8,** *Currency:* **CFA franc,** *Official Language:* **French,** *Nationality:* **Burkinabe**

Country: **BURUNDI,** *Capital:* **Bujumbura,** *Area:* **27.8,** *Population:* **9.0** *Literacy:* **59.3,** *Currency:* **Burundi franc** *Official Language:* **Kirundi, French,** *Nationality:* **Burundian(s)**

Country: **CAMEROON,** *Capital:* **Yaounde,** *Area:* **475.4,** *Population:* **19.7** *Literacy:* **67.9,** *Currency:* **CFA franc** *Official Language:* **English, French** *Nationality:* **Cameroonian(s)**

Country: **CAPE VERDE,** *Capital:* **Praia,** *Area:* **4.0,** *Population:* **0.5,** *Literacy:* **76.6** *Currency:* **Cape Verdean escudo,** *Official Language:* **Portuguese, Crioulo,** *Nationality:* **Cape Verdean(s)**

Country: **CENTRAL AFRICAN REPUBLIC,** *Capital:* **Bangui,** *Area:* **623.0,** *Population:* **4.5,** *Literacy:* **48.6** *Currency:* **CFA franc,** *Official Language:* **French, Sangho,** *Nationality:* **Central African(s)**

Country: **CHAD,** *Capital:* **N'Djamena** *Area:* **1284.0,** *Population:* **10.8,** *Literacy:* **25.7,** *Currency:* **CFA franc,** *Official Language:* **French , Arabic,** *Nationality:* **Chadian(s)**

Country: **COMOROS,** *Capital:* **Moroni** *Area:* **2.2,** *Population:* **0.8,** *Literacy:* **56.5,** *Currency:* **Comoran franc,** *Official Language:* **Arabic, French & Shikomoro,** *Nationality:* **Comoran(s)**

Country: **CONGO,** *Capital:* **Brazzaville,** *Area:* **342.0,** *Population:* **4.0** *Literacy:* **83.8,** *Currency:* **CFA franc,** *Official Language:* **French, Lingala & Monokutuba,** *Nationality:* **Congolese**

Country: **CONGO, DEMOCRATIC REPUBLIC OF,** *Capital:* **Kinshasa,** *Area:* **2345.4,** *Population:* **71.7,** *Literacy:* **67.2,** *Currency:* **Congolese franc,** *Official Language:* **French, Lingala & Kingwana,** *Nationality:* **Congolese**

Country: **COTE D'IVOIRE,** *Capital:* **Yamoussoukro,** *Area:* **322.5,** *Population:* **21.5,** *Literacy:* **48.7,** *Currency:* **CFA franc,** *Official Language:* **French, Dioula,** *Nationality:* **Ivoirian(s)**

Country: **DJIBOUTI,** *Capital:* **Djibouti** *Area:* **23.0,** *Population:* **0.8,** *Literacy:* **67.9,** *Currency:* **Djiboutian franc,** *Official Language:* **French, Arabic,** *Nationality:* **Djiboutian(s)**

Country: **EGYPT,** *Capital:* **Cairo,** *Area:* **1001.4,** *Population:* **82.1,** *Literacy:* **71.4** *Currency:* **Egyptian £,** *Official Language:* **Arabic,** *Nationality:* **Egyptian(s)**

Country: **EQUATORIAL GUINEA** *Capital:* **Malabo,** *Area:* **28.0,** *Population:* **0.7,** *Literacy:* **87.0,** *Currency:* **CFA franc,** *Official Language:* **Spanish, French,** *Nationality:* **Equatoguinean(s)**

Country: **ERITREA,** *Capital:* **Asmara** *Area:* **117.6,** *Population:* **5.9,** *Literacy:* **58.6,** *Currency:* **Nakfa,** *Official Language:* **Tigrinya, Arabic & English,** *Nationality:* **Eritrean(s)**

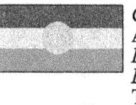

Country: **ETHIOPIA,** *Capital:* **Addis Ababa,** *Area:* **1104.3,** *Population:* **90.8,** *Literacy:* **42.7,** *Currency:* **Birr,** *Official Language:* **Amarigna,Orominga Tigrigna, English & Arabic,** *Nationality:* **Ethiopian(s)**

Country: **GABON,** *Capital:* **Libreville,** *Area:* **267.7,** *Population:* **1.6,** *Literacy:* **63.2,** *Currency:* **CFA franc,** *Official Language:* **French,** *Nationality:* **Gabonese**

Country: **GAMBIA, THE,** *Capital:* **Banjul,** *Area:* **11.3,** *Population:* **1.8,** *Literacy:* **40.1,** *Currency:* **Dalasi,** *Official Language:* **English,** *Nationality:* **Gambian(s)**

Country: **GHANA,** *Capital:* **Accra,** *Area:* **238.5,** *Population:* **24.8,** *Literacy:* **57.9,** *Currency:* **Cedi,** *Official language:* **English, Asante, Ewe & Fante,** *Nationality:* **Ghanaian(s)**

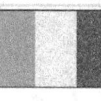

Country: **GUINEA,** *Capital:* **Conakry** *Area:* **245.8,** *Population:* **10.6,** *Literacy:* **29.5,** *Currency:* **Guinean franc,** *Official Language:* **French,** *Nationality:* **Guinean(s)**

Country: **GUINEA-BISSAU,** *Capital:* **Bissau,** *Area:* **36.1,** *Population:* **1.6** *Literacy:* **42.4,** *Currency:* **CFA franc** *Official Language:* **Portuguese** *Nationality:* **Guinean(s)**

Country: **KENYA,** *Capital:* **Nairobi,** *Area:* **580.4,** *Population:* **41.1,** *Literacy:* **85.1,** *Currency:* **Kenyan shilling,** *Official Language:* **English, Kiswahili,** *Nationality:* **Kenyan(s)**

Country: **LESOTHO,** *Capital:* **Maseru** *Area:* **30.3,** *Population:* **1.9,** *Literacy:* **84.8,** *Currency:* **Maloti,** *Official Language:* **English, Sesotho,** *Nationality:* **Mosotho (singular), Basotho (plural)**

Country: **LIBERIA,** *Capital:* **Monrovia** *Area:* **111.4,** *Population:* **3.8,** *Literacy:* **57.5,** *Currency:* **Liberian $,** *Official Language:* **English,** *Nationality:* **Liberian(s)**

Country: **LIBYA,** *Capital:* **Tripoli,** *Area:* **1759.5,** *Population:* **6.6,** *Literacy:* **82.6** *Currency:* **Libyan dinar,** *Official Language:* **Arabic, Italian & English,** *Nationality:* **Libyan(s)**

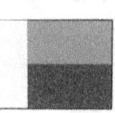

Country: **MADAGASCAR,** *Capital:* **Antananarivo,** *Area:* **587.0,** *Population:* **21.9,** *Literacy:* **68.9,** *Currency:* **Malagasy ariary,** *Official Language:* **French Malagasy,** *Nationality:* **Malagasy**

Country: **MALAWI,** *Capital:* **Lilongwe** *Area:* **118.5,** *Population:* **15.9,** *Literacy:* **62.7,** *Currency:* **Malawian kwacha** *Official Language:* **Chichewa** *Nationality:* **Malawian(s)**

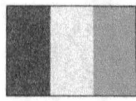

Country: **MALI,** *Capital:* **Bamako,** *Area:* **1240.1,** *Population:* **14.2,** *Literacy:* **46.4** *Currency:* **CFA franc,** *Official Language:* **French, Bambara,** *Nationality:* **Malian(s)**

Country: **MAURITANIA,** *Capital:* **Nouakchott,** *Area:* **1030.7,** *Population:* **3.3,** *Literacy:* **51.2,** *Currency:* **Ouguiya** *Official Language:* **Arabic,** *Nationality:* **Mauri tanian(s)**

Country: **MAURITIUS,** *Capital:* **Port Louis,** *Area:* **2.0,** *Population:* **1.3,** *Literacy:* **84.4,** *Currency:* **Mauritian rupee,** *Official Language:* **Creole, Bhojpuri, French & English,** *Nationality:* **Mauri tian(s)**

Country: **MOROCCO,** *Capital:* **Rabat** *Area:* **446.5,** *Population:* **32.0,** *Literacy:* **52.3,** *Currency:* **Moroccan dirham,** *Official Language:* **Arabic,** *Nationality:* **Moroccan(s)**

Country: **MOZAMBIQUE,** *Capital:* **Maputo,** *Area:* **799.4,** *Population:* **22.9** *Literacy:* **47.8,** *Currency:* **Metical** *Official Language:* **Portuguese, Emakhuwa Xichangana & Elomwe,** *Nationality:* **Mozambican(s)**

Country: **NAMIBIA,** *Capital:* **Windhoek,** *Area:* **824.2,** *Population:* **2.1** *Literacy:* **85.0,** *Currency:* **Namibian $** *Official Language:* **English, Afrikaan & German,** *Nationality:* **Namibian(s)**

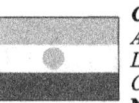

Country: **NIGER,** *Capital:* **Niamey,** *Area:* **1267.0,** *Population:* **16.5,** *Literacy:* **28.7** *Currency:* **CFA franc,** *Official Language:* **French,** *Nationality:* **Nigerien(s)**

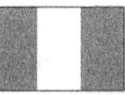

Country: **NIGERIA,** *Capital:* **Abuja** *Area:* **923.8,** *Population:* **155.2,** *Literacy:* **68.0,** *Currency:* **Naira,** *Official Language:* **English,** *Nationality:* **Nigerien(s)**

Country: **RWANDA,** *Capital:* **Kigali** *Area:* 26.3, *Population:* 11.4, *Literacy:* **70.4,** *Currency:* **Rwandan franc,** *Official Language:* **Kinyarwanda, French & English,** *Nationality:* **Rwandan(s)**

Country: **SAO TOME AND PRINCIPE,** *Capital:* **Sao Tome,** *Area:* **1.0,** *Population:* **0.2,** *Literacy:* **84.9** *Currency:* **Dobra,** *Official Language:* **Portuguese,** *Nationality:* **Sao Tomean(s)**

Country: **SENEGAL,** *Capital:* Dakar *Area:* **196.7,** *Population:* **12.6,** *Literacy:* **39.3,** *Currency:* **CFA franc,** *Official Language:* **French,** *Nationality:* **Senegalese**

Country: **SEYCHELLES,** *Capital:* **Victoria,** *Area:* **0.4,** *Population:* **0.09** *Literacy:* 91.8, *Currency:* **Seychelles rupee,** *Official Language:* **Creole English,** *Nationality:* **Seychellois**

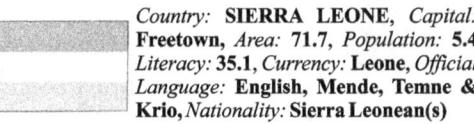

Country: **SIERRA LEONE**, *Capital:* **Freetown**, *Area:* **71.7**, *Population:* **5.4** *Literacy:* **35.1**, *Currency:* **Leone**, *Official Language:* **English, Mende, Temne & Krio**, *Nationality:* **Sierra Leonean(s)**

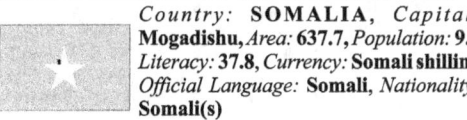

Country: **SOMALIA**, *Capital:* **Mogadishu**, *Area:* **637.7**, *Population:* **9.9** *Literacy:* **37.8**, *Currency:* **Somali shilling** *Official Language:* **Somali**, *Nationality:* **Somali(s)**

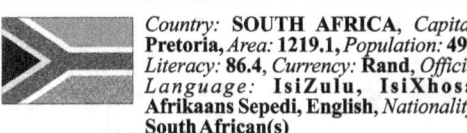

Country: **SOUTH AFRICA**, *Capital:* **Pretoria**, *Area:* **1219.1**, *Population:* **49.0** *Literacy:* **86.4**, *Currency:* **Rand**, *Official Language:* **IsiZulu, IsiXhosa, Afrikaans Sepedi, English**, *Nationality:* **South African(s)**

Country: **SOUTH SUDAN**, *Capital:* **Juba**, *Area:* **644.3**, *Population:* **8.3**, *Literacy:* **28.0**, *Currency:* **Sudanese £**, *Official Language:* **Arabic, English**, *Nationality:* **Sudanese**

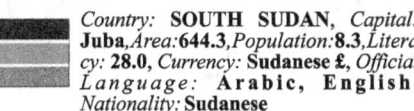

Country: **SUDAN**, *Capital:* **Khartoum** *Area:* **2505.8**, *Population:* **45.0**, *Literacy:* **61.1**, *Currency:* **Sudanese £**, *Official Language:* **Arabic, English**, *Nationality:* **Sudanese**

Country: **SWAZILAND**, *Capital:* **Mbabane**, *Area:* **17.4**, *Population:* **1.4**, *Literacy:* **81.6**, *Currency:* **Emalangeni**, *Official Language:* **English, si Swati**, *Nationality:* **Swazi(s)**

Country: **TANZANIA**, *Capital:* **Dodoma**, *Area:* **947.3**, *Population:* **42.7**, *Literacy:* **69.4**, *Currency:* **Tanzanian shilling**, *Official Language:* **Kiswahili English & Arabic**, *Nationality:* **Tanzanian(s)**

Country: **TOGO**, *Capital:* **Lome**, *Area:* **56.8**, *Population:* **6.7**, *Literacy:* **60.9**, *Currency:* **CFA franc**, *Official Language:* **French**, *Nationality:* **Togolese**

Country: **TUNISIA**, *Capital:* **Tunis**, *Area:* **163.6**, *Population:* **10.6**, *Literacy:* **74.3**, *Currency:* **Tunisian dinar**, *Official Language:* **Arabic, French**, *Nationality:* **Tunisian(s)**

Country: **UGANDA**, *Capital:* Kampala *Area:* **241.0**, *Population:* **34.6**, *Literacy:* **66.8**, *Currency:* **Ugandan shilling** *Official Language:* **English**, *Nationality:* **Ugandan(s)**

Country: **ZAMBIA**, *Capital:* **Lusaka**, *Area:* **752.6**, *Population:* **13.9**, *Literacy:* **80.6**, *Currency:* **Zambian kwacha**, *Official Language:* **Bemba, Nyanja Tonga, Lozi Lunda, Kaonde, Luvale & English**, *Nationality:* Zambian(s)

Country: **ZIMBABWE**, *Capital:* **Harare**, *Area:* **390.8**, *Population:* **12.1**, *Literacy:* **90.7**, *Currency:* **Zimbabwean $**, *Official Language:* **English**, *Nationality:* **Zimbabwean(s)**

ASIA

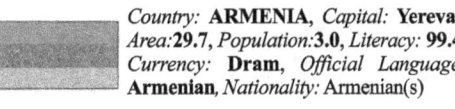

Country: **AFGHANISTAN**, *Capital:* **Kabul**, *Area:* **652.2**, *Population:* **29.8** *Literacy:* **28.1**, *Currency:* **Afghani**, *Official Language:* **Afghan persian (or) Dari, Pashto**, *Nationality:* **Afghan(s)**

Country: **ARMENIA**, *Capital:* **Yerevan** *Area:* **29.7**, *Population:* **3.0**, *Literacy:* **99.4**, *Currency:* **Dram**, *Official Language:* **Armenian**, *Nationality:* Armenian(s)

Country: **AZERBAIJAN**, *Capital:* **Baku**, *Area:* **86.6**, *Population:* **8.4**, *Literacy:* **98.8**, *Currency:* **Azerbaijani manat**, *Official Language:* **Azerbaijani (Azeri)**, *Nationality:* **Azerbaijani(s)**

Country: **BAHRAIN**, *Capital:* **Manama**, *Area:* **0.7**, *Population:* **12**, *Literacy:* **86.5**, *Currency:* **Bahraini dinar**, *Official Language:* **Arabic**, *Nationality:* **Bahraini(s)**

Country: **BANGLADESH**, *Capital:* **Dhaka**, *Area:* **144.0**, *Population:* **158.6** *Literacy:* **47.9**, *Currency:* **Taka**, *Official Language:* **Bangla**, *Nationality:* **Bangladeshi(s)**

Country: **BHUTAN**, *Capital:* **Thimphu** *Area:* **38.4**, *Population:* **0.7**, *Literacy:* **47.0**, *Currency:* **Ngultrum**, *Official Language:* **Dzongkha**, *Nationality:* **Bhutanese**

Country: **BRUNEI**, *Capital:* **Bandar Serf Begawan**, *Area:* **5.8**, *Population:* **0.4**, *Literacy:* **92.7**, *Currency:* **Bruneian $**, *Official Language:* **Malay**, *Nationality:* **Bruneian(s)**

Country: **CAMBODIA**, *Capital:* **Phnom Penh**, *Area:* **181.0**, *Population:* **14.7**, *Literacy:* **73.6**, *Currency:* **Riel**, *Official Language:* **Khmer**, *Nationality:* **Cambodian(s)**

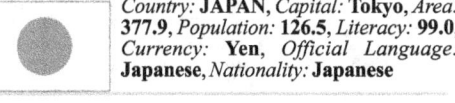

Country: **CHINA**, *Capital:* **Beijing**, *Area:* **9597.0**, *Population:* 1336.7, *Literacy:* **91.6**, *Currency:* **Renminbi yuan**, *Official Language:* **Mandarin, Yue, Wu & Minbei**, *Nationality:* **Chinese**

Country: **CYPRUS**, *Capital:* **Nicosia**, *Area:* **9.2**, *Population:* **1.1**, *Literacy:* **97.6**, *Currency:* **Turkish new lira**, *Official Language:* **Greek, Turkish & English** *Nationality:* **Cypriot(s)**

Country: **GEORGIA**, *Capital:* **Tbilisi** *Area:* **69.7**, *Population:* **4.6**, *Literacy:* **100.0**, *Currency:* **Lari**, *Official Language:* **Georgian, Russian & Armenian** *Nationality:* Georgian(s)

Country: **EAST TIMOR**, *Capital:* **Dili** *Area:* **15.0**, *Population:* **1.2**, *Literacy:* **58.6**, *Currency:* **US $**, *Official Language:* **Tetum, Portuguese**, *Nationality:* **Timorese**

Country: **INDIA**, *Capital:* **Delhi**, *Area:* **3287.3**, *Population:* **1210.2**, *Literacy:* **74.0**, *Currency:* **₹**, *Official Language:* **Hindi, English**, *Nationality:* **Indian(s)**

Country: **INDONESIA**, *Capital:* **Jakarta** *Area:* 1905.0, *Population:* 245.6, *Literacy:* **90.4**, *Currency:* **Indonesian rupiah** *Official Language:* Bahasa Indonesia **English & Dutch**, *Nationality:* **Indonesian(s)**

Country: **IRAN**, *Capital:* **Tehran**, *Area:* **1648.2**, *Population:* **77.9**, *Literacy:* **77.0** *Currency:* **Iranian rial**, *Official Language:* **Persian, Turkic & Kurdish**, *Nationality:* **Iranian(s)**

Country: **IRAQ**, *Capital:* **Baghdad**, *Area:* **438.3**, *Population:* **30.4**, *Literacy:* **74.1**, *Currency:* **Iraqi dinar**, *Official Language:* **Arabic, Kurdish**, *Nationality:* **Iraqi(s)**

Country: **ISRAEL**, *Capital:* **Jerusalem** *Area:* **20.8**, *Population:* **7.5**, *Literacy:* **97.1**, *Currency:* **New Israeli shekel**, *Official Language:* **Hebrew, Arabic**, *Nationality:* **Israeli(s)**

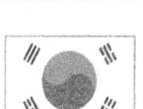

Country: **JAPAN**, *Capital:* **Tokyo**, *Area:* **377.9**, *Population:* **126.5**, *Literacy:* **99.0**, *Currency:* **Yen**, *Official Language:* **Japanese**, *Nationality:* **Japanese**

Country: **JORDAN**, *Capital:* **Amman**, *Area:* **89.3**, *Population:* **6.5**, *Literacy:* **89.9**, *Currency:* **Jordania dinar**, *Official Language:* **Arabic**, *Nationality:* **Jordanian(s)**

Country: **KAZAKHSTAN**, *Capital:* **Astana**, *Area:* **2724.9**, *Population:* **15.5**, *Literacy:* **99.5**, *Currency:* **Tenge**, *Official Language:* **Kazakh, Russian**, *Nationality:* **Kazakhstani(s)**

Country: **KOREA, NORTH**, *Capital:* **Pyongyang**, *Area:* **120.5**, *Population:* **24.5**, *Literacy:* **99.0**, *Currency:* **North Korean won**, *Official Language:* **Korean**, *Nationality:* **Korean(s)**

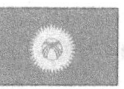

Country: **KOREA, SOUTH**, *Capital:* **Seoul**, *Area:* **99.7**, *Population:* **48.7**, *Literacy:* **97.9**, *Currency:* **South Korean won**, *Official Language:* **Korean**, **English** *Nationality:* **Korean(s)**

Country: **KUWAIT**, *Capital:* **Kuwait**, *Area:* **17.8**, *Population:* **2.6**, *Literacy:* **93.3**, *Currency:* **Kuwaiti dinar**, *Official Language:* **Arabic**, *Nationality:* **Kuwaiti(s)**

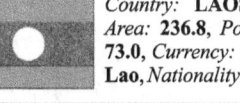

Country: **KYRGYZSTAN**, *Capital:* **Bishkek**, *Area:* **199.9**, *Population:* **5.6**, *Literacy:* **98.7**, *Currency:* **Som**, *Official Language:* **Kyrgyz, Russian & Uzbek**, *Nationality:* **Kyrgyzstani(s)**

Country: **LAOS**, *Capital:* **Vientiane**, *Area:* **236.8**, *Population:* **6.5**, *Literacy:* **73.0**, *Currency:* **Kip**, *Official Language:* **Lao**, *Nationality:* **Lao(s) or Laotian(s)**

Country: **LEBANON**, *Capital:* **Beirut**, *Area:* **10.4**, *Population:* **4.1**, *Literacy:* **87.4**, *Currency:* **Lebanese £**, *Official Language:* **Arabic**, *Nationality:* **Lebanese**

Country. **MALAYSIA**, *Capital:* **Kuala Lumpur**, *Area:* **329.8**, *Population:* **28.7**, *Literacy:* **88.7**, *Currency:* **ringgit**, *Official Language:* **Bahasa Malaysia**, *Nationality:* **Malaysian(s)**

Country: **MALDIVES**, *Capital:* **Male**, *Area:* **0.3**, *Population:* **0.4**, *Literacy:* **93.8**, *Currency:* **rufiyaa**, *Official Language:* **Maldivian Dhivehi**, *Nationality:* **Maldivian(s)**

Country: **MONGOLIA**, *Capital:* **Ulan Bator**, *Area:* **1564.1**, *Population:* **3.1**, *Literacy:* **97.8**, *Currency:* **Togrok/Tugrik**, *Official Language:* **Khalkha Mongol**, *Nationality:* **Mongolian(s)**

Country: **MYANMAR**, *Capital:* **Naypyidaw**, *Area:* 677.0, *Population:* 54.0 *Literacy:* **89.9**, *Currency:* **kyat**, *Official Language:* **Burmese**, *Nationality:* **Burmese**

Country: **NEPAL**, Capital: **Kathmandu**, Area: **147.2**, Population: **29.4**, Literacy: **48.6**, Currency: **Nepalese rupee**, Official Language: **Nepali, Maithali & Bhojpuri**, Nationality: Nepalese

Country: **OMAN**, Capital: **Muscat**, Area: **309.5**, Population: **3.0**, Literacy: **81.4**, Currency: **Omani rial**, Official Language: **Arabic**, Nationality: **Omani(s)**

Country: **PAKISTAN**, Capital: **Islamabad**, Area: **796.1**, Population: **187.3**, Literacy: **49.9**, Currency: **Pakistani rupee**, Official Language: **Urdu, Punjabi, Sindhi, Siraiki & Pashtu**, Nationality: **Pakistani(s)**

Country: **PHILIPPINES**, Capital: **Manila**, Area: **300.0**, Population: **101.8**, Literacy: **92.6**, Currency: **Philippine peso**, Official Language: **Filipino English**, Nationality: **Filipino(s)**

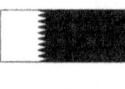
Country: **QATAR**, Capital: **Doha**, Area: **11.6**, Population: **0.8**, Literacy: **89.0**, Currency: **Qatari riyal**, Official Language: **Arabic**, Nationality: **Qatari(s)**

Country: **RUSSIA**, Capital: **Moscow**, Area: **17098.2**, Population: **138.7**, Literacy: **99.4**, Currency: **Russian ruble**, Official Language: **Russian**, Nationality: **Russian(s)**

Country: **SAUDI ARABIA**, Capital: **Riyadh**, Area: **2149.7**, Population: **26.1**, Literacy: **78.8**, Currency: **Saudi riyal**, Official Language: **Arabic**, Nationality: **Saudi(s)**

Country: **SINGAPORE**, Capital: **Singapore**, Area: **0.7**, Population: **4.7**, Literacy: **92.5**, Currency: **Singapore $**, Official Language: **Mandarin, English, Malay & Hokkien & Tamil**, Nationality: **Singaporean(s)**

Country: **SRI LANKA**, Capital: **Colombo**, Area: **65.6**, Population: **21.3**, Literacy: **90.7**, Currency: **Sri Lankan rupee**, Official Language: **Sinhala, Tamil**, Nationality: **Sri Lankan(s)**

Country: **SYRIA**, Capital: **Damascus**, Area: **185.2**, Population: **22.5**, Literacy: **79.6**, Currency: **Syrian £**, Official Language: **Arabic**, Nationality: **Syrian(s)**

Country: **TAIWAN**, Capital: **Taipei**, Area: **36.0**, Population: **23.1**, Literacy: **96.1**, Currency: **New Taiwan $**, Official Language: **Mandarin Chinese**, Nationality: **Taiwanese**

Country: **TAJIKISTAN**, Capital: **Dushanbe**, Area: **143.1**, Population: **7.6**, Literacy: **99.5**, Currency: **Tajikistani somoni**, Official Language: **Tajik**, Nationality: **Tajikistani(s)**

Country: **THAILAND**, Capital: **Bangkok**, Area: **513.1**, Population: **66.7**, Literacy: **92.6**, Currency: **baht**, Official Language: **Thai, English**, Nationality: **Thai**

Country: **TURKEY**, Capital: **Ankara**, Area: **783.6**, Population: **78.8**, Literacy: **87.4**, Currency: **Turkish lira**, Official Language: **Turkish**, Nationality: **Turk(s)**

Cotmfn/: **TURKMENISTAN**, Capital: **Ashgabat**, Area: **488.1**, Population: **5.0**, Literacy: **98.8**, Currency: **Turkmen manat**, Official Language: **Turkmen Russian & Uzbek**, Nationality: **Turkmen(s)**

Country: **UNITED ARAB EMIRATES**, Capital: **Abu Dhabi**, Area: **83.6**, Population: **5.2**, Literacy: **77.9**, Currency: **Emirati dirham**, Official Language: **Arabic**, Nationality: **Emirati(s)**

Country: **UZBEKISTAN**, Capital: **Toshkent**, Area: **447.4**, Population: **28.1**, Literacy: **99.3**, Currency: **Uzbekistani soum**, Official Language: **Uzbek Russian**, Nationality: **Uzbekistani**

Country: **VIETNAM**, Capital: **Hanoi**, Area: **331.2**, Population: **90.5**, Literacy: **90.3**, Currency: **Dong**, Official Language: **Vietnamese**, Nationality: **Vietnamese**

Country: **YEMEN**, Capital: **San'a**, Area: **528.0**, Population: **24.1**, Literacy: **50.2**, Currency: **Yemeni riyal**, Official Language: **Arabic**, Nationality: **Yemeni(s)**

AUSTRALIA AND OCEANIA

Country: **AUSTRALIA**, Capital: **Canberra**, Area: **7741.2**, Population: **21.8**, Literacy: **99.0**, Currency: **Australian $**, Official Language: **English**, Nationality: **Australian(s)**

Country: **FIJI**, Capital: **Suva**, Area: **18.3**, Population: **0.9**, Literacy: **93.7**, Currency: **Fijian $**, Official Language: **English, Fijian**, Nationality: **Fijian(s)**

Country: **KIRIBATI**, Capital: **Tarawa**, Area: **0.8**, Population: **0.10**, Literacy: **95.0**, Currency: **Australian $**, Official Language: **I-Kiribati, English**, Nationality: **I-Kiribati**

Country: **MARSHALL ISLANDS**, Capital: **Majuro**, Area: **0.2**, Population: **0.07**, Literacy: **93.7**, Currency: **US $**, Official Language: **Marshallese, English**, Nationality: **Marshallese**

Country: **MICRONESIA FEDERATED STATES OF**, Capital: **Palikir**, Area: **0.7**, Population: **0.1**, Literacy: **89.0**, Currency: **US $**, Official Language: **English**, Nationality: **Micronesian(s)**

Country: **NAURU**, Capital: **Yaren**, Area: **0.02**, Population: **0.01**, Literacy: **97.0**, Currency: **Australian $**, Official Language: **Nauruan, English**, Nationality: **Nauruan(s)**

Country: **NEW ZEALAND**, Capital: **Wellington**, Area: **268.7**, Population: **4.3**, Literacy: **99.0**, Currency: **New Zealand $**, Official Language: **English, Maori & Sign**, Nationality: **New Zealander(s)**

Country: **PALAU**, Capital: **Melekeok**, Area: **0.5**, Population: **0.02**, Literacy: **92.0**, Currency: **US $**, Official Language: **Palauan, Sonsoralese, Tobi, Angaur Japanese & English**, Nationality: **Palauan(s)**

Country: **PAPUA NEW GUINEA**, Capital: **Port Moresby**, Area: **462.8**, Population: **6.2**, Literacy: **57.3**, Currency: **kina**, Official Language: **Tok Pisin English & Hiri Motu**, Nationality: **Papua New Guinean(s)**

Country: **SAMOA**, Capital: **Apia**, Area: **2.8**, Population: **0.2**, Literacy: **99.7**, Currency: **Tala**, Official Language: **Samoan, English**, Nationality: **Samoan(s)**

Country: **SOLOMON ISLANDS**, Capital: **Honiara**, Area: **28.9**, Population: **0.6**, Literacy: **76.6**, Currency: **Solomon Islands $**, Official Language: **English Melanesian Pidgin**, Nationality: **Solomon Islander(s)**

Country: **TONGA**, Capital: **Nuku'alofa**, Area: **0.7**, Population: **0.1**, Literacy: **98.9**, Currency: **Pa'anga**, Official Language: **Tongan, English**, Nationality: **Tongan(s)**

Country: **TUVALU**, Capital: **Funafuti**, Area: **0.02**, Population: **0.01**, Literacy: **95.0**, Currency: **Tuvaluan $ or Australian $**, Official Language: **Tuvaluan, English**, Nationality: **Tuvaluan(s)**

Country: **VANUATU**, Capital: **Port Vila**, Area: **12.2**, Population: **0.2**, Literacy: **74.0**, Currency: **Vatu**, Official Language: **Bislama, English & French**, Nationality: **Ni-Vanuatu**

EUROPE

Country: **ALBANIA**, Capital: **Tirana**, Area: **28.7**, Population: **3.0**, Literacy: **98.7**, Currency: **Leke**, Official Language: **Albanian**, Nationality: **Albanian(s)**

Country: **ANDORRA**, Capital: **Andorra la Vella**, Area: **0.5**, Population: **0.08**, Literacy: **100.0**, Currency: **Euro**, Official Language: **Catalan**, Nationality: **Andorran(s)**

Country: **AUSTRIA**, Capital: **Vienna**, Area: **83.9**, Population: **8.2**, Literacy: **98.0**, Currency: **Euro**, Official Language: **German, Croatian, Slovene & Hungarian**, Nationality: **Austrian(s)**

Country: **BELARUS**, Capital: **Minsk**, Area: **207.6**, Population: **9.6**, Literacy: **99.6**, Currency: **Belarusian ruble**, Official Language: **Belarusian, Russian**, Nationality: **Belarusian(s)**

Country: **BELGIUM**, Capital: **Brussels**, Area: **30.5**, Population: **10.4**, Literacy: **99.0**, Currency: **Euro**, Official Language: **Dutch, French & German**, Nationality: **Belgian(s)**

Country: **BOSNIA-HERZEGOVINA** *Capital:* **Sarajevo**, *Area:* **51.2**, *Population:* **4.6**, *Literacy:* **96.7**, *Currency:* **Konvertibilna Marka**, *Official Language:* **Bosnian, Croatian & Serbian**, *Nationality:* **Bosnian(s) Herzegovinian(s)**

Country: **BULGARIA**, *Capital:* **Sofia**, *Area:* **110.9**, *Population:* **7.1**, *Literacy:* **98.2**, *Currency:* **Lev**, *Official Language:* **Bulgarian, Turkish & Roma**, *Nationality:* **Bulgarian(s)**

Country: **CROATIA**, *Capital:* **Zagreb**, *Area:* **56.5**, *Population:* **4.5**, *Literacy:* **98.1**, *Currency:* **Kuna**, *Official Language:* **Croatian, Serbian**, *Nationality:* **Croat(s), Croatian(s)**

Country: **CZECH REPUBLIC**, *Capital:* **Prague**, *Area:* **78.9**, *Population:* **10.2**, *Literacy:* **99.0**, *Currency:* **koruny**, *Official Language:* **Czech, Slovak**, *Nationality:* **Czech(s)**

Country: **DENMARK**, *Capital:* **Copenhagen**, *Area:* **43.1**, *Population:* **5.5**, *Literacy:* **99.0**, *Currency:* **Danish kroner**, *Official Language:* **Danish, Faroese Greenlandic & English**, *Nationality:* **Dane(s)**

Country: **ESTONIA**, *Capital:* **Tallinn** *Area:* **45.2**, *Population:* **1.3**, *Literacy:* **99.8**, *Currency:* **kroon**, *Official Language:* **Estonian, Russian**, *Nationality:* **Estonian(s)**

Country: **FINLAND**, *Capital:* **Helsinki** *Area:* **338.1**, *Population:* **5.3**, *Literacy:* **100.0**, *Currency:* **Euro**, *Official Language:* **Finnish, Swedish**, *Nationality:* **Finn(s)**

Country: **FRANCE**, *Capital:* **Paris**, *Area:* **551.5**, *Population:* **65.3**, *Literacy:* **99.0**, *Currency:* **Euro**, *Official Language:* **French**, *Nationality:* **Frenchman(men) Frenchwoman (women)**

Country: **GERMANY**, *Capital:* **Berlin**, *Area:* **357.0**, *Population:* **81.5**, *Literacy:* **99.0**, *Currency:* **Euro**, *Official Language:* **German**, *Nationality:* **German(s)**

Country: **GREECE**, *Capital:* **Athens**, *Area:* **132.0**, *Population:* **10.8**, *Literacy:* **96.0**, *Currency:* **Euro**, *Official Language:* **Greek**, *Nationality:* **Greek(s)**

Country: **HUNGARY**, *Capital:* **Budapest**, *Area:* **93.0**, *Population:* **10.0**, *Literacy:* **99.4**, *Currency:* **Forint**, *Official Language:* **Hungarian**, *Nationality:* **Hungarian(s)**

Country: **ICELAND**, *Capital:* **Reykjavik**, *Area:* **103.0**, *Population:* **0.3** *Literacy:* **99.0**, *Currency:* **Icelandic kronur**, *Official Language:* **Icelandic English, Nordic & German**, *Nationality:* **Icelander(s)**

Country: **IRELAND**, *Capital:* **Dublin**, *Area:* **70.3**, *Population:* **4.4**, *Literacy:* **99.0**, *Currency:* **Euro**, *Official Language:* **English, Irish**, *Nationality:* **Irish**

Country: **ITALY**, *Capital:* **Rome**, *Area:* **301.3**, *Population:* **61.0**, *Literacy:* **98.4**, *Currency:* **Euro**, *Official Language:* **Italian**, *Nationality:* **Italian(s)**

Country: **KOSOVO**, *Capital:* **Pristina**, *Area:* **10.9**, *Population:* **1.8**, *Literacy:* **91.9**, *Currency:* **Euro**, *Official Language:* **Albanian & Serbanian**, *Nationality:* **Kosovar (Albanian), Kosovac (Serbian)**

Country: **LATVIA**, *Capital:* **Riga**, *Area:* **64.6**, *Population:* **2.2**, *Literacy:* **99.7**, *Currency:* **lat**, *Official Language:* **Latvian, Russian**, *Nationality:* **Latvian(s)**

Country: **LIECHTENSTEIN**, *Capital:* **Vaduz**, *Area:* **0.16**, *Population:* **0.03**, *Literacy:* **100.0**, *Currency:* **Swiss franc**, *Official Language:* **German**, *Nationality:* **Liechtensteiner(s)**

Country: **LITHUANIA**, *Capital:* **Vilnius**, *Area:* **65.3**, *Population:* **3.5**, *Literacy:* **99.6**, *Currency:* **Litas**, *Official Language:* **Lithuanian**, *Nationality:* **Lithuanian(s)**

Country: **LUXEMBOURG**, *Capita/:* **Luxembourg**, *Area:* **2.6**, *Population:* **0.5**, *Literacy:* **100.0**, *Currency:* **Euro**, *Official Language:* **Luxembourgish, French & German**, *Nationality:* **Luxembouxger(s)**

Country: **MACEDONIA**, *Capital:* **Skopje**, *Area:* **25.7**, *Population:* **2.1**, *Literacy:* **96.1**, *Currency:* **Macedonian denar**, *Official Language:* **Macedonian Albanian**, *Nationality:* **Macedonian(s)**

Country: **MALTA**, *Capital:* **Valletta** *Area:* **0.3**, *Population:* **0.4**, *Literacy:* **92.8**, *Currency:* **Titixo**, *Official Language:* **Maltese, English**, *Nationality:* **Maltese**

Country: **MOLDOVA**, *Capital:* **j Chisinau**, *Area:* **33.8**, *Population:* **4.3**, *Literacy:* **99.1**, *Currency:* **Moldovan leu**, *Official Language:* **Moldovan**, *Nationality:* **Moldovan(s)**

Country: **MONACO**, *Capital:* **Monaco-Ville**, *Area:* **0.002**, *Population:* **0.03** *Literacy:* **99.0**, *Currency:* **Euro**, *Official Language:* **French**, *Nationality:* **Monegasque(s) or Monacan(s)**

Country: **MONTENEGRO**, *Capital:* **j Podgorica**, *Area:* **14.0**, *Population:* **0.7**, *Literacy:* **97.0**, *Currency:* **Euro**, *Official Language:* **Serbian, Montenegro** *Nationality:* **Montenegrin(s)**

Country: **NETHERLANDS**, *Capital:* **Amsterdam**, *Area:* **41.5**, *Population:* **16.8**, *Literacy:* **99.0**, *Currency:* **Euro**, *Official Language:* **Dutch, Frisian**, *Nationality:* **Dutchman (men.), Dutchwoman (women)**

Country: **NORWAY**, *Capital:* **Oslo**, *Area:* **323.8**, *Population:* **4.7**, *Literacy:* **100.0**, *Currency:* **Norwegian krone**, *Official Language:* **Bokmal Norwegian Nynorsk Norwegian & Sami**, *Nationality:* **Norwegian(s)**

Country: **POLAND**, *Capital:* **Warsaw** *Area:* **312.7**, *Population:* **38.4**, *Literacy:* **99.8**, *Currency:* **Zloty**, *Official Language:* **Polish**, *Nationality:* **Pole(s)**

Country: **PORTUGAL**, *Capital:* **Lisbon**, *Area:* **92.1**, *Population:* **10.8**, *Literacy:* **93.3**, *Currency:* **Euro**, *Official Language:* **Portuguese, Mirandese**, *Nationality:* **Portuguese**

Country: **ROMANIA**, *Capital:* **Bucharest**, *Area:* **238.4**, *Population:* **21.9**, *Literacy:* **97.3**, *Currency:* **Leu**, *Official Language:* **Romanian**, *Nationality:* **Romania n(s)**

Country: **SAN MARINO**, *Capital:* **San Marino**, *Area:* **0.06**, *Population:* **0.03**, *Literacy:* **96.0**, *Currency:* **Euro**, *Official Language:* **Italian**, *Nationality:* **Sami**

Country: **SERBIA**, *Capital:* **Belgrade** *Area:* **77.5**, *Population:* **7.3**, *Literacy:* **96.4**, *Currency:* **Serbian dinar**, *Official Language:* **Serbian, Romanian Hungarian, Slovak, Ukrainian & Croatian**, *Nationality:* **Seib(s)**

Country: **SLOVAKIA**, *Capital:* **Bratislava**, *Area:* **49.0**, *Population:* **5.5**, *Literacy:* **99.6**, *Currency:* **Slovak koruna**, *Official Language:* **Slovak, Hungarian** *Nationality:* **Slovak(s)**

Country: **SLOVENIA**, *Capital:* **Ljubljana**, *Area:* **20.3**, *Population:* **2.0**, *Literacy:* **99.7**, *Currency:* **Euro**, *Official Language:* **Slovenian, Serbo-Croatian Italian & Hungarian**, *Nationality:* **Slovene(s)**

Country: **SPAIN**, *Capital:* **Madrid**, *Area:* **505.4**, *Population:* **46.7**, *Literacy:* **97.9**, *Currency:* **Euro**, *Official Language:* **Castilian Spanish, Catalan, Galician**

Country: **SWEDEN**, *Capital:* **Stockholm** *Area:* **450.3**, *Population:* **9.1**, *Literacy:* **99.0**, *Currency:* **Swedish krona**, *Official Language:* **Swedish Sami & Finnish** *Nationality:* **Swede(s)**

Country: **SWITZERLAND**, *Capital:* **Bern**, *Area:* **41.3**, *Population:* **7.6**, *Literacy:* **99.0**, *Currency:* **Swiss franc**, *Official Language:* **German, French, Italian & Romansch**. *Nationality:* **Swiss**

Country: **UKRAINE**, *Capital:* **Kiev** *Area:* **603.5**, *Population:* **45.1**, *Literacy:* **99.4**, *Currency:* **Hryvnia**, *Official Language:* **Ukrainian, Russian** *Nationality:* **Ukrainian(s)**

Country: **UNITED KINGDOM**, *Capital:* **London**, *Area:* **244.8**, *Population:* **62.7**, *Literacy:* **99.0**, *Currency:* **British £**, *Official Language:* **English, Welsh & Scottish** *Nationality:* **British**

Country: **VATICAN CITY**, *Capital:* **Vatican City**, *Area:* **0.0004**, *Population:* **0.0008**, *Literacy:* **100.0**, *Currency:* **Euro**, *Official Language:* **Italian, Latin & French**, *Nationality:* **none**

NORTH AMERICA

Country: **ANTIGUA AND BARBUDA**, *Capital:* **Saint John's**, *Area:* **0.4**, *Population:* **0.08**, *Literacy:* **85.8**, *Currency:* **E. Caribbean $**, *Official Language:* **English**, *Nationality:* **Antiguan(s), Barbudan(s)**

Country: **BAHAMAS, THE**, *Capital:* **Nassau**, *Area:* **13.9**, *Population:* **0.3**, *Literacy:* **95.6**, *Currency:* **Bahamian $**, *Official Language:* **English**, *Nationality:* **Bahamian(s)**

Country: **BARBADOS**, *Capital:* **Bridgetown**, *Area:* **0.4**, *Population:* **0.3**, *Literacy:* **99.7**, *Currency:* **Barbadian $**, *Official Language:* **English**, *Nationality:* **Barbadian(s) or Bajan (colloquial)**

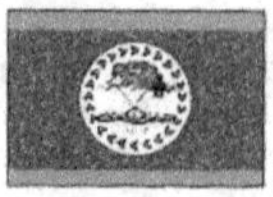
Country: **BELIZE,** *Capital:* **Belmopan** *Area:* **23.0,** *Population:* **0.3,** *Literacy:* **76.9,** *Currency:* **Belizean $,** *Official Language:* **Spanish, Creole, Mayan & English,** *Nationality:* **Belizean(s)**

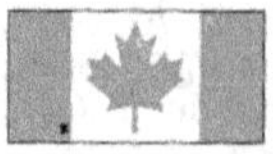
Country: **CANADA,** *Capital:* **Ottawa** *Area:* **9984.7,** *Population:* **34.0,** *Literacy:* **99.0,** *Currency:* **Canadian $,** *Official Language:* **English, French,** *Nationality:* **Canadian(s)**

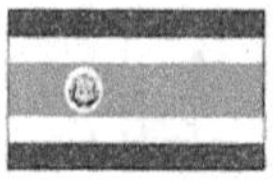
Country: **COSTA RICA,** *Capital:* **San Jose,** *Area:* **51.1,** *Population:* **4.6,** *Literacy:* **94.9,** *Currency:* **Costa Rican colon,** *Official Language:* **Spanish, English,** *Nationality:* **Costa Rican(s)**

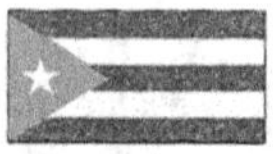
Country: **CUBA,** *Capital:* **Havana,** *Area:* **110.9,** *Population:* **11.1,** *Literacy:* **99.8,** *Currency:* **Cuban peso & Cuban convertible peso,** *Official Language:* **Spanish,** *Nationality:* **Cuban(s)**

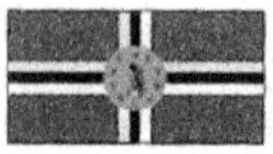
Country: **DOMINICA,** *Capital:* **Roseau** *Aea:* **0.7,** *Population:* **0.07,** *Literacy:* **94.0,** *Currency:* **E. Caribbean $,** *Official Language:* **English,** *Nationality:* **Dominican(s)**

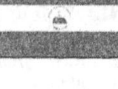

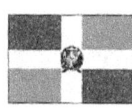

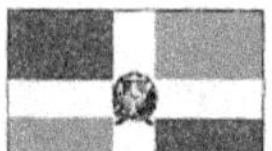
Country: **DOMINICAN REPUBLIC** *Capital:* **Santo Domingo,** *Area:* **48.7** *Population:* **10.0,** *Literacy:* **87.0,** *Currency:* **Dominican peso,** *Official Language:* **Spanish,** *Nationality:* **Dominican(s)**

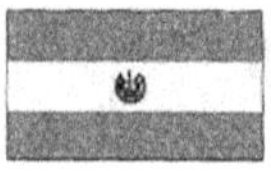
Country: **EL SALVADOR,** *Capital:* **San** Salvador, *Area:* **21.0,** *Population:* **6.1** *Literacy:* **81.1,** *Currency:* **US $,** *Official Language:* **Spanish, Nahua,** *Nationality:* **Salvadoran(s)**

Country: **GRENADA,** *Capital:* **Saint George's,** *Area:* **0.3,** *Population:* **0.1** *Literacy:* **96.0,** *Currency:* **E. Caribbean $** *Official Language:* **English,** *Nationality:* **Grenadian(s)**

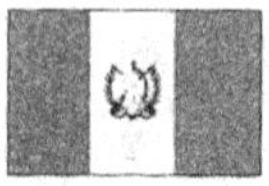
Country: **GUATEMALA,** *Capital:* **Guatemala City,** *Area:* **108.9,** *Population:* **13.8,** *Literacy:* **69.1,** *Currency:* **Quetzal** *Official Language:* **Spanish, Amerindian** *Nationality:* **Guatemalan (s)**

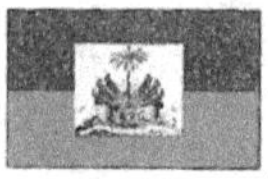
Country: **HAITI,** *Capital:* **Port-au-Prince,** *Area:* **27.7,** *Population:* **9.7** *Literacy:* **52.9,** *Currency:* **Gourde,** *Official Language:* **French, Creole,** *Nationality:* **Haitian(s)**

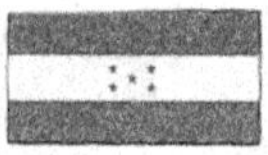
Country: **HONDURAS,** *Capital:* **Tegucigalpa,** *Area:* **112.1,** *Population:* **8.1** *Literacy:* **80.0,** *Currency:* **lempira,** *Official Language:* **Spanish, Amerindian,** *Nationality:* **Honduran(s)**

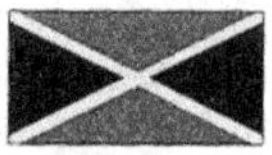
Country: **JAMAICA,** *Capital:* **Kingston** *Area:* **11.0,** *Population:* **2.9,** *Literacy:* 87.9 *Currency:* **Jamaican $,** *Official Language:* **English, English Patois,** *Nationality:* **Jamaican(s)**

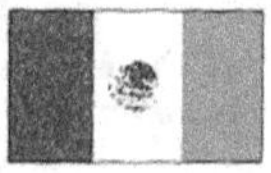
Country: **MEXICO,** *Capital:* **Mexico** City, *Area:* **1964.4,** *Population:* **113.7** *Literacy:* **86.1,** *Currency:* **Mexican peso** *Official Language:* **Spanish,** *Nationality:* **Mexican(s)**

Country: **NICARAGUA,** *Capital:* **Managua,** *Area:* **130.4,** *Population:* **5.7** *Literacy:* **67.5,** *Currency:* **cordoba** *Official Language:* **Spanish,** *Nationality:* **Nicaraguan(s)**

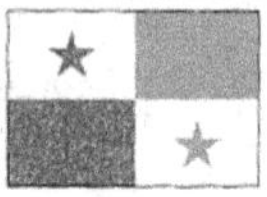
Country: **PANAMA,** *Capital:* **Panama City,** *Area:* **75.4,** *Population:* **3.5,** *Literacy:* **91.9,** *Currency:* **Balboa,** *Official Language:* **Spanish, English** *Nationality:* **Panamanian(s)**

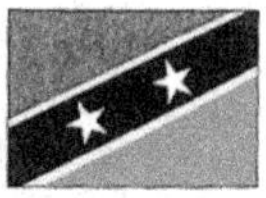
Country: **SAINT KITTS AND NEVIS** *Capital:* **Basseterre,** *Area:* **0.3,** *Population:* **0.05,** *Literacy:* **97.8,** *Currency:* **E. Caribbean $,** *Official Language:* **English,** *Nationality:* **Kittitian(s) Nevisian(s)**

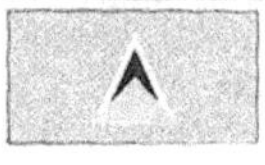
Country: **SAINT LUCIA,** *Capital:* **Castries,** *Area:* **0.6,** *Population:* **0.2** *Literacy:* **90.1,** Currency: **E. Caribbean $** *Official Language:* **English,** *Nationality:* **Saint Lucian(s)**

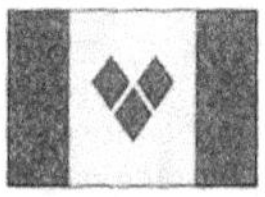
Country: **SAINT VINCENT AND THE GRENADINES,** *Capital:* **Kingstown** *Area:* **0.4,** *Population:* **0.1** *Literacy:* **96.0** *Currency:* **E. Caribbean $,** *Official Language:* **English, French Patois** *Nationality:* **Saint Vincentian(s) or Viti(s)**

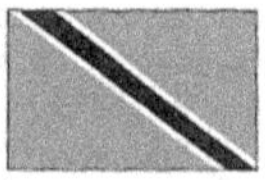
Country: **TRINIDAD AND TOBAGO** *Capital:* **Port of Spain,** *Area:* **5.1,** *Population:* **1.2,** *Literacy:* **98.6,** *Currency:* **Trinidad and Tobago $,** *Official Language:* **English,** *Nationality:* **Trinidadian(s), Tobagonian(s)**

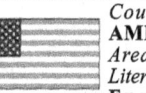

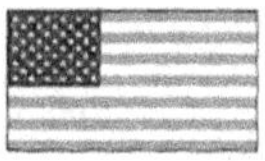
Country: **UNITED STATES OF AMERICA,** *Capital:* **Washington,** *Area:* **9826.7,** *Population:* **313.2,** *Literacy:* **99.0** *Currency:* **US $,** *Official* **English, Spanish & Hawaiian** *Nationality:* **American(s)**

SOUTH AMERICA

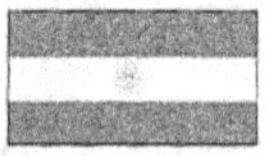
Country: **ARGENTINA,** *Capital:* **Buenos Aires,** *Area:* **2780.4,** *Population:* **41.8,** *Literacy:* **97.2,** *Currency:* **Argentine peso,** *Official Language:* **Spanish,** *Nationality:* **Argentine(s)**

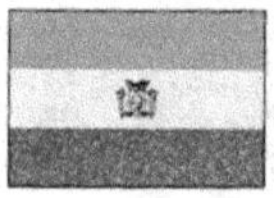
Country: **BOLIVIA,** *Capital:* **La Paz,** *Area:* **1098.6,** *Population:* **10.1,** *Literacy:* **86.7,** *Currency:* **Boliviano,** *Official Language:* **Spanish, Quechua & Aymara,** *Nationality:* **Bolivian(s)**

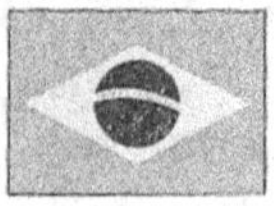
Country: **BRAZIL,** *Capital:* **Brasilia** ***Ana:*** **8514.9,** *Population:* **203.4,** *Literacy:* **88.6,** *Currency:* **Real,** *Official Language:* **Portuguese,** *Nationality:* **Brazilian(s)**

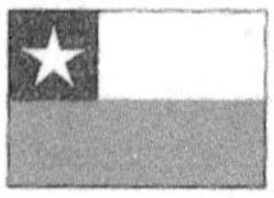
Country: **CHILE,** *Capital:* **Santiago** *Area:* **756.1,** *Population:* **16.9,** *Literacy:* **95.7,** *Currency:* **Chilean peso,** *Official Language:* **Spanish,** *Nationality:* **Chilean(s)**

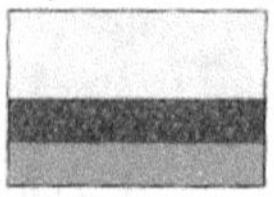
Country: **COLOMBIA,** *Capital:* **Bogota** *Area:* **1138.9,** *Population:* **44.7,** *Literacy:* **90.4,** *Currency:* **Colombian peso,** *Official Language:* **Spanish,** *Nationality:* **Colombian(s)**

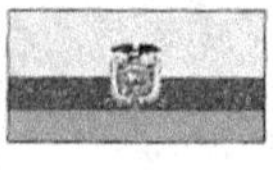
Country: **ECUADOR,** *Capital:* **Quito** *Area:* **283.6,** *Population:* **15.0,** *Literacy:* **91.0,** *Currency:* **US $,** *Official Language:* **Spanish, Quechua,** *Nationality:* **Ecuadorian(s)**

Country; **GUYANA,** *Capital:* **Georgetown,** *Area:* **215.0,** *Population:* **0.7,** *Literacy:* **91.8,** *Currency:* **Guyanese $** *Official Language:* **English, Amerindian & Creole,** *Nationality:* **Guyanese**

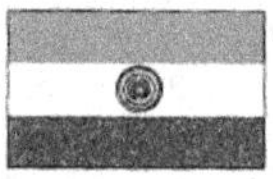
Country: **PARAGUAY,** *Capital:* **Asuncion,** *Area:* **406.7,** *Population:* **6.5** *Literacy:* **94.0,** *Currency:* **guarani** *Official Language:* **Spanish, Guarani,** *Nationality:* **Paraguayan(s)**

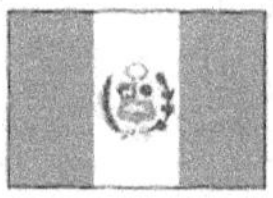
Country: **PERU,** *Capital;* **Lima,** *Area:* **1285.2,** *Population:* **29.2,** *Literacy:* **92.9** *Currency:* **Neuvo sol,** *Official Language:* **Spanish, Quechua & Aymara** *Nationality:* **Peruvian(s)**

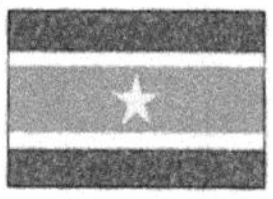
Country: **SURINAME,** *Capital:* Paramaribo, *Area:* **163.8,** *Population:* **0.5** *Literacy:* **89.6,** *Currency:* **Suriname $** *Official Language:* **Dutch,** *Nationality:* **Surinamer(s)**

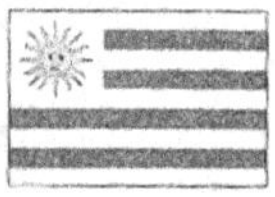
Country: **URUGUAY,** *Capital:* Montevideo, *Area:* **176.2,** *Population:* **3.3,** *Literacy:* **98.0,** *Currency:* **Uruguayan peso,** *Official Language:* **Spanish,** *Nationality:* **Uruguayan(s)**

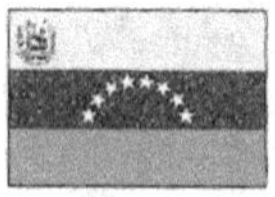
Country: **VENEZUELA,** *Capital:* Caracas, *Area:* **912.0,** *Population:* **27.6** *Literacy:* **93.0,** *Currency:* **Bolivar,** *Official Language:* **Spanish,** *Nationality:* **Venezuelan(s)**

Notes:

1. The area for India includes the 78,114 sq.km of under unlawful occupation of Pakistan; 5,180 sq. km. of area handed over to China by Pakistan and 37, 555 sq. km of area under unlawful occupation of China.
2. The population for India excludes the population of the area under unlawful occupation of Pakistan and China. The population figures are 2011 provisional census data.
3. Literacy percent for India is of the population aged 7 years and above as per 2011 provisional census data.
4. Communaute Financiere Africaine has been abbreviated as CFA.
5. Statistics for Morocco include the Western Sahara region.
6. The dollar and the pound have been shown as $ and £ respectively.
7. Israel declared Jerusalem as its capital in 1950, but India, U.K., U.S.A. and most other countries maintain their embassies in TelAviv-Yafo.

How to use the Index

The following system is used to locate a place or a geographical feature on any map in this *School Atlas*. Each entry starts with the name of the place or feature followed by the name of the country or region in which it is located. Placed next to it is the alphanumeric reference followed by the coordinate reference (i.e., latitude and longitude reference). Take Delhi for example. The entry reads **Delhi,** Delhi, India 28°36'N 77°12'E. You can locate Delhi using coordinate reference by finding latitude 28 degree north and estimating 36 minute north from 28 degrees north in order to locate 28 degree 36 minute north. You can then find longitude 76 degree east and estimate 1 degree 12 minute east from 76 degrees east in order to find *77* degrees 12 minutes east. The symbol for Delhi lies on the intersection formed by latitude 28°36'N and longitude 77°12'E.

A name may appear on several maps, but this index lists only the best presentation. The names of rivers have been indexed either according to their origins or according to their mouths.

The physical feature entry is followed by the description of the feature. For example: *Great Himalaya*, Ra. This descriptive term is usually abbreviated. A list of abbreviations is included for your reference.

List of Abbreviations

A.&N.Is.	- Andaman and Nicobar Islands	Cro.	- Croatia	Jam.	- Jamaica	N.T.	- Northern Territory	Sing.	- Singapore
A.C.T.	- Australian Capital Territory	Czech Rep.	- Czech Republic	Jhar.	- Jharkhand	N.Y.	- New York	Slov.	- Slovakia
A.P.	- Andhra Pradesh	D.&D.	- Daman and Diu	Kar.	- Karnataka	N.Z.	- New Zealand	Slove.	- Slovenia
Afgh.	- Afghanistan	D.C.	- District of Columbia	Kazak.	- Kazakhstan	Naga.	- Nagaland	Solomon Is.	- Solomon Islands
Ala.	- Alabama	D.N.H.	- Dadra and Nagar Haveli	Ky.	- Kentucky	Nam.	- Namibia	Soma.	- Somalia
Alb.	- Albania			Kyr.	- Kyrgyzstan	Nebr.	- Nebraska	St.-e.	- Saint-e
Alg.	- Algeria	Del.	- Delaware	L.	- Lake	Neth.	- Netherlands	St.K.&N.	- Saint Kitts and Nevis
Amer. Samoa	- American Samoa	Dem.Rep. of Congo	- Democratic Republic of Congo	La.	- Louisiana	Neth. Ant.	- Netherlands Antilles		
Ando.	- Andorra			Lak.	- Lakshadweep	New Cal.	- New Caledonia	St.Vin.& Gren.	- Saint Vincent and The Grenadines
Antarc.	- Antarctica	Den.	- Denmark	Leb.	- Lebanon	Nicar.	- Nicaragua		
Antig. &Barb.	- Antigua and Barbuda	Des.	- Desert	Lib.	- Liberia	Nig.	- Nigeria	Sta., Sto.	- Santa, Santo
		Dom.	- Dominica	Liech.	- Liechtenstein	Nor.	- Norway	Str.	- Strait
Ar.P.	- Arunachal Pradesh	Dom.Rep.	- Dominican Republic	Lith.	- Lithuania	Okla.	- Oklahoma	Suri.	- Suriname
				Lux.	- Luxembourg	P.	- Pass	Switz.	- Switzerland
Arc.Oc.	- Arctic Ocean	E.	- East-ern	M.P.	- Madhya Pradesh	P.N.G.	- Papua New Guinea	T.&C.Is.	- Turks and Caicos Islands
Arch.	- Archipelago	Ecu.	- Ecuador	Mace.	- Macedonia				
Arg.	- Argentina	ElSalv.	- El Salvador	Madag.	- Madagascar	P.R.	- Puerto Rico	T.N.	- Tamil Nadu
Ariz.	- Arizona	Eng.	- England	Maha.	- Maharashtra	Pa.	- Pennsylvania	Tajik.	- Tajikistan
Ark.	- Arkansas	Eq.Guinea	- Equatorial Guinea	Malay.	- Malaysia	Pac.Oc.	- Pacific Ocean	Tanz.	- Tanzania
Atl.Oc.	- Atlantic Ocean	Eri.	- Eritrea	Mani.	- Manipur	Pak.	- Pakistan	Tas.	- Tasmania
Aus.	- Austria	Est.	- Estonia	Marshall Is.	- Marshall Islands	Para.	- Paraguay	Tenn.	- Tennessee
Aust.	- Australia	Eth.	- Ethiopia	Mart.	- Martinique	Pass.	- Passage	Terr.	- Territory
Azer.	- Azerbaijan	F.	- Firth	Mass.	- Massachusetts	Pen.	- Peninsula	Thai.	- Thailand
B.	- Bay/Bight	F.S.M.	- Federated States of Micronesia	Maur.	- Mauritania	Phil.	- Philippines	Tr.	- Trench
Baha.	- The Bahamas			Maus.	- Mauritius	Pi.	- Puduchcheri	Tri.	- Tripura
Bangla.	- Bangladesh	Falk.Is.	- Falkland Islands	Md.	- Maryland	Pk.	- Peak	Trin.& Tob.	- Trinidad and Tobago
Bel.	- Belarus	Fin.	- Finland	MeditSea	- Mediterranean Sea	Plat.	- Plateau		
Belg.	- Belgium	Fla.	- Florida			Port.	- Portugal	Tun.	- Tunisia
Bol.	- Bolivia	Fr.	- France	Megh.	- Meghalaya	Pt.-o	- Point-Puerto	Turk.	- Turkmenistan
Bos.Herz.	- Bosnia-Herzegovina	Fr.Poly.	- French Polynesia	Mich.	- Michigan	Pta.	- Punta	U.A.E.	- United Arab Emirates
				Minn.	- Minnesota	Queens.	- Queensland		
Bots.	- Botswana	G.	- Gulf	Missi.	- Mississippi	R.	- River	U.K.	- United Kingdom
Bulg.	- Bulgaria	Ga.	- Georgia	Misso.	- Missouri	R.I.	- Rhode Island	U.P.	- Uttar Pradesh
Bur.Faso	- Burkina Faso	Ger.	- Germany	Miz.	- Mizoram	Ra.-s.	- Range-s	U.S.A.	- United States of America
Bum.	- Burundi	Green.	- Greenland	Mong.	- Mongolia	Raj.	- Rajasthan		
C.	- Cape	Gren.	- Grenada	Mont.	- Montana	Res.	- Reservoir	Ukr.	- Ukraine
C.A.R.	- Central African Republic	Gt.	- Great-er	Monte.	- Montenegro	Rom.	- Romania	Urug.	- Uruguay
		Guad.	- Guadeloupe	Monts.	- Montserrat	S.	- South-ern	Utta.	- Uttarakhand
C.Rica	- Costa Rica	Guat.	- Guatemala	Mor.	- Morocco	S.A.	- South Australia	Uzbek.	- Uzbekistan
C.S.I. Terr.	- Coral Sea Islands Territory	Guj.	- Gujarat	Mozam.	- Mozambique	S.Africa	- South Africa	Va.	- Virginia
		H.P.	- Himachal Pradesh	Ms.	- Mouths	S.Amer.	- South America	Ven.	- Venezuela
C.Verde	- Cape Verde	Har.	- Haryana	Mt.-n.-s.	- Mount-ain-s	S.Ar.	- Saudi Arabia	Vic.	- Victoria
Calif.	- California	Hd.	- Head	Mte.	- Monte	S.C.	- South Carolina	Viet.	- Vietnam
Cam.	- Cameroon	Hond.	- Honduras	Mtn.Ra.,	- Mountain Range	S.Dak.	- South Dakota	Vir.Is.	- Virgin Islands
Camb.	- Cambodia	Hung.	- Hungary	Myan.	- Myanmar	S.Korea	- South Korea	Vol.	- Volcan, Volcano
Cay.Is.	- Cayman Islands	Ice.	- Iceland	N.	- North-ern	S.Lanka	- Sri Lanka	Vt.	- Vermont
Ch.	- Chandigarh	Ill.	- Illinois	N.Amer.	- North America	S.M.	- San Marino	W.	- West-ern
Chan.	- Channel	Ind.	- Indiana	N.C.	- North Carolina	S.Sudan	- South Sudan	W.A.	- Western Australia
Chhat.	- Chhattisgarh	Ind.Oc.	- Indian Ocean	N.Dak.	- North Dakota	S.Tom. &P.	- Sao Tome and Principe	W.B.	- West Bengal
Co.	- Cerro	Indo.	- Indonesia	N.H.	- New Hampshire			W.Sahara	- Western Sahara
Col.	- Colombia	Ire.	- Ireland	N.Ire.	- Northern Ireland	Sa.	- Serra, Sierra	W.Va.	- West Virginia
Colo.	- Colorado	Is.	- Island-s	N.J.	- New Jersey	Sa.Leone	- Sierra Leone	Wash.	- Washington
Com.	- Comoros	Isth.	- Isthmus	N.Korea	- North Korea	Scot.	- Scotland	Wis.	- Wisconsin
Conn.	- Connecticut	J.&K.	- Jammu and Kashmir	N.Mariana Is.	- Northern Mariana Islands	Sd.	- Sound	Wyo.	- Wyoming
Cook Is.	- Cook Islands			N.Mex.	- New Mexico	Sen.	- Senegal	Zimb.	- Zimbabwe
Cord.	- Cordillera			N.S.W.	- New South Wales	Sey.	- Seychelles		

110 Index

Aalborg Aniak

A

Aalborg, Den.	61	57°02'N	09°54'E
Aba as Su'ud, S.Ar.	51	17°28'N	44°06'E
Abadan, Iran	51	30°22'N	48°20'E
Abakan, Russia	53	53°40'N	91°10'E
Abashiri, Japan	54	44°00'N	144°15'E
Abaya, L., Eth.	65	06°30'N	37°50'E
Abbot Ice Shelf, Antarc.	82	73°00'S	92°00'W
Abbottabad, Pak.	48	34°10'N	73°15'E
Abd al Kuri, I., Yemen	51	12°05'N	52°20'E
Abeche, Chad	66	13°50'N	20°35'E
Aberdeen L., Canada	73	64°28'N	99°00'W
Aberdeen, S.Dak., U.S.A.	77	45°28'N	98°29'W
Aberdeen, Scot., U.K.	64	57°09'N	02°05'W
Aberystwyth, Wales, U.K.	64	52°25'N	04°05'W
Abha, S.Ar.	51	18°00'N	42°34'E
Abhayapuri, Assam, India	30	26°24'N	90°38'E
Abidjan, Cote d'Ivoire	66	05°26'N	03°58'W
Abilene, Texas, U.S.A.	77	32°28'N	99°43'W
Abisko, Sweden	61	68°22'N	18°47'E
Abohar, Punjab, India	21	30°10'N	74°10'E
Abor Hills, India	30	28°17'N	94°20'E
Absaroka Ra., U.S.A.	77	44°45'N	109°50'W
Abu Dhabi, U.A.E.	51	24°28'N	54°22'E
Abu Road, Raj., India	29	24°30'N	72°58'E
Abu, Raj., India	29	24°41'N	72°50'E
Abuja, Nig.	66	09°16'N	07°02'E
Abuna, Brazil	80	09°40'S	65°20'W
Acapulco, Mexico	74	16°51'N	99°56'W
Accra, Ghana	66	05°35'N	00°06'W
Achill I., Ire.	64	53°58'N	10°01'W
Acklins I., Baha.	78	22°30'N	74°00'W
Aconcagua, Co., Mtn., Arg.	79	32°39'S	70°00'W
Acquaviva, S.M.	61	43°57'N	12°25'E
Ad Dahna, Des., S.Ar.	51	24°30'N	48°10'E
Ad Dakhla, W.Sahara	66	23°50'N	15°53'W
Ad Dammam, S.Ar.	51	26°20'N	50°05'E
Adam, Oman	51	22°15'N	57°28'E
Adam's Bridge, Is., India	27	09°15'N	79°40'E
Adamawa Highlands, Cam.-Nig.	65	07°20'N	12°20'E
Adana, Turkey	51	37°00'N	35°16'E
Adapazari, Turkey	51	40°48'N	30°25'E
Adare C., Antarc.	82	71°00'S	171°00'E
Addis Ababa, Eth.	66	09°02'N	38°42'E
Addu Atoll, Maldives	48	00°38'S	73°10'E
Adelaide I., Antarc.	82	67°15'S	68°30'W
Adelaide, S.A., Aust.	70	34°52'S	138°30'E
Adelie Land, Antarc.	82	68°00'S	140°00'E
Aden, Yemen	51	12°45'N	45°00'E
Aden,G.of, Asia-Africa	51	12°30'N	47°30'E
Adi, I., Indo.	52	04°15'S	133°30'E
Adige, R., Italy	60	45°09'N	12°20'E
Adilabad, A.P., India	27	19°33'N	78°20'E
Adoni, A.P., India	27	15°36'N	77°18'E
Adra, W.B., India	30	23°30'N	86°42'E
Adrar, Alg.	66	27°51'N	00°11'W
Adriatic Sea, Europe	60	43°00'N	16°00'E
Advent, I., Panama	78		
Adwa, Eth.	66	14°15'N	38°52'E
Aegean Sea, Greece-Turkey	60	38°30'N	25°00'E
AFGHANISTAN, Asia	48	33°00'N	65°00'E
Afognak I., U.S.A.	73	58°15'N	152°30'W
Afyon, Turkey	51	38°45'N	30°33'E
Agadez, Niger	66	16°58'N	07°59'E
Agadir, Mor.	66	30°28'N	09°55'W
Agar, M.P., India	24	23°42'N	76°00'E
Agartala, Tri., India	30	23°48'N	91°18'E
Agatti I., India	27	10°50'N	72°11'E
Agatti, Lak., India	27	10°50'N	72°12'E
Aghil P., India	21	36°12'N	76°41'E
Agra, U.P., India	22	27°06'N	78°00'E
Aguascalientes, Mexico	74	22°00'N	102°20'W
Aguja, Pta., Peru	79	05°47'S	81°06'W
Agulhas, C., S.Africa	65	34°52'S	20°00'E
Ahaggar Mts., Alg.	65	23°00'N	06°30'E
Ahipara Bay, N.Z.	70	35°05'S	173°05'E
Ahmadabad, Guj., India	29	23°00'N	72°36'E
Ahmadpur East, Pak.	48	29°12'N	71°10'E
Ahobilam, A.P., India	27	15°04'N	78°32'E
Ahrax Pt., Malta	61	35°59'N	14°22'E
Ahvaz, Iran	51	31°20'N	48°40'E
Ahwa, Guj., India	29	20°44'N	73°42'E
Air(Azbine), Mts., Niger	65	18°30'N	08°00'E
Aivalli, Kar., India	27	16°00'N	75°53'E
Aixirivall, Ando.	61		
Aizawl, Miz., India	30	23°42'N	92°42'E
Aizu-wakamatsu, Japan	54	37°30'N	139°56'E
Ajaccio, France	61	41°55'N	08°40'E
Ajaigarh, M.P., India	27	24°52'N	80°17'E
Ajanta Ra., India	27	20°28'N	75°50'E
Ajay, R., India	30	23°40'N	88°09'E
Ajjer,Tassili-n-, Plat., Alg.	65	26°05'N	06°00'E
Ajmer, Raj., India	29	26°24'N	74°36'E
Ajnala, Punjab, India	21	31°51'N	74°50'E
Akanthou, Cyprus	57	35°21'N	33°44'E
Akbarpur, U.P., India	22	26°22'N	79°57'E
Akbarpur, U.P., India	22	26°26'N	82°35'E
Akhdar Mts., Oman	51	23°10'N	57°25'E
Akhisar, Turkey	51	38°56'N	27°48'E
Akhnur, J.&K., India	21	32°52'N	74°45'E
Akita, Japan	54	39°45'N	140°07'E
Aklera, Raj., India	29	24°25'N	76°34'E
Akobo, S.Sudan	66	07°46'N	32°59'E
Akron, Ohio, U.S.A.	77	41°05'N	81°31'W
Aksai Chin, Region, India	21	35°15'N	79°55'E
Aksehir, Turkey	51	38°18'N	31°30'E
Aksu, China	50	41°05'N	80°10'E
Aktau, Kazak.	53	44°35'N	50°23'E
Aktobe, Kazak.	53	50°17'N	57°10'E
Akureyri, Ice.	61	65°40'N	18°06'W
Al Ahmadi, Kuwait	51	29°05'N	48°10'E
Al Alamayn, Egypt	66	30°48'N	28°58'E
Al Amarah, Iraq	51	31°55'N	47°15'E
Al Bayda, Libya	66	32°50'N	21°44'E
Al Buraymi, Oman	51	24°14'N	55°46'E
Al Fayyum, Egypt	66	29°19'N	30°50'E
Al Ghaydah, Yemen	51	16°13'N	52°11'E
Al Ghurdaqah, Egypt	66	27°15'N	33°50'E
Al Hadithah, Iraq	51	34°00'N	41°13'E
Al Hamad, Plain, Jordan-S.Ar.	51	31°30'N	39°30'E
Al Hasakah, Syria	51	36°35'N	40°45'E
Al Hufuf, S.Ar.	51	25°25'N	49°45'E
Al Irqah, Yemen	66	13°39'N	47°22'E
Al Jaghbub, Libya	51	29°42'N	24°38'E
Al Jahrah, Kuwait	66	29°25'N	47°40'E
Al Jawf, Libya	51	24°10'N	23°24'E
Al Jawf, S.Ar.	51	29°55'N	39°40'E
Al Khaburah, Oman	51	23°57'N	57°05'E
Al Khasab, Oman	66	26°11'N	56°14'E
Al Khums, Libya	51	31°20'N	14°10'E
Al Kut, Iraq	51	32°30'N	46°00'E
Al Ladhiqiyah, Syria	51	35°30'N	35°45'E
Al Lith, S.Ar.	51	20°09'N	40°15'E
Al Liwa, Oasis, U.A.E.	51	24°31'N	56°36'E
Al Mubarraz, S.Ar.	51	25°30'N	49°40'E
Al Mukalla, Yemen	51	14°33'N	49°02'E
Al Mukha, Yemen	51	13°18'N	43°15'E
Al Qatif, S.Ar.	66	26°35'N	50°00'E
Al Qatrun, Libya	51	24°56'N	15°03'E
Al Qunfidhah, S.Ar.	51	19°03'N	41°04'E
Al Qurnah, Iraq	51	31°01'N	47°25'E
Al Ula, S.Ar.	51	26°35'N	38°00'E
Al Wafrah, Kuwait	51	28°33'N	47°56'E
Al Wajh, S.Ar.	51	26°10'N	36°30'E
Al Widyan, Des., Iraq-S.Ar.	51	31°30'N	42°00'E
Ala Kul, L., Kazak.	53	46°00'N	81°40'E
Ala Shan, Mts., China	50	40°00'N	104°00'E
Alabama, R., U.S.A.	77	31°08'N	87°57'W
ALABAMA, U.S.A.	77	33°00'N	87°00'W
Alagoinhas, Brazil	80	12°07'S	38°20'W
Alajuela, C.Rica	78	10°02'N	84°08'W
Alaknanda, R., India	21	30°09'N	78°38'E
Alakurtti, Russia	61	67°00'N	30°30'E
Aland, Kar., India	27	17°36'N	76°35'E
Alappuzha, Kerala, India	27	09°30'N	76°18'E
Alaska Pen., U.S.A.	77	56°00'N	159°00'W
Alaska Ra., U.S.A.	77	62°50'N	151°00'W
ALASKA, U.S.A.	77	64°00'N	154°00'W
Alaska,G.of, U.S.A.	77	58°00'N	145°00'W
Albacete, Spain	61	38°50'N	02°00'W
ALBANIA, Europe	61	41°00'N	20°00'E
Albany, Ga., U.S.A.	77	31°35'N	84°10'W
Albany, N.Y., U.S.A.	77	42°39'N	73°45'W
Albany, R., Canada	73	52°17'N	81°31'W
Albany, W.A., Aust.	70	35°01'S	117°58'E
Albert Lea, Minn., U.S.A.	77	43°39'N	93°22'W
Albert, L., Uganda-Dem.Rep.ofCongo	65	01°30'N	31°00'E
Albuquerque, N.Mex., U.S.A.	77	35°05'N	106°39'W
Albury, N.S.W., Aust.	70	36°03'S	146°56'E
Aldabra Is., Sey.	65	09°22'S	46°28'E
Aldan, R., Russia	53	58°40'N	125°30'E
Aldan, Russia	53	58°40'N	125°30'E
Alderney, I., U.K.	64	49°42'N	02°11'W
Alenuihaha Chan., U.S.A.	77	20°30'N	156°00'W
Aleppo, Syria	51	36°10'N	37°15'E
Alesund, Norway	61	62°28'N	06°12'E
Aleutian Is., U.S.A.	77	52°00'N	175°00'W
Aleutian Tr., Pac.Oc.	44	48°00'N	180°00'E
Alexander Arch., U.S.A.	77	57°00'N	135°00'W
Alexander I., Antarc.	82	69°00'S	70°00'W
Alexandra, N.Z.	70	45°14'S	169°25'E
Alexandria, Egypt	66	31°00'N	30°00'E
Alexandria, Va., U.S.A.	77	38°48'N	77°03'W
ALGERIA, Africa	66	28°30'N	02°00'E
Algiers, Alg.	66	36°42'N	03°08'E
Algoa B., S.Africa	65	33°50'S	25°45'E
Ali Kheyl, Afgh.	48	33°57'N	69°43'E
Alicante, Spain	61	38°30'N	00°37'W
Alice Springs, N.T., Aust.	70	23°40'S	133°50'E
Alice, Texas, U.S.A.	77	27°45'N	98°05'W
Aligarh, U.P., India	22	27°54'N	78°06'E
Alihe, China	50	50°34'N	123°43'E
Alipur Duar, W.B., India	30	26°30'N	89°35'E
Alipur, Pak.	48	29°25'N	70°55'E
Alipur, W.B., India	30	22°31'N	88°20'E
Alirajpur, M.P., India	24	22°16'N	74°24'E
Allahabad, U.P., India	22	25°30'N	81°54'E
Allegheny Mts., U.S.A.	77	38°15'N	80°10'W
Allen, L., Ire.	64	54°08'N	08°04'W
Alliance, Nebr., U.S.A.	77	42°06'N	102°52'W
Almaty, Kazak.	53	43°15'N	76°57'E
Almeria, Spain	61	37°20'N	02°20'W
Almora, Utta., India	21	29°36'N	79°36'E
Alnwick, Eng., U.K.	64	55°24'N	01°42'W
Alofi, Niue (N.Z.)	70	19°03'S	169°55'W
Along, Ar.P., India	30	28°08'N	94°43'E
Alor Setar, Malay.	52	06°07'N	100°22'E
Alor, I., Indo.	52	08°15'S	124°30'E
Alot, M.P., India	24	23°45'N	75°40'E
Alpena, Mich., U.S.A.	77	45°04'N	83°27'W
Alpine, Texas, U.S.A.	77	30°22'N	103°40'W
Alps, Mts., Europe	60	46°30'N	09°30'E
Alta, Norway	61	69°57'N	23°10'E
Altai Mts., Asia	50	46°40'N	92°45'E
Altamira, Brazil	80	03°12'S	52°10'W
Altanbulag, Mong.	50	50°16'N	106°30'E
Altay, Mong.	50	46°18'N	96°15'E
Altoona, Pa., U.S.A.	77	40°31'N	78°24'W
Altun Shan, Mts., China	50	38°30'N	88°00'E
Aluva, Kerala, India	27	10°06'N	76°22'E
Alwar, Raj., India	29	27°36'N	76°36'E
Amadeus, L., Aust.	70	24°54'S	131°00'E
Amami I., Japan	54	28°20'N	129°30'E
Amami Is., Japan	54	27°16'N	129°21'E
Amapa, Brazil	70	02°05'N	50°50'W
Amarapura, Myan.	55	21°54'N	96°03'E
Amaravati, A.P., India	27	16°35'N	80°20'E
Amaravati, R., India	27	11°00'N	78°15'E
Amarillo, Texas, U.S.A.	77	35°13'N	101°50'W
Amarnath, J.&K., India	21	19°12'N	73°22'E
Amarpatan, M.P., India	24	24°19'N	80°59'E
Amarpur, Tri., India	30	25°05'N	87°00'E
Amarwara, M.P., India	24	22°18'N	79°11'E
Amasya, Turkey	51	40°40'N	35°50'E
Amazon Basin, Brazil	79	02°30'S	60°00'W
Amazon, R., S.Amer.	79	00°05'S	50°00'W
Ambala, Har., India	21	30°24'N	76°54'E
Ambalangoda, S.Lanka	49	06°15'N	80°05'E
Ambarchik, Russia	53	69°40'N	162°20'E
Ambasa, Tri., India	30	23°51'N	91°48'E
Ambergris Cay, Belize	78	18°00'N	88°00'W
Ambikapur, Chhat., India	25	23°06'N	83°12'E
Ambon, Indo.	52	03°35'S	128°20'E
Ambovombe, Madag.	66	25°11'S	46°05'E
Amboyna Cay, S.China Sea	52	07°50'N	112°50'E
Amderma, Russia	53	69°45'N	61°30'E
American High Land, Antarc.	82	73°00'S	75°00'E
Amery Ice Shelf, Antarc.	82	69°30'S	72°00'E
Amet, Raj., India	29	25°16'N	73°59'E
Amga, R., Russia	53	62°38'N	134°32'E
Amgun, R., Russia	53	52°56'N	139°38'E
Amindivi Is., India	27	11°30'N	72°30'E
Amini, Lak., India	27	11°07'N	72°45'E
Amirante Is., Sey.	87	06°00'S	53°00'E
Amla, M.P., India	24	21°54'N	78°10'E
Amlekhganj, Nepal	49	27°12'N	85°00'E
Amman, Jordan	51	31°57'N	35°52'E
Ammassalik, Green. (Den.)	74	65°40'N	37°20'W
Amod, Guj., India	29	21°58'N	72°56'E
Ampara, S.Lanka	49	07°19'N	81°38'E
Amreli, Guj., India	29	21°35'N	71°17'E
Amritsar, Punjab, India	21	31°36'N	74°54'E
Amroha, U.P., India	22	28°53'N	78°30'E
Amsterdam, I., France	87	37°30'S	77°30'E
Amsterdam, Neth.	61	52°23'N	04°54'E
Amu Darya, R., Asia	53	43°58'N	59°34'E
Amundsen G., Canada	73	71°00'N	124°00'W
Amundsen Sea, Antarc.	82	72°00'S	115°00'W
Amur, R., Russia	53	52°56'N	141°10'E
An Nafud (Gt.Sandy Des.), S.Ar.	51	28°15'N	41°00'E
An Najaf, Iraq	51	32°03'N	44°15'E
An Nasiriyah, Iraq	51	31°00'N	46°15'E
Anabar, R., Russia	53	73°08'N	113°36'E
Anadyr, R., Russia	53	64°55'N	176°05'E
Anadyr, Russia	53	64°35'N	177°20'E
Anadyr,G.of, Russia	53	64°00'N	180°00'E
Anah, Iraq	51	34°25'N	42°00'E
Anai Mudi, Pk., India	27	10°12'N	77°04'E
Anaimalai Hills, India	27	10°20'N	76°40'E
Anakapalle, A.P., India	27	17°42'N	83°06'E
Anambas Is., Indo.	52	03°20'N	106°30'E
Anand, Guj., India	29	22°32'N	72°59'E
Anandapur, Odisha, India	25	21°16'N	86°13'E
Anandpur Sahib, Punjab, India	21	31°12'N	76°34'E
Anantapur, A.P., India	27	14°42'N	77°36'E
Anantnag, J.&K., India	21	33°42'N	75°06'E
Anardara, Afgh.	48	32°46'N	61°39'E
Anatolia, Plat., Turkey	51	39°00'N	35°00'E
Anchorage, Alaska, U.S.A.	77	61°13'N	149°54'W
Ancona, Italy	61	43°38'N	13°30'E
Ancud, Chile	80	42°00'S	73°50'W
Andalsnes, Norway	61	62°35'N	07°43'E
Andalusia, Region, Spain	60	37°35'N	05°00'W
ANDAMAN AND NICOBAR IS., India	27	10°00'N	93°00'E
Andaman Sea, Indian Ocean	27	11°00'N	96°00'E
Anderson, R., Canada	73	69°42'N	129°00'W
Andes, Mts., S.Amer.	79	20°00'S	68°00'W
ANDHRA PRADESH, India	27	17°00'N	80°00'E
Andijon, Uzbek.	53	41°10'N	72°15'E
Andkhvoy, Afgh.	48	36°56'N	65°05'E
Andong, S.Korea	54	36°40'N	128°43'E
Andorra la Vella, Ando.	61	42°31'N	01°32'E
ANDORRA, Europe	61	42°33'N	01°33'E
Andreanof Is., U.S.A.	77	52°00'N	178°00'W
Andros I., Baha.	78	24°30'N	78°00'W
Andrott I., India	27	10°48'N	73°41'E
Anegada, I., Vir.Is. (U.K)	78	18°45'N	64°20'W
Aneto, Pk., Spain	60	42°37'N	00°40'E
Angara, R., Russia	53	58°30'N	97°00'E
Angarsk, Russia	53	52°30'N	104°00'E
Angel Falls, Ven.	79	05°57'N	62°30'W
Angerman, R., Sweden	60	62°40'N	18°00'E
Angers, France	61	47°30'N	00°35'W
Anglesey, I., U.K.	64	53°17'N	04°20'W
ANGOLA, Africa	66	12°00'S	18°00'E
ANGUILLA(U.K.), I., N.Amer.	78	18°15'N	63°05'W
Aniak, U.S.A.	74	61°32'N	159°40'W

Anini   Bambari

112 Index

Bamian Bijnor

Bamian, Afgh. 48 34°48'N 67°48'E
Banaba, I., Kiribati 70 00°45'S 169°50'E
Banas, R., India 29 24°20'N 72°15'E
Banda Aceh, Indo. 52 05°35'N 95°20'E
Banda Sea, Indo. 52 06°00'S 130°00'E
Banda, M.P., India 24 24°02'N 78°58'E
Banda, U.P., India 22 25°30'N 80°26'E
Bandar Abbas, Iran 57 27°15'N 56°15'E
Bandar Lampung, Indo. 52 05°20'S 105°10'E
Bandar Seri Begawan, Brunei 52 04°52'N 115°00'E
Bandarpunch, Pk., India 21 30°58'N 78°36'E
Band-e Baba, Upland, Afgh. 48 34°37'N 62°40'E
Band-e Torkestan, Mts., Afgh. 48 35°30'N 64°00'E
Bandeira, Pico da, Brazil 79 20°26'S 41°47'W
Bandipur, Kar., India 27 11°40'N 76°37'E
Bandipura, J.&K., India 21 34°25'N 74°39'E
Bandung, Indo. 52 06°54'S 107°36'E
Banei, Odisha, India 25 21°47'N 85°02'E
Banganapalle, A.P., India 27 15°19'N 78°12'E
Bangarapet, Kar., India 27 12°59'N 78°10'E
Banggi, I., Malay. 52 07°17'N 117°12'E
Bangka, I., Indo. 52 02°00'S 105°50'E
Bangkok, Thai. 55 13°44'N 100°33'E
Bangkok, Bight of, Thai. 55 13°30'N 100°31'E
BANGLADESH, Asia 48 24°00'N 90°00'E
Bangor, Maine, U.S.A. 77 44°48'N 68°46'W
Bangor, N.Ire., U.K. 64 54°40'N 05°40'W
Bangor, Wales, U.K. 64 53°14'N 04°08'W
Bangriposi, Odisha, India 25 22°11'N 86°38'E
Bangui, C.A.R. 66 04°23'N 18°35'E
Bangweulu, L., Zambia 65 11°00'S 30°00'E
Banihal P., India 21 33°30'N 75°12'E
Baniyas, Syria 51 35°10'N 36°00'E
Banja Luka, Bos.Herz. 61 44°49'N 17°11'E
Banjar, H.P., India 21 31°37'N 77°24'E
Banjarmasin, Indo. 52 03°20'S 114°35'E
Banjul, The Gambia 66 13°28'N 16°40'W
Banka, Bihar, India 23 24°53'N 86°55'E
Banks I., Canada 73 73°15'N 121°30'W
Banks Peninsula, N.Z. 70 43°45'S 173°15'E
Banks Strait, Aust. 70 40°40'S 148°10'E
Bankura, W.B., India 30 23°11'N 87°18'E
Banmanki, Bihar, India 23 25°53'N 87°12'E
Banmauk, Myan. 55 24°26'N 95°55'E
Bannu, Pak. 48 32°54'N 70°36'E
Banow, Afgh. 48 35°38'N 69°15'E
Banswara, Raj., India 29 23°32'N 74°24'E
Bantry B., Ire. 64 51°37'N 09°44'W
Bantry, Ire. 64 51°41'N 09°27'W
Banyak Is., Indo. 55 02°10'N 97°10'E
Banzare Coast, Antarc. 82 68°00'S 125°00'E
Baoding, China 50 38°50'N 115°28'E
Baoji, China 50 34°20'N 107°05'E
Baotou, China 50 40°32'N 110°02'E
Bapatla, A.P., India 27 15°55'N 80°30'E
Bara Banki, U.P., India 22 26°53'N 81°12'E
Bara Lacha La, P., India 21 32°42'N 77°31'E
Baragarh, Odisha, India 25 21°20'N 83°37'E
Barahona, Dom.Rep. 78 18°13'N 71°07'W
Barail Ra., India 80 25°15'N 93°20'E
Barakar, R., India 23 24°10'N 86°20'E
Baraki Barak, Afgh. 48 33°55'N 68°58'E
Barakot, Odisha, India 25 21°33'N 84°59'E
Barakpur, W.B., India 30 22°44'N 88°30'E
Baramula, J.&K., India 21 34°15'N 74°20'E
Baran, Raj., India 29 25°06'N 76°30'E
Barasat, W.B., India 30 22°46'N 88°31'E
BARBADOS, N.Amer. 78 13°10'N 59°30'W
Barbuda, I., Leeward Is. 78 17°30'N 61°40'W
Barcelona, Spain 61 41°21'N 02°10'E
Barcelona, Ven. 80 10°10'N 64°40'W
Barda Hills, India 29 21°50'N 69°30'E
Barddhaman, W.B., India 30 23°14'N 87°39'E
Bardoli, Guj., India 29 21°12'N 73°05'E
Bareilly, U.P., India 22 28°24'N 79°30'E
Barengapara, Megh., India 30 25°13'N 90°12'E
Barents Sea, Arc.Oc. 53 73°00'N 39°00'E
Barguna, Bangla. 48 22°09'N 90°08'E
Barharwa, Jhar., India 23 24°51'N 87°49'E
Barhi, Jhar., India 23 24°18'N 85°30'E
Barhi, M.P., India 22 23°54'N 80°49'E
Bari Doab, Pak. 48 30°20'N 73°00'E
Bari Sadri, Raj., India 29 24°21'N 74°46'E
Bari, Italy 61 41°08'N 16°51'E
Bari, Raj., India 29 26°39'N 77°39'E
Barigello, R., Italy 61
Baripada, Odisha, India 25 21°57'N 86°45'E
Barisal, Bangla. 48 22°42'N 90°18'E
Barisan Mts., Indo. 52 03°30'S 102°30'E
Barito, R., Indo. 52 04°00'S 114°50'E
Barkly Tableland, Region, Aust. 70 17°50'S 136°40'E
Barkol, China 50 43°37'N 93°02'E
Barkot, Utta., India 21 30°49'N 78°15'E
Barkuhi, M.P., India 24 22°13'N 78°42'E
Barlee, L., Aust. 70 29°15'S 119°30'E
Barmer, Raj., India 29 25°42'N 71°24'E
Barnagar, M.P., India 24 23°07'N 75°19'E
Barnala, Punjab, India 21 30°25'N 75°35'E
Barnaul, Russia 53 53°20'N 83°40'E
Barnsley, Eng., U.K. 64 53°34'N 01°27'W
Barnstaple, Eng., U.K. 64 51°05'N 04°04'W
Baroda, M.P., India 24 25°29'N 76°35'E
Barpali, Odisha, India 25 21°11'N 83°35'E
Barpeta, Assam, India 30 26°20'N 91°10'E
Barquisimeto, Ven. 80 10°04'N 69°19'W
Barra, I., U.K. 64 57°00'N 07°29'W
Barrancas, Ven. 80 08°55'N 62°05'W
Barranquilla, Col. 80 11°00'N 74°50'W
Barreiros, Brazil 80 08°49'S 35°12'W
Barren I., India 27 12°18'N 93°48'E
Barrier Ra., Aust. 70 31°00'S 141°30'E
Barro Colorado, I., Panama 78 09°12'N 79°50'W
Barrow Creek, N.T., Aust. 70 21°30'S 133°55'E
Barrow I., Aust. 70 20°45'S 115°20'E
Barrow, R., Ire. 64 52°25'N 06°58'W
Barrow, U.S.A. 82 71°18'N 156°47'W
Barrow, Pt., U.S.A. 73 71°30'N 156°00'W
Barrow-in-Furness, Eng., U.K. 64 54°07'N 03°14'W
Barsalpur, Raj., India 29 28°12'N 72°18'E
Bartang, R., Tajik. 48 37°54'N 71°34'E
Bartica, Guyana 80 06°25'N 58°40'W
Bartin, Turkey 51 41°38'N 32°21'E
Baruun Urt, Mong. 50 46°31'N 113°22'E
Barwah, M.P., India 24 22°16'N 76°05'E
Barwani, M.P., India 24 22°00'N 74°54'E
Basar, Ar.P., India 30 27°59'N 94°37'E
Basavakalyan, Kar., India 27 17°52'N 76°57'E
Basavana Bagevadi, Kar., India 27 16°34'N 75°57'E
Basel, Switz. 61 47°35'N 07°35'E
Bashi Chan., Phil.-Taiwan 52 21°40'N 121°20'E
Basilan, I., Phil. 52 06°35'N 122°00'E
Basildon, Eng., U.K. 64 51°34'N 00°28'E
Basirhat, W.B., India 30 22°40'N 88°54'E
Basoda, M.P., India 24 23°52'N 77°54'E
Basoli, J.&K., India 21 32°29'N 75°51'E
Basra, Iraq 51 30°30'N 47°50'E
Bass Strait, Aust. 70 39°15'S 146°30'E
Bassein, Myan. 55 16°45'N 94°44'E
Basse-Terre, Guad. (Fr.) 78 16°00'N 61°44'W
Basseterre, St.K.&N. 78 17°17'N 62°43'W
Basti, U.P., India 22 26°52'N 82°55'E
Bata, Eq.Guinea 66 01°57'N 09°50'E
Batabano, G.of, Cuba 78 22°30'N 82°30'W
Batala, Punjab, India 21 31°47'N 75°18'E
Batan Is., Phil. 52 20°30'N 121°50'E
Batangas, Phil. 52 13°35'N 121°10'E
Batdambang, Camb. 55 13°06'N 103°14'E
Bath, Eng., U.K. 64 51°23'N 02°22'W
Bathinda, Punjab, India 21 30°12'N 74°54'E
Bathurst I., Aust. 70 11°30'S 130°10'E
Bathurst I., Canada 73 76°00'N 100°30'W
Bathurst, C., Canada 73 70°34'N 128°00'W
Bathurst, N.S.W., Aust. 70 33°25'S 149°31'E
Baton Rouge, La., U.S.A. 77 30°27'N 91°11'W
Batot, J.&K., India 21 33°13'N 75°19'E
Batticaloa, S.Lanka 49 07°48'N 81°42'E
Batu Is., Indo. 52 00°30'S 98°25'E
Baubau, Indo. 52 05°25'S 122°38'E
Bauchi, Nig. 66 10°22'N 09°48'E
Bauda, Odisha, India 25 20°49'N 84°24'E
Bawani Khera, Har., India 21 28°57'N 76°01'E
Bay Is., Hond. 78 16°10'N 86°30'W
Bayamo, Cuba 78 20°20'N 76°40'W
Bayamon, P.R.(U.S.A.) 78 18°24'N 66°10'W
Bayan Har Shan, Mts., China 50 34°00'N 98°00'E
Bayana, Raj., India 29 26°55'N 77°18'E
Bayanhongor, Mong. 50 46°08'N 100°41'E
Baydaratskaya B., Russia 53 70°00'N 66°00'E
Baykal, L., Russia 53 53°08'N 108°00'E
Baykit, Russia 53 61°50'N 95°50'E
Bayonne, France 61 43°30'N 01°28'W
Bazdar, Pak. 48 26°18'N 65°13'E
Bazman, Mt., Iran 51 28°04'N 60°01'E
Be'er Menuha, Israel 51 30°17'N 35°07'E
Beacon Hill, Hong Kong, China 50
Beagle Gulf, Aust. 70 12°00'S 130°00'E
Beas, R., India 21 31°10'N 75°01'E
Beata, C., Dom.Rep. 78 17°40'N 71°30'W
Beau Bassin, Maus. 66 20°13'S 57°27'E
Beaufort Sea, Canada 73 70°00'N 135°00'W
Beaufort West, S.Africa 66 32°18'S 22°36'E
Beaumont, Texas, U.S.A. 77 30°05'N 94°06'W
Beawar, Raj., India 29 26°03'N 74°18'E
Bechar, Alg. 66 31°38'N 02°18'W
Bedford, Eng., U.K. 64 52°08'N 00°28'W
Bedok Res., Sing. 52 01°21'N 103°56'E
Beersheba, Israel 51 31°15'N 34°48'E
Begamganj, M.P., India 24 23°36'N 78°21'E
Begusarai, Bihar, India 23 25°24'N 86°09'E
Behbehan, Iran 51 30°30'N 50°15'E
Bei Shan, Mts., China 50 41°30'N 96°00'E
Beihai, China 50 21°28'N 109°06'E
Beijing, China 50 39°55'N 116°20'E
Beira, Mozam. 66 19°50'S 34°52'E
Beirut, Leb. 51 33°53'N 35°31'E
Beitbridge, Zimb. 66 22°12'S 30°00'E
Bejaia, Alg. 66 36°42'N 05°02'E
Bela, Pak. 48 26°12'N 66°20'E
Bela, U.P., India 22 26°49'N 79°40'E
Bela, U.P., India 22 25°50'N 82°00'E
Belagavi, Kar., India 27 15°48'N 74°30'E
BELARUS, Europe 53 53°30'N 27°00'E
Belaya, R., Russia 60 54°40'N 56°00'E
Belcher Is., Canada 73 56°15'N 78°45'W
Beldanga, W.B., India 30 23°56'N 88°15'E
Belem, Brazil 80 01°20'S 48°30'W
Belen, N.Mex., U.S.A. 77 34°40'N 106°46'W
Belfast, N.Ire., U.K. 64 54°37'N 05°56'W
BELGIUM, Europe 61 50°30'N 05°00'E
Belgorod, Russia 61 50°35'N 36°35'E
Belgrade, Serbia 61 44°50'N 20°37'E
Belitung, I., Indo. 52 03°10'S 107°50'E
Belize City, Belize 78 17°25'N 88°00'W
BELIZE, N.Amer. 78 17°00'N 88°30'W
Belle Isle,Str.of, Canada 73 51°30'N 56°30'W
Bellingshausen Sea, Antarc. 82 66°00'S 80°00'W
Belmopan, Belize 78 17°18'N 88°30'W
Belo Horizonte, Brazil 80 19°55'S 43°56'W
Belomorsk, Russia 53 64°35'N 34°54'E
Belonia, Tri., India 30 23°15'N 91°30'E
Belo-Tsiribihina, Madag. 66 19°40'S 44°30'E
Belukha, Mt., Russia 53 49°50'N 86°50'E
Belur, Kar., India 27 13°08'N 75°50'E
Belyando, R., Aust. 70 21°38'S 146°50'E
Bemetara, Chhat., India 25 21°43'N 81°33'E
Bemidji, Minn., U.S.A. 77 47°28'N 94°53'W
Bend, Oregon, U.S.A. 77 44°04'N 121°19'W
Bendern, Liech. 61 47°13'N 09°30'E
Bendigo, Vic., Aust. 70 36°40'S 144°15'E
Bengal, B.of, Indian Ocean 44 16°00'N 88°00'E
Bengaluru, Kar., India 27 12°54'N 77°36'E
Bengbu, China 50 32°58'N 117°20'E
Benghazi, Libya 66 32°11'N 20°03'E
Benghisa Pt., Malta 61 35°48'N 14°32'E
Bengkulu, Indo. 52 03°50'S 102°12'E
Benguela, Angola 66 12°37'S 13°25'E
Beni, Nepal 49 28°22'N 83°34'E
Beniganj, U.P., India 22 27°19'N 80°27'E
BENIN, Africa 66 10°00'N 02°00'E
Benin, B.of, G.of Guinea 65 05°00'N 03°00'E
Benue, R., Nig. 65 07°48'N 06°46'E
Benxi, China 50 41°20'N 123°48'E
Beohari, M.P., India 24 24°06'N 81°24'E
Beppu, Japan 54 33°15'N 131°30'E
Berasia, M.P., India 24 23°39'N 77°26'E
Berau, B., Indo. 52 02°30'S 132°30'E
Berber, Sudan 66 18°00'N 34°00'E
Berbera, Soma. 66 10°30'N 45°02'E
Berdychiv, Ukr. 61 49°57'N 28°30'E
Berezniki, Russia 53 59°24'N 56°46'E
Berezovo, Russia 82 64°00'N 65°00'E
Bergen, Norway 61 60°20'N 05°20'E
Berhala Str., Indo. 52 01°00'S 104°15'E
Bering Sea, Russia-U.S.A. 77 58°00'N 171°00'E
Bering Str., U.S.A. 77 65°30'N 169°00'W
Berkner I., Antarc. 82 79°30'S 50°00'W
Berlin, Ger. 61 52°30'N 13°25'E
BERMUDA IS.(U.K.), N.Amer. 74 32°45'N 65°00'W
Bern, Switz. 61 46°57'N 07°28'E
Berwick-upon- Tweed, Eng., U.K 64 55°46'N 02°00'W
Bethel, U.S.A. 74 60°48'N 161°45'W
Betpak Dala, Plain, Kazak. 53
Bettiah, Bihar, India 23 26°48'N 84°33'E
Bettlerjoch P., Aus.-Liech. 61
Betul Plat., India 24 21°40'N 77°40'E
Betul, M.P., India 24 21°54'N 77°54'E
Betwa, R., India 24 26°00'N 79°30'E
Beverley, Eng., U.K. 64 53°51'N 00°26'W
Beypore, Kerala, India 27 11°10'N 75°46'E
Beypore, R., India 27 11°10'N 75°47'E
Beysehir, L., Turkey 51 37°41'N 31°33'E
Bhabua, Bihar, India 23 24°58'N 83°41'E
Bhachau, Guj., India 29 23°14'N 70°20'E
Bhadar, R., India 29 21°28'N 69°49'E
Bhadasar, Raj., India 29 27°06'N 70°48'E
Bhadohi, U.P., India 22 25°23'N 82°38'E
Bhadra Dam, India 27
Bhadra Res., India 27 13°42'N 75°45'E
Bhadra, R., India 27 13°10'N 75°20'E
Bhadra, Raj., India 29 29°07'N 75°15'E
Bhadrachalam, A.P., India 27 17°42'N 80°54'E
Bhadrak, Odisha, India 25 21°06'N 86°30'E
Bhadrapur, Nepal 49 26°31'N 88°06'E
Bhadravati, Kar., India 27 13°49'N 75°40'E
Bhagalpur, Bihar, India 23 25°12'N 87°00'E
Bhagirathi, R., India 21 31°00'N 78°42'E
Bhaidar I., India 29 22°28'N 69°19'E
Bhainsdehi, M.P., India 24 21°39'N 77°37'E
Bhairab Bazar, Bangla. 48 24°04'N 90°58'E
Bhairab, R., Bangla. 48 22°51'N 89°34'E
Bhairabi, Miz., India 30
Bhakra Dam, India 21 31°30'N 76°30'E
Bhaktapur, Nepal 49 27°42'N 85°30'E
Bhalukpong, Ar.P., India 30 27°00'N 92°36'E
Bhamo, Myan. 55 24°18'N 97°17'E
Bhander Plat., India 24 24°20'N 80°21'E
Bhander, M.P., India 24 25°42'N 78°43'E
Bhanjanagar, Odisha, India 25 19°57'N 84°41'E
Bhanvad, Guj., India 29 21°56'N 69°47'E
Bharatpur, Nepal 49 27°40'N 84°24'E
Bharatpur, Raj., India 29 27°15'N 77°30'E
Bharthana, U.P., India 22 26°44'N 79°17'E
Bharuch, Guj., India 29 21°42'N 72°54'E
Bhatapara, Chhat., India 25 21°44'N 81°57'E
Bhatiapara Ghat, Bangla. 48 23°13'N 89°42'E
Bhatkal, Kar., India 27 13°54'N 74°30'E
Bhatpara, W.B., India 30 22°50'N 88°25'E
Bhavani Sagar Res., India 27 11°30'N 77°06'E
Bhavani, R., India 27 11°00'N 76°50'E
Bhavani, T.N., India 27 11°27'N 77°43'E
Bhavnagar, Guj., India 29 21°48'N 72°06'E
Bhawanipatna, Odisha, India 25 19°54'N 83°12'E
Bhera, Pak. 48 32°29'N 72°57'E
Bhilai, Chhat., India 25 21°12'N 81°25'E
Bhilwara, Raj., India 29 25°18'N 74°36'E
Bhim, Raj., India 29 25°45'N 74°08'E
Bhima, R., India 27 16°25'N 77°17'E
Bhimavaram, A.P., India 27 16°30'N 81°30'E
Bhimunipatnam, A.P., India 27 17°53'N 83°25'E
Bhind, M.P., India 24 26°30'N 78°46'E
Bhinga, U.P., India 22 27°40'N 81°58'E
Bhinmal, Raj., India 29 24°59'N 72°21'E
Bhiwani Bagar, Region, India 21
Bhiwani, Har., India 21 28°48'N 76°12'E
Bhognipur, U.P., India 22 26°13'N 79°51'E
Bhojpur, Nepal 49 27°10'N 87°02'E
Bhola, Bangla. 48 22°45'N 90°35'E
Bhopal, M.P., India 24 23°18'N 77°24'E
Bhuban, Odisha, India 25 20°54'N 85°54'E
Bhubaneshwar, Odisha, India 25 20°18'N 85°48'E
Bhuj, Guj., India 29 23°12'N 69°36'E
Bhumiphol Dam, Thai. 55
BHUTAN, Asia 48 27°25'N 90°30'E
Biak, I., Indo. 52 01°10'S 136°06'E
Bialystok, Poland 61 53°10'N 23°10'E
Biaora, M.P., India 24 23°55'N 76°55'E
Bidar, Kar., India 27 17°55'N 77°35'E
Bie Plat., Angola 65 12°00'S 16°00'E
Bien Hoa, Viet. 55 10°55'N 106°49'E
Bighorn Mts., U.S.A. 77 44°30'N 107°30'W
Bihar Sharif, Bihar, India 23 25°06'N 85°24'E
BIHAR, India 23 25°43'N 86°00'E
Bijapur, Chhat., India 25 18°50'N 80°50'E
Bijni, Assam, India 30 26°30'N 90°40'E
Bijnor, U.P., India 22 29°27'N 78°11'E

Index 113

Bikaner — Campeche

Bikaner, Raj., India 29 28°00'N 73°18'E
Bikini, Atoll, Marshall Is. 70 12°00'N 167°30'E
Bikramganj, Bihar, India 23 25°13'N 84°17'E
Bilara, Raj., India 29 26°14'N 73°53'E
Bilasipara, Assam, India 30 26°13'N 90°14'E
Bilaspur, Chhat., India 25 22°06'N 82°06'E
Bilaspur, H.P., India 21 31°19'N 76°50'E
Bilauktaung Range, Mts., Myan.-Thai. 55 13°00'N 99°00'E
Bilbao, Spain 61 43°16'N 02°56'W
Billings, Mont., U.S.A. 77 45°47'N 108°30'W
Bilma Oasis, Niger 65 18°30'N 14°00'E
Bilma, Niger 66 18°50'N 13°30'E
Bina, M.P., India 24 24°13'N 78°14'E
Bindra Nawagarh, Chhat., India 25 20°40'N 82°12'E
Bingol, Turkey 51 38°53'N 40°29'E
Binika, Odisha, India 25 21°02'N 83°52'E
Binjai, Indo. 52 03°20'N 98°30'E
Bintan, I., Indo. 52 01°00'N 104°00'E
Bioco, I., Eq.Guinea 65 03°30'N 08°40'E
Bir Mogrein, Maur. 66 25°10'N 11°25'W
Biramitrapur, Odisha, India 25 22°24'N 84°46'E
Biratnagar, Nepal 48 26°31'N 87°21'E
Birdsville, Queens., Aust. 70 25°51'S 139°20'E
Birendranagar, Nepal 49 28°40'N 81°35'E
Birganj, Nepal 49 27°00'N 84°54'E
Birhan, Mt., Eth. 65 10°43'N 37°52'E
Birjand, Iran 51 32°53'N 59°08'E
Birkenhead, Eng., U.K. 64 53°23'N 03°02'W
Birkirkara, Malta 61 35°54'N 14°27'E
Birmingham, Ala., U.S.A. 77 33°31'N 86°48'W
Birmingham, Eng., U.K. 64 52°29'N 01°52'W
Bisalpur, U.P., India 22 28°14'N 79°48'E
Biscay, Bay of, France-Spain 60 45°00'N 02°00'W
Bishkek, Kyr. 53 42°54'N 74°46'E
Bishnupur, Mani., India 30 24°37'N 93°45'E
Bishnupur, W.B., India 30 23°08'N 87°20'E
Bishrampur, Chhat., India 25 23°15'N 82°56'E
Bismarck Arch., P.N.G. 70 02°30'S 150°00'E
Bismarck Ra., P.N.G. 70 05°35'S 145°00'E
Bismarck, N.Dak., U.S.A. 77 46°48'N 100°47'W
Bissau, Guinea-Bissau 66 11°45'N 15°45'W
Biswan, U.P., India 22 27°29'N 81°02'E
Bitra I., India 27 11°37'N 72°11'E
Bitterfontein, S.Africa 66 31°01'S 18°32'E
Bitterroot Ra., U.S.A. 77 46°00'N 114°20'W
Bixessarri, Ando. 61
Biysk, Russia 53 52°40'N 85°00'E
Black Forest, Mts., Ger. 60 48°30'N 08°20'E
Black River, Jam. 78 18°00'N 77°50'W
Black Sea, Europe 60 43°30'N 35°00'E
Black Volta, R., Africa 65 08°41'N 01°33'W
Blackall, Queens., Aust. 70 24°25'S 145°45'E
Blackburn, Mt., U.S.A. 77
Blackpool, Eng., U.K. 64 53°49'N 03°03'W
Blackwater, R., Ire. 64 52°04'N 07°52'W
Blagoveshchensk, Russia 53 50°20'N 127°30'E
Blanc, C., Maur. 65 20°44'N 17°05'W
Blanc, Mont, France-Italy 60 45°48'N 06°50'E
Blanca Bay, Arg. 79 39°10'S 61°30'W
Blanca P., Ando.-Fr. 61
Blanca Pk., U.S.A. 77 37°35'N 105°29'W
Blanco, C., C.Rica 78 09°34'N 85°08'W
Blanco, C., U.S.A. 61 42°51'N 124°34'W
Blanquilla, I., Ven. 78 11°51'N 64°37'W
Blantyre, Malawi 66 15°45'S 35°00'E
Blenheim, N.Z. 70 41°38'S 173°57'E
Bloemfontein, S.Africa 66 29°06'S 26°07'E
Blue Mt., Pk., Jam. 78 18°03'N 76°36'W
Blue Mts., U.S.A. 77 45°15'N 119°00'W
Blue Nile, R., Sudan-Eth. 65 15°38'N 32°31'E
Blue Ridge, Mts., U.S.A. 73 36°30'N 80°15'W
Bluefields, Nicar. 78 12°20'N 83°50'W
Bluff Knoll, Mt., Aust. 70 34°24'S 118°15'E
Blumenau, Brazil 80 27°00'S 49°00'W
Blyth, Eng., U.K. 64 55°08'N 01°31'W
Blytheville, Ark., U.S.A. 77 35°56'N 89°52'W
Bo Hai, G., China 50 39°00'N 119°00'E
Bo, Sa.Leone 66 07°55'N 11°50'W
Boa Vista, Brazil 80 02°48'N 60°30'W
Boa Vista, I., C.Verde 66 16°00'N 22°50'W
Boac, Phil. 52 13°27'N 121°50'E
Bobaomby, C., Madag. 65 11°58'S 49°14'E
Bobbili, A.P., India 27 18°35'N 83°30'E
Bobo-Dioulasso, Bur.Faso 66 11°08'N 04°13'W
Bodaybo, Russia 53 57°50'N 114°00'E
Bodh Gaya, Bihar, India 23 24°43'N 84°58'E
Bodhan, A.P., India 27 18°40'N 77°44'E
Bodo, Norway 61 67°17'N 14°24'E
Bogale, Myan. 55 16°16'N 95°22'E
Bogda Shan, Mtn., China 50 43°35'N 89°40'E
Bogota, Col. 80 04°35'N 74°04'W
Bogra, Bangla. 48 24°48'N 89°18'E
Bohemian Forest, Mts., Ger. 60 49°08'N 13°14'E
Bohol Sea, Phil. 52 09°00'N 124°00'E
Bohol, I., Phil. 52 09°50'N 124°10'E
Boise, Idaho, U.S.A. 77 43°37'N 116°13'W
Bojeador, C., Phil. 52 18°30'N 120°50'E
Bojnurd, Iran 51 37°30'N 57°20'E
Bokajan, Assam, India 30 26°02'N 93°50'E
Bokaro, Jhar., India 23 23°46'N 85°58'E
Bol'shevik I., Russia 53 78°30'N 102°00'E
Bol'shezemel'skaya Tundra, Plain, Russia 60 67°30'N 58°00'E
Bol'shoy Lyakhov I., Russia 53 73°35'N 142°00'E
Bolan P., Pak. 48 29°50'N 67°20'E
Bolivar, Pk., Ven. 79 08°33'N 70°59'W
BOLIVIA, S.Amer. 80 17°06'S 64°00'W
Bolivian Plat., S.Amer. 79 20°00'S 67°30'W
Bologna, Italy 61 44°29'N 11°20'E
Bolpur, W.B., India 30 23°40'N 87°45'E
Bolton, Eng., U.K. 64 53°35'N 02°26'W
Bolzano, Italy 61 46°31'N 11°22'E
Boma, Dem.Rep.of Congo 66 05°48'S 13°03'E
Bomberai, Pen., Indo. 52 03°00'S 133°00'E
Bomdila, Ar.P., India 30 27°18'N 92°24'E
Bomdo, Ar.P., India 30 28°47'N 94°48'E
Bomu, R., C.A.R.-Dem. Rep.of Congo 65 04°40'N 22°30'E
Bon, C., Tun. 65 37°01'N 11°02'E
Bonaire, I., Neth.Ant. 78 12°10'N 68°15'W
Bondo, Dem.Rep. of Congo 66 03°48'N 23°42'E
Bone, G.of, Indo. 52 04°10'S 120°50'E
Bongaigaon, Assam, India 30 26°26'N 90°31'E
Bongor, Chad 66 10°35'N 15°20'E
Bonifacio, Str.of, France-Italy 60 41°12'N 09°15'E
Bonin Is., Japan 44 27°00'N 142°00'E
Bonn, Ger. 61 50°46'N 07°06'E
Boothia Pen., Canada 73 71°00'N 94°00'W
Boothia, G.of, Canada 73 71°00'N 90°00'W
Booue, Gabon 66 00°05'S 11°55'E
Boras, Sweden 61 57°43'N 12°56'E
Borborema, Plat.of, Brazil 79 07°00'S 37°00'W
Bordeaux, France 61 44°50'N 00°36'W
Borger, Texas, U.S.A. 77 35°39'N 101°24'W
Borgo Maggiore, S.M. 61 43°56'N 12°27'E
Borisoglebsk, Russia 61 51°27'N 42°05'E
Borneo, I., Indo. 52 01°00'N 115°00'E
Bornholm, I., Den. 60 55°10'N 15°00'E
Borujerd, Iran 51 33°55'N 48°50'E
Borzya, Russia 53 50°24'N 116°31'E
Bose, China 50 23°53'N 106°35'E
BOSNIA-HERZEGOVINA, Europe 61 44°00'N 17°00'E
Bosporus, Str., Turkey 51 41°10'N 29°10'E
Bostan, Pak. 48 30°26'N 67°02'E
Bosten Hu, L., China 50 41°55'N 87°40'E
Boston, Mass., U.S.A. 77 42°22'N 71°04'W
Botad, Guj., India 29 22°15'N 71°40'E
Bothnia, G.of, Fin.-Sweden 60 63°00'N 20°15'E
BOTSWANA, Africa 66 22°00'S 24°00'E
Bouake, Cote d'Ivoire 66 07°40'N 05°02'W
Bouar, C.A.R. 66 06°00'N 15°40'E
Bougainville, I., P.N.G. 70 06°00'S 155°00'E
Boulder, W.A., Aust. 70 30°54'S 121°33'E
Boulia, Queens., Aust. 70 22°52'S 139°51'E
Bounty Is., N.Z. 70 48°00'S 178°30'E
Bourke, N.S.W., Aust. 70 30°08'S 145°55'E
Bournemouth, Eng., U.K. 64 50°43'N 01°52'W
BOUVET I.(Nor.), S.Atl.Oc. 87 54°26'S 03°24'E
Bowman I., Antarc. 82 65°00'S 104°00'E
Boyle, Ire. 64 53°59'N 08°18'W
Boyni Qara, Afgh. 48 36°20'N 67°00'E
Boyoma Falls, Dem. Rep.of Congo 65 00°15'N 25°29'E
Bradford, Eng., U.K. 64 53°47'N 01°45'W
Braemar, Scot., U.K. 64 57°00'N 03°24'W
Brahmanbaria, Bangla. 48 23°58'N 91°15'E
Brahmani, R., India 25 20°39'N 86°46'E
Brahmapur, Odisha, India 25 19°18'N 84°48'E
Brahmaputra, R., India 30 26°30'N 92°24'E
Branco, C., Brazil 79 07°09'S 34°47'W
Branco, I., C.Verde 66
Branco, R., Brazil 79 01°20'S 61°50'W
Brandon, Canada 74 49°50'N 99°57'W
Brani I., Sing. 52 01°16'N 103°50'E
Brasilia, Brazil 80 15°47'S 47°55'W
Brasov, Rom. 61 45°38'N 25°35'E
Bratislava, Slov. 61 48°10'N 17°07'E
Bratsk, Russia 53 56°10'N 101°30'E
Brava, I., C.Verde 66 14°52'N 24°43'W
Brawley, Calif., U.S.A. 77 32°59'N 115°31'W
Bray, Ire. 64 53°13'N 06°07'W
BRAZIL, S.Amer. 80 12°00'S 50°00'W
Brazilian Highlands, Brazil 79 18°00'S 46°30'W
Brazos, R., U.S.A. 77 28°53'N 95°23'W
Brazzaville, Congo 66 04°09'S 15°12'E
Bream Bay, N.Z. 70 35°56'S 174°28'E
Brecon, Wales, U.K. 64 51°57'N 03°23'W
Bremen, Ger. 61 53°04'N 08°47'E
Bressay, I., U.K. 64 60°10'N 01°01'W
Brest, Bel. 53 52°10'N 23°40'E
Brest, France 61 48°24'N 04°31'W
Brett, C., N.Z. 70 35°10'S 174°20'E
Bridgetown, Barbados 78 13°05'N 59°30'W
Bridgetown, W.A., Aust. 70 33°58'S 116°07'E
Brighton, Eng., U.K. 64 50°49'N 00°07'W
Brindisi, Italy 61 40°39'N 17°55'E
Brisbane, Queens., Aust. 70 27°25'S 153°02'E
Bristol B., U.S.A. 77 58°00'N 160°00'W
Bristol Chan., U.K. 64 51°18'N 04°30'W
Bristol, Eng., U.K. 64 51°26'N 02°35'W
BRITISH INDIAN OCEAN TERRITORY 87
British Isles, Is., Europe 60 54°00'N 04°00'W
Brno, Czech Rep. 61 49°10'N 16°35'E
Brocken, Hill, Ger. 60 51°47'N 10°37'E
Broken Hill, N.S.W., Aust. 70 31°58'S 141°29'E
Brooks Ra., U.S.A. 77 68°40'N 147°00'W
Broome, W.A., Aust. 70 18°00'S 122°15'E
Brothers,The, Is., Yemen 51
Brownsville, Texas, U.S.A. 77 25°54'N 97°30'W
Bruce, Mt., Aust. 70 22°37'S 118°08'E
BRUNEI, Asia 52 04°50'N 115°00'E
Brunner, L., N.Z. 70 42°37'S 171°27'E
Brussels, Belg. 61 50°51'N 04°21'E
Bryansk, Russia 53 53°13'N 34°25'E
Bubiyan, I., Kuwait 51 29°45'N 48°15'E
Bucaramanga, Col. 80 07°00'N 73°00'W
Buchan Ness, C., U.K. 64 57°29'N 01°46'W
Buchanan, Lib. 66 05°57'N 10°02'W
Bucharest, Rom. 61 44°27'N 26°10'E
Budapest, Hung. 61 47°29'N 19°05'E
Budaun, U.P., India 22 28°06'N 79°06'E
Bude, Eng., U.K. 64 50°49'N 04°34'W
Buea, Cam. 66 04°10'N 09°09'E
Buenaventura, Col. 80 03°53'N 77°04'W
Buenos Aires, Arg. 80 34°30'S 58°20'W
Buffalo, N.Y., U.S.A. 77 42°53'N 78°53'W
Bug, R., Poland 53 52°31'N 21°05'E
Bug, R., Ukr. 60 46°59'N 31°58'E
Bugun Shara, Mts., Mong. 50 49°00'N 104°00'E
Builth Wells, Wales, U.K. 64 52°09'N 03°25'W
Buir Nur, L., Mong. 50 47°50'N 117°42'E
Bujumbura, Buru. 66 03°16'S 29°18'E
Bukama, Dem.Rep. of Congo 66 09°10'S 25°50'E
Bukavu, Dem.Rep. of Congo 66 02°20'S 28°52'E
Bukittinggi, Indo. 52 00°20'S 100°20'E
Bukum I., Sing. 52 01°14'N 103°46'E
Bula, Indo. 52 03°06'S 130°30'E
Bulandshahr, U.P., India 22 28°28'N 77°51'E
Bulawayo, Zimb. 66 20°07'S 28°32'E
Bulgan, Mong. 50 48°48'N 103°28'E
BULGARIA, Europe 61 42°35'N 25°30'E
Buli B., Indo. 52 01°05'N 128°25'E
Buller, R., N.Z. 70 41°44'S 171°36'E
Bulu, Mtn., Indo. 52 02°51'N 116°01'E
Bum La, P., India 30 27°24'N 91°54'E
Bunbury, W.A., Aust. 70 33°20'S 115°35'E
Bundaberg, Queens., Aust. 70 24°54'S 152°22'E
Bundi, Raj., India 29 25°24'N 75°36'E
Bundu, Jhar., India 23 23°09'N 85°38'E
Bungo Channel, Japan 54 33°00'N 132°15'E
Bunji, J.&K., India 21 35°45'N 74°40'E
Buntok, Indo. 52 01°40'S 114°58'E
Buon Me Thuot, Viet. 55 12°38'N 108°05'E
Buran Darat, I., Sing. 52 01°15'N 103°51'E
Buraydah, S.Ar. 51 26°20'N 44°08'E
Burgas, Bulg. 61 42°33'N 27°29'E
Burhanpur, M.P., India 24 21°18'N 76°14'E
Burhi Gandak, R., India 23 25°27'N 86°31'E
Burica Pt., C.Rica-Panama 78 08°03'N 82°51'W
Buriram, Thai. 55 14°59'N 103°07'E
BURKINA FASO, Africa 66 12°00'N 01°00'W
Burlington, Vt., U.S.A. 78 44°29'N 73°12'W
Burnpur, W.B., India 30 23°40'N 86°57'E
Bursa, Turkey 51 40°15'N 29°05'E
Buru, I., Indo. 52 03°30'S 126°30'E
BURUNDI, Africa 66 03°15'S 30°00'E
Burzil P., India 21 34°47'N 75°07'E
Bushehr, Iran 51 28°20'N 51°45'E
Busing I., Sing. 52 01°14'N 103°45'E
Busselton, W.A., Aust. 70 33°42'S 115°15'E
Buta, Dem.Rep.of Congo 66 02°50'N 24°53'E
Butaritari, I., Kiribati 70 03°30'N 174°00'E
Buton, I., Indo. 52 05°00'S 122°45'E
Butte, Mont., U.S.A. 77 46°00'N 112°32'W
Butuan, Phil. 52 08°57'N 125°33'E
Butwal, Nepal 49 27°33'N 83°31'E
Buxar, Bihar, India 23 25°34'N 83°58'E
Buxoro, Uzbek. 53 39°48'N 64°25'E
Bydgoszcz, Poland 61 53°16'N 17°33'E
Bylot I., Canada 73 73°13'N 78°34'W
Byramgore Reef, India 27 11°54'N 71°47'E
Byron,C., Aust. 70 28°40'S 153°37'E
Byrranga Mts., Russia 53 75°00'N 100°00'E

C

C.Breton I., Canada 73 46°00'N 60°30'W
Ca Mau, Pt.,Viet. 55 08°38'N 104°44'E
Ca Mau, Viet. 55 09°10'N 105°09'E
Ca'chiavello, R., S.M. 61 43°55'N 12°28'E
Cabanatuan, Phil. 52 15°30'N 120°58'E
Cabaneta Pk., Ando.-Fr. 61
Cabinda, Angola 66 05°33'S 12°11'E
Cachoeira, Brazil 80 12°30'S 39°00'W
Cadiz, Spain 61 36°30'N 06°20'W
Caen, France 61 49°10'N 00°22'W
Caernarfon, Wales, U.K. 60 53°08'N 04°16'W
Cagayan de Oro, Phil. 52 08°30'N 124°40'E
Cagayan Sulu I., Phil. 52 07°01'N 118°30'E
Cagliari, Italy 61 39°13'N 09°07'E
Caguas, P.R.(U.S.A.) 78 18°14'N 66°02'W
Caicos Is., T.&C.Is. (U.K.) 78 21°40'N 71°40'W
Caicos Pass., T.&C.Is. (U.K.) 78 22°45'N 72°45'W
Caird Coast, Antarc. 82 75°00'S 25°00'W
Cairns, Queens., Aust. 70 16°57'S 145°45'E
Cairo, Egypt 66 30°01'N 31°14'E
Cajamarca, Peru 80 07°05'S 78°28'W
Calabria, Region, Italy 60 39°00'N 16°30'E
Calafate, Arg. 80 50°19'S 72°15'W
Calais, France 61 50°57'N 01°56'E
Calama, Chile 80 22°30'S 68°55'W
Calang, Indo. 52 04°37'N 95°37'E
Calbayog, Phil. 52 12°04'N 124°38'E
Calgary, Canada 74 51°00'N 114°10'W
Cali, Col. 80 03°25'N 76°35'W
California, G.of, Mexico 73 27°00'N 111°00'W
CALIFORNIA, U.S.A. 72 37°30'N 119°30'W
Calimere, Pt., India 27 10°17'N 79°52'E
Callao, Peru 80 12°00'S 77°00'W
Caloocan, Phil. 52 14°39'N 120°58'E
Cam Ranh, Viet. 55 11°56'N 109°14'E
Camaguey, Cuba 78 21°20'N 78°00'W
Camaron, C., Hond. 78 16°00'N 85°05'W
CAMBODIA, Asia 55 12°15'N 105°00'E
Cambrian Mts., U.K. 64 52°03'N 03°57'W
Cambridge Bay, Canada 74 69°10'N 105°00'W
Cambridge, Eng., U.K. 64 52°12'N 00°08'E
Cambridge, Jam. 78 18°18'N 77°54'W
CAMEROON, Africa 66 06°00'N 12°30'E
Cameroon, Mt., Vol., Cam. 65 04°13'N 09°10'E
Camorta I., India 27 08°12'N 93°32'E
Campbel Town, Scot., U.K. 64 55°26'N 05°36'W
Campbell I., N.Z. 70 52°30'S 169°00'E
Campbellpore, Pak. 48 33°46'N 72°26'E
Campbelltown, N.S.W., Aust. 70 34°04'S 150°49'E
Campeche Bay, Mexico 78 19°30'N 93°00'W
Campeche, Mexico 74 19°50'N 90°32'W

Chongp'yong

Davis Str.

116 Index

Dawa Elgon

Dawa, R., Eth.	65	04°11'N	42°06'E
Dawna Ra., Mts., Myan.-Thai.	55	16°30'N	98°30'E
Dawson Creek, Canada	74	55°45'N	120°15'W
Dawson, Canada	74	64°10'N	139°30'W
Daxue Shan, Mts., China	50	30°30'N	101°30'E
Dayr az Zawr, Syria	51	35°20'N	40°05'E
Dayton, Ohio, U.S.A.	77	39°45'N	84°12'W
Daytona Beach, Fla., U.S.A.	77	29°13'N	81°01'W
De Aar, S.Africa	66	30°39'S	24°00'E
De Long Is., Russia	53	76°40'N	149°20'E
Dead Sea, Israel-Jordan	51	31°30'N	35°30'E
Death Valley, U.S.A.	77	36°15'N	116°50'W
Debrecen, Hung.	61	47°33'N	21°42'E
Decatur, Ill., U.S.A.	77	39°51'N	88°57'W
Deccan, Plat., India	27	18°00'N	79°00'E
Dechhu, Raj., India	29	26°47'N	72°20'E
Dee, R., U.K.	60	57°09'N	02°05'W
Dee, R., U.K.	60	53°22'N	03°17'W
Deep Bay, Hong Kong, China	50		
Degana, Raj., India	29	26°46'N	74°16'E
Deh Shu, Afgh.	48	30°27'N	63°24'E
Dehiwala-Mt.Lavinia, S.Lanka	49	06°50'N	79°51'E
Dehra Dun, Utta., India	21	30°18'N	78°00'E
Dehri, Bihar, India	23	24°50'N	84°15'E
Del Rio, Texas, U.S.A.	77	29°22'N	100°54'W
Delaware B., U.S.A.	77	39°00'N	75°10'W
DELAWARE, U.S.A.	77	39°00'N	75°20'W
Delgado, C., Mozam.	65	10°45'S	40°40'E
Delhi, Delhi, India	21	28°36'N	77°12'E
DELHI, India	21	28°45'N	77°15'E
Denham, Mt., Jam.	78	18°14'N	77°31'W
Denham, W.A., Aust.	70	25°56'S	113°31'E
Denizli, Turkey	51	37°42'N	29°02'E
Denmark Str., Green.(Den.)-Ice.	73	65°00'N	28°00'W
DENMARK, Europe	61	55°30'N	09°00'E
Denpasar, Indo.	52	08°45'S	115°14'E
Denver, Colo., U.S.A.	77	39°44'N	104°59'W
Deoband, U.P., India	22	29°42'N	77°43'E
Deogarh, Odisha, India	25	21°32'N	84°45'E
Deori, MP, India	**24**	**23°22'N**	**79°02'E**
Deoria, U.P., India	22	26°31'N	83°48'E
Deosai Mts., India	21	35°40'N	75°00'E
Deosai Plains, India	21	34°48'N	75°31'E
Deothang, Bhutan	48	26°51'N	91°27'E
Depsang Plains, India	21	35°15'N	78°00'E
Dera Baba Nanak, Punjab, India	21	32°01'N	75°07'E
Dera Bugti, Pak.	48	29°03'N	69°12'E
Dera Ghazi Khan, Pak.	48	30°05'N	70°43'E
Dera Ismail Khan, Pak.	48	31°50'N	70°50'E
Derbent, Russia	53	42°05'N	48°15'E
Derby, Eng., U.K.	64	52°56'N	01°28'W
Derby, W.A., Aust.	70	17°18'S	123°38'E
Derg, L., Ire.	64	53°00'N	08°20'W
Des Moines, Iowa, U.S.A.	77	41°35'N	93°37'W
Des Moines, R., U.S.A.	77	40°23'N	91°25'W
Dese, Eth.	66	11°05'N	39°40'E
Deseado, Arg.	80	47°55'S	66°00'W
Deshgaon, M.P., India	24	21°54'N	76°12'E
Deshnok, Raj., India	29	27°47'N	73°24'E
Desna, R., Ukr.-Russia	60	50°33'N	30°32'E
Detroit, Mich., U.S.A.	77	42°20'N	83°03'W
Devenport, Tas., Aust.	70	41°10'S	146°22'E
Devgadh Bariya, Guj., India	29	22°40'N	73°55'E
Devghar, Jhar., India	23	24°30'N	86°42'E
Devikolam, Kerala, India	27	10°04'N	77°05'E
Devikot, Raj., India	29	26°38'N	71°09'E
Devli, Raj., India	29	25°50'N	75°20'E
Devon I., Canada	73	75°10'N	85°00'W
Dewas, M.P., India	24	22°59'N	76°03'E
Dezful, Iran	51	32°20'N	48°30'E
Dhahran, S.Ar.	51	26°10'N	50°07'E
Dhaka, Bangla.	48	23°42'N	90°24'E
Dhamar, Yemen	51	14°30'N	44°20'E
Dhamtari, Chhat., India	23	20°42'N	81°36'E
Dhanbad, Jhar., India	23	23°48'N	86°24'E
Dhandhuka, Guj., India	29	22°21'N	71°58'E
Dhangadhi, Nepal	49	28°41'N	80°38'E
Dhankuta, Nepal	49	26°54'N	87°24'E
Dhanushkodi, T.N., India	27	09°13'N	79°24'E
Dhaola Dhar Ra., India	21	32°30'N	76°05'E
Dhar, M.P., India	24	22°35'N	75°26'E
Dharamgarh, Odisha, India	25	19°52'N	82°47'E
Dharampur, Guj., India	29	20°32'N	73°17'E

Dharan Bazar, Nepal	49	26°52'N	87°19'E
Dhari, Guj., India	29	21°19'N	71°02'E
Dharmanagar, Tri., India	30	24°24'N	92°07'E
Dharmapuri, T.N., India	27	12°10'N	78°10'E
Dharmastala, Kar., India	27	12°59'N	75°12'E
Dharmavaram, A.P., India	27	14°29'N	77°44'E
Dharmjaygarh, Chhat., India	25	22°28'N	83°13'E
Dharmshala, H.P., India	21	32°16'N	76°23'E
Dharwad, Kar., India	27	15°22'N	75°15'E
Dhasan, R., India	24	25°44'N	79°24'E
Dhaulagiri, Mtn., Nepal	49	28°48'N	83°24'E
Dhaulpur, Raj., India	29	26°40'N	77°57'E
Dhebar L., India	29	24°10'N	74°00'E
Dhemaji, Assam, India	30	27°32'N	94°33'E
Dhenkanal, Odisha, India	25	20°45'N	85°35'E
Dholka, Guj., India	29	22°44'N	72°29'E
Dhoraji, Guj., India	29	21°45'N	70°37'E
Dhorimanna, Raj., India	29	25°10'N	71°26'E
Dhrangadhra, Guj., India	29	22°59'N	71°31'E
Dhuburi, Assam, India	30	26°00'N	90°00'E
Dhunche, Nepal	49	28°06'N	85°14'E
Dhupgarh, Pk., India	24	22°27'N	78°22'E
Dhuri, Punjab, India	21	30°22'N	75°53'E
Di'er Songhua Jiang, R., China	54	45°20'N	124°40'E
Diamantina, Brazil	80	18°17'S	43°40'W
Diamantina, R., Aust.	70	26°45'S	139°10'E
Diamond Harbour, W.B., India	30	22°11'N	88°14'E
Dibang or Sikang, R., India	30	28°30'N	95°48'E
Dibrugarh, Assam, India	30	27°30'N	94°54'E
Dickinson, N.Dak., U.S.A.	77	46°53'N	102°47'W
Didwana, Raj., India	29	27°23'N	74°36'E
Dig, Raj., India	29	27°28'N	77°20'E
Digboi, Assam, India	30	27°24'N	95°42'E
Digha, W.B., India	30	21°38'N	87°32'E
Diglipur, A.&N.Is., India	27	13°16'N	93°00'E
Digri, Pak.	48	25°09'N	69°08'E
Digul, R., Indo.	52	07°07'S	138°42'E
Dihang or Siang, R., India-China	30	28°10'N	94°59'E
Dijon, France	61	47°20'N	05°03'E
Dikson, Russia	53	73°40'N	80°05'E
Dili, East Timor	52	08°39'S	125°34'E
Dimapur, Naga., India	30	25°54'N	93°45'E
Dimjor La, P., India	21	34°03'N	79°11'E
Dimona, Israel	51	31°04'N	35°02'E
Dinagat, I., Phil.	52	10°15'N	125°30'E
Dinajpur, Bangla.	48	25°33'N	88°43'E
Dinaric Alps, Mts., Bos.Herz.-Cro.	60	44°00'N	16°30'E
Dindi, R., India	27	16°24'N	78°15'E
Dindigul, T.N., India	27	10°25'N	78°00'E
Dindori, M.P., India	24	22°55'N	81°09'E
Dingle B., Ire.	64	52°03'N	10°20'W
Dingle, Ire.	64	52°09'N	10°17'W
Dingli, Malta	61	35°52'N	14°22'E
Dingwall, Scot., U.K.	64	57°36'N	04°26'W
Dinhata, W.B., India	30	26°08'N	89°27'E
Dipayal, Nepal	49	29°14'N	80°54'E
Diphu P., India	30	28°09'N	97°20'E
Diphu, Assam, India	30	25°49'N	93°26'E
Diplo, Pak.	48	24°35'N	69°35'E
Dir, Pak.	48	35°12'N	71°54'E
Dirang Dzong, Ar.P., India	30	27°24'N	92°06'E
Dire Dawa, Eth.	66	09°35'N	41°45'E
Dirk Hartog I., Aust.	70	25°50'S	113°05'E
Disa, Guj., India	29	24°18'N	72°10'E
Disappointment, L., Aust.	70	23°20'S	122°40'E
Dispur, Assam, India	30	26°06'N	91°54'E
Diu, D.&D., India	29	20°42'N	70°54'E
Divi Pt., India	27	15°59'N	81°09'E
Diwal Qol, Afgh.	48	34°23'N	67°52'E
Dixon Entrance, U.S.A.-Canada	77	54°30'N	132°00'W
Diyarbakir, Turkey	51	37°55'N	40°18'E
Diz, Pak.	48	26°38'N	63°33'E
Djanet, Alg.	66	24°35'N	09°32'E
DJIBOUTI, Africa	66	12°00'N	43°00'E
Djibouti, Djibouti	66	11°30'N	43°05'E
Dmitriy Laptev Str., Russia	53	73°00'N	140°00'E
Dnieper, R., Europe	60	46°30'N	32°18'E

Dniester, R., Ukr.-Moldova	60	46°18'N	30°17'E
Dnipropetrovsk, Ukr.	53	48°30'N	35°00'E
Doba, Chad	66	08°40'N	16°50'E
Dod Ballapur, Kar., India	27	13°18'N	77°30'E
Doda Betta, Pk., India	27	11°26'N	76°45'E
Doda, J.&K., India	21	33°10'N	75°34'E
Dodge City, Kansas, U.S.A.	77	37°45'N	100°01'W
Dodoma, Tanz.	66	06°08'S	35°45'E
Dogo, I., Japan	54	36°15'N	133°16'E
Doha, Qatar	51	25°15'N	51°35'E
Dohrighat, U.P., India	22	26°14'N	83°36'E
Dolak, I., Indo.	52	08°00'S	138°30'E
Dolungmukh, Ar.P., India	30	27°35'N	94°17'E
Dom, Mtn., Indo.	52	02°43'S	137°06'E
Domagnano, S.M.	61		
Dombas, Norway	61	62°04'N	09°08'E
Dominica Pass., Dom.-Guad.	78	15°40'N	61°20'W
DOMINICA, N.Amer.	78	15°20'N	61°20'W
DOMINICAN REPUBLIC, N.Amer.	78	19°00'N	70°30'W
Don, R., Russia	60	47°04'N	39°18'E
Don, R., U.K.	64	57°11'N	02°05'W
Doncaster, Eng., U.K.	64	53°32'N	01°06'W
Dondra Hd., S.Lanka	49	05°55'N	80°40'E
Donegal B., Ire.	64	54°31'N	08°49'W
Donegal, Ire.	64	54°39'N	08°05'W
Donets, R., Ukr.- Russia	60	47°33'N	40°55'E
Donetsk, Ukr.	53	48°00'N	37°45'E
Dong Hoi, Viet.	55	17°26'N	106°36'E
Dongargarh, Chhat., India	25	21°10'N	80°40'E
Dongchuan, China	50	26°08'N	103°01'E
Dongola, Sudan	66	19°09'N	30°22'E
Dongting Hu, L., China	50	29°18'N	112°45'E
Donostia-San Sebastian, Spain	61	43°17'N	01°58'W
Dorchester, Eng., U.K.	64	50°42'N	02°27'W
Dori, Bur.Faso	66	14°03'N	00°02'W
Dornakal, A.P., India	27	17°26'N	80°11'E
Dornoch Firth, U.K.	64	57°51'N	04°04'W
Dornoch, Scot., U.K.	64	57°53'N	04°02'W
Dortmund, Ger.	61	51°30'N	07°28'E
Dothan, Ala., U.S.A.	77	31°13'N	85°24'W
Douala, Cam.	66	04°00'N	09°45'E
Doubtless Bay, N.Z.	70	34°55'S	173°26'E
Douglas, Isle of Man (U.K.)	64	54°10'N	04°28'W
Douro, R., Port.-Spain	60	41°08'N	08°40'W
Dover, Del., U.S.A.	77	39°10'N	75°32'W
Dover, Eng., U.K.	64	51°07'N	01°19'E
Dover, Str.of, U.K.-France	64	51°00'N	01°30'E
Dowl at Yar, Afgh.	48	34°33'N	65°47'E
Dowlatabad, Afgh.	48	36°30'N	64°53'E
Dowshi, Afgh.	48	35°35'N	68°43'E
Dozen, I., Japan	54	36°05'N	133°05'E
Drake Pass., Antarc.	84	58°00'S	68°00'W
Drakensberg, Mts., Lesotho-S.Africa	64	31°00'S	28°00'E
Drammen, Norway	61	59°42'N	10°12'E
Dras, J.&K., India	21	34°25'N	75°48'E
Drava, R., Europe	60	45°33'N	18°55'E
Dresden, Ger.	61	51°03'N	13°44'E
Drogheda, Ire.	64	53°43'N	06°22'W
Dry Harbour Mts., Jam.	78	18°19'N	77°24'W
Duars, Plains, India	30	26°30'N	90°00'E
Dubai, U.A.E.	51	25°18'N	55°20'E
Dubawnt L., Canada	73	63°04'N	101°42'W
Dubawnt, R., Canada	73	64°33'N	100°06'W
Dubbo, N.S.W., Aust.	70	32°11'S	148°35'E
Dublin, Ire.	64	53°21'N	06°15'W
Dubrovnik, Cro.	61	42°39'N	18°06'E
Duc Trong, Viet.	55	11°45'N	108°23'E
Ducie I., Pitcairn Is. (U.K.)	70	24°40'S	124°48'W
Dudhana, R., India	27	19°18'N	76°56'E
Dudhinagar, U.P., India	22	24°12'N	83°18'E
Dudhwa, U.P., India	22	28°30'N	80°39'E
Dudinka, Russia	53	69°30'N	86°13'E
Dukhan, Qatar	51	25°25'N	50°50'E
Duki, Pak.	48	30°14'N	68°25'E
Dukou, China	50	26°35'N	101°43'E
Dulan, China	50	36°14'N	98°03'E
Dulce Gulf, C.Rica	78	08°40'N	83°20'W
Duluth, Minn., U.S.A.	77	46°47'N	92°06'W
Dum Dum, W.B., India	30	22°39'N	88°33'E
Dum Duma, Assam, India	30	27°32'N	95°33'E
Dumaguete, Phil.	52	09°17'N	123°15'E
Dumfries, Scot., U.K.	64	55°04'N	03°37'W
Dumka, Jhar., India	23	24°12'N	87°15'E
Dumraon, Bihar, India	23	25°33'N	84°08'E

Dun Laoghaire, Ire.	64	53°17'N	06°08'W
Dunagiri, Pk., India	21	30°27'N	79°50'E
Duncan Pass., India	27	11°04'N	92°40'E
Duncansby Hd., U.K.	64	58°39'N	03°01'W
Dundalk, Ire.	64	54°01'N	06°24'W
Dundee, Scot., U.K.	64	56°28'N	02°59'W
Dunedin, N.Z.	70	45°53'S	170°30'E
Dungarpur, Raj., India	29	23°52'N	73°45'E
Dungarvan, Ire.	64	52°05'N	07°37'W
Dunhuang, China	50	40°08'N	94°36'E
Dunmore Town, Baha.	78	25°30'N	76°39'W
Durango, Colo., U.S.A.	77	37°16'N	107°53'W
Durango, Mexico	74	24°03'N	104°39'W
Durban, S.Africa	66	29°49'S	31°01'E
Durg, Chhat., India	25	21°12'N	81°18'E
Durgapur, W.B., India	30	23°30'N	87°20'E
Durham, Eng., U.K.	64	54°47'N	01°34'W
Durham, N.C., U.S.A.	77	35°59'N	78°54'W
Durmitor, Mtn., Monte.	60	43°10'N	19°00'E
Durres, Alb.	61	41°19'N	19°28'E
Dushanbe, Tajik.	53	38°33'N	68°48'E
Duyun, China	50	26°18'N	107°29'E
Dwarka, Guj., India	29	22°12'N	68°54'E
Dyer, C., Canada	73	66°40'N	61°00'W
Dzamin Uud, Mong.	50	43°50'N	111°58'E
Dzavhan Gol, R., Mong.	50	48°48'N	93°24'E
Dzerzhinsk, Russia	61	56°14'N	43°30'E
Dzhugdzhur Ra., Russia	53	57°30'N	138°00'E
Dzungarian Basin, China	50	44°30'N	86°00'E

E

E.Siberian Sea, Russia	53	73°00'N	160°00'E
Earnslaw, Mt., N.Z.	70	44°32'S	168°27'E
East C., Russia	53	66°05'N	169°40'W
East Cape, N.Z.	70	37°42'S	178°35'E
East China Sea, Asia	50	30°05'N	126°00'E
East Coast Bays, N.Z.	70	36°46'S	174°46'E
East Kilbride, Scot., U.K.	64	55°45'N	04°09'W
East Korea Bay, N.Korea	54	39°30'N	128°00'E
East Lamma Chan., Hong Kong, China	50		
East London, S.Africa	66	33°00'S	27°55'E
EAST TIMOR, Asia	52	08°50'S	125°45'E
Eastbourne, Eng., U.K.	64	50°46'N	00°18'E
Easter I., Chile	86	27°00'S	109°00'W
Eastern Channel, Japan	54	34°00'N	129°30'E
Eastern Des., Egypt	65	28°15'N	31°55'E
Eastern Ghats, India	27	14°00'N	78°50'E
Eastern Sayan Mts., Russia	53	53°30'N	98°00'E
Eastern, Cord., Col.	79	05°00'N	74°30'W
Eastmain, R., Canada	73	52°27'N	78°26'W
Ebetsu, Japan	54	43°07'N	141°34'E
Ebinur Hu, L., China	50	45°00'N	83°00'E
Ebro, R., Spain	60	40°43'N	00°54'E
ECUADOR, S.Amer.	80	02°00'S	78°00'W
Ed Damer, Sudan	66	17°27'N	34°00'E
Ed Debba, Sudan	66	18°00'N	30°51'E
Ed, Eri.	66	14°00'N	41°38'E
Edinburgh, Scot., U.K.	64	55°57'N	03°13'W
Edmonton, Canada	74	53°30'N	113°30'W
Edrengiyn Nuruu, Mong.	50	44°15'N	97°45'E
Edward, L., Uganda-Dem. Rep.of Congo	65	00°25'S	29°40'E
Edwards Plat., U.S.A.	77	30°45'N	101°20'W
Egmont, C., N.Z.	70	39°16'S	173°45'E
EGYPT, Africa	66	26°30'N	29°30'E
Eight Degree Chan., India	27	08°00'N	73°00'E
Eighty Mile Beach, Aust.	70	19°30'S	120°40'E
Eivissa, I., Spain	60	39°00'N	01°23'E
El Djouf, Des., Mali-Maur.	65	21°00'N	08°00'W
El Fasher, Sudan	66	13°33'N	25°26'E
El Geneina, Sudan	66	13°26'N	22°26'E
El Golea, Alg.	66	30°30'N	02°50'E
El Muglad, Sudan	66	11°01'N	27°44'E
El Obeid, Sudan	66	13°08'N	30°10'E
El Paso, Texas, U.S.A.	77	31°45'N	106°29'W
EL SALVADOR, N.Amer.	78	13°50'N	89°00'W
El Serrat, Ando.	61	42°37'N	01°33'E
El Turbio, Arg.	80	51°46'S	72°07'W
Elat, Israel	51	29°30'N	34°56'E
Elazig, Turkey	51	38°37'N	39°14'E
Elbe, R., Ger.	60	53°50'N	09°00'E
Elbert, Mt., U.S.A.	77	39°07'N	106°27'W
Elbrus, Mtn., Russia	60	43°21'N	42°30'E
Elburz Mts., Iran	51	36°00'N	52°00'E
Eleuthera I., Baha.	78	25°00'N	76°20'W
Elgin, Scot., U.K.	64	57°39'N	03°19'W
Elgon, Mt., Kenya-Uganda	65	01°10'N	34°30'E

120 Index

Ipoh Kandangan

Ipoh, Malay.	52	04°35'N	101°05'E
Ipswich, Eng., U.K.	64	52°04'N	01°10'E
Iquique, Chile	80	20°19'S	70°05'W
Iquitos, Peru	80	03°45'S	73°10'W
Iraklion, Greece	61	35°20'N	25°12'E
IRAN, Asia	57	33°00'N	53°00'E
Iran, Plat.of, Iran	57	32°00'N	55°00'E
Iranshahr, Iran	57	27°15'N	60°40'E
IRAQ, Asia	57	33°00'N	44°00'E
Irazu, Vol., C.Rica	78	09°59'N	83°52'W
Irbid, Jordan	57	32°35'N	35°48'E
Irbil, Iraq	57	36°11'N	44°01'E
IRELAND, Europe	64	53°50'N	07°52'W
Iringa, Tanz.	66	07°48'S	35°43'E
Iriomote I., Japan	54	24°19'N	123°48'E
Irish Sea, U.K.- Ire.	64	53°38'N	04°48'W
Irkutsk, Russia	53	52°18'N	104°20'E
Ironword, Mich., U.S.A.	77	46°27'N	90°09'W
Irrawaddy, Mouths of the, Myan.	55	15°41'N	95°05'E
Irrawaddy, R., Myan.	55	15°48'N	95°05'E
Irtysh, R., Asia	53	61°04'N	68°52'E
Irvine, Scot., U.K.	64	55°37'N	04°41'W
Isabela, Phil.	52	06°40'N	122°10'E
Isabelia, Cord., Nicar.	78	13°30'N	85°25'W
Isafjordur, Ice.	61	66°05'N	23°09'W
Isbister, Scot., U.K.	64	60°36'N	01°19'W
Ishigaki I., Japan	55	24°20'N	124°10'E
Ishim, R., Russia-Kazak.	53	57°45'N	71°10'E
Ishinomaki, Japan	54	38°32'N	141°20'E
Ishkoshim, Afgh.	48	36°44'N	71°37'E
Ishkuman, J.& K., India	21	36°30'N	73°50'E
Isiro, Dem.Rep.of Congo	66	02°53'N	27°40'E
Iskenderun, Turkey	57	36°32'N	36°10'E
Islamabad, Pak.	48	33°42'N	73°06'E
Islampur, W.B., India	30	26°16'N	88°11'E
Islands, Bay of, N.Z.	70	35°15'S	174°06'E
Islay, I., U.K.	64	55°46'N	06°10'W
Ismailiyah Canal, Egypt	65	30°36'N	32°15'E
Ismoili Somoni, Mtn., Tajik.	53	39°00'N	72°02'E
Isparta, Turkey	57	37°47'N	30°30'E
ISRAEL, Asia	57	32°00'N	34°50'E
Issyk Kul, L., Kyr.	53	42°25'N	77°15'E
Istanbul, Turkey	61	41°00'N	29°00'E
Itaituba, Brazil	80	04°10'S	55°50'W
ITALY, Europe	45	42°00'N	13°00'E
Itanagar, Ar.P., India	30	27°06'N	93°37'E
Itarsi, M.P., India	24	22°36'N	77°51'E
Ittoqqortoormiit, Green.(Den.)	82	70°20'N	23°00'W
Iturup, I., Russia	53	45°00'N	148°00'E
Ivanovo, Russia	61	57°05'N	41°00'E
Ivory Coast, Cote d'Ivoire	65		
Iwaki, Japan	54	37°03'N	140°55'E
Izabal, L., Guat.	78	15°30'N	89°10'W
Izhevsk, Russia	53	56°51'N	53°14'E
Izmir, Turkey	57	38°25'N	27°08'E
Izu Is., Japan	54	34°30'N	140°00'E
Izumo, Japan	54	35°20'N	132°46'E

J

Jabalpur, M.P., India	24	23°12'N	79°54'E
Jackson Bay, N.Z.	70	43°58'S	168°42'E
Jackson, Missi., U.S.A.	77	32°18'N	90°12'W
Jacksonville, Fla., U.S.A.	77	30°20'N	81°39'W
Jacmel, Haiti	78	18°14'N	72°32'W
Jacobabad, Pak.	48	28°20'N	68°29'E
Jadcherla, A.P., India	27	16°44'N	78°05'E
Jaddi, Ras, C., Pak.	48	25°14'N	63°31'E
Jafarabad, Guj., India	29	20°50'N	71°25'E
Jaffna, S.Lanka	49	09°42'N	80°00'E
Jagadhri, Har., India	21	30°10'N	77°20'E
Jagannathganj Ghat, Bangla.	48	24°44'N	89°50'E
Jagatsinghapur, Odisha, India	25	20°13'N	86°18'E
Jagdalpur, Chhat., India	25	19°06'N	82°00'E
Jagdishpur, U.P., India	22	26°26'N	81°39'E
Jagraon, Punjab, India	21	30°48'N	75°36'E
Jagtial, A.P., India	27	18°50'N	79°00'E
Jahanabad, Bihar, India	23	25°13'N	85°05'E
Jaintia Hills, India	30	25°12'N	92°23'E
Jaintiapur, Bangla.	48	25°08'N	92°07'E
Jaipur, Raj., India	29	26°54'N	75°48'E
Jais, U.P., India	22	26°16'N	81°37'E
Jaisalmer, Raj., India	29	26°52'N	70°56'E
Jaisinghnagar, M.P., India	24	23°39'N	81°26'E
Jaitaran, Raj., India	29	26°08'N	74°00'E
Jajarkot, Nepal	49	28°42'N	82°11'E
Jajpur, Odisha, India	25	20°53'N	86°22'E
Jakarta, Indo.	52	06°09'S	106°49'E
Jakhau, Guj., India	29	23°12'N	68°47'E
Jalalabad, Afgh.	48	34°30'N	70°29'E
Jalalabad, Punjab, India	21	30°35'N	74°17'E
Jalalabad, U.P., India	22	27°41'N	79°42'E
Jalandhar, Punjab, India	21	31°18'N	75°36'E
Jaldak, Afgh.	48	31°58'N	66°43'E
Jalor, Raj., India	29	25°19'N	72°44'E
Jalpaiguri, W.B., India	30	26°32'N	88°46'E
Jam Jodhpur, Guj., India	29	21°54'N	70°01'E
JAMAICA, N.Amer.	78	18°10'N	77°30'W
Jamalpur, Bangla.	48	24°52'N	89°56'E
Jambi, Indo.	52	01°38'S	103°30'E
Jambusar, Guj., India	29	22°03'N	72°51'E
James B., Canada	73	51°30'N	80°00'W
James Ross I., Antarc.	82	63°58'S	57°50'W
James, R., U.S.A.	77	42°52'N	97°18'W
JAMMU AND KASHMIR, India	21	34°00'N	76°00'E
Jammu, J.& K., India	21	32°42'N	74°54'E
Jamnagar, Guj., India	29	22°24'N	70°00'E
Jampur, Pak.	48	29°42'N	70°36'E
Jamshedpur, Jhar., India	23	22°48'N	86°12'E
Jamtara, Jhar., India	23	23°59'N	86°49'E
Jamui, Bihar, India	23	24°55'N	86°13'E
Jamuna, R., Bangla.	48	24°54'N	89°42'E
JAN MAYEN (NOR.), I., Arctic Region	82	71°00'N	09°00'W
Janakpur, Nepal	49	26°45'N	85°59'E
Jangipur, W.B., India	30	24°27'N	88°04'E
Janjgir, Chhat., India	25	22°02'N	82°35'E
Januaria, Brazil	80	15°25'S	44°25'W
Jaora, M.P., India	24	23°40'N	75°10'E
Japan Tr., N.Pa.Oc.	44	32°00'N	142°00'E
JAPAN, Asia	54	36°00'N	138°00'E
Japan, Sea of (East Sea), Asia	54	40°00'N	135°00'E
Japura, R., Brazil	79	03°08'S	65°46'W
Jara La, P., India	21	32°47'N	77°35'E
Jaranwala, Pak.	48	31°15'N	73°26'E
Jaria Jhanjail, Bangla.	48	25°00'N	90°39'E
Jarvis I., Line Is.	70	00°15'S	159°55'W
Jasdan, Guj., India	29	22°02'N	71°15'E
Jashipur, Odisha, India	25	21°59'N	86°05'E
Jashpur, Chhat., India	25	22°53'N	84°09'E
Jask, Iran	57	25°38'N	57°45'E
Jatara, M.P., India	24	24°57'N	79°07'E
Jatobal, Brazil	80	04°35'S	49°33'W
Jaunpur, U.P., India	22	25°48'N	82°42'E
Java Sea, Indo.	52	04°35'S	107°15'E
Java Tr., Ind.Oc.	52	09°00'S	105°00'E
Java, I., Indo.	44	07°00'S	110°00'E
Javadi Hills, India	27	12°40'N	78°40'E
Jawala Mukhi, H.P., India	21	31°51'N	76°22'E
Jawhar, Maha., India	27	19°54'N	73°18'E
Jaya, Pk., Indo.	52	03°57'S	137°17'E
Jayanti, W.B., India	30	26°45'N	89°40'E
Jayapura, Indo.	52	02°28'S	140°38'E
Jayawijaya Mts., Indo.	52	05°00'S	139°00'E
Jaynagar, Bihar, India	29	26°35'N	86°07'E
Jaypur, Odisha, India	24	18°51'N	82°40'E
Jaz Murian L., Iran	57	27°24'N	58°49'E
Jeddah, S.Ar.	57	21°29'N	39°10'E
Jefferson City, Misso., U.S.A.	77	38°34'N	92°10'W
Jelep La, P., India	20	27°22'N	88°43'E
Jember, Indo.	52	08°11'S	113°41'E
Jeremie, Haiti	78	18°40'N	74°10'W
JERSEY(U.K.), Europe	64	49°11'N	02°07'W
Jerusalem, Israel	57	31°47'N	35°10'E
JERVIS BAY TERRITORY, Aust.	70	35°08'S	150°46'E
Jessore, Bangla.	48	23°12'N	89°12'E
Jetpur, Guj., India	29	21°45'N	70°10'E
Jhabua, M.P., India	24	22°43'N	74°37'E
Jhajjar, Har., India	21	28°37'N	76°42'E
Jhal Jhao, Pak.	48	26°20'N	65°35'E
Jhalarapatan, Raj., India	29	24°32'N	76°10'E
Jhalawar, Raj., India	29	24°40'N	76°10'E
Jhalida, W.B., India	30	23°22'N	85°59'E
Jhalod, Guj., India	29	23°06'N	74°09'E
Jhang Maghiana, Pak.	48	31°15'N	72°22'E
Jhansi, U.P., India	22	25°24'N	78°36'E
Jhargram, W.B., India	30	22°27'N	87°00'E
JHARKHAND, India	23	23°27'N	85°00'E
Jharsuguda, Odisha, India	25	21°48'N	84°00'E
Jhelum, R., Pak.-India	21	32°30'N	73°00'E
Jhunjhunun, Raj., India	29	28°10'N	75°30'E
Ji'an, China	50	27°06'N	114°59'E
Jialing Jiang, R., China	50	29°30'N	106°20'E
Jiangmen, China	50	22°32'N	113°00'E
Jiayuguan, China	50	39°45'N	98°15'E
Jilin, China	50	43°44'N	126°30'E
Jima, Eth.	66	07°40'N	36°47'E
Jinan, China	50	36°38'N	117°01'E
Jind, Har., India	21	29°19'N	76°22'E
Jingdezhen, China	50	29°20'N	117°11'E
Jining, China	50	35°22'N	116°34'E
Jinsha Jiang, R., China	55	28°46'N	104°36'E
Jintur, Maha., India	27	19°36'N	76°39'E
Jinzhou, China	50	41°05'N	121°03'E
Jiujiang, China	50	29°42'N	115°58'E
Jiwani, Pak.	48	25°07'N	61°48'E
Jiwani, Ras, C., Pak.	48		
Jixi, China	50	45°20'N	130°50'E
Jizan, S.Ar.	57	17°00'N	42°20'E
Joao Pessoa, Brazil	80	07°10'S	34°52'W
Jobat, M.P., India	24	22°25'N	74°35'E
Jodhpur, Raj., India	29	26°12'N	73°00'E
Jodiya, Guj., India	29	22°39'N	70°21'E
Joetsu, Japan	54	37°10'N	138°14'E
Jog Falls, India	27	14°13'N	74°46'E
Jogbani, Bihar, India	23	26°24'N	87°12'E
Jogindarnagar, H.P., India	21	31°51'N	76°49'E
Johannesburg, S.Africa	66	26°10'S	28°02'E
Johor Strait, Sing.	52	01°28'N	103°52'E
Joinville I., Antarc.	82	65°00'S	55°30'W
Joinville, Brazil	80	26°15'S	48°55'W
Jolarpettai, T.N., India	27	12°35'N	78°32'E
Joliet, Ill., U.S.A.	77	41°32'N	88°05'W
Jolo, I., Phil.	52	06°00'N	121°09'E
Jolo, Phil.	45	06°00'N	121°00'E
Jomolhari, Pk., Bhutan	48	27°51'N	89°22'E
Jonkoping, Sweden	61	57°45'N	14°10'E
Jonquiere, Canada	74	48°27'N	71°14'W
Jora, M.P., India	24	26°18'N	77°46'E
JORDAN, Asia	57	31°00'N	36°00'E
Jorhat, Assam, India	30	26°48'N	94°12'E
Jorm, Afgh.	48	36°49'N	70°55'E
Joseph Bonaparte G., Aust.	70	14°35'S	128°50'E
Joshimath, Utta., India	21	30°33'N	79°36'E
Jowai, Megh., India	30	25°26'N	92°12'E
Juan de Fuca, Str.of, Canada-U.S.A.	73	48°15'N	124°00'W
Juan Fernandez Is., Chile	79	33°50'S	80°00'W
Juan Gallegos, I., Panama	78		
Juazeiro, Brazil	80	09°30'S	40°30'W
Juba, S.Sudan	66	04°53'N	31°38'E
Jubba, R., Soma.	65	00°15'S	42°37'E
Juberri, Ando.	61		
Juiz de I, Brazil	80	21°43'S	43°19'W
Juliaca, Peru	80	15°25'S	70°10'W
Jumla, Nepal	49	29°12'N	82°12'E
Junagadh, Guj., India	29	21°30'N	70°24'E
Juneau, Alaska, U.S.A.	77	58°18'N	134°25'W
Junnar, Maha., India	27	19°12'N	73°58'E
Jur, R., S.Sudan	65	08°45'N	29°15'E
Jura Mts., France-Switz.	60	46°40'N	06°05'E
Jura, I., U.K.	64	56°00'N	05°50'W
Jurong I., Sing.	52		
Jurong Strait, Sing.	52	01°18'N	103°43'E
Jurong, R., Sing.	52	01°18'N	103°44'E
Jurua, R., Brazil	79	02°37'S	65°44'W
Juticalpa, Hond.	80	14°40'N	86°12'W
Jutland, Pen., Den.	60	56°25'N	09°30'E
Juventud I., Cuba	78	21°40'N	82°40'W
Juymand, Iran	57	34°18'N	58°38'E

K

K², Pk., India	21	35°48'N	76°30'E
Kaashidhoo, Maldives	48	04°58'N	73°28'E
Kabaena, I., Indo.	52	05°15'S	122°00'E
Kabala, Sa.Leone	66	09°38'N	11°37'W
Kabalo, Dem.Rep.of Congo	66	06°00'S	27°00'E
Kabani, R., India	27	12°13'N	76°52'E
Kabul, Afgh.	48	34°30'N	69°06'E
Kabul, R., Afgh.	48	34°30'N	70°18'E
Kabwe, Zambia	66	14°30'S	28°29'E
Kachchh Pen., India	29	23°24'N	69°30'E
Kachchh, G.of, India	29	22°30'N	69°30'E
Kachchh, Rann of, India	29	24°00'N	70°00'E
Kackar, Mt., Turkey	57	40°45'N	41°10'E
Kadamatt I., India	27	11°12'N	72°45'E
Kadapa, A.P., India	27	14°30'N	78°48'E
Kadi, Guj., India	29	23°18'N	72°23'E
Kadiri, A.P., India	27	14°12'N	78°13'E
Kaduna, Nig.	66	10°30'N	07°21'E
Kadur, Kar., India	27	13°32'N	76°01'E
Kaedi, Maur.	66	16°09'N	13°28'W
Kaesong, N.Korea	54	37°58'N	126°35'E
Kagal, Maha., India	27	16°35'N	74°19'E
Kagoshima, Japan	54	31°35'N	130°33'E
Kahan, Pak.	48	29°20'N	68°57'E
Kahoolawe, I., U.S.A.	78	20°33'N	156°37'W
Kahramanmaras, Turkey	51	37°37'N	36°53'E
Kai Is., Indo.	52	05°55'S	132°45'E
Kaiapoi, N.Z.	70	43°23'S	172°39'E
Kaieteur Falls, Guyana	79	05°01'N	59°10'W
Kaifeng, China	50	34°48'N	114°21'E
Kaikoura, N.Z.	70	42°25'S	173°43'E
Kailashahar, Tri., India	30	24°19'N	92°00'E
Kaimana, Indo.	52	03°39'S	133°45'E
Kaimanawa Mts., N.Z.	70	39°15'S	175°56'E
Kaimganj, U.P., India	22	27°33'N	79°24'E
Kainji Res., Nig.	65	10°01'N	04°40'E
Kaipara Harbour, N.Z.	70	36°25'S	174°14'E
Kairana, U.P., India	22	29°24'N	77°15'E
Kaitaia, N.Z.	70	35°08'S	173°17'E
Kaithal, Har., India	21	29°48'N	76°26'E
Kaiwi Chan., U.S.A.	77	21°15'N	157°30'W
Kajalgaon, Assam, India	30		
Kakdwip, W.B., India	30	21°53'N	88°12'E
Kakhovka Res., Ukr.	60	47°05'N	34°00'E
Kakkanad, Kerala, India	27	09°59'N	76°21'E
Kakinada, A.P., India	27	17°00'N	82°12'E
Kala Oya, R., S.Lanka	49	08°20'N	79°45'E
Kalabagh, Pak.	49	33°00'N	71°28'E
Kaladan, R., India-Myan.	55	20°15'N	92°59'E
Kaladi, Kerala, India	27	10°14'N	76°24'E
Kalahari Des., Africa	65	23°00'S	22°00'E
Kalam, Pak.	48	35°30'N	72°30'E
Kalamata, Greece	61	37°03'N	22°10'E
Kalamazoo, Mich., U.S.A.	77	42°17'N	85°35'W
Kalambo Falls, Tanz.-Zambia	65	08°37'S	31°35'E
Kalanwali, Har., India	21	29°50'N	75°01'E
Kalat, Pak.	48	29°08'N	66°31'E
Kalavad, Guj., India	29	22°13'N	70°26'E
Kalburgi, Kar., India	27	17°24'N	76°48'E
Kalemie, Dem.Rep. of Congo	66	05°55'S	29°09'E
Kaleymo, Myan.	55	23°11'N	94°05'E
Kalgoorlie, W.A., Aust.	70	30°50'S	121°30'E
Kali Sindh, R., India	29	25°27'N	76°17'E
Kaligandaki, R., Nepal	49	27°45'N	84°23'E
Kalimpong, W.B., India	30	27°06'N	88°30'E
Kalinga, Odisha, India	25	20°11'N	84°25'E
Kaliningrad, Russia	53	54°42'N	20°32'E
Kaliveli Tank, India	27	12°05'N	79°50'E
Kaliyaganj, W.B., India	30	25°38'N	88°19'E
Kalka, Har., India	21	30°46'N	76°57'E
Kallam, Maha., India	27	18°35'N	76°04'E
Kallang, R., Sing.	52	01°18'N	103°52'E
Kalmar, Sweden	61	56°40'N	16°20'E
Kalol, Guj., India	29	23°15'N	72°33'E
Kalpa, H.P., India	21	31°32'N	78°15'E
Kalpeni I., India	27	10°04'N	73°37'E
Kalpetta, Kerala, India	27	11°37'N	76°04'E
Kalsubai, Pk., India	27	19°35'N	73°45'E
Kaluga, Russia	61	54°35'N	36°10'E
Kalutara, S.Lanka	49	06°35'N	80°00'E
Kalyan, Maha., India	27	19°16'N	73°11'E
Kalyandurg, A.P., India	27	14°32'N	77°05'E
Kama Res., Russia	60		
Kama, R., Russia	60	55°45'N	52°00'E
Kamaishi, Japan	54	39°16'N	141°53'E
Kamalia, Pak.	48	30°44'N	72°42'E
Kamalpur, Tri., India	30	24°10'N	91°50'E
Kaman, Raj., India	29	27°37'N	77°12'E
Kamaran, I., Yemen	57	15°21'N	42°35'E
Kamareddi, A.P., India	27	18°17'N	78°19'E
Kamchatka Pen., Russia	53	57°00'N	160°00'E
Kamet, Mtn., India	21	30°55'N	79°39'E
Kamina, Dem.Rep.of Congo	66	08°45'S	25°00'E
Kamloops, Canada	74	50°40'N	120°20'W
Kampala, Uganda	66	00°20'N	32°30'E
Kampire Dior, Pk., India	21	36°38'N	74°23'E
Kampong Cham, Camb.	55	11°59'N	105°26'E
Kampong Chhnang, Camb.	55	12°12'N	104°42'E
Kampong Spoe, Camb.	55	11°23'N	104°34'E
Kampong Thum, Camb.	55	12°39'N	104°53'E
Kampot, Camb.	55	10°36'N	104°12'E
Kamthi, Maha., India	27	21°13'N	79°12'E
Kananga, Dem.Rep.of Congo	66	05°55'S	22°18'E
Kanazawa, Japan	54	36°30'N	136°38'E
Kanchenjunga, Mtn., India	30	27°50'N	88°10'E
Kanchipuram, T.N., India	27	12°48'N	79°42'E
Kandahar, Afgh.	48	31°32'N	65°30'E
Kandahar, Maha., India	27	18°54'N	77°13'E
Kandalaksha, Russia	53	67°09'N	32°30'E
Kandangan, Indo.	52	02°50'S	115°20'E

Kandi — Kola Pen.

Kolaka   Leticia

Index 125

Mersin — Naga Hills

Place	Page	Latitude	Longitude
Mersin, Turkey	57	36°51'N	34°36'E
Mersing, Malay.	52	02°25'N	103°50'E
Merta Road, Raj., India	29	26°41'N	73°55'E
Merta, Raj., India	29	26°39'N	74°04'E
Meru, Kenya	66	00°03'N	37°40'E
Mesa, Ariz., U.S.A.	77	33°25'N	111°50'W
Mesopotamia, Region, Iraq-Syria	51	33°30'N	44°00'E
Messina, Italy	61	38°11'N	15°34'E
Messina, Str.of, Italy	60	38°15'N	15°35'E
Meta, R., Col.	79	06°12'N	67°28'W
Mettur Dam, India	27		
Metz, France	61	49°08'N	06°10'E
Meulaboh, Indo.	52	04°11'N	96°03'E
Mexicali, Mexico	74	32°40'N	115°30'W
Mexican Plat., Mexico	73	25°00'N	104°00'W
Mexico City, Mexico	74	19°20'N	99°10'W
Mexico, G.of, N.Amer.	73	25°00'N	90°00'W
MEXICO, N.Amer.	74	25°00'N	105°00'W
Meymaneh, Afgh.	48	35°54'N	64°43'E
Mezen, R., Russia	60	65°44'N	44°22'E
Mezen, Russia	53	65°50'N	44°20'E
Mhow, M.P., India	24	22°33'N	75°50'E
Miami, Fla., U.S.A.	77	25°47'N	80°11'W
Mianawali, Pak.	48	32°36'N	71°30'E
Mianyang, China	50	31°22'N	104°47'E
Michigan, L., U.S.A.	77	44°00'N	87°00'W
MICHIGAN, U.S.A.	77	44°00'N	85°00'W
Michurinsk, Russia	61	52°58'N	40°27'E
MICRONESIA, FEDERATED STATES OF, Oceania	70	09°00'N	150°00'E
Micronesia, Is., Pac.Oc.	84	08°00'N	160°00'E
Middle America Tr., Pac.Oc.	73		
Middle Andaman, I., India	27	12°36'N	92°48'E
Middle Atlas, Mts., Mor.	65	34°00'N	06°00'W
Middle Coral Reef, India	27	12°30'N	92°23'E
Middlesbrough, Eng., U.K.	64	54°35'N	01°13'W
Midway I., U.S.A	86	28°13'N	177°22'W
Mikir Hills, India	30	26°20'N	93°30'E
Mikkeli, Fin.	61	61°43'N	27°15'E
Mikura I., Japan	54	33°52'N	139°36'E
Milan, Italy	61	45°28'N	09°12'E
Mildura, Vic., Aust.	70	34°13'S	142°09'E
Milford Sound, N.Z.	70	44°41'S	167°47'E
Mili, Atoll, Marshall Is.	70	06°05'N	171°55'E
Milk, R., Canada-U.S.A.	77	48°04'N	106°19'W
Milk, Wadi el, R., Sudan	65	18°01'N	30°58'E
Milton Keynes, Eng., U.K.	64	52°01'N	00°44'W
Milwaukee Deep, P.R.Trench, Atl.Oc.	73	19°50'N	68°00'W
Milwaukee, Wis., U.S.A.	77	43°02'N	87°55'W
Min Chiang, R., China	50	26°00'N	119°35'E
Min Jiang, R., China	50	28°45'N	104°40'E
Minahassa Pen., Indo.	52	01°00'N	124°35'E
Minbu, Myan.	55	20°10'N	94°53'E
Minch, The, Chan., U.K.	64	58°05'N	05°55'W
Mindanao, I., Phil.	52	08°00'N	125°00'E
Mindelo, C.Verde	66	16°52'N	24°59'W
Mindoro Str., Phil.	52	12°30'N	120°30'E
Mindoro, I., Phil.	52	13°00'N	121°00'E
Minicoy I., India	27	08°18'N	73°00'E
Minneapolis, Minn., U.S.A.	77	44°59'N	93°16'W
Minnesota, R., U.S.A.	73	44°55'N	93°11'W
MINNESOTA, U.S.A.	77	46°00'N	94°15'W
Minorca, I., Spain	60	40°00'N	04°00'E
Minot, N.Dak., U.S.A.	77	48°14'N	101°18'W
Minsk, Bel.	53	53°52'N	27°30'E
Mintaka P., India	21	36°54'N	74°54'E
Minto, L., Canada	73	57°15'N	74°50'W
Minya, Egypt	66	28°07'N	30°33'E
Miraflores Locks, Panama	78		
Miraj, Maha., India	27	16°50'N	74°45'E
Miram Shah, Pak.	48	33°00'N	70°02'E
Mirbat, Oman	57	17°00'N	54°45'E
Miri Hills, India	30	27°50'N	94°00'E
Miri, Malay.	52	04°23'N	113°59'E
Miri, Mt., Pak.	48	29°10'N	62°50'E
Mirim, L., Brazil-Urug.	79	32°45'S	52°50'W
Mirjaveh, Iran	57	28°59'N	61°26'E
Mirpur Khas, Pak.	48	25°30'N	69°00'E
Mirpur Sakro, Pak.	48	24°33'N	67°41'E
Mirpur, J.&K., India	21	33°32'N	73°56'E
Mirs Bay, Hong Kong, China	50		
Mirzapur, U.P., India	22	25°12'N	82°36'E
Mishmi Hills, India	30	29°00'N	96°00'E
Misima I., P.N.G.	70	10°40'S	152°45'E
Miskolc, Hung.	61	48°07'N	20°50'E
Misool, I., Indo.	52	01°52'S	130°10'E
Misratah, Libya	66	32°24'N	15°03'E
Misrikh, U.P., India	22	27°21'N	80°35'E
Mississippi River Delta, U.S.A.	77	29°10'N	89°15'W
Mississippi, R., U.S.A.	77	29°09'N	89°15'W
MISSISSIPPI, U.S.A.	77	33°00'N	90°00'W
Missoula, Mont., U.S.A.	77	46°52'N	114°01'W
Missouri, Coteau du, U.S.A.	77	47°00'N	100°00'W
Missouri, R., U.S.A.	77	38°49'N	90°07'W
MISSOURI, U.S.A.	77	38°25'N	92°30'W
Mistassini, L., Canada	73	51°00'N	73°30'W
Misti, Vol., Peru	79	16°18'S	71°24'W
Mitchell, Mt., U.S.A.	73	35°46'N	82°16'W
Mitchell, R., Aust.	70	15°12'S	141°35'E
Mitchell, S.Dak., U.S.A.	77	43°43'N	98°02'W
Mito, Japan	54	36°20'N	140°30'E
Mitu, Col.	80	01°08'N	70°03'W
Mitumba Mts., Dem. Rep.of Congo	65	07°00'S	27°30'E
Miyake I., Japan	54	34°05'N	139°30'E
Miyako I., Japan	54	24°45'N	125°20'E
Miyako, Japan	54	39°40'N	141°59'E
Miyakonojo, Japan	54	31°40'N	131°05'E
Miyazaki, Japan	54	31°56'N	131°30'E
Mizo Hills, India	30	23°25'N	92°50'E
MIZORAM, India	30	23°30'N	92°48'E
Moa I., Aust.	70		
Moba, Dem. Rep.of Congo	66	07°00'S	29°48'E
Mobile, Ala., U.S.A.	77	30°41'N	88°03'W
Mocambique, Mozam.	66	15°03'S	40°42'E
Modasa, Guj., India	29	23°30'N	73°21'E
Moe, Vic., Aust.	70	38°12'S	146°19'E
Moffat, Scot., U.K.	64	55°21'N	03°27'W
Moga, Punjab, India	21	30°48'N	75°08'E
Mogadishu, Soma.	66	02°02'N	45°25'E
Mogaung, Myan.	55	25°17'N	96°53'E
Mogocha, Russia	53	53°40'N	119°50'E
Mohaka, R., N.Z.	70	39°07'S	177°12'E
Mohala, Chhat., India	25	20°34'N	80°48'E
Mohana, M.P., India	24	25°53'N	77°45'E
Mohanganj, Bangla.	48	24°52'N	90°59'E
Mohania, Bihar, India	23	25°09'N	83°37'E
Moheli, I., Com.	65	12°15'S	43°50'E
Moirang, Mani., India	30	24°28'N	93°44'E
Mojave Des., U.S.A.	77	35°00'N	116°30'W
Mokau, R., N.Z.	70	38°35'S	174°35'E
Mokochung, Naga., India	30	26°18'N	94°30'E
Mokp'o, S.Korea	54	34°47'N	126°23'E
Mold, Wales, U.K.	64	53°09'N	03°08'W
Molde, Norway	61	62°54'N	07°09'E
MOLDOVA, Europe	53	47°00'N	28°00'E
Mollendo, Peru	80	17°00'S	72°00'W
Molokai, I., U.S.A.	77	21°08'N	157°00'W
Molucca Sea, Indo.	52	02°00'S	124°00'E
Moluccas, Is., Indo.	52	01°00'S	127°00'E
Mombasa, Kenya	66	04°02'S	39°43'E
Mon, Naga., India	30	26°40'N	95°01'E
Mona Pass., Dom. Rep.-P.R.	78	18°30'N	67°45'W
MONACO, Europe	61	43°46'N	07°23'E
Monaco, Port of, Monaco	61		
Monaco-Ville, Monaco	61	43°42'N	07°22'E
Monaghan, Ire.	64	54°15'N	06°57'W
Monasterevan, Ire.	64	53°08'N	07°03'W
Monbetsu, Japan	54	44°21'N	143°22'E
Monchegorsk, Russia	61	67°54'N	32°58'E
Moncton, Canada	74	46°07'N	64°51'W
Mong Hsat, Myan.	55	20°32'N	99°16'E
Mongar, Bhutan	48	27°15'N	91°12'E
MONGOLIA, Asia	50	47°00'N	103°00'E
Mongolia, Plat.of, Mong.	50	46°30'N	110°00'E
Mongu, Zambia	66	15°16'S	23°12'E
Monkoto, Dem. Rep.of Congo	66	01°38'S	20°35'E
Monowai, L., N.Z.	70	45°53'S	167°25'E
Monroe, La., U.S.A.	77	32°30'N	92°07'W
Monrovia, Lib.	66	06°18'N	10°47'W
MONTANA, U.S.A.	77	47°00'N	110°00'W
Monte Giardino, S.M.	61	43°55'N	12°29'E
Montego Bay, Jam.	78	18°30'N	78°00'W
MONTENEGRO, Europe	61	42°30'N	19°18'E
Monteria, Col.	80	08°46'N	75°53'W
Monterrey, Mexico	74	25°40'N	100°30'W
Montes Claros, Brazil	80	16°30'S	43°50'W
Montevideo, Urug.	80	34°50'S	56°11'W
Montgomery, Ala., U.S.A.	77	32°23'N	86°19'W
Montpelier, Vt., U.S.A.	77	44°16'N	72°35'W
Montpellier, France	61	43°37'N	03°52'E
Montreal, Canada	74	45°31'N	73°34'W
Montrose, Scot., U.K.	64	56°44'N	02°27'W
MONTSERRAT(U.K.), N.Amer.	78	16°40'N	62°10'W
Monturull, Pk., Ando.-Spain	61		
Monywa, Myan.	55	22°05'N	95°13'E
Monze, C., Pak.	48	24°47'N	66°37'E
Moore, L., Aust.	70	29°50'S	117°35'E
Moosonee, Canada	74	51°17'N	80°39'W
Mopti, Mali	66	14°30'N	04°00'W
Moqor, Afgh.	48	32°50'N	67°42'E
Moradabad, U.P., India	22	28°48'N	78°48'E
Moranhat, Assam, India	30	27°08'N	94°54'E
Morant Pt., Jam.	78	17°55'N	76°12'W
Moratuwa, S.Lanka	49	06°45'N	79°55'E
Morava, R., Serbia	60	44°43'N	21°02'E
Moravian Heights, Czech Rep.	60	49°30'N	15°40'E
Moray Firth, U.K.	64	57°40'N	03°52'W
Morbi, Guj., India	29	20°50'N	70°42'E
More Assynt, Ben, U.K.	64	58°08'N	04°52'W
Morecambe, Eng., U.K.	64	54°05'N	02°52'W
Moree, N.S.W., Aust.	70	29°28'S	149°54'E
Moreh, Mani., India	30	24°21'N	94°21'E
Morena, M.P., India	24	26°30'N	78°00'E
Morena Mts., Spain	60	38°20'N	04°00'W
Moriah, Trin.&Tob.	78	11°15'N	60°43'W
Morioka, Japan	54	39°45'N	141°08'E
Moro G., Phil.	52	06°30'N	123°00'E
MOROCCO, Africa	66	32°00'N	05°50'W
Moron, Mong.	50	49°28'N	100°08'E
Moroni, Comoros	66	11°39'S	43°14'E
Morotai, I., Indo.	52	02°10'N	128°30'E
Morpeth, Eng., U.K.	64	55°10'N	01°41'W
Moruga, Trin.&Tob.	78	10°06'N	61°17'W
Morven, Queens., Aust.	70	26°22'S	147°05'E
Moscow, Russia	53	55°45'N	37°35'E
Moshi, Tanz.	66	03°22'S	37°18'E
Mosjoen, Norway	61	65°51'N	13°12'E
Mosquito Coast, Nicar.	78	13°00'N	84°00'W
Mosquitos, G.of, Panama	78	09°15'N	81°10'W
Moss, Norway	61	59°27'N	10°40'E
Mossel Bay, S.Africa	66	34°11'S	22°08'E
Mosta, Malta	61	35°55'N	14°25'E
Mostar, Bos.Herz.	61	43°22'N	17°50'E
Mosul, Iraq	57	36°15'N	43°05'E
Motagua, R., Guat.	78	15°44'N	88°14'W
Moth, U.P., India	22	25°41'N	78°58'E
Motherwell, Scot., U.K.	64	55°47'N	03°58'W
Motihari, Bihar, India	23	26°42'N	84°54'E
Mottama, G.of, Myan.	55	16°05'N	96°30'E
Motueka, N.Z.	70	41°07'S	173°01'E
Moulmein, Myan.	55	16°30'N	97°40'E
Moundou, Chad	66	08°40'N	16°10'E
Mount Gambier, S.A., Aust.	70	37°50'S	140°46'E
Mount Isa, Queens., Aust.	70	20°42'S	139°26'E
Mount Magnet, W.A., Aust.	70	28°02'S	117°47'E
Mount Maunganui, N.Z.	70	37°40'S	176°14'E
Moyobamba, Peru	80	06°00'S	77°00'W
Mozambique Chan., Africa	65	20°00'S	43°00'E
MOZAMBIQUE, Africa	66	19°00'S	35°00'E
Mt.Hagen, P.N.G.	70	05°52'S	144°16'E
Mtwara, Tanz.	66	10°20'S	40°20'E
Mu Us Shamo, Des., China	50	39°00'N	109°00'E
Muang Phon Hong, Laos	55	18°29'N	102°27'E
Muara, Brunei	52	05°02'N	115°03'E
Muchinga Mts., Zambia	65	11°30'S	31°30'E
Mudan Jiang, R., China	54	46°15'N	129°31'E
Mudanjiang, China	50	44°38'N	129°30'E
Muddebihal, Kar., India	27	16°20'N	76°10'E
Mudgal, Kar., India	27	16°01'N	76°27'E
Mughal Sarai, U.P., India	22	25°15'N	83°11'E
Mugla, Turkey	57	37°15'N	28°22'E
Mugugau, Nepal	49	29°45'N	82°30'E
Muhleholz, Liech.	61		
Mukadahan, Thai.	55	16°30'N	104°44'E
Mukher, Maha., India	27	18°42'N	77°23'E
Muktsar, Punjab, India	21	30°30'N	74°30'E
Mula, R., India	27	19°38'N	75°03'E
Mulaku Atoll, Maldives	49	03°00'N	73°30'E
Mulanje, Mt., Malawi-Mozam.	65	15°54'S	35°35'E
Mulhacen, Pk., Spain	60	37°04'N	03°20'W
Muling Ja, P., India	21	31°12'N	79°17'E
Mull, I., U.K.	64	56°25'N	05°56'W
Mullaittivu, S.Lanka	49	09°18'N	80°48'E
Muller Mts., Indo.	50	00°30'N	113°30'E
Mullingar, Ire.	64	53°31'N	07°21'W
Multai, M.P., India	24	21°50'N	78°21'E
Multan, Pak.	49	30°06'N	71°30'E
Mumbai, Maha., India	27	19°00'N	72°48'E
Mun, R., Thai.	55	15°16'N	105°29'E
Muna, I., Indo.	52	05°00'S	122°30'E
Munabao, Raj., India	29	25°45'N	70°18'E
Mundra, Guj., India	29	22°54'N	69°48'E
Mungaoli, M.P., India	24	24°24'N	78°07'E
Mungbere, Dem. Rep.of Congo	66	02°36'N	28°28'E
Mungeli, Chhat., India	25	22°05'N	81°43'E
Munger, Bihar, India	23	25°24'N	86°30'E
Munich, Ger.	61	48°08'N	11°34'E
Munnar, Kerala, India	27	10°07'N	77°03'E
Murai Res., Sing.	52	01°24'N	103°41'E
Murat, R., Turkey	57	38°46'N	40°00'E
Murchison, R., Aust.	70	27°45'S	114°00'E
Murcia, Spain	61	38°05'N	01°10'W
Mures, R., Rom.	60	46°15'N	20°13'E
Murgap, R., Turk.	48	37°15'N	62°26'E
Murghab, R., Afgh.	48	35°50'N	63°07'E
Murmansk, Russia	53	68°57'N	33°10'E
Muroran, Japan	54	42°25'N	141°00'E
Muroto Pt., Japan	54	33°15'N	134°10'E
Murray Bridge, S.A., Aust.	70	35°06'S	139°14'E
Murray, R., Aust.	70	35°20'S	139°22'E
Murshidabad, W.B., India	30	24°11'N	88°19'E
Murtajapur, Maha., India	27	20°40'N	77°25'E
Murud, Maha., India	27	18°19'N	72°59'E
Murwara, M.P., India	24	23°48'N	80°18'E
Murzuq, Libya	66	25°53'N	13°57'E
Mus, Turkey	57	38°45'N	41°30'E
Musa Khel Bazar, Pak.	48	30°59'N	69°52'E
Musa Qal'eh, Afgh.	48	32°20'N	64°50'E
Muscat, Oman	57	23°37'N	58°36'E
Musgrave Ranges, Aust.	70	26°00'S	132°00'E
Musi, R., India	27	16°41'N	79°40'E
Musi, R., Indo.	52	02°20'S	104°56'E
Musiri, T.N., India	27	10°58'N	78°26'E
Muskogee, Okla., U.S.A.	77	35°45'N	95°22'W
Mussoorie, Utta., India	21	30°27'N	78°06'E
Mustang, Nepal	49	29°10'N	83°55'E
Mut, Egypt	66	25°28'N	28°58'E
Mutare, Zimb.	66	18°58'S	32°38'E
Mutsu, Japan	54	41°05'N	140°55'E
Muyun Kum, Des., Kazak.	53	44°12'N	71°00'E
Muzaffarabad, J.&K., India	21	34°25'N	73°30'E
Muzaffargarh, Pak.	48	30°00'N	71°12'E
Muzaffarnagar, U.P., India	22	29°30'N	77°42'E
Muzaffarpur, Bihar, India	23	26°06'N	85°24'E
Muztag, Mtn., China	50	36°19'N	87°23'E
Mwanza, Tanz.	66	02°30'S	32°58'E
Mweru, L., Dem.Rep. of Congo-Zambia	65	09°00'S	28°40'E
My Tho, Viet.	55	10°20'N	106°23'E
Myajlar, Raj., India	29	26°15'N	70°20'E
MYANMAR, Asia	55	21°00'N	96°30'E
Myaungmya, Myan.	55	16°34'N	94°54'E
Myeik Arch., Myan.	55	12°27'N	98°37'E
Myeik, Myan.	55	12°27'N	98°37'E
Myingyan, Myan.	55	21°25'N	95°23'E
Myitkyina, Myan.	55	25°26'N	97°26'E
Mykolayiv, Ukr.	61	46°58'N	32°00'E
Mymensingh, Bangla.	48	24°42'N	90°30'E
Mysuru, Kar., India	27	12°18'N	76°36'E

N

Place	Page	Latitude	Longitude
N.Dvina, R., Russia	60	64°32'N	40°30'E
N.IRELAND, U.K.	64	54°45'N	07°00'W
N.Platte, Nebr., U.S.A.	77	41°08'N	100°46'W
N.Ronaldsay, I., U.K.	64	59°22'N	02°26'W
N.Saskatchewan, R., Canada	73	53°15'N	105°05'W
N.Siberian Lowland, Russia	53	72°00'N	104°00'E
N.Uist, I., U.K.	64	57°40'N	07°15'W
N.W.Cape, Aust.	70	21°45'S	114°09'E
N.York Moors, Hills, U.K.	64	54°23'N	00°53'W
Nabarangapur, Odisha, India	25	19°17'N	82°37'E
Nabha, Punjab, India	21	30°26'N	76°14'E
Nacala, Mozam.	66	14°31'S	40°34'E
Nachingwea, Tanz.	66	10°23'S	38°49'E
Nadiad, Guj., India	29	22°42'N	72°54'E
Naenwa, Raj., India	29	25°44'N	75°56'E
Naga Hills, India	30	25°55'N	94°13'E

Naga

North Dakota

Princess Ragnhild Coast — Ritchie's Arch.

Riva

Santo Domingo — Sirohi

Swakopmund

Todupulai

Index 135

Vanern Xam Nua

Vanern, L., Sweden	60	58°47'N	13°30'E
Vanlaiphai, Miz., India	30	23°07'N	93°06'E
Vanthli, Guj., India	29	21°29'N	70°20'E
Vanua Levu, I., Fiji	70	16°33'S	179°15'E
VANUATU, Oceania	70	15°00'S	168°00'E
Varada, R., India		15°00'N	75°40'E
Varanasi, U.P., India	22	25°20'N	83°04'E
Vardo, Norway	82	70°23'N	31°05'E
Varna, Bulg.	61	43°13'N	27°56'E
Vasco-da-Gama, Goa, India	27	15°19'N	73°54'E
VATICAN CITY, Europe	61	41°54'N	12°27'E
Vatican City, Vatican City	61		
Vattaru Falhu, Maldives	48	03°16'N	73°25'E
Vattern, L., Sweden	60	58°25'N	14°30'E
Vav, Guj., India	29	24°20'N	71°32'E
Vavuniya, S.Lanka	49	08°45'N	80°27'E
Vedaranniyam, T.N., India	27	10°21'N	79°50'E
Velanganni, T.N., India	27	10°43'N	79°50'E
Velikaya, R., Russia	73	64°32'N	176°06'E
Velikiy Novgorod, Russia	61	58°30'N	31°25'E
Vellar, R., India	27	11°24'N	79°30'E
Vellore, T.N., India	27	12°57'N	79°10'E
Vembanad L., India	27	09°36'N	76°15'E
Venezuela, G.of, Ven.	78	11°30'N	71°00'W
VENEZUELA, S.Amer.	80	07°00'N	65°20'W
Venezuelan Basin, Caribbean Sea	73		
Venice, Italy	61	45°27'N	12°21'E
Venkatagiri, A.P., India	27	14°00'N	79°35'E
Veraval, Guj., India	29	20°52'N	70°27'E
Verde, C., Sen.	65	14°45'N	17°32'W
Verkhoyansk Ra., Russia	53	66°00'N	129°00'E
Verkhoyansk, Russia	53	67°35'N	133°25'E
VERMONT, U.S.A.	77	44°00'N	73°00'W
Verona, Italy	61	45°27'N	11°00'E
Vesteralen, Is., Nor.	60	68°45'N	15°00'E
Vesuvius, Vol., Italy	60	40°49'N	14°26'E
Vetluga, R., Russia	60	56°36'N	46°04'E
Victoria Falls, Zambia-Zimb.	65	17°58'S	25°52'E
Victoria I., Canada	73	71°00'N	111°00'W
Victoria Land, Antarc.	82	75°00'S	160°00'E
VICTORIA, Aust.	70	37°20'S	144°10'E
Victoria, Canada	71	48°30'N	123°25'W
Victoria, L., Africa	65	01°00'S	33°00'E
Victoria, Malta	61	36°03'N	14°14'E
Victoria, Mt., Myan.	55	21°11'N	93°56'E
Victoria, R., Aust.	70	15°10'S	129°40'E
Victoria, Seychelles	87	05°00'S	55°40'E
Vidin, Bulg.	61	43°59'N	22°50'E
Vidisha, M.P., India	24	23°31'N	77°48'E
Viedma, Arg.	80	40°50'S	63°00'W
Vienna, Aus.	61	48°12'N	16°22'E
Vienne, R., France	60	47°13'N	00°05'E
Vientiane, Laos	55	17°58'N	102°37'E
Viet Tri, Viet.	55	21°17'N	105°25'E
VIETNAM, Asia	55	15°00'N	108°00'E
Vieux Fort, St.Lucia	78	13°46'N	60°58'W
Vigan, Phil.	52	17°35'N	120°28'E
Vigo, Spain	61	42°12'N	08°41'W
Vijapur, Guj., India	29	23°32'N	72°47'E
Vijapura, Kar., India	27	16°48'N	75°42'E
Vijayanagar, Ar.P., India	30	27°15'N	96°55'E
Vijayawada, A.P., India	27	16°31'N	80°39'E
Vikarabad, A.P., India	27	17°20'N	77°52'E
Vil'kitskiy Str., Russia	53	78°00'N	103°00'E
Vila de Sena, Mozam.	66	17°25'S	35°00'E
Villa Montes, Bol.	80	21°10'S	63°30'W
Villarrica, Para.	80	25°40'S	56°30'W
Vilnius, Lith.	53	54°38'N	25°19'E
Viluppuram, T.N., India	27	11°59'N	79°31'E
Vilyuy, R., Russia	53	64°24'N	126°26'E
Vinh Long, Viet.	55	10°11'N	105°59'E
Vinh, Viet.	55	18°38'N	105°42'E
Vinnytsya, Ukr.	53	49°15'N	28°30'E
Vinson Massif, Mt., Antarc.	82	79°50'S	84°17'W
Viramgam, Guj., India	29	23°05'N	72°00'E
Virarajendrapet, Kar., India	27	12°10'N	75°50'E
VIRGIN IS.(U.K.), N.Amer.	78	18°30'N	64°30'W
VIRGIN IS.(U.S.A.), N.Amer.	78	18°20'N	65°00'W
Virginia, Minn., U.S.A.	77	47°31'N	92°32'W
VIRGINIA, U.S.A.	77	37°30'N	78°45'W
Virudunagar, T.N., India	27	09°30'N	77°58'E
Viscount Melville Sd., Canada	73	74°10'N	108°00'W
Vishakhapatnam, A.P., India	27	17°45'N	83°20'E
Vishwanath, Assam, India	30	26°37'N	93°11'E
Visnagar, Guj., India	29	23°45'N	72°32'E
Vistula, R., Poland	60	54°22'N	18°55'E
Vitebsk, Bel.	61	55°10'N	30°15'E
Viti Levu, I., Fiji	70	17°30'S	177°30'E
Vitim, R., Russia	53	59°26'N	112°34'E
Vizianagaram, A.P., India	27	18°06'N	83°30'E
Vladikavkaz, Russia	61	43°00'N	44°35'E
Vladimir, Russia	61	56°15'N	40°30'E
Vladivostok, Russia	61	43°10'N	131°53'E
Vlore, Alb.	61	40°32'N	19°28'E
Vohimena, C., Madag.	65	25°34'S	45°10'E
Voi, Kenya	66	03°25'S	38°32'E
Volga Upland, Russia	60	51°00'N	46°00'E
Volga, R., Russia	60	46°00'N	48°30'E
Volgograd Res., Russia	60	50°00'N	45°20'E
Volgograd, Russia	53	48°40'N	44°25'E
Volkhov, R., Russia	60	60°08'N	32°20'E
Vologda, Russia	53	59°13'N	39°54'E
Volta, L., Ghana	65	07°30'N	00°15'E
Vorkuta, Russia	53	67°48'N	64°20'E
Voronezh, Russia	53	51°40'N	39°10'E
Voss, Norway	61	60°38'N	06°27'E
Vostok I., Kiribati	70	10°05'S	152°23'W
Vrindavan, U.P., India	22	27°37'N	77°40'E
Vung Tau, Viet.	55	10°22'N	107°05'E
Vyara, Guj., India	29	21°08'N	73°28'E
Vyatka, R., Russia	60	55°37'N	51°28'E
Vyborg, Russia	53	60°43'N	28°47'E
Vychegda, R., Russia	60	61°18'N	46°36'E

W

W.Dvina, R., Bel.-Russia	60	57°04'N	24°03'E
Wabash, R., U.S.A.	77	37°48'N	88°02'W
Waco, Texas, U.S.A.	77	31°33'N	97°09'W
Wad Medani, Sudan	66	14°28'N	33°30'E
Wad Thana, Pak.	48	27°22'N	66°23'E
Waddington, Mt., Canada	73	51°21'N	125°18'W
Wadhwan, Guj., India	29	22°43'N	71°40'E
Wadi Halfa, Sudan	66	21°53'N	31°19'E
Wadi, Kar., India	27	17°06'N	77°00'E
Wagga Wagga, N.S.W., Aust.	70	35°07'S	147°24'E
Waghai, Guj., India	29	20°44'N	73°36'E
Wah, Pak.	48	33°45'N	72°40'E
Wahiawa, Hawaii, U.S.A.	77	21°30'N	158°02'W
Waiapu, R., N.Z.	70	37°47'S	178°29'E
Waiau, R., N.Z.	70	46°12'S	167°37'E
Waiau, R., N.Z.	70	42°47'S	173°22'E
Waidhan, M.P., India	24		
Waigeo, I., Indo.	52	00°20'S	130°40'E
Waihou, R., N.Z.	70	37°15'S	175°40'E
Waikaremoana, L., N.Z.	70	38°49'S	177°09'E
Wailuku, Hawaii, U.S.A.	77	20°54'N	156°30'W
Waimate, N.Z.	70	44°45'S	171°03'E
Waingapu, Indo.	52	09°35'S	120°11'E
Wainwright, Alaska, U.S.A.	77	70°39'N	159°51'W
Waipa, R., N.Z.	70	37°40'S	175°08'E
Wairarapa, L., N.Z.	70	41°14'S	175°15'E
Wairau, R., N.Z.	70	41°32'S	174°07'E
Wairoa, R., N.Z.	70	36°05'S	173°59'E
Waishnodevi, J.&K., India	21	33°00'N	74°59'E
Waitaki, R., N.Z.	70	44°56'S	171°07'E
Wakatipu, L., N.Z.	70	45°05'S	168°33'E
Wakayama, Japan	54	34°15'N	135°15'E
Wake, I., U.S.A.	87	19°17'N	166°36'E
Wakefield, Eng., U.K.	64	53°41'N	01°29'W
Wakhan, Region, Afgh.	48	37°00'N	73°00'E
Wakhan Darya, R., Afgh.	21	37°01'N	72°40'E
Wakkanai, Japan	54	45°28'N	141°35'E
Walachia, Region, Rom.	60		
Walawe Ganga, R., S.Lanka	49	06°06'N	81°01'E
WALES, U.K.	64	52°30'N	03°45'W
Wales, U.S.A.	74	65°37'N	168°05'W
Walgreen Coast, Antarc.	82	75°15'S	105°00'W
Walla Walla, Wash., U.S.A.	77	46°04'N	118°20'W
WALLIS & FUTUNA IS. (FR.), Oceania	70	13°18'S	176°10'W
Walong, Ar.P., India	30	28°06'N	97°00'E
Waltair, A.P., India	27	17°44'N	83°23'E
Walvis B., Nam.	65		
Walvis Bay, Nam.	66	23°00'S	14°28'E
Wana, Pak.	48	32°20'N	69°32'E
Wanaka, L., N.Z.	70	44°33'S	169°07'E
Wanaka, N.Z.	70	44°42'S	169°09'E
Wanaparthy, A.P., India	27	16°22'N	78°04'E
Wanganui, N.Z.	70	39°56'S	175°03'E
Wanganui, R., N.Z.	70	39°55'S	175°04'E
Wangdue Phodrang, Bhutan	48	27°28'N	89°54'E
Wangerberg, Liech.	61		
Wankaner, Guj., India	29	22°35'N	71°00'E
Wanxian, China	50	30°42'N	108°20'E
Warangal, A.P., India	27	18°00'N	79°30'E
Waraseoni, M.P., India	24	21°46'N	80°03'E
Warkworth, N.Z.	70	36°24'S	174°41'E
Warrego, R., Aust.	70	30°24'S	145°21'E
Warrington, Eng., U.K.	64	53°24'N	02°35'W
Warsaw, Poland	61	52°13'N	21°00'E
Warwick, Eng., U.K.	64	52°18'N	01°35'W
Wash, The, B., U.K.	64	52°58'N	00°20'E
Washington, D.C., U.S.A.	77	38°54'N	77°02'E
Washington, Mt., U.S.A.	73	44°16'N	71°18'W
WASHINGTON, U.S.A.	77	47°30'N	120°30'W
Washir, Afgh.	48	32°16'N	63°51'E
Washuk, Pak.	48	27°42'N	64°45'E
Watampone, Indo.	52	04°29'S	120°25'E
Waterford, Ire.	64	52°15'N	07°08'W
Waterloo, Iowa, U.S.A.	77	42°30'N	92°21'W
Wau, S.Sudan	53	07°45'N	28°01'E
Wausau, Wis., U.S.A.	77	44°58'N	89°38'W
Wazay, Afgh.	48	33°22'N	69°26'E
Wazi Khwa, Afgh.	48	32°07'N	68°16'E
Wazirabad, Pak.	48	32°30'N	74°08'E
Weda B., Indo.	52	00°30'N	127°50'E
Weddell Sea, Antarc.	82	73°00'S	42°00'W
Weifang, China	50	36°44'N	119°07'E
Weligama, S.Lanka	49	05°58'N	80°25'E
Welkom, S.Africa	66	28°00'S	26°46'E
Wellesley Islands, Aust.	70	16°42'S	139°30'E
Wellington I., Chile	79	49°30'S	75°00'W
Wellington, N.Z.	70	41°19'S	174°46'E
Wells, L., Aust.	70	26°44'S	123°15'E
Wenshan, China	50	23°20'N	104°18'E
Wenzhou, China	50	28°00'N	120°38'E
Weser, R., Ger.	60	53°36'N	08°28'E
Wessel Is., Aust.	70	11°10'S	136°45'E
WEST BENGAL, India	30	23°00'S	87°30'W
West Bromwich, Eng., U.K.	64	52°32'N	01°59'W
West Coral Reef, India	27		
West Ice Shelf, Antarc.	82	67°00'S	85°00'E
West Lamma Chan., Hong Kong, China	50		
West Palm Beach, Fla., U.S.A.	77	26°43'N	80°03'W
West Siberian Plain, Russia	53	62°00'N	75°00'E
WEST VIRGINIA, U.S.A.	77	38°45'N	80°30'W
WESTERN AUSTRALIA, Aust.	70	25°00'S	123°00'E
Western Channel, Japan-S.Korea	54	34°30'N	128°00'E
Western Des., Egypt	65	30°12'N	30°10'E
WESTERN SAHARA, Africa	66	25°00'N	13°30'W
Western Sayan Mts., Russia	53	53°00'N	92°00'E
Western, Cord., Col.	79	05°00'N	76°15'W
Westland Bight, N.Z.	70	42°55'S	170°05'E
Weston, Malay.	52	05°10'N	115°35'E
Weston-super-Mare, Eng., U.K.	52	51°21'N	02°58'W
Westport, N.Z.	70	41°46'S	171°37'E
Westray, I., U.K.	64	59°18'N	03°00'W
Wetar Str., East Timor-Indo.	52	08°20'S	126°30'E
Wetar, I., Indo.	52	07°45'S	126°00'E
Wewak, P.N.G.	70	03°38'S	143°41'E
Wexford, Ire.	64	52°20'N	06°28'W
Weymouth, Eng., U.K.	64	50°37'N	02°28'W
Whakatane, N.Z.	70	37°57'S	177°01'E
Whalsay, I., U.K.	64	60°22'N	00°59'W
Whangaehu, R., N.Z.	70	40°03'S	175°06'E
Whangarei, N.Z.	70	35°43'S	174°21'E
White Coomb, Mtn., U.K.	64	55°25'N	03°19'W
White Nile, R., S.Sudan	65	15°38'N	32°31'E
White Sea, Russia	60	65°30'N	38°00'E
White Volta, R., Ghana-Bur.Faso	65	09°10'N	01°15'W
White, R., U.S.A.	77	43°34'N	100°45'W
White, R., U.S.A.	77	33°59'N	91°09'W
Whitehorse, Canada	74	60°43'N	135°03'W
Whitney, Mt., U.S.A.	77	36°35'N	118°18'W
Wholdaia, L., Canada	73	60°43'N	104°20'W
Whyalla, S.A., Aust.	70	33°02'S	137°30'E
Wichita Falls, Texas, U.S.A.	77	33°54'N	98°30'W
Wichita, Kansas, U.S.A.	77	37°42'N	97°20'W
Wick, Scot., U.K.	64	58°26'N	03°05'W
Wicklow Mts., Ire.	64	53°06'N	06°20'W
Wicklow, Ire.	64	52°59'N	06°03'W
Wight, Isle of, U.K.	64	50°40'N	01°20'W
Wilhelm, Mt., P.N.G.	70	05°50'S	145°01'E
Wilkes Land, Antarc.	82	69°00'S	120°00'E
Willemstad, Neth. Ant.	78	12°06'N	68°56'W
Williamnagar, Megh., India	30	25°30'N	90°38'E
Williston, N.Dak., U.S.A.	77	48°09'N	103°37'W
Wilmington, Del., U.S.A.	77	39°45'N	75°33'W
Wilmington, N.C., U.S.A.	77	34°14'N	77°55'W
Winchester, Eng., U.K.	64	51°04'N	01°18'W
Windhoek, Nam.	66	22°35'S	17°04'E
Windsor, Eng., U.K.	64	51°29'N	00°36'W
Windward Is., Lesser Antilles	78	13°00'N	61°00'W
Windward Pass., Cuba-Haiti	78	20°00'N	74°00'W
Winisk, R., Canada	73	55°17'N	85°05'W
Winnipeg, Canada	74	49°54'N	97°09'W
Winnipeg, L., Canada	73	52°00'N	97°00'W
Winnipegosis, L., Canada	73	52°30'N	100°00'W
Winslow, Ariz., U.S.A.	77	35°02'N	110°42'W
Winston-Salem, N.C., U.S.A.	77	36°06'N	80°15'W
Winton, Queens., Aust.	70	22°24'S	143°03'E
WISCONSIN, U.S.A.	77	45°00'N	90°00'W
Wokam, I., Indo.	52	05°45'S	134°28'E
Wokha, Naga., India	30	26°06'N	94°16'E
Wollaston L., Canada	73	58°07'N	103°10'W
Wollongong, N.S.W., Aust.	70	34°25'S	150°54'E
Wolverhampton, Eng., U.K.	64	52°35'N	02°07'W
Wonju, S.Korea	54	37°22'N	127°58'E
Wonsan, N.Korea	54	39°11'N	127°27'E
Woodroffe, Mt., Aust.	70	26°20'S	131°45'E
Woods, L., Aust.	70	17°50'S	133°30'E
Woods, L.of the, Canada-U.S.A.	77	49°15'N	94°45'W
Woomera, S.A., Aust.	70	31°14'S	136°50'E
Worcester, Eng., U.K.	64	52°11'N	02°12'W
Worcester, S.Africa	66	33°39'S	19°27'E
Wowoni, I., Indo.	52	04°05'S	123°05'E
Wrangel I., Russia	53	71°00'N	180°00'E
Wrangell Mts., U.S.A.	77	61°30'N	142°00'W
Wrath, C., U.K.	70	58°38'N	05°01'W
Wreck Reef, Aust.	61		
Wroclaw, Poland	50	51°05'N	17°05'E
Wu Jiang, R., China	50	29°40'N	107°20'E
Wuhan, China	50	30°31'N	114°18'E
Wuhu, China	21	31°22'N	118°21'E
Wular L., India	50	34°17'N	74°29'E
Wuliang Shan, Mts., China	55	24°30'N	100°40'E
Wuntho, Myan.	50	23°54'N	95°42'E
Wutai Shan, Mtn., China	50	39°00'N	113°30'E
Wuwei, China	50	37°57'N	102°34'E
Wuxi, China	50	31°33'N	120°18'E
Wuyi Shan, Mts., China	50	27°00'N	117°00'E
Wuzhi Shan, Mtn., China	50	18°45'N	109°45'E
Wuzhou, China	50	23°30'N	111°18'E
Wye, R., U.K.	64	51°38'N	02°40'W
Wyndham, W.A., Aust.	70	15°33'S	128°03'E
WYOMING, U.S.A.	77	43°00'N	108°00'W

X

Xaghra, Malta	61	36°03'N	14°16'E
Xaignabouli, Laos	61	19°16'N	101°46'E
Xam Nua, Laos	55	20°25'N	104°02'E